THREE MEN IN HER LIFE . . .
ONE TERRIBLE SECRET

Aging and arrogant, the Earl of Maybridge would tell Erin Benson anything except the truth about what had happened to her mother at Amberley so long ago.

Heir to the Maybridge title and estate, the brilliant and ruthless Simon Hogarth is one step away from the highest office in the land, but Erin holds the power to destroy him.

And David Lennox, half-American, half-Scot, part noble, part commoner, makes Erin forget her doubts in a wave of desire that sweeps her into a passion she has not planned for and toward a revelation she never suspected.

Erin is about to discover what shaped her mother's fate—but the choices she makes now will determine her own. . . .

FAMILY SECRETS

by

Susan Bowden

SIGNET
Published by the Penguin Group
Penguin Books USA Inc., 375 Hudson Street,
New York, New York 10014, U.S.A.
Penguin Books Ltd, 27 Wrights Lane,
London W8 5TZ, England
Penguin Books Australia Ltd, Ringwood,
Victoria, Australia
Penguin Books Canada Ltd, 10 Alcorn Avenue,
Toronto, Ontario, Canada M4V 3B2
Penguin Books (N.Z.) Ltd, 182–190 Wairau Road,
Auckland 10, New Zealand

Penguin Books Ltd, Registered Offices:
Harmondsworth, Middlesex, England

First published by Signet, an imprint of Dutton Signet,
a division of Penguin Books USA Inc.

First Printing, August, 1996
10 9 8 7 6 5 4 3 2

Printed in Canada

For Philip Goodchild,
beloved uncle and dear friend.

There are secrets in all families.

—John Farquhar

Prologue

The child stood on the deck of the large ship, her hands clutching the railing. The sight of the water far below terrified her, but she couldn't escape from it. The other children behind her were crushing her against the ship's side, the hard edge of the cardboard box that held her gas mask digging into her chest.

Some of the children were screaming for their mothers, noses running, faces filthy from the smoke. One boy was hitting out at the grown-up who was trying to calm him, using words that Kate knew were bad.

Kate swallowed hard, determined not to cry. "You must be very brave, Katie," her mother had told her almost two weeks ago, as she buttoned up her coat with trembling fingers. "No crying, mind. You'll be safe from the bombs in Canada." Her mother's eyes had been all red and swollen, as if *she'd* been crying a lot.

The ship's horn blared, the noise making Kate's ears go deaf for a moment. The small boy beside her—the one who'd wet his trousers on the bus—screamed. Then the ship shuddered and slowly began to slip away from the shore.

"Wave good-bye to England," one of the ladies-in-charge said. Kate waved her little paper Union Jack. Some of the grown-ups on the shore shouted, their smiling faces upturned, arms waving. Others just stood there, not moving, their faces like white stones.

Kate's heart beat faster as she became aware of the gap between the ship and the crowd of people. Then the gap widened and she saw the swiftly increasing expanse of black, oily water that divided her from the land.

Terror flooded her. Her mouth opened. "Mummy!"

she screamed, even though she knew her mother wasn't there. "Mummy!"

It had been eleven days since she'd seen her mother. She'd been counting the days ever since her mother had said good-bye. After her mam had left the house, the lady had ordered one of the maids to take her up to that scary attic that smelled of mice and mothballs. When she left the house, there was the long train journey to this horrid black town. The last two nights she'd slept in the school hall that had been made into a dormitory with beds on the floors for all the children who were going on the boats to Canada.

Maybe she'd never see her mam again.

Chapter One

"Mummy!"

The thin wail of a terrified child broke into Erin's sleep. "Oh no, not again," she muttered, throwing back the bedclothes. "It's okay, Mom, I'm coming," she shouted. "Everything's okay." She fumbled for the light switch in the hall and ran across the landing to her parents' room.

Not her parents' room anymore, she reminded herself, sadness engulfing her. Just her mother's room now.

Her mother was sitting bolt upright, looking like a small child in the king-size bed. She reached out a hand to Erin, her face wet with tears. "Oh, Erin," she said, her face crumpling.

Erin put her arms around her and held her close, rocking her back and forth. How strange it felt to be comforting her own mother. Mom had always been a worrier, of course, mainly about Erin, but in herself she'd always seemed so strong, so invincible. Not anymore. Not since that day, six weeks and five days ago, when a speeding car had skidded on the icy road, plowing into Dad's car as he was driving home from seeing a patient at Grace Hospital.

When the ambulance had taken Dr. Jim Benson back to the Grace, he was declared dead on arrival.

"Was it the same dream as before?" Erin asked her mother, rubbing her back, the cotton nightdress damp beneath her hand.

Kate Benson nodded.

"Tell me again. Everything. All the smallest details."

"I can't. I don't want to," her mother whispered. "It's too painful to think about."

"I understand," Erin said. "But talking about it might

help. You're bottling it all up. It's better that it comes out."

Her mother's spine stiffened under Erin's hand. "I don't want to be analyzed by my own daughter, thank you very much."

Erin held back her annoyance. "I'm not trying to analyze you, Mom. But these nightmares of yours are getting worse. You yourself said last night that you were afraid of going to sleep in case you had one again."

Her mother turned her head away to gaze at the watercolor she'd painted and hung above the bed several years ago, but Erin sensed that she didn't really see it, that her mind was still focused on the nightmare.

"Why don't you tell me as much as you can recall about the dream, before you forget?" Erin suggested. "Then I'll make us both a cup of hot chocolate and we'll watch one of the old *Rockford Files* I taped last week."

Her mother gave a shuddering sigh and then moved away from the circle of her arms, as if she needed distance to be able to talk. She sat on the edge of the bed, her face still averted from Erin, and began to recount the dream in a low voice.

Her description of her nightmare was much the same as before. The young child on the ship, parting from her mother. The feelings of terror as the ship glided away from the shore. "I don't think I've ever felt so frightened, so alone," she whispered, when she'd finished.

Erin touched her mother's knee. "Poor Mom. It's quite natural that you'd dream about being sent away from England and your mother now, when you've suffered another traumatic loss. Post-traumatic stress, they call it. What we must do is—"

Erin stopped short, seeing her mother's eyes fill with tears. She tried to blink back her own. It wasn't easy to cope with her mother's distress when she herself was still trying to get over the shock of her father's death. She'd been so close to her father. It was still hard to believe that she'd lost him without any warning. After all, he was only sixty-three, a comparatively young man.

"Let's go and get that chocolate, shall we?" she said gently. She put her hand beneath her mother's elbow to help her up.

Kate pulled her arm away. "I'm not an invalid, you know," she snapped. "Nor am I in my dotage."

"No need to bite my head off. I was just trying to help. I'll go and put the kettle on."

Erin ran downstairs, annoyed as much at herself as at her mother. What the hell was the matter with her, that she couldn't keep her cool with her grieving mother?

Her father's sudden violent death had shattered their lives like a stone flung against the smooth surface of a mirror. What bothered Erin most was that the crack seemed to be spreading wider and wider. She'd hoped that by now she would have been able to move back to her downtown apartment, but these nightmares had become so bad that she couldn't leave her mother alone in the house.

When the kettle boiled she filled the two mugs and stirred the chocolate powder into them. A familiar ritual from her childhood. Hot chocolate and talking in the kitchen. Communicating with her parents had always seemed easier in the stillness of the night.

Except that it had usually been Dad who'd waited up for her when she'd come in late.

The thought that he'd never again be there to exult with her highs and commiserate with her lows was unbearable.

She heard her mother descending the stairs. The slow slap of her slippers made her sound like an old woman of eighty, not the vibrant woman of sixty who used to water-ski at the lake every summer. Erin doubted she'd ever see her mother on water skis again.

She set the mugs on the table by the patio window. "There we are," she said, trying to sound bright and cheerful. "Steaming hot chocolate. What would you like to eat with it?"

Her mother sat down at the table and cupped her hands around the mug. "I'm not hungry." She tried to smile. "Sorry I woke you again. You haven't been getting much sleep recently."

"I'm fine, Mom."

Her mother continued as if she hadn't heard her. "I feel so guilty. I can catch up with sleep during the day, but you have to go into the studio every morning, however little sleep you get."

Erin sat across from her. "Don't you worry about me. It's you I'm worried about. You're the one who should be sleeping." She frowned. "I wonder if it could be those new sleeping pills Jean gave you that are causing these dreams."

"I doubt it."

Erin hesitated, knowing that her mother didn't want to talk about the nightmares. On the other hand, it was important that she not stifle whatever it was that was troubling her. "You said that you don't consciously recall the time before you came to Canada, right?"

"I don't want to talk about it," Kate said flatly, picking up her spoon to stir the hot chocolate.

"I'm just trying to find out if you can remember what parts of the dream actually happened to you and what is imaginary."

The stirring became more agitated. "And I've told you that I don't remember any of it."

"Yet it must have happened a bit like your dream, mustn't it?" Erin prompted gently. "You were evacuated from England to Canada with a large group of children in 1940. Your boat sailed from Liverpool. Gran's told us that. When I asked her years ago, she said your parents had been killed in the London blitz."

"That's right," her mother said.

Erin allowed the silence to stretch on between them.

"I'd been in Winnipeg for several months," her mother said, after a long pause, "and all the other parents had written from England to the people who'd taken their children in. Gran said she couldn't understand why she hadn't heard a thing from my family, so she made inquiries. That's when she was told that my parents had been killed."

Erin stretched a hand across the table. "Poor Mom. I hate to think of you as a little orphan of six or seven, stranded in Canada."

"But she wasn't there," Kate whispered, staring across the kitchen at something unseen.

"Who wasn't? Oh, you mean in the dream. You mean your mother wasn't there?"

"That's right. She wasn't at the railway station in London, either. All the other mothers were there."

This was something new. Her mother hadn't mentioned a railway station before. She sat staring into space, turning her teaspoon over and over.

"I expect she was working that day and couldn't get away," Erin said, after what seemed like several minutes, but was probably only a few seconds.

Her mother's dark eyes widened. "No. She left the house before I did. She left me there in the big house and she went away. I kept waiting for her, but she never came back. They said she wasn't coming back, ever."

Erin didn't want to interrupt this flow of new information, but when her mother's distressed voice once more lapsed into silence she said, "I thought you said your mother *was* there. She was doing up your coat, right? And she told you that the bombs wouldn't be able to hurt you in Canada."

"That was before. She went away before they took us to the train. Days before. After she left, they put me in the hard iron bed in the attic with that horrid Betty who pinched me."

Erin didn't dare make a move. Her mother's voice had risen to the higher pitch of a young child.

"And she always had dirty hands, Betty did. She used to do the grate blacking and then she'd rub her hands on me and I'd get into trouble for dirtying my Sunday dress."

Erin waited for more, but it didn't come. "Can you remember anything else about the house?" she asked.

"It was very big, with lots of rooms. The floors shone like glass. I could look down and see myself. And there was a painted ceiling with pictures of fat babies with wings floating in the sky."

"You mean cherubs?"

As soon as she asked the question Erin knew she'd broken the spell. Damn! Her mother's eyes focused on her. "Cherubs?" she repeated, looking puzzled.

"You were talking about painted ceilings with what I take were cherubs on them."

"Was I?" Her mother yawned and reached for the mug. "I must have been talking in my sleep." She drank down the rest of the chocolate and got to her feet. "I think I can go back to bed now. I feel much better, thanks to you, sweetie."

But Erin's curiosity was piqued now. "It sounds to me as if you lived in some sort of stately home in England, before you came to Canada."

"What makes you say that?"

"Painted ceilings. A servant girl called Betty blacking grates. Hardly your average little villa, is it?"

"I expect it's something from a book I read. *The Little Princess* or probably *The Secret Garden.* Those were two favorites of mine. I used to read them to you, remember? That Betty sounds like a character out of *The Secret Garden,* doesn't she? It's years since I read that book. Isn't it amazing what the mind can recall?"

She was right, of course, but, having taken several psychology courses at the University of Winnipeg, Erin also knew that it was even more amazing what the mind could suppress. There was an element of panic in her mother's voice as she rattled on about the books.

"Time we went back to bed," Kate said abruptly. She went to the sink to rinse out her mug. Automatically, her fingers reached out to check the earth in the pot of herbs on the windowsill. Tutting to herself, she watered them and then carefully polished up the drops of water on the counter with a paper towel.

Behind her back, Erin shook her head, clamping her lips together to avoid telling her mother that she'd had more important things on her mind than watering the plants.

"That's better," her mother said, drying her hands. She bent to kiss Erin's cheek. "Good night, darling. And thank you."

"Good night, Mom. Nothing to thank me for. Sleep well."

"I think I will now. Don't sit up for too long, will you? You need your sleep more than I do."

"I'll be up in a couple of minutes." Erin went to the foot of the stairs and watched her mother go up. She might sleep well for the rest of the night, but Erin was sure that this wasn't the last of the nightmares. Dad's sudden death had resurrected those buried memories.

She very much doubted that they'd become dormant again.

She went back to the kitchen and took up the pad of paper by the telephone. Then she sat down at the table and wrote down everything she could remember of what her mother had said about that house. She felt completely wide awake now. She'd dig out her old copy of *The Secret Garden* from the bookshelves in the basement and read it, just in case there was a character called Betty in it who blackened grates. Somehow she doubted it.

Then, tomorrow, she'd go and visit Gran on the way home from the television studio. Gran's body might be crippled with arthritis, but her mind was still pretty sharp for an eighty-two-year-old. She might come up with something new. Erin decided it might be best not to tell her mother she was going to see Gran.

She scanned the list she'd made. *Missing parents. Cherubs. Blackened grates. Sunday dress* . . . In order to help her mother, she must garner as many facts as possible from the woman who had not only given the little English evacuee a home, but also adopted her.

After all, Erin thought, *I know all about Dad's background.* Jim Benson's father, and his father before him, had been ranchers in Alberta, descendants of English stock from Ontario who'd come out west for a better life, and with their marriages they'd added a dash of German and Dutch to make a good Canadian mix.

Her mother's past, on the other hand, was a void, shrouded in mystery. Even if her mother's parents had died in the London blitz, surely there would have been grandparents, aunts, and uncles. Why had none of them contacted Gran?

Her mother's depression seemed to be getting worse. She was also increasingly afraid of leaving the house. Just the thought of going to the local drugstore made her anxious. What if she became a chronic agoraphobic? Erin had already lost one parent. She couldn't bear the thought of losing another to a living death.

"Oh, God," she whispered. "What if I have to move back home permanently?" The thought of losing her independence made her feel as if a huge weight were bearing down on her chest, crushing her.

Breathing hard, she stood up and tore the sheet of paper off the pad, folding it into three.

For her own sake, as well as her mother's, she had to do something before things became worse. If she asked the right questions, perhaps Gran would come up with some new answers.

Chapter Two

The Honorable Simon Hogarth M.P. was not looking forward to this visit to Amberley Court. His grandfather, the Earl of Maybridge, was a difficult man to deal with at any time, but what he was about to tell him would stretch the limits of their relationship almost to breaking point.

"He'll go through the raftered roof when I tell him," he said to Paul Ransome as they sped along the M25. "I just hope the old chap doesn't have a heart attack."

Ransome looked uneasy. "Perhaps you should have brought your wife with you. You say she gets on well with your grandfather."

"Olivia offered to come. I told her I didn't want to subject her to one of my grandfather's tirades." Simon glanced across at Ransome, his lips quirking into a little smile. "Don't tell me you're afraid, Paul. You, one of the elder statesmen of the Tory party."

"What you're proposing to do is pretty bloody incredible."

"Not if I get to be Prime Minister of Great Britain in exchange, it isn't. Besides, it's been done before."

"Lord Hailsham, you mean?" Ransome looked concerned. "You do understand that there are no guarantees you'll be chosen. It's not in the bag yet, you know."

Simon swiftly maneuvered the Saab across three lanes to take the Sevenoaks exit. "I'm well aware of that. Publicly, I'm not burning any bridges. But I realize that the caucus must know that I'm willing to do this before they can even consider me for the leadership."

"It's a big sacrifice."

"Not really. All I shall give up is the actual title and

the entailed estates attached to it. They consist mainly of a dilapidated castle and some rather good shooting land up in Yorkshire. The rest, including Amberley, will be mine. And when I die, the title will go to my son." *If I ever have one,* was his unspoken thought.

As he drove along the familiar winding country road that led to Amberley, he knew that Ransome was glancing at his profile, trying to fathom him. Simon smiled to himself. No one who studied his face would find out what made him tick. Long ago, even before he'd become the youngest member of Parliament in the House of Commons, he'd made sure that he would have three, not two, personas. One for the public, one for the backroom boys in the party, and a third, for himself alone. Even Olivia rarely caught a glimpse of *that* Simon Hogarth. It appeared only when he lost control, in a rare burst of fury or, even more rare, during sex.

He had to admit, though, as he swung through the gates of Amberley Court, that he was going to have to exert even more self-control than usual to deal with his irascible grandfather today.

The broad drive that led to the great house was lined with venerable old lime trees. As far as Simon was concerned everything at Amberley was too bloody venerable and too bloody old. The place was like a museum.

Come to think of it, he could recall his father telling him he considered Amberley to be more like a mausoleum. His father had been drunk at the time—when hadn't he been?—but Simon remembered experiencing a rare feeling of affinity with him on that particular occasion. It was then that his father had told him that he had no desire to live at Amberley. "By the time my father shuffles off this mortal coil," he'd said, "I'll be off living in the Bahamas. I shall just turn it all over to you, Simon, my boy, and wish you the best of bloody British luck."

In fact, his father hadn't had the choice of living or not at Amberley, because he'd keeled over in his favorite bar one day and was dead before the ambulance arrived. That made Simon the heir apparent to the peerage and the ancient—and crumbling—family seat in Yorkshire, Maybridge Castle, which was used mainly for the shooting season. He would also inherit the far more valuable Amberley estate in Kent. Amberley Court was not tied in with the ancient Maybridge title. It had come into the family in the seventeenth century as the result of a highly profitable arranged marriage.

His father had died nine years ago, but the old earl was still alive. Giles Hogarth, Lord Maybridge, was a thriving eighty-one.

Now the imposing house came into sight, its ancient rose-red brick bathed in spring sunlight. On the roofs of both the central wing and the two side wings, tall white chimneys stood out against the bright blue sky.

"Very impressive," Ransome said. "I'd seen photographs, of course, but they never do a place justice, do they?"

"The tour guides tell us that some people are rather disappointed when they see the interior of the house. I suppose the word *court* conjures up images of glass-lined halls, like Versailles. My great-grandfather, being a true Victorian, took advantage of all the new inventions of his age. The interior was refurbished in his time to make it more comfortable. New kitchens and bathrooms added etcetera. It's time it was done again, brought up-to-date."

Amberley was one of the few stately homes left that still employed a butler and there he was, standing at the top of the broad sweep of stone steps, looking as if a puff of wind might blow him over. Another venerable—and ancient—part of Amberley. It was high time that the place was managed by a young, go-ahead team and run properly, thought Simon, like a business venture.

When he inherited Amberley, the first thing he intended to do was sweep away all the ancient retainers his grandfather had surrounded himself with. They were ridiculous, money-wasting anachronisms.

"Hello, Harrington," he said, as he got out of the car. He held out his hand to the butler. "Wonderful to see you again. You don't look a day older."

"Thank you, Master Simon. It has been quite a while since we had the pleasure of seeing you."

Simon caught the hint of reproach in the old man's

voice. Damn his insolence! "This is Mr. Ransome, Harrington."

"Good morning, sir." Harrington made a little bow in Ransome's direction. "You will find his lordship in the library."

Mrs. Edwards, the housekeeper, greeted them in the hall. "A pleasure to have you here again, Mr. Simon," she said briskly.

Now, Mrs. Edwards he would keep on, Simon thought. She was the one member of the staff who held this place together.

Although his grandfather didn't care much for Mrs. Edwards, preferring to have Harrington to serve him personally, he did recognize her ability. "That woman is as efficient as a public school matron and just as ruthless," he'd recently told Simon.

Simon had smiled to himself, knowing that he'd been the one who had first interviewed Mrs. Edwards. He'd vetted all the applicants for the housekeeper's position. Of course it hadn't been necessary to tell his grandfather that.

Simon led the way across the highly polished floor of the great hall, ignoring Harrington's attempt to maneuver himself in front of him. "Thank you, Harrington. We'll announce ourselves," he told him when they reached the library door.

The old man inclined his head in a slight nod and turned away. Simon raised his eyebrows at Ransome and led him into the library.

At first he thought the room was empty, but then he saw his grandfather's angular body slumped in a wing chair by the fireplace, pages of *The Times* scattered at his feet. The mouth beneath the bristling mustache was wide open, emitting a loud rasping sound.

"Grandfather," Simon said softly.

With a start and then a series of snorts, Lord Maybridge awoke. "What the devil . . . !" He glared at Simon. "Why didn't Harrington warn me you were here?"

"My fault, Grandfather. I'm sorry," Simon said. "I showed myself in. Do you want us to give you time to wake up?" He gave his grandfather a sympathetic smile.

"Nothing worse than being woken from a deep sleep, is there?"

"No need to speak to me as if I'm a child in the nursery." Lord Maybridge heaved himself up from his chair, growling at Simon's offer of assistance. "Lie still, you silly blighters," he commanded his dogs, who'd scrambled to their feet as soon as they saw him move. "Help yourself to drinks," he told Simon in much the same tone as he'd used with his dogs. "I have to empty the old water tank."

Simon watched as he shuffled across the carpeted floor, leaning heavily on his cane. The door opened and then crashed shut.

"Every time I see him he's a little slower and a great deal more bad-tempered," he said, speaking half to himself. "What can I get you to drink, Ransome. Whiskey? G and T?"

"Whiskey. A little water. No ice. Spoils the taste."

Simon poured himself a glass of tonic water and added several ice cubes.

"You don't drink at all, eh?" Ransome asked. "I know you don't when we're sitting, but I thought you might socially. I mean, when you're at home."

Simon sat down, moving the plump cushion away from his back. He held his glass up to the autumn sunlight streaming in from the long, mullioned windows. "When you have a father who drinks himself into an early grave, you either emulate him or make a vow never to be like him. I chose the latter."

That was one accusation his opponents within the party and across the floor of the House would never be able to make: that Simon Hogarth was a drunk like his father.

Flushing with embarrassment, Ransome hurriedly cleared his throat. "Quite right. Good thing. Didn't mean to put you on the spot."

"You didn't," Simon said calmly. "This is your first visit to Amberley. What do you think of this room?"

Ransome looked around, obviously glad to have the subject changed. "What a superb collection." He waved his hand at the leather-bound volumes lining the walls from floor to ceiling.

"My grandfather has made a vow to read each and every one of those books before he dies."

"How far has he got?"

"You'd have to ask him yourself. That desk over there by the window is Chippendale. My favorite piece in here is the set of library steps. I loved climbing those when I was a boy." Simon leaned back, lifting his head to gaze at the ceiling. "That's the only thing that doesn't work, as far as I'm concerned. The ceiling. Those gaudy cherubs with their floating draperies are totally incongruous in a library of any kind, but particularly in this one."

"Is it your intention to have the paintings whitewashed when you take over?"

Simon stifled the impulse to start at the sound of his grandfather's voice. The old man had entered so quietly he hadn't heard him. "Definitely not."

His grandfather crossed the room and slowly lowered himself into his chair again. "Quiet, you foolish beasts," he told his two dogs, who'd bounded up from the hearth rug to welcome him back. "What will you do with the ceiling, then?"

Simon met the searching gaze without flinching. The old man's eyes were still an astonishing blue, despite his age. "This is neither the place nor time to discuss that."

"You're not proposing to turn Amberley over to the National Trust, are you? If you are, say so now and I'll go to court to fight your right to manage the estate, like Marlborough has done with his son. You'd have the title, then, but you wouldn't have Amberley."

It was the perfect opening. "No, I won't have the title," Simon said. "That's my reason for coming down today. I wanted you to know that I'm about to announce to the media my intention to relinquish my right to the title."

Giles Hogarth's long-fingered hand tightened on the gold knob of his cane, the knotted veins standing out. He drew in such a long breath that Simon was half afraid that he might explode. "You'll do nothing of the sort. When I die, you will take your place in the House of Lords as the fourteenth Earl of Maybridge."

"I'm sorry, Grandfather, but that's not possible," Simon told him. "You must have known this was coming, when I stood for Parliament."

"I fought you on that, as well. However, your father said it was best to let you get it out of your system, that you could be a member of the House of Commons for as long as I and then he lived."

"But my father didn't live, did he? He died before you did."

"Drank himself to death, the bloody fool."

"Yes, well that's all in the past. What matters now is that I intend to formally renounce the title."

"Can't formally disclaim the title until I'm dead. And I'm not dead yet, as you can see." Giles glowered at Simon and then fixed his gaze on Ransome, who was pretending intense interest in his almost empty glass. "We'll talk about this another time," Giles said. "When we're alone," he added pointedly.

"I'm afraid not. Ransome is here at my request."

Paul Ransome looked as if he would rather be anywhere else at the moment.

Giles slammed his palm down on the arm of his chair. "I fail to see what Mr. Ransome has to do with any of this."

Simon gave a faint smile. "Tell him, Paul."

Ransome cleared his throat and leaned forward, glad to have the chance to get down to his reason for being there. "Your grandson is one of the brightest stars in the Conservative party, Lord Maybridge. He has more than fulfilled the feelings of expectation many of us had when he was first elected."

Lord Maybridge shifted impatiently in his chair. "Yes, yes, we know all that. Get to the point."

"The point is that the Labour Party is now in power. Their leader, Ian Rutherford, is young, dynamic and charismatic. Whereas our leader—"

"We know all about your leader," Giles said. "Pickard was a disaster as Prime Minister."

"As I was going to say, Michael Pickard has given his all to the party and needs a well-deserved rest."

Giles snorted. "God defend me from political gobbledygook. You mean you're about to toss him out."

Ransome folded his hands, slowly interlacing his fingers. "We shall need a dynamic new leader. One who can match Rutherford in age and charisma. Someone energetic and progressive. A new face for the new millennium. Many of us feel that your grandson is that man."

Giles looked from Ransome to Simon, and back again. "Many, but not all, eh? You'll have a fight on your hands from the establishment, those who want a piece of the pie themselves."

"Simon is a member of the shadow cabinet. He hasn't exactly stayed in the background himself. He has an excellent record of performance."

Giles turned to look at his grandson, who sat on the chaise longue to his left. "So you propose to abandon the title that has been in our family for more than four hundred years on the slight chance that you might become Prime Minister four or five years from now, is that it?"

Simon could see from the knotted muscles in his grandfather's neck how hard he was struggling to maintain control over his temper. "I know how much this must hurt you, Grandfather, and I regret that very much."

"If you give up the title on my death, you realize that there will be no Earl of Maybridge until you die? It isn't as if someone else can take over in the interim." The old man slammed his open hand on his knee. "In fact, it might be better if you did die. At least, that way, Lennox would inherit the title, considering you haven't managed to father a son yet."

The barb bit deep, but Simon displayed no emotion. "We've already discussed this before. If I don't have a son, I am sure David Lennox will manage very well. I know he's not a Hogarth, but he is your cousin Lucy's grandson and, therefore, carries Hogarth blood in his veins."

"You know what I think of Cousin Lucy. Besides, Lennox is a damned American."

"Not really." It pleased Simon to see his grandfather rise to his bait. The more he pretended to support David Lennox, the more his grandfather would oppose him. "David's mother's American, but his father was Scottish, as you well know."

"And his grandfather was nothing but a damned pill-pusher in a chemist shop." Giles waved an impatient hand. "Whatever he is, Lennox can't get the title if you give it up. Not unless you die without leaving a male heir, that is."

"Precisely." Simon smiled. "So there's really no point in discussing it now, is there?"

His grandfather's eyes narrowed. "I warn you, Simon. If you persist in this, I shall be forced to do something drastic."

Simon met his grandfather's furious gaze without flinching. "I'm sorry, but I told you when I first ran for Parliament that politics meant more to me than anything else in the world."

"That's a lot of claptrap! We allowed you to do it, your father and I, because we felt you had at least twenty years to get it out of your system. Goddammit, Simon, your father was less than fifty at the time. We thought we had all the time in the world."

"I would never have been satisfied with being a mere member of Parliament, Grandfather. You should have known that. To have any chance of being elected leader of the Tory party, I have to announce that I am giving up my right to the peerage. No peer can be a member of the House of Commons."

"Don't speak to me as if I'm some sort of imbecile." Lord Maybridge's roar made the dogs spring up from their slumber and set them barking again. He rose, his eyes bright with fury. "Shut up, you stupid beasts." He pounded his cane on the floor. "Stop that bloody noise!"

Simon and Paul Ransome scrambled to their feet. Simon went to his grandfather, taking him by the arm, but he flung him off, raising his cane as if to strike him with it.

"Get off me, damn you. You're no better than your father was. A couple of ungrateful curs. These two dogs are more loyal than you and your useless father." His breathing came in ragged gasps, his chest heaving, the gleaming blue eyes almost starting from his head.

"Sit down, Grandfather," Simon said, genuinely concerned. "Please sit down. Let me send for Harrington."

But Harrington was already there, hurrying into the room, holding out a bottle of pills and a glass of water.

"Who the devil sent for you?" Giles demanded, his breathing still labored.

Harrington made no reply. He shook out a pill and handed it to Lord Maybridge, who took it and then swallowed it down with some water.

"I think it would be better if you were to leave us for a while, Mr. Simon," Harrington said, "and allow his lordship to rest."

"I think you should send for Dr. Alexander."

"All he needs is rest," Harrington assured him.

"I shall be fine. Just made me so bloody angry," Giles said as he sank into his chair. He added something about not coming to a hasty decision. Simon couldn't hear the exact words, but he caught the gist of it.

"I won't," he said. "I promise I shall consider it all very carefully in the light of your strong objections." He pressed his grandfather's shoulder and then motioned to Ransome that they should leave.

"I'll call later to make sure he has recovered," Simon said to Harrington at the door. "It would be best to call in Dr. Alexander, just in case."

The butler's eyes were filled with hostility. "That is for his lordship to decide. While he is able to do so for himself," he added pointedly.

Simon smiled. "Of course. I also know that he's in the best hands with you caring for him, Harrington. You have my telephone number if you need to contact me. I should be back in my office by three o'clock. Or you can call me on my car phone."

As they drove off down the gravel driveway, Ransome mopped his face with his handkerchief. "My God, Simon, I thought your grandfather was going to pop off right there and then."

"Not him. He just likes to get his own way and employs whatever methods he has in his power to do so."

"Still, you must admit that he has just cause to be upset. What you are proposing means the end of centuries of tradition."

"Well, you know what I feel about traditions, Paul.

They are there to be broken. It's tradition that kept Britain stagnant for so long."

"You may have to keep that particular opinion to yourself, at least until you've been made leader. It's a young man's idea."

"I *am* a young man. I thought that was the point, to choose someone who'll be around the age of forty in the year two thousand. That new face for the new millennium you were talking about."

"Yes, yes, but remember you'll need the vote of the traditionalists in the party to get the leadership in the first place."

"I'll remember. Thanks for reminding me, Paul. I don't know what I'd do without you. Thank God I have you on my side." Simon drove through the open wrought-iron gates and down to the crossroads. Then he took the Sevenoaks road, passing the Fox and Hounds pub, which used to be a particular favorite of his father's.

"You told Lord Maybridge that you would reconsider your decision," Ransome said, his voice worried.

"I told him that because it was what he wanted to hear. I would have told him anything to calm him down. Those temper tantrums of his are always worrying. Although I should have grown used to them by now, one never knows when he will give himself a heart attack."

"Then you won't reconsider?"

"Of course not. My mind is made up. If they want me, I shall be happy to accept the leadership of the Conservative party. And I see no reason why they shouldn't want me. Not only am I an experienced politician, but I'm also a family man, with an attractive, photogenic wife and two lovely little daughters, to whom I'm devoted."

"True, true. Very important that, nowadays. There have been too many scandals in the party recently."

"Well, that's one problem you won't have with me, Ransome. Not a hint of scandal can be attached to my name or that of any member of my family."

The specter of his father hung in the air, but neither mentioned him. His father was dead, gone.

"Not many people can say that," Ransome said.

"Exactly. All it needs is that final, very public—and,

I trust, well publicized—announcement that I intend to relinquish my right to the title for the good of the country, and the leadership should be in the bag."

Ransome beamed at Simon. "Excellent. Wonderful publicity for the party."

Simon gave Paul an amused glance. "It's a foolproof plan. Absolutely nothing can go wrong."

Chapter Three

Anna Bartley, Erin's grandmother, had lived in East Kildonan, in the white stuccoed bungalow with the dark green shutters, for as long as Erin could remember. When her husband, Joseph, had died, the family had tried to persuade her to move into a seniors' apartment block, but she wouldn't hear of it.

"I'm not in my dotage yet," she'd told them, her spine stiff with disapproval. "I want to hear children shouting in the street outside my home, not the thump of walkers."

When Anna made up her mind about something, there was no moving her. So Erin's mother had resigned herself to the fact that she would have to continue worrying about Anna falling down the basement stairs or slipping in the bath.

At least it means that Mom doesn't have as much time to worry about me, Erin thought, as she waded through the snow that had drifted across the path. Although it had been recently cleared by the snow-clearing service her mother had insisted on paying for, the gusty March winds had blown snow across the path again.

She mounted the three wooden steps up to the doorway and pressed the bell.

It seemed to take her grandmother far longer than usual to get to the door. When she opened it, Erin saw that she was leaning on the walking stick they'd given her. She'd adamantly refused to use it . . . until now.

Erin suddenly realized that Gran had been growing increasingly frail since the day of the accident. She'd been very fond of her son-in-law and his death had come as a great shock to her. Gran was yet another victim of that bastard who'd plowed into her father's car.

Erin blinked away the tears that filled her eyes and summoned up a smile. "Hi, Gran." She hugged the thin figure, feeling the outline of her spine beneath the navy sweater.

Never one to prolong an embrace, her grandmother stepped back to survey her. "You've cut your hair again."

"Yes. Do you like it?"

"Not much. You looked better with your hair longer."

Erin grimaced. "Sorry about that. It's easier to look after this way."

"Hmm!" was the only response she got. Her grandmother led the way into the small living room, which was as neat as always. The natural pine floor gleamed, the smell of floor wax telling Erin that it had been newly polished. The little table in the window alcove was set for tea, the china cups and saucers and silver carefully laid out on a white cloth embroidered with bright blue forget-me-nots.

"Sit down," her grandmother said, clearing away a pile of books and papers from the sofa. "I'll just go and put the kettle on."

"Were you working?" Erin asked, looking at the papers.

Her grandmother's neat gray head poked around the kitchen door. "Yes. Homework from my two adult students, the ones who are learning English. I was filling in time until you came," she added pointedly, retreating again into the kitchen.

Knowing she couldn't be seen, Erin grimaced. Thank heavens she'd never had her grandmother for a teacher. She went to the kitchen door. "Sorry I was a bit late. We were editing next week's show."

"How is your work going?"

"Okay."

"Just okay?" Anna frowned at her over her glasses, her hands busying themselves with setting out oatmeal cookies on a plate.

Erin shrugged. "I just get bored with the same old things, I suppose. Producing a talk show and making local documentaries can hardly compete with Oprah or Ricki Lake."

"Who in the world is Ricki Lake?"

"I don't think you'd want to know, Gran." Erin stifled a giggle at the thought of her grandmother watching the Ricki Lake show.

"I hope you realize how lucky you are to have such an interesting job," her grandmother said severely. "Many young women would give their eyeteeth to work in television. Or to have any job at all, for that matter."

Erin sighed. "I know. I keep telling myself that. But I've been so restless . . . Ever since Dad . . ." She turned away.

Her grandmother made no move to touch her, but when she spoke there was warm sympathy in her voice. "It's been particularly hard on you, Erin. You have to worry about your mother as well as yourself. She's taking it very badly. I worry about her. How is she today?"

"Not good. That's why I wanted to speak to you. It's about these nightmares she's having. I thought you might be able to help."

"Hold on. The tea is just about ready. Tea first and then we'll talk. Although how I can help, I really don't know. I feel increasingly useless with this wretched arthritis."

Erin helped her grandmother in with the tray and then sat beside her on the sofa, noticing how her twisted hands shook as she poured the tea. Everyone she cared about seemed to be falling apart. Or leaving her. Or, worse still, dying. It made her feel scared and vulnerable and very alone. Recent events had reminded her that the people she loved were not immortal. Nor was love itself, despite what the poets said. She shivered.

"Turn the heat up if you're cold," her grandmother told her.

Erin had to smile. Old, she might be, but Gran didn't miss a thing. "I'm fine." She took a sip of tea, which was far too weak for her liking.

"Have you heard from Rob Harris?"

Erin gave her grandmother a sharp look. Now she was reading minds.

"Don't look at me like that. You can talk about the man, can't you?"

Erin crumbled the cookie on her plate into several

pieces. "I can, but I don't really want to. It still hurts." She felt her cheeks flush. "I got a note from him a couple of weeks ago. He'd just heard about Dad."

"And is he enjoying Toronto?"

"He didn't say."

"I always liked Rob."

"Yes, I know you did, Gran," Erin said angrily. "But he's gone to Toronto. It's five months since he left. We're no longer together."

"You should have gone with him."

Erin felt like yelling at her. She took a deep breath. "I'm surprised to hear you say that, considering how horrified you were when we first moved in together."

"It's not easy to adjust to all the changes that have happened since I was young. Despite that, I still think you should have gone to Toronto with him."

"And given up my job here? You just told me a moment ago that I was lucky to have a good job."

"You might have found something better, something that excited you, in Toronto."

"I doubt it very much. Besides, Rob made it very clear that our relationship wasn't a permanent one. He told me there'd be no guarantees if I came with him."

"Since when did life give guarantees? You should have taken the chance when you had it. So what if it didn't work out. You're still young."

Erin was amazed. Was this her straitlaced grandmother talking?

"No need to look so surprised, young woman. You've been in Winnipeg all your life. You even went to university here. Perhaps it's time you saw the world before it's too late."

Erin tried to smile, but couldn't. "It's too late already, Gran. I'm thirty years old."

"What drivel! Thirty's a child."

Erin felt her mouth trembling. She put up a hand to cover it. "No, it's not. I feel my time is running out. I know I have a good job and a nice apartment, but that's not enough." She met her grandmother's gaze. "I want to travel, see the world. I also want to share my life with someone, to have children. The older I get the further away I seem to be from what I want in life. When I was younger, a good career was what I wanted. Then a lover who was fun to be with. Now, I see my friends with children *and* professions, and I feel incredibly envious."

"Then find yourself the right man and have your children."

Erin gave a harsh laugh. "It's not that easy. All the good ones seem to have been taken. And I refuse to have a child by myself. That's selfish. I'd rather adopt a child who needs a home than do that."

"That's not such a bad idea, you know. After all, that's what I did with your mother."

Erin jumped at this opportunity to get away from the subject of her love life—or lack of it—and onto the reason she was here. "That's what I wanted to speak to you about."

"What? Adopting a child?"

"No. About Mom. I've told you about these nightmares she's having. She starts grief counseling next week, as you know. Meanwhile, I thought I could help her sort out what is real and what is imaginary in these dreams she's having."

"They're getting worse, then?"

"I'm afraid so. I don't want to worry you, but . . ." Erin hesitated. Just by being here, talking about it, she was worrying her grandmother. But who else could help her?

"I'm her mother, Erin," Anna said softly. "I'll worry more if you don't tell me the truth. Tell me about the nightmares."

Erin did so, including all the details she could remember, referring to the notes she'd made to make sure she'd covered everything. "I think that's all," she said, when she'd finished.

To Erin's surprise, her grandmother said nothing.

"Have you heard any of this before, Gran?"

"Not that I recall." Anna took off her metal-rimmed glasses to polish them with her paper napkin.

It was an obvious evasion tactic. Erin was sure she knew more than she was willing to tell. "When Mom started talking about her mother not being there to see her off at the railway station, she went into a sort of a trance, as if she were seeing everything as it happened.

The big house, the servant girl who pinched her, the painted ceiling . . ."

"Your mother always had a vivid imagination."

Erin frowned. "No, that's the point. It all came pouring out, as—as if it had been hidden away for a long time, and was now bursting out. I'm quite sure these were actual memories."

Her grandmother picked up the china teapot. "Perhaps they were. More tea, dear?"

"Please," Erin said, trying to hide her impatience. She wished her grandmother would show more interest. "What I want to find out from you, Gran, is what you know for sure about Mom's background. Did she ever talk to you about a big house with a painted ceiling?"

"I can't remember, dear. It's all so long ago. More than fifty years. Shall I cut you a piece of cake? I know you like this orange coffee cake, so I made it for you. You can take the rest away with you when you go. It's too sweet for my taste."

Erin clamped her hand over her grandmother's wrist, as she began to cut the cake. "Forget the cake. This is vitally important."

Looking surprised, her grandmother put down the knife.

"You asked for the truth, Gran. So I'll give it to you. I'm very concerned about Mom. She seems to be retreating into a world of her own. I'm really scared." Erin was so close to her grandmother, she could smell the fustiness of old age, mixed with a hint of lemon, from the dried lemon balm Gran kept in all her clothing drawers. "You are the only one who knows anything about her past. It's my past, too, I would remind you. I know absolutely nothing about my mother's family."

"None of us do," Anna retorted. "Her parents died in the London blitz. That's all I know."

"So you've told me before. What I can't understand is why no one contacted you. There must have been grandparents or aunts—or some relative. How could they just abandon a little girl like that?"

Anna blinked. "War affects people in strange ways, I suppose."

"No one wrote to you about her?"

Anna shook her head.

"What about when you and Grandpa adopted her. Didn't you need papers for that?"

"They were all lost in the bombing." Her grandmother turned her face away from Erin, so that Erin could see the wrinkled skin stretched against the bones of her neck.

Suddenly Erin knew that her grandmother was lying. She also knew that, if she accused her of lying, her grandmother was likely to clam up altogether. She stood up, picked up the tray, and took it into the kitchen. Then she came back and moved the little table that had been separating them, the table her grandmother was using as a shield.

All this time, her grandmother sat, hands folded in her lap, staring out the window at the fresh fall of snow that blanketed the lawn and coated the branches of the maple tree. It was far too large for her small backyard, but she refused to have it cut down.

Heart pounding, Erin sat beside her, and sought for the right words. "Gran, this is terribly important," she said, taking her grandmother's hand. It felt disconcertingly like a dead bird in her hands. "For Mom's sake, I have to know the truth."

"The truth would only do her more harm now," Anna whispered, her iron-gray head still averted.

"Then tell me, at least, so that I know how to help her."

Silence.

"Gran, she's still a comparatively young woman!" Erin cried. "I can't lose her as well."

A spasm of the hand in hers. Then, Anna said: "I don't see how what happened more than fifty years ago will help her now."

"I don't, either. All I know is that Dad's death has resurrected all these memories she's hidden away for so long. Unless she can work out what happened to her in the past, she might get even more depressed. She's afraid to leave the house. She talks about not being able to face the future without Dad. I'm beginning to feel," Erin said in a flat voice, "as if I've lost both my parents, not just Dad."

For the first time since Erin had cleared the table away, her grandmother looked at her. Gazing into the pale gray eyes, Erin shivered, suddenly afraid of what her grandmother was going to say.

"We've never told another living soul this," Anna whispered. "Jo made me swear never to tell anyone."

Erin stared at her grandmother. So there *was* a family secret. "Grandpa would have understood," she said, her heart beating fast in anticipation.

"I hope you're right." Anna fumbled with the papers at the end of the sofa. Then her hands stilled and she folded them in her lap. There was another long spell of silence that Erin did not dare break. Then her grandmother began speaking.

"When the Canadian government offered to take evacuees from Britain, they asked for volunteers to care for them in their homes. Jo and I had no children of our own. We were one of the first to offer our home. When we first saw your mother our hearts went out to her. She was only five years old, as you know."

It was hard to believe. Five years old, torn from her home and family, and sent across the Atlantic to strangers.

"She was painfully thin," her grandmother continued, "and she'd been sick on the boat and on the long train journey across Canada, so she smelled terrible. Poor little mite, she hadn't been able to eat for days. She was well dressed in a coat with a little velvet collar. She carried her gas mask in a cardboard box slung across her on a string."

Tears filled Erin's eyes. "Poor little thing."

"They'd rounded the children up and taken them into a school to be sorted out. Some of them were crying, because they'd been separated from brothers or sisters. Your mother stood apart, those brown eyes of hers looking as big as saucers in her thin little face. Like all the other children, she had a label pinned to her coat, with her name and address on it. Mary Selden, it said."

"Wait a minute. Mary Selden? That wasn't Mom's name."

"So we learned. When we called her that, she kept telling us that wasn't her name. Her name was Kate or

Katie, she told us. Thinking there had been an error, we immediately contacted the authorities, but they said her name was definitely Mary Selden. That the separation from her family must have confused her. Call her whatever she wants, they said, until she settles in. Then we found the book and—"

"What book?"

"I'll show it to you in a minute," Anna said sharply, annoyed at being interrupted. "So Kate she was. And always has been."

"How very strange." Erin was about to ask more, but she thought it best to let her grandmother finish before she asked questions. She was on a roll now.

"After a few weeks had gone by, we began to think it kind of odd that we hadn't heard from the child's mother. But we knew that there was heavy bombing in London by this time. In fact, Kate's group of evacuees was the last to reach Canada. Two of the subsequent evacuee boats were torpedoed. The second one, *City of Benares,* was sunk and seventy-three children were killed. After that, there were no more children sent to Canada."

"I'm not surprised. I think it was wrong, anyway, to tear children away from their parents, even if there was a war on."

"I wonder if you'd have felt the same way, if you knew that your child could be blasted away by a bomb at any moment. At the time, many thought it was the right thing to do. To save as many children as possible. After all, Hitler was threatening to invade Britain. They wanted to save the children and . . ." Her voice trailed away. "Now I've lost my train of thought," she said, her voice sharp with annoyance. "Where was I?"

"Wondering why you hadn't heard from little Kate's mother."

"Oh, yes. So I got in touch with the authorities again and they said they'd look into it."

Again, Anna subsided into silence.

"And?" prompted Erin, after a few moments.

"They wrote me a letter. It said that the address they'd been given was a false one. So was the name. They couldn't trace Kate's parents."

"Oh, my God."

"At first Jo and I thought there'd been some bureaucratic mix-up. We got in touch with our M.P. He took up our case and had his office make inquiries. They came up with the same results. There was no such address in London. Of course, all this time poor little Kate was asking us where her mother was, why hadn't she written to her, as she'd promised to do. I had to make excuses. She used to cry herself to sleep, asking for her 'Mummy' or her 'Mam,' as she sometimes called her. Eventually she stopped asking for her, but I had the feeling that she hadn't forgotten her."

"We know now that she hadn't. She'd just pushed it all away into her subconscious, because it was too painful to think about." Erin hesitated, not quite knowing how to couch her next question. "Are you saying that her parents hadn't been killed in the blitz at all?"

"We don't know what happened to them. I just made that up as an excuse."

Erin was amazed at the matter-of-fact tone her grandmother used to tell her this monumental news. "What about the false name and address?"

"I'm afraid Kate's mother must have thought that the evacuation scheme would be a good way of getting rid of an unwanted child."

Erin stared at her. "No," she said flatly. "I can't believe any mother could be that callous."

Anna raised her thin shoulders slowly and then released them with a long sigh. "War makes people do strange things, Erin. She was probably an unwed mother. In those days that was a terrible stigma."

"It's still no excuse," Erin said, her voice rising. "I can't believe anyone would do such a thing." This was her flesh and blood they were talking about. Her real grandmother! "So you adopted Mom. Didn't you need papers for that?"

"We waited six years. The war had been over for quite a while. Kate was almost twelve by then. In all that time, no one had claimed her."

Erin wanted to cry. She also felt like pounding something or someone.

"They told us we could adopt her," her grandmother

said, "as there'd been no claim made to her. By that time, she seemed to have settled in very well with us, and called us Mom and Dad." There was a hint of defensiveness in Anna's voice. "We loved that child just as much as if she was our very own."

"Of course you did, Gran. You were the best parents." Impulsively, Erin leaned over and hugged her grandmother, although she knew she didn't much like being hugged. "The best grandparents, too."

"I'm afraid that's all I can tell you," Anna said in a quavering voice. "As you can see, it's not much help to your mother now. In fact, I think it would be devastating for her to find out that her mother had abandoned her. Far better for her to think that she died in the blitz."

"I'm not so sure about that. It depends on whether her mother actually did abandon her."

Her grandmother's eyes widened. "You're surely not going to tell her," she protested.

"I'll talk to Dr. Wainwright about it, see what she says. Meanwhile, Gran, you said something about a book?"

Her grandmother stiffly rose to her feet and grasped her stick. "It's locked away in the dresser."

"Can I get it for you?"

"No, you most certainly cannot. I shall get it for myself."

Slowly, Anna crossed the room and went to the old oak dresser that had stood in the same corner for as long as Erin could remember. She'd always thought of it as Gran's treasure chest. The repository of bags of sticky peppermints, bits of rolled-up string, small notepads with animal pictures on the covers, and greeting cards—usually flowery ones—for every possible occasion.

Her grandmother unlocked one of the lower drawers and dragged it out. Reaching right into the back, she drew out a package wrapped in brown paper and tied with string.

She walked back and threw the package on Erin's lap. "There you are, Miss Nosy-Parker."

Erin ignored the jibe. This wasn't the time to get into one of her fights with her grandmother. The string was tied with her notoriously difficult knots. "Have you got some scissors?"

"Oh, give it to me." Anna grabbed it from her and began painstakingly picking at the knots until Erin felt like screaming. "There you are. All it needs is a little patience."

Erin breathed deeply and then drew the book from its wrappings. It was a slim volume bound in red, and bore the title in faded gilt lettering: *The Secret Garden.*

"How strange! Mom mentioned *The Secret Garden* last night when she'd told me about her nightmare."

"It was one of her favorite books when she was a child."

"Why did you wrap it up and hide it away, then?"

"Because once I knew that she'd been abandoned, I thought it best in the circumstances that she not be reminded of her past." Anna leaned across to open the book to the front page, pointing at it with her crooked index finger.

There was an inscription there, written in round, childish handwriting. As she read it, Erin held her breath.

To Katie, from your Mam. I shall love you always, my darling daughter.

She released her breath in a long sigh, tears welling in her eyes. "*I shall love you always.* That doesn't sound like a mother who would abandon her daughter, does it?"

"It sounds pretty final to me. We didn't notice the inscription until a long while after Kate arrived. It confirmed, of course, that Kate—or Katie—was her correct Christian name, but told us absolutely nothing else about her parentage. When we discovered that her surname and address were false, I decided it was best to take away the book."

Erin considered it cruel to have taken away the only memento of her mother little Kate had, but didn't say so. She began to riffle through the pages, years of dust tickling her nose. The illustrations were old-fashioned and faded. She noticed that the lining inside the back cover had almost peeled away and began picking at it. It lifted easily. Inside was tucked a small envelope, its whiteness mottled and yellowed. There was nothing written on it.

"What's that?" her grandmother asked.

"I don't know. It's open." Erin drew out a black-and-white photograph, cracked with age.

"Bless me!" her grandmother said. "I never saw that before." She held out her hand for the picture, but Erin ignored her, taking it to the window to look at it in the better light there.

The faded photograph showed a pretty, dark-haired young woman dressed simply in a light-colored blouse and a three-quarter-length straight dark skirt. She was smiling up at the young man who was standing by a sleek and extremely expensive-looking sports car. The man—not much more than a boy, really—was classically handsome, his long legs clad in white or cream trousers. With his air of assurance, almost arrogance, no one could mistake him for anything other than a member of the English upper class.

Erin became aware that her heart was hammering in her chest. She gave the photograph to her grandmother.

"Those were the clothes of the thirties," Anna said.

"This could be Mom's mother, couldn't it?"

"Not very likely," her grandmother said dryly. "She'd hardly have sent her away if she'd had a car like that, would she?"

"It was probably the man's car. He might have been her lover," Erin said, thinking out loud.

"You mean that the man in the photograph was the reason for her sending her child away? I suppose that's possible."

"No. No, I don't think that's how it was at all." Erin shook her head vehemently. "If that was the case, there's no way she would have put the photograph in the book for her daughter." She took the photograph back from her grandmother.

"Who says she did? It's probably a picture of complete strangers. Give it to me." Anna held out her hand.

"No way. You'd tear it up."

"If you intend to show it your mother and make her even more upset, I certainly would. Don't tell her, Erin,"

Anna pleaded. "She mustn't know anything about all this."

Erin slipped the photograph into its envelope and put it inside the book again, snapping it shut. "Sorry, but I'm keeping this, Gran. It could be part of my heritage, too, you know."

"Romantic garbage," Anna muttered, stomping across the floor to the sofa.

"Garbage or not, I want you to try to remember every little detail that Mom told you when she first came to you as a child in 1940. With this book and photograph and Mom's dreams, we've already got some clues. But we need more."

"What on earth for?" her grandmother demanded.

"Because," Erin said, "there's obviously some big mystery about Mom's past. I intend to find out the truth about her parentage and why she was abandoned."

Chapter Four

That morning, Kate had decided that she would try once again to go downtown. She needed several things. More mohair wool to finish the sweater she was knitting for Erin, some paint for the basement wall . . . Besides, it was time she got out again, she told herself, trying to ignore the fact that her heart was pounding furiously at the very thought of leaving the house.

Surely she'd feel fine in the familiar environment of Eaton's department store. Perhaps she should phone Pam Thiessen to see if she could meet her for lunch in the Grill Room. It was ages since she'd tasted Eaton's chicken pot pie.

She had actually pressed the first three digits of Pam's number when she set the receiver down again. After all, if she committed herself to meeting someone, she wouldn't be able to escape if she had another one of those "feelings." Better to go alone this time. Next time she'd call Pam.

She had a long shower, washed her hair, even did her nails properly for the first time since Jim had died. "Oh, Jim," she whispered, tears oozing from her eyes. She seemed to have a never-ending supply of tears, always at the ready. They came at the most unexpected times, when she watched the news, for instance, or when she saw a Huggies diaper ad. Perhaps it would be better not to turn on the television at all.

Her hands began shaking when she was putting on her lipstick. Then the shaking spread to her legs, so that she had to sit down. The black cloud that had been lurking somewhere in a corner of her mind began to spread.

The phone rang, making her jump, so that her heart

beat even faster. She picked up the receiver in her bedroom.

"Hello, Kate."

Oh, lord. It was Pam. "Hi, Pam."

"I just wondered if you felt like lunch today? You said you might feel like it at the end of this week. And here we are, Friday. My day off without pay, courtesy of the provincial government cutbacks. How about it?"

Pam sounded her usual bubbly self, but there was a hint of tension in her voice. This was about the sixth time she'd called to suggest going out. Each time Kate had found an excuse not to go.

"Well, I . . ."

Don't be an idiot, Kate told herself. You're all dressed up, ready to go. She drew in a deep breath, determined to ignore her trembling legs and pounding heart. "Why not? I need some things at Eaton's. What about lunch at the Grill Room?"

"Sounds great." Kate sensed Pam's relief. "I'll pick you up. What time?"

"Could you make it soon?" Kate knew that she might change her mind if she had too much time to think.

"I can come right away. I'll be there in fifteen minutes. Okay?"

"Yes, yes. Fine," Kate said breathlessly.

But she knew as soon as she set the receiver down that it wasn't fine at all. She was feeling sick now and sweating, as if she were going through the menopause again. *Oh God, I don't think I can do this,* she thought, as she made her way downstairs, her damp palms sticking to the banister.

By the time Pam's car drew up at the front of the house, Kate was so tense she could hardly breathe. Pam honked the horn twice. Kate rechecked that the back door was locked, set the alarm, and walked unsteadily to the front door.

"Hold on a minute," she shouted to Pam. "I just have to lock the back door." Anything to gain a little more time.

The alarm was beeping. Had she left herself enough time to get out or should she reset it? Oh, God, why was she such a mess? What had happened to her old organized self? She hated this weepy, shaking, insecure person she'd become.

She locked the front door and started down the path, wishing she had a railing to hold on to. When she slid into the passenger seat Pam leaned over to give her a hug. Kate tried not to shrink away. Nowadays, any physical contact made her feel as if she would shatter into a thousand tiny pieces.

"Boy, it's great to see you," Pam said. "You look terrific."

"I'm feeling much better," Kate lied. "It's funny you should call. It was such a lovely day, I was going to phone you. That's why I was ready to go so quickly."

"That's great. It won't be long before you're back running everything again. The volunteer bureau's not the same without you."

Kate gave her a faint smile. They'd have to miss her for a darned long time, the way she was feeling. "I need a little more time," she told Pam.

"Of course you do," Pam said. "But you'll be surprised how quickly you'll get back to your old self, once you get out into the world again."

The pressure of everyone's expectations pressed down on Kate like a heavy gray blanket.

By the time they reached Eaton's car park, she was answering Pam in monosyllables, her entire being concentrating on keeping herself from falling apart, making a fool of herself in public.

"Do you want to shop first?" Pam asked. "Or eat?"

Kate stood by the Estée Lauder counter, the mixture of exotic scents making her feel faint. The floor was unsteady beneath her feet. Everything seemed to be heaving up and down around her.

"I'm not feeling too good," she heard herself say, as if she were a long way off.

Pam took her elbow. "Let's take the elevator up to the fifth floor then. You can sit down and rest in the Grill Room."

She led Kate to the elevator, but when the doors opened Kate couldn't go in. She wrenched her arm away. "I can't," she said distractedly. "I must go home I have to go home."

People were staring at her, white faces looming. She wanted to run, run . . . but she couldn't because her legs were weighed down with lead. Her heart was pounding so fast she was afraid she'd have a heart attack. *You can't do that,* she told herself. *If you die, Erin will be an orphan.*

Orphan, orphan, orphan. The words seemed to boom in the hollow inside her head.

"I have to go home. I'll be fine once I get home."

Pam led her to the side door. "Take deep breaths. You're hyperventilating," she said quite calmly, as if it was an everyday occurrence.

Which it is, thought Kate.

"Slowly now. Breathe slowly."

Kate tried to breathe slowly, but it was almost impossible with her mind screaming at her to run before the danger that hid behind every counter jumped out at her.

"That's better," Pam said.

To her utter embarrassment, Kate began to cry. She was aware of people turning to look at her, wondering what on earth was wrong with her.

"Oh, Kate." Pam's arm went around her.

"Please take me home," Kate pleaded. "I want to go home."

"Of course I will. Can you walk to the car park? I don't want to leave you alone here while I bring the car around."

"Yes, yes, I'll walk." Anything, to get out of there. The relief at the thought of going home, being safe again, was overwhelming. She should never have come out in the first place. Kate walked as fast as possible to the car park, ahead of Pam, the snow-covered path—trodden into mud in places—slowing her down. She wished she could break into a run.

"Does your doctor know you're having panic attacks?" Pam asked her in the car, as she drove down to Portage Avenue.

"Panic attacks?" Kate repeated. It sounded so ordinary, so mundane, hardly describing the blind terror, the dissolution of self, the utter disintegration that she'd just undergone. "Yes, I told her. She said the grief counseling would help."

"So it will. You'll be amazed how quickly you'll get better." Thus spoke Pam, her dear friend, the professional social worker, unwittingly exerting pressure on her again.

Blinking, Kate turned to look out the car window. There was a German shepherd in the open back of the truck in the next lane. As the truck bounced along, he was fighting to keep on his feet. Poor thing, Kate thought. She knew exactly how he felt. "I don't think I'll ever get better," she told Pam, bleak despair washing over her.

"What garbage! Depression can be treated with medication. Once you've dealt with the grief, you'll be a new person. It's very important to take time to mourn the loss of someone you love, to adjust to the differences in your life."

"Then why are you telling me how quickly it will all be better?" Kate demanded. "You keep pressuring me, everyone keeps pressuring me, to get better *quickly.* Then you tell me that it takes time. I wish you'd damned well make up your mind."

"I'm sorry, Kate. I didn't mean to exert pressure on you." Pam sounded hurt. "You take all the time you need. Your friends will be here for you, however long it takes."

"I'm not sure I want to wait that long."

Pam phoned Erin that evening. "It's Pam. Is your mother around? Can you speak without her hearing?"

"Yes. She went to bed early. She seemed extra quiet, as if she didn't want to talk."

"Did she tell you what happened today?"

"Today? No. What happened?"

"She didn't tell you we went to Eaton's today, then."

"No. She never said a word. Eaton's? That's great."

"Not so great, I'm afraid. She had a bad panic attack there and fell to pieces."

Erin's heart sank. "Oh, no."

"I hadn't realized how bad things were. She should be seeing someone right away, Erin. I'm concerned about her."

"We all are," Erin said, stung. She felt as if Pam was suggesting that she was neglecting her mother.

"She said something about not wanting to wait to get better."

"Do you mean you think she's suicidal?"

"I don't really think so, but she's certainly very depressed."

"I'll speak to Dr. Wainwright first thing tomorrow. Thanks, Pam." Erin hesitated. "I think there's more to it than just Dad's death."

"What do you mean?"

"There's Mom's childhood. You know about that."

"Sort of. She was an English evacuee whose parents were killed, right? Oh . . . you mean Jim's death has made her think about losing her parents."

"I think so. She's having nightmares about that, anyway. I was speaking to my grandmother about it today."

"Any help there?"

"Perhaps." Erin wasn't about to tell Pam what she'd learned from her grandmother. "We'll see. I'm sorry about today. It can't have been easy for you."

"Who cares about it being easy for me! It was Kate who was suffering, not me. She's my friend, Erin. I want her back, too, just like you do."

"You're right."

When Erin put down the receiver, she didn't hear the slight click of the bedroom receiver being replaced.

Upstairs, Kate sat in the dark bedroom, staring at the telephone on Jim's chest of drawers. People were discussing her as if she no longer existed. She felt totally out of control of her own life. And what was all this about Erin talking to her grandmother today? She was determined to find out what was going on.

She stood up, meaning to go and speak to Erin, ask her what she and Anna had been discussing, but then decided against it. She was seized with a feeling of unbearable fatigue, as if just raising her arm was too much effort, never mind going downstairs to confront Erin. What she really wanted to do was sleep. The sleeping pill was taking effect, making her feel woozy. She'd just lie down and see what happened.

Please God, she prayed, as she pulled the quilt over her, let there be no bad dreams tonight.

After her mother went to bed, Erin sat for a long time making notes in a new black notebook. It was what she always did when she was embarking on research for a new program. This time was different. This time the research was of vital personal importance both to her and her family.

She'd learned a great deal about her mother's childhood today. Not only from her grandmother's story and the book and photograph, but also from the realization that everything possible had been done to eradicate all Mom's memories of her background, even to taking away the only gift her mother had given her.

Erin shook her head and made another note in her book.

She was sure that her grandmother had done it for the best, but it was easy to see why now, when she was undergoing another trauma, her mother's repressed memories were coming out in the form of nightmares and panic attacks.

When she'd made all her notes, listing the pros and cons of telling her mother what she'd learned today, Erin took out *The Secret Garden* again and reread the inscription. Then she began to read the book itself. She was so immersed that it took several seconds before she realized that her mother was crying out.

Another nightmare. Would it never end?

Erin looked around. She opened one of the cupboards and thrust the book into a large casserole dish. Then she hesitated for a moment, the casserole lid in her hand. Perhaps this was the time, after all, to return the book to its owner. She took it out again and set it down on the table. Then she raced upstairs.

Her mother was sitting up in bed, eyes wide open, screaming: "Mummy! Mummy! I can't see you! Where are you, Mummy?"

Erin hugged her mother. Her body was stiff with terror, her arms extended. "It's okay, Mom. Just another bad dream," she said soothingly, by now used to the routine.

She felt her mother shudder and then relax against her. "Erin?"

"Yes, it's me, Mom. You had another bad dream, that's all."

Her mother's hair and nightdress were wringing wet. "Oh, Erin, it was so real," she whispered. "We were going down a street lined with houses, but there was no light anywhere. All the houses were in darkness, with black curtains over the windows. Someone was holding my hand, dragging me along, and I was crying. There was a scary droning sound overhead and they yelled at me to run. Then they took me down some steps into this horrible crowded place deep in the ground that smelled of petrol fumes and people. It was full of other children and a lot of them were crying, including me. That's when you woke me up."

"It could have been an air raid, from the sound of it. We're going to have to start doing some research into 1940 in wartime England, to see what it was like. But before we do that, I've got something to show you."

The words were out before she knew it. Too late now to retract them.

"What?" asked her mother, her tone suspicious.

"Put on a dry nightdress—"

"There are pajamas in the drawer."

"Okay. Put them on and I'll put the kettle on." Her mother was shivering now. "Would you like to have a quick bath?"

"No. I don't want to be alone," Kate said through chattering teeth.

"I'd stay with you."

"No. I don't want a bath. But I will have a cup of tea. What's this surprise?"

Erin smiled. "Wait and see."

She went downstairs, put the book away in the nearest drawer, and then put the kettle on.

"What's the surprise?" her mother asked again when she came down to the kitchen.

"There's your tea. Sit down and I'll show you." Her mother pulled a chair out and sat at the pine table in the windowed alcove that overlooked the long veranda and the back garden. Erin pushed the book across the table to her.

"What's this?" Her mother frowned. "Oh, *The Secret Garden.* That's strange. I could have sworn yours was a paperback. Did you find anything in it that was like my dream? Like the house in the dream, I mean." Kate opened the book as she spoke. Her eyes widened as she read the inscription. She put her hand to her mouth. "Oh, my God," she whispered.

Erin held her breath.

Her mother's fingers stroked lightly along the faded lines her mother had written, as if the page was made of the softest velvet.

"Did you remember she'd given you the book?" Erin asked, after a few seconds of silence.

Her mother looked at her blankly, as if she'd forgotten she was there. "No, of course not. I'd have told you, shown you, if I had. Where did you find this?"

"Gran had it."

"What do you mean, she had it?"

Erin hesitated, searching for the right words. "She put it away when you were a child. She thought it was better for you not to think about your mother, when you were making a new life in Canada."

Tears welled in her mother's eyes as she ran her fingers over the inscription again. "My mother's writing," she whispered.

"There's something else." Erin drew out the photograph. "This was in the book. It fell out when I opened it. Gran said she'd never seen it before."

Kate took the picture and stared at it. Again, she said nothing.

"Do you think it's your mother?" Erin asked.

Kate shook her head slowly. "I have no idea. I keep telling you, I can't remember what she looked like."

"I think it's your mother. She looks exactly like you in your wedding picture. The same dark eyes and wavy hair."

"You're jumping to conclusions," her mother told her, frowning.

"The man's gorgeous. Much better looking than Hugh Grant. He could be your father."

Her mother slapped the photograph down on the table. "Don't talk such nonsense, Erin. My father worked in a bakery. That's what it said on my identification card. This man is definitely not a baker. My parents lived in a street of terraced houses in Wandsworth. Someone told my mother—I mean Anna—that, when she inquired. The entire street was flattened by a land mine."

Erin hesitated. Gran had warned her not to tell her mother the truth, but surely the discovery of the book shed a new light on the mystery. Besides, her mother deserved the truth. She took a deep breath. "That wasn't true."

"What wasn't?"

"The bomb killing your parents. That wasn't true. Gran made it up."

"Stop talking garbage, Erin."

"I mean it. I went to see Gran today."

"So I gathered. To talk about me behind my back?"

"No, not really. We both love you, Mom, and we're worried about you."

"If you'd all leave me alone and stop expecting so much of me, I'd be fine. Pam's the same. 'You'll be your old self very soon.' I'll never be my old self!" Kate shouted, tears filling her eyes. "Never!"

"I know that, Mom. I know things will never be the same for you." Erin handed her the box of tissues from the top of the fridge. "They'll never be the same for me, either, you know," she said in a muffled voice. "Don't forget he was my father."

"Oh, Erin, I'm sorry." Her mother shook her head, fighting to hold back the tears. "I'm such a mess at the moment, I don't seem to be able to cope. I hate being like this," she said, pounding her fist on the table. "I hate it."

"I know that. I also know that this won't last. Even though you think you'll never get over it, you will. We both will. And I think that solving the mystery of your background might help." Erin ran her fingers over the photograph.

"There is no mystery."

"Ask Gran, if you don't believe me."

"I will."

Damn, Erin thought. Gran's going to *kill* me.

"Why would she make up the story about the bomb?" her mother asked.

Erin grimaced. "That's the sticky part. It seems that the address and name you were given were false."

"False?"

"They didn't exist."

"What do you mean?"

"They were invented."

Her mother stared at her. "And that's supposed to make me feel better? If what you say is true, it means that my mother wanted to get rid of me, doesn't it?" Her eyes widened. "Doesn't it?" she repeated, her voice rising, when Erin didn't reply.

"I thought that, too, at first, until I found the book. That wasn't the message of an uncaring mother."

"Oh, Erin," her mother said with a sigh. "You've a lot to learn about life. There are plenty of mothers who've given up their children so they can make a better life for themselves . . . or because of a man." She picked up the photograph again. "Had it occurred to you that, far from being my father, this man might have been the reason for my mother wanting to get rid of me?"

"Yes."

"That would make more sense, in the circumstances." Kate stared down at the photograph and then turned her head to gaze out the window at the darkness outside.

Erin began to wonder if she'd been right to tell her. "I thought so, too—for a moment. But then I decided it couldn't be her lover. Your mother would never have put the photo in your book if it was."

"It might have been the only picture she had."

"Then she would have cut the man out of the picture."

"Oh, Erin. You're such a romantic. It's probably not my mother at all." Kate pushed aside the photograph and the book, and picked up her teacup.

Erin went to stand over her. "Yes, it is. And you know it is. And you know something else? We're going to get to the bottom of this, you and I."

"You do what you want, dear," her mother said resignedly. "Just don't ask me to get involved." She drank down her tea, and then stared gloomily into the empty cup. "I'm just not capable of thinking about anything at the moment."

"I know you're not, but I intend to start looking into this right away." Erin's investigative spirit was up. "Once I get going, I bet you'll want to become involved. I think it will be good for both of us."

Her mother gave her a faint smile and shook her head.

Despite her mother's seeming disinterest, Erin couldn't contain her excitement. "You do realize, Mom, don't you, that your mother could still be alive?"

"I doubt that very much. She'd be in her eighties, wouldn't she? Besides, I don't care. I'm not interested in that part of my life."

Erin didn't believe her. "Not only your mother, but your father might still be alive, too. Whoever he is!"

Chapter Five

Several weeks had passed since the last time Simon had been to Amberley Court. He couldn't wait any longer. The party's pressure on him to make a public announcement had become too intense.

To ensure that he had to spend as little time as possible at Amberley, he didn't leave London until after lunch on Saturday. And this time he brought Olivia and the girls with him as backup.

"Maytime at Amberley," Olivia said with a satisfied sigh as they drove beneath the flowering horse-chestnut trees. Smiling, she turned her head to look out the side window. She could catch glimpses of the indigo mist of violets and forget-me-nots and the last bluebells that carpeted the woodland, as if patches of the blue sky were reflected there. The country aroma of rain-wet earth wafted through the open window.

Simon glanced at Olivia's profile, the silvery-blond hair curving against her white neck. "You really love coming to Amberley, don't you?" he said.

Olivia turned her head. "Sorry, but I do. I know you're not so keen, but that's because Amberley is all tied up with unhappy memories for you."

"Once it's mine, I shall enjoy it," Simon said. His eyes were fixed on the road winding ahead.

"For me," Olivia said, "Amberley has no bad memories. So I'm free to love it."

"I suppose you'll want to live here when my grandfather dies."

"Not permanently, darling. It's too far from good schools for the girls. But I would like to spend our summers—"

"Is our great-grandpa going to die soon?" Nicola asked in her clear voice.

"No, of course he's not," Olivia told her, giving Simon a warning frown.

"But Daddy said—"

"Daddy was talking about a long time in the future, not now," her mother told her.

"I don't want Daddy to die," Perdita wailed and then began to sob. From her cage behind the rear seat, their spaniel, Trixie, whined in sympathy.

"Silly," Nicola said. "Daddy isn't going to die. It's Great-grandpa who's going to die."

"No one's going to die," Simon shouted. Hell! What a start to what was bound to be a disastrous weekend.

Olivia gave him a surprised look. Simon rarely lost his temper. "We can't arrive with Perdita crying," she said. "Stop for a moment, Simon."

Muttering to himself, Simon pulled the car into the side of the drive.

"Perdy, stop that stupid noise at once," Olivia said.

The five-year-old sniffed and gulped. "But Daddy said—"

"You didn't listen properly," Nicola told her with all the scorn of an older sister. "You never do."

Simon reached over to haul Perdita from the back seat and sat her on his lap. "Hush, sweetheart," he said, drying her eyes. "Everyone's going to live for a very long time, including Great-grandpa."

As he calmed his daughter's fears, the thought came into Simon's mind that, in fact, it would be better for him if the old man were to die as soon as possible. His death would make Simon's renunciation of the title far more effective. The thought gave him a spasm of what might, in another person, be guilt. However, Simon recognized it for what it really was, a quirk of irony.

Once peace was restored, they continued up the driveway and came to a halt in front of the house. All smiles, they climbed out of the car, to be greeted first by Lord Maybridge himself, and then Harrington and Mrs. Edwards.

Olivia kissed Giles's cheek. "How lovely to see you," she told him. "I've missed you so much."

"Then you should make sure that husband of yours brings you here more often," Giles said gruffly. "And how are my two little beauties?" he asked, turning to the girls, leaning heavily on his walking stick to bend to their level.

"Hello, Great-grandpa," Nicola said, lifting her face to be kissed.

But Perdita hung back, suddenly shy. She stared up at Giles, her blue eyes wide. "Well, Princess Perdita, you look as if you've seen a ghost," her great-grandfather said, beaming down at her. "Do I get a kiss or not?"

She nodded, and held up her arms to him. He scooped her up with one arm, hugging her against him.

Olivia was annoyed. Simon's grandfather never tried to hide the fact that he favored shy Perdita over the more confident Nicola. Their mother didn't believe in showing favoritism. Not openly, anyway.

They all went inside, led by Trixie, who danced around them, barking wildly with excitement. Lord Maybridge's more sedate golden retriever and Airedale were content to walk beside the group, their nails clicking on the tiled floor.

"That bitch of yours needs some discipline," Giles said.

"She's young and very excited," Olivia said. "She's not used to all this space."

Nor, for that matter, was Olivia. She had been brought up in a large detached house in Barnes, the child of middle-class parents, her father a bank manager, her mother a teacher of languages in a private school.

Very occasionally, when Simon was in one of his strange, abstract moods, Olivia wondered if he'd chosen her for political reasons rather than love. Perhaps he'd considered someone like her—with her good solid background—would make the perfect wife for a politician. Simon had always been eager to distance himself from his aristocratic background, knowing that it turned off a large part of the voting population.

But whatever his original reason for being attracted to her, she knew that Simon loved her now and was faithful to her. Which was more than could be said for some other Tory members. The party had been riddled with scandals recently, both personal and financial. So much so that a new set of guidelines, a sort of members' moral code, had been prepared the previous year.

As they started up the wide staircase to go to their room, Olivia linked her arm in Simon's, pressing his against the side of her breast. He responded with an appreciative look. *Later,* it said.

Not only was Simon faithful, but Olivia meant to keep it that way. For one thing, she found him extremely exciting. There was a sense of unexplored, potentially dangerous, territory to Simon that she found sexually stimulating. And, emotionally, she loved him more than any other man she'd ever known. Although sometimes she wondered whether she knew Simon at all.

No, keeping Simon faithful was not difficult. Apart from her confidence in her own ability to excite him, Olivia was well aware that if Simon was to gain their joint ambition, not a breath of scandal must touch either of them.

When Mrs. Edwards had borne the children off to their room and Simon closed the door, Olivia stood in the center of the bedroom and slowly dragged off her heavy wool sweater.

Simon released his breath in a low whistle. "My God, Olivia. You mean you weren't wearing a bra all this time? A good thing I didn't know that while I was driving or I'd have been dragging you into the woods for a quickie on the way down."

He dropped the large briefcase he was carrying and came to her, his hands encircling her breasts, thumbs firming her nipples, so that they stood erect, eager for his mouth to suck on them.

She excited him so much that he dragged down her jeans and took her there, in the middle of the room that had once been his parents', defying the convention that sex should be performed in the four-poster bed, beneath the tapestry cover, and never in broad daylight.

Afterward, they stood there in a pool of sunlight, gazing into each other's eyes, laughing.

"Simon, you didn't even draw the curtains," Olivia said, through her laughter. "Anyone from the garden could have seen us if they'd looked up." She reached for her silk dressing gown.

"Let them. This old place needs a bit of livening up. Don't cover yourself up yet."

She let the dressing gown fall, but instinctively folded her arms across her abdomen to cover the scar. "I don't know how you can bear to look at me in the daylight."

"I love every part of you. And *that* part tells me what you went through to give me our two lovely daughters." He gently moved her arms away and bent his head to press kisses along the faded scar. Then he turned away to pick up his jeans and shirt.

Olivia's heart quickened. *God, how I love this man,* she thought. There was nothing she wouldn't do for him. She pulled on her dressing gown and went into the bathroom to turn on the water for a bath. "Do you want a bath first?" she shouted.

"No, I'll have one later, before we change for dinner."

Olivia poured in some of her Yves Saint Laurent *Champagne* bath essence and then came back into the room. "After I've had my bath, we should take some time to plan your strategy with your grandfather."

Simon was pulling on his cable-knit sweater. When his face appeared, Olivia saw, with a sinking feeling in the pit of her stomach, that it bore that blank expression she knew so well, the one that meant he was beginning to shut her out.

"No need for strategy," he said lightly. He sat on the edge of the wing chair to tie his shoes. "There's nothing he can say or do to change my decision."

"We don't want to upset him again, do we? I worry about making him ill."

"Olivia, we've discussed this ad nauseam. I have waited two months to give him my final decision. That is quite long enough. I refuse to let the old man and his feigned illnesses scare me off."

She drew the tasseled belt of her dressing-gown through her fingers. "He might decide to change his will."

"So? What would that do?"

"We could lose Amberley."

Simon gave her a cold look. "I would remind you that that possibility worries you far more than it does me."

"You once told me that Amberley was the only part of the Maybridge estate worth having."

"Don't worry, Darling." Simon tightened the knot in his shoelace with a jerk. "You'll get your precious Amberley. It's been in the family since the end of the seventeenth century. The old man would never divide up the estate."

"I hope you're right."

"Besides, who would he give it to?"

Olivia raised her shoulders and lowered them slowly. "I don't know."

"Exactly. However angry he might be with me, do you really think my grandfather would leave his beloved Amberley to some stranger?"

"I don't suppose so."

"Family is all important to my grandfather. You know that."

"What about David Lennox, though? After all, he is the heir to the title after you."

"The old man loathes the thought of Lennox inheriting the title. There's no way he'd leave anything to him. As you know, the only time David Lennox comes to Amberley is for the annual family gathering for Grandfather's birthday. Apart from that, he's virtually a stranger to the family. I don't think he's even spent Christmas at Amberley."

"He did, once, about five years ago, remember? Your grandfather was so incredibly rude to him he never came again. Why *does* he treat David so badly?"

"I've told you before," Simon said impatiently. "It's something to do with David's grandmother. Old Cousin Lucy married against the twelfth earl's wishes. She was tossed out of Amberley and never allowed to return. Besides that, the old man dislikes David because his mother's an American and he was brought up in the States."

For obvious reasons, Simon did not tell Olivia about his grandfather's recent warning that Lennox *would* inherit if Simon failed to have a son.

But Olivia voiced his thoughts. "I wish we could do

something about this stupid entail. It's ridiculous in this so-called emancipated age. Why should the girls lose their inheritance because we haven't had a son? Can't anything be done about it?"

"They've tried to change the law on entailed estates, but it would never get through the House of Lords."

Olivia turned away, tears stinging her eyes. "Maybe we should—"

"Don't even say it. You know what the doctors said last time. Two cesareans are enough."

Blinking rapidly, Olivia bent to pick up her shoes and set them neatly by the chair. "Are you absolutely sure you should tell him this weekend?"

"Absolutely."

"Couldn't it wait? After all, you can't officially renounce the title until he dies, can you?"

"No. But it's time it was made public. The caucus wants me to do it before they make their announcement. We've discussed this already, Olivia. That is why we're here." He spoke to her in an eminently reasonable tone, as if she were a child.

"He looks so much more frail than the last time I saw him." She put her hand on Simon's arm. "Supposing he has a stroke when you tell him? It could kill him."

"All the better. The timing would be perfect. Excuse me, I have to use the bathroom before you take your bath."

The bathroom door closed. Although he'd shut it quietly, Olivia felt as if Simon had slammed it in her face.

The atmosphere that evening was definitely strained. Nothing important had been discussed while the children were still with them. Once the girls had eaten their supper in the kitchen, followed by a romp in the garden with their great-grandfather and the dogs—all of them returning in a flurry of excitement because they'd found a curled-up hedgehog by the woodshed—Mrs. Edwards had taken them off for their baths.

Even then, when the three adults gathered in the library for their predinner drinks, nothing was said, as if there were a tacit agreement among them that they wait until after dinner before broaching the subject occupying everyone's mind.

I'll be damned if I'll leave them to their port and brandy after dinner like the good little woman, Olivia thought. She was an important part of Simon's decision and she intended to be at his side when he told Giles.

She ran her hand down the side of the velvet dress she'd bought for the occasion. It was the color of rich claret and had cost a great deal. She rarely wore anything this opulent, preferring elegant understatement in her clothes. But somehow Amberley deserved clothes from another era. She also knew that Giles liked women to dress up for dinner.

He was looking at her now over his glass of whiskey. "You look marvelous in that dress, my dear Olivia, very Elizabethan. Amberley is the perfect setting for it."

Olivia glowed. "Thank you. I thought you might like it."

"You're a bloody lucky man to have such an exquisite wife," Giles told Simon.

Simon's gaze met Olivia's across the hearth. "You don't have to tell me that," he said softly. "I know."

They exchanged small smiles. Olivia felt the tension slipping from her, knowing that this was Simon's apology for his earlier coldness.

The dinner was a fine one. Although Giles favored plain English cooking rather than fancy continental cuisine, the fillets of lamb were pink and succulent, served with a delicious purée of leeks with potato-and-sage fritters. The meal ended with the usual fine array of cheeses Amberley always provided, and a delicious pear-and-walnut tart.

When he'd finished his cheese, Giles pushed his plate aside. "Well, Simon. Shall we take our brandy in here?"

Olivia knew that Giles was expecting her to say that she would go and wait in the drawing room with the coffee until the men were ready to join her. She looked down at the small piece of glacéed fruit on her plate, picked up a speck of sugar with her finger, licked it, wiped her hand on her napkin . . . and said nothing.

"Why don't we go to the library?" Simon said. "It's warmer than the drawing room."

"Very well." His grandfather pushed back his chair, looking displeased, but he waited at the door for Olivia to go ahead of him.

Once Harrington had carried the tray of drinks and coffee to the library and Simon had thrown another log on the fire, an uneasy silence fell on them. It was broken at last by Giles.

"So . . ." he said, and waited for Simon to speak. When Simon said nothing, his grandfather's face flushed plum-red. "I take it that you haven't come here merely for a pleasant visit. Have you come to a decision about the title?"

"I have."

Olivia was sitting on the edge of her seat. *For God's sake, tell him, Simon,* she wanted to scream at him. It was almost as if Simon enjoyed making his grandfather drag it out of him.

Giles's face flushed an even darker red. "For Christ's sake, man, stop arsing around. Let's have it."

Simon leaned forward, fingertips touching. "I have told the caucus that if they wish to propose me for leader of the party I shall announce my intention to renounce my title to the media immediately."

"How the devil can you renounce a title you don't even have yet?" Giles demanded. Sensing his anger, his Airedale sprang to his feet, coat bristling, legs stiff, poised to defend him. His master grasped his collar, hauling him back.

"I can't," Simon said calmly. "Not officially, anyway. But the intent is there when the occasion arises."

"When I kick the bucket, you mean. And what happens if they change their mind, like Macmillan did with Hailsham? Do you meekly say, 'On second thoughts I think I'll be the Earl of Maybridge after all,' eh?"

"I get a year's grace to make that decision—"

"Once I'm dead," his grandfather reminded him.

Simon did not flinch from his grandfather's fury. "When you die," he agreed.

"So, willy-nilly, whatever happens, you will not be the next Earl of Maybridge. Is that right?"

Olivia's palms felt uncomfortably damp against the

soft velvet of her dress. She clutched her hands together in her lap.

"That is right," Simon said.

"You will leave our ancient title in a vacuum for all the years of your life, for thirty, perhaps forty, years?"

"I will."

"And I will see you damned in hell first." The words exploded from Giles in a spray of spittle. Leaning on his cane, he scrambled to his feet and stood swaying.

Olivia went to him. "Giles, you mustn't let yourself get overwrought. Please, sit down."

He pushed her from him, holding his stick in front of him to fend her off. "Get away from me. You could have stopped this if you'd wanted to," he told her. "He would have listened to you."

She looked up at him. Despite his stooped shoulders, Lord Maybridge had never before seemed quite so tall. "It's what Simon wants to do. Therefore, I want it, too."

He looked past her at Simon, who'd risen to his feet, but had made no move to approach him. "You're power hungry, that's what you are. You've always been driven by ambition."

"If you mean I'm not content to sit on my backside and live off the hard work of my ancestors, you're right."

"By God, you're proving yourself to be your mother's son after all, aren't you?"

Simon's mouth tightened into a thin line. "We will keep my mother out of this."

"Oh, will we?" Giles thumped his stick on the floor to emphasize each word. "I knew when your father married his secretary that no good would come of it. Now we see the result."

"You used to say that she was the best thing that ever happened to my father," Simon reminded him coldly.

Olivia tensed, knowing how Simon had revered his mother, who had died when he was only twelve. "She was a good woman, your mother. Only a saint could have put up with my son. But she wasn't the right stock. Her father pushed a barrow in Covent Garden."

"He was a clerk in a florist's office there."

"Whatever." Giles waved his hand impatiently. "It's all the same. Wrong stock. Never works."

"My mother's background has nothing to do with this, I assure you. I have based my decision solely on my desire to serve my country."

"Codswallop! You've based it on your desire for power." Giles's eyes glared at him from beneath extravagant eyebrows. "I warn you, Simon, if you make this announcement I shall do everything in my power to thwart you."

"There's nothing you can do, Grandfather. The old school has lost its power base in the party."

"To hell with the party. I'm talking about money, my boy. Money. I'll make sure you don't get a penny from me or from my estates."

"It's only the title I'm renouncing, not the estates. Those will come to me upon your death."

His smile infuriated Giles even further. "We shall see about that." He moved forward to thrust his head close to Simon. "I would remind you that Amberley is not part of the original Maybridge entail. It came into the family through marriage. Therefore, it can be willed elsewhere. And if it is, I would also remind you that it will be lost to you and your family forever, not for just one generation."

Simon's face became as hard and white as the marble bust on its plinth in the corner. "And I remind you, sir, that by doing so, you would lose all contact with the only family you have left in the world."

"Ah, but you will never know until my death what exactly I have done, will you?"

Olivia decided it was time she intervened before things went too far. "I think we're all feeling tired," she said firmly. "Why don't we calm down and go to bed? We'll see everything much more clearly in the morning, when we've had a good sleep."

Giles rounded on her. "I can see everything very clearly tonight, thank you, Olivia. I see a man who has no sense of tradition or familial duty. A man who would grasp at any opportunity to feed his vaunting ambition. Well, if he abandons the family, the family will abandon him." He glared down at them both. "I do not like to ask you to leave my library, so I myself will go elsewhere."

Olivia took his arm. "Please, Giles. If you would only listen to Simon. He has such wonderful ideas for the country. He intends to—"

He pushed her hand off. "I have no wish to hear his intentions. All I know is that he has broken my heart." Head averted, he pushed past them and limped from the room, his dogs following him.

They left Amberley the next morning, before nine, without seeing Lord Maybridge again: Simon having achieved his goal, Olivia uneasily aware that they might have lost Amberley, the children complaining at having to leave before they'd seen the new kittens in the barn Mrs. Edwards had promised to show them. Perdita, of course, was crying.

It wasn't until they'd rounded the corner and were driving up to the locked gates that they saw the cars and vans and television cameras waiting for them on the other side.

Spotting them, the media surged to the gates, cameras clicking and whirring, shouting their questions even before the car had come to a halt.

Chapter Six

Kate was standing on the step stool, vacuuming the den walls the night the picture came on the television screen. When she saw the magnificent red-brick house behind the wrought-iron gates she almost toppled off the step stool.

Scrambling down, she switched off the vacuum, only to discover that she'd left the television sound on mute. "Damn!" By the time she'd located the remote control beneath the drapes she'd taken down, the news had moved on to report about the European Common Market.

Heart hammering, she checked the channel. It was the CBC Newsworld channel, but the news wasn't on until eleven and it was now only ten minutes to eleven. She flicked through the television guide, her hands shaking. Thursday Evening. There it was: The British Broadcasting World Service. That made sense. Obviously, the house was somewhere in England.

Perhaps the news item, whatever it was, would be repeated. Forgetting all about the rest of the cleaning, Kate sat down and waited for the eleven o'clock CBC news. But when it came on, the only item from Britain was something about an earl's grandson being chosen as the new leader of the Conservative party. They showed a still picture of him with his wife and children and then a quick clip of him walking outside the House of Commons. That was all. Nothing about a large house with dozens of rooms and a rocking horse in the nursery.

Kate started. Rocking horse? Where had that come from? She began to shiver. Oh no, she thought. Not again.

The antidepressants the doctor had started her on several weeks ago had really helped her. The panic attacks had lessened and her strength was coming back. Now, just when she thought she was beginning to get back to normal, this had to happen. Would it never end?

The back door slammed. "Hi, Mom. I'm home," Erin shouted.

Kate remained seated in the reclining leather chair that had been Jim's. She was beginning to wonder if she'd imagined the entire thing. Wasn't that how paranoia began: seeing things on television that weren't really there?

"Where are you?" Erin shouted.

Kate found her voice. "I'm in here," she shouted back. "In the den." She turned the television off.

Erin came down the hallway. "Are you okay?" she said quickly, when she saw her mother's face.

"No. Not really."

"What on earth have you been doing?" Erin asked, looking around the room.

"What does it look like? I was spring-cleaning the den."

"At eleven o'clock at night?"

"I was sitting in here, watching *ER* and then I saw a cobweb in the corner of the wall. I meant to tackle this room tomorrow, but decided to start tonight instead."

Erin glanced at the upturned step stool in the middle of the floor. "You didn't fall, did you?"

"No, I didn't fall. I just had a—a . . ." Kate sought for the right words. "I had a shock, that's all."

"What sort of shock?"

"I just hope I didn't imagine it."

"Imagine what?"

"The house."

"What house?" Erin was trying not to show her impatience. She hoped to God this wasn't a relapse. She threw her sweater over the back of the sofa and sat down.

Her mother stared straight ahead at the blank television screen. "I saw a house on the news. I had the strangest feeling that I'd seen it before."

"A house? You mean . . ."

"A stately home-type house," Kate said impatiently. "In England."

Erin's heart pounded with sudden excitement. "Where did you see it? I mean, which channel?"

"On CBC Newsworld."

"Oh well, that's easy to trace."

"No, no. It was on that channel, but it was the BBC world news program. You know, the one that comes on before the CBC news."

"Did you watch the CBC as well?"

"Yes, but it wasn't on there."

Erin sprang up. "Don't worry. It'll be easy to track it down. What was this place like?"

"I only caught a glimpse of it, really, but it was a lovely old house. Red brick with lots of windows. Then I got an image of a rocking horse in a nursery."

"They showed the nursery on the news?" Erin asked, puzzled.

"No, of course not," her mother said in one of her scathing 'Don't be so ridiculous' tones. "I mean I suddenly remembered this rocking horse. It came almost immediately after my memory of the house."

Erin bent down to hug her. "Mom, I do believe we may have a breakthrough here."

"Perhaps." Her mother gave her one of her old quirky smiles. Then it faded. "Perhaps not. Besides, I wonder if we're not tempting fate by tampering with my past this way."

"What else can we do? Your past is demanding to be heard, isn't it? You know what Dr. Prentice says. By confronting your past, you can make yourself strong enough to face the future."

"Dr. Prentice speaks a lot of mumbo-jumbo," Kate said acidly.

"Don't knock it. She's really helped you. You're a new person already."

"I'm sure I'd be just as much improved if I'd gone through the normal grieving process by myself."

Erin was tempted to remind her of how she'd been only two short months ago. It was a manifestation of her mother's improved health that she refused to acknowledge how much her doctors had helped her.

"This calls for a celebration. How about a drink?"

"Mine's a rye and ginger." Her mother's sarcastic tone was inescapable.

Erin sighed. "Sorry, Mom. That was tactless of me. I forgot about your medication. How about a good strong cup of tea?"

Kate's face relaxed and she stood up. "Sounds good to me. Then I'm going to have a hot bath. I'm sore all over."

"You haven't overdone it, have you?"

"No, Erin, I haven't overdone it. It's the May long weekend next week. I always have the house thoroughly cleaned before the Victoria Day weekend." She went ahead of Erin to the kitchen.

"Didn't Maria come in today?" Erin said, following her.

"She did, but we spent the day cleaning the upstairs rooms. Have you eaten?"

"We got some Chinese food sent in. We were editing that show on children's breakfast programs in the inner city I was telling you about. I didn't want to leave until I'd finished it."

Erin watched as her mother set a wedge of carrot cake topped with cream icing on a plate. She sighed inwardly. If she didn't get away from here soon she'd balloon into a blimp. What was it about mothers that they always felt they had to keep feeding you?

She sat down at the kitchen table, watching as her mother poured the tea. "Now tell me again what that house looked like."

Although she was snowed under with work, Erin phoned the Newsworld office in Toronto first thing the next morning. When she got through and told them what she was after, the woman at the other end of the line laughed. "What on earth would Winnipeg want with that story?" she asked. Rather condescendingly, Erin thought, bristling at her tone.

"Until I know what the story was, I'm not sure," Erin said, her voice cold.

"It was the Conservative leadership story in Britain."

"That was on the eleven o'clock news," Erin said. "There was no stately home in that coverage." At least, that was what her mother had said.

"No, I know there wasn't. We didn't have that clip, but the BBC did."

"Can you tell me where the house is?"

"It's a place called Amberley. Amberley Court."

"How does it fit into the story about the Tory leadership?"

"It's the family seat of the Earl of Maybridge, apparently. Simon Hogarth, the new leader, is the heir to the title."

"So his father lives there?"

"No, his grandfather. His father's dead."

"Amberley Court," Erin repeated.

"That's it. I have to go. If you want to know any more I'll put you on to my assistant."

"Thanks. Oh, just one more thing. Where is this Amberley? I mean, what part of England?"

"Kent, I believe. Or was it Sussex? One of the home counties near London, anyway."

"Would it be possible to send me a copy of that BBC clip?"

"Sure. Give me the address." Erin did so. "If you use it, don't forget to give BBC a reference, will you?"

Erin bit her lip to hold back a caustic comment. *What sort of moron do you think I am?* she wanted to ask. Instead, she said, "Thanks a lot. You've been a great help."

"If you don't mind my asking, what *is* your interest in this story?"

"Oh, you never know. Perhaps there's a Winnipeg connection none of us know about."

"A Winnipeg connection?" the woman repeated incredulously. "You must be kidding."

"You never know, do you?" Erin said. "Thanks again. 'Bye." She quickly replaced the receiver.

For more than a minute she sat at her desk, staring at the telephone, her heart galloping. She always felt this way when she sensed a story, but this was more than just an interesting news item. This story involved her own mother and, therefore, herself.

Automatically her fingers went to the computer keyboard and she set up a new subdirectory.

The name of the new directory was *Amberley*.

Chapter Seven

When Erin awoke on Saturday morning she felt a surge of excitement, followed almost immediately by such an overwhelming sense of disappointment that she dragged the covers over herself again, turning away from the sunlight that was filtering through the curtains.

The Victoria Day weekend was traditionally the May holiday when lakeside cottages were opened up after the long winter. Erin could remember the childhood excitement of packing up the Volvo station wagon with boxes of groceries, bedding and quilts in plastic coverings, cans of paint . . . and then driving the familiar Trans-Canada Highway to West Hawk Lake.

Once they left the city behind, she'd always experienced that special thrill of excitement, watching the ribbon of road unfurling before them, edged by the pines that heralded the beginning of the great Canadian Shield.

Last summer had been their last time together at the cottage. In the fall, her parents had sold it to friends. It was too much work, her mother had said, she was too busy with her volunteer work to spend two isolated months at the lake. It had been just one more example of her mother's growing impatience with the traditions she'd been perfectly happy to carry out for so many years. Although her father had said very little, Erin suspected that there'd been heated discussion on the subject for quite a while before they'd decided to sell.

She herself had felt a tangle of emotions at the news. Although she had rarely gone there for longer than a weekend in recent years, the thought of losing their cottage made her feel angry and impotent.

The family cottage was the repository of so many

happy memories. Barbecues—with the sizzle of steaks and the light from the coals illuminating familiar faces. The midnight swims in the cool depths of the lake, the only sound the calling of the loons. Her first kiss—when Brian Kelly caught her behind the boathouse. And the long talks with her father as they sat late at night on the dock, the water lapping against the pilings.

Now, however, she was glad they'd sold it. The thought of returning there, of experiencing all the reminders of those happy times would have been unbearable. Not only had she lost her father, with whom memories of the cottage were inextricably intertwined, she had also lost Rob. It was at the cottage that she and Rob had first made love.

They'd gone down for a couple of days by themselves in the middle of the week. As her mind went back to that time, two years ago, Erin recalled again the smell of wet wool, when a rain shower had soaked Rob's Aran sweater as they ran back from the shore to the cottage. Rob had drawn her to him in the doorway, pulling her against him. They'd made love on her mother's hooked rug in front of the log fire.

Erin groaned and threw back the bedclothes. No point in this masochistic reliving of the past. All that was gone, behind her. Two people she would never see again. Tears stung her eyes as she sat on the side of the bed. Problem was, her life at present was nothing but work and her mother. Not at all promising.

Then she remembered the videotape. It had arrived at the studio yesterday, but when she'd got home, eager to show it to her mother, she'd found Gran there for dinner and knew she'd have to wait.

She could hear her mother clattering dishes in the kitchen. It was a nostalgic sound, reminiscent of her years of growing up in this large house beside the Assiniboine River. When she went out onto the landing, the smell of newly perked coffee wafted up to her.

"That smells good," she called down.

Her mother came out of the kitchen. "So you're awake at last. I'll make some waffles."

Erin was about to say, "No waffles," but didn't. A few weeks ago her mother hadn't had the energy to make instant coffee, never mind waffles. The least she could do was eat her mother's waffles and be grateful for the change in her.

"Let's look at that tape after breakfast, shall we?" she suggested as she was pouring maple syrup on her waffles.

"I'm not sure I want to." Her mother took up the bottle of syrup and wiped the lip before screwing the cap back on. She leaned over the table to look out the window. "There's a couple of blue jays on the bird feeder. What a racket they make, don't they? Frightens off all the other birds."

"Why don't you want to watch it?" Erin demanded, ignoring her mother's attempt to change the subject.

Kate resolutely stared out the window. "I didn't like the way it made me feel when I saw it last week. It brought back all those weird feelings I'm trying to avoid."

"Then I'll watch it by myself." Erin jumped up and put her dishes away in the dishwasher. Not wanting to force the issue, she went into the family room and slid the tape into the VCR. She'd already watched it in her office at work, but she wasn't about to tell her mother that.

The picture of Amberley Court came on the screen, the voice-over explaining that the Court had been the home of the earls of Maybridge for more than three hundred years, although Maybridge Castle, in Yorkshire, was the original family seat.

The old Earl of Maybridge, whose picture was shown—a strong face with an aquiline nose—had declined to comment on the subject of his grandson's appointment as leader of the Conservative party. From the look of him, Erin guessed that he wouldn't couch his refusal to comment in polite terms. With his bristling mustache, he looked like a retired general, one of the survivors of the good old British Empire.

As she rewound the tape to watch it again, Erin became aware that her mother was standing in the doorway. She said nothing, but watched again as the camera panned across the scenes of vast parkland, the artificial lake with a fountain spewing up from a statue at its center, and the sweep of steps up to the front of the magnificent red-brick house.

"They never let me play at the front of the house, of course," her mother said in a hollow voice. "Mostly in the kitchen garden."

Erin automatically pressed the pause button, freezing the picture of the house on the screen. She held her breath for a moment and then slowly released it. "Show me where it is," she said at last.

"I can't, can I? It's around the back." Her mother went to the television and pointed to the large window on the right of the house. "That was a room with lots of books and a big window." Her voice slid up to the higher-pitched tones of a small child. "There was a big table with a globe on it. My mam let me turn it once when she was dusting the room. But then there was an awful fight with the lady. She said I had no right to be there. The only other times I was in the book room was when he showed me some pretty pictures in a large book on the table."

"He?" Erin asked.

Her mother's eyes gazed at her blankly. "He went away," she said finally. "I never saw him again."

"Do you really think it was this very house?" Erin asked her softly.

Her mother's hand dropped from the screen and she looked bewildered. "What?"

"Do you think this was the house where you lived before you came to Canada?"

"I don't know. I just remember a house like this, that's all." Her mother's voice had returned to its normal tone. "I should think a great many stately homes look like this one. Big park. Stone steps. Gardens."

"Yes, but we've watched programs about old English houses and you haven't had the same reaction to them. *Brideshead Revisited,* for instance. I don't remember the pictures of Castle Howard making you feel that way."

"Castle Howard's quite different."

"That's my point. Sit down a minute, Mom. I've got an idea."

Her mother looked uneasy. "I should go and clean up the kitchen."

"Relax. I'll do the kitchen."

"No. I have to get back to normal again. No more mollycoddling me. Which reminds me," her mother added, sitting down on the couch. "The volunteer bureau phoned me to see if I felt able to put in a few hours a week."

"What did you say?"

"I told them I thought I could. I want to start helping at the hospital again, too, but I don't think I'm quite ready for that yet." Kate's voice wavered and she covered her eyes with her hand for a moment.

Erin swallowed the lump in her throat. "No, I think that should wait a while. Don't rush things, Mom. Take it slowly."

Her mother nodded. She fumbled in her sleeve for a tissue. "I keep thinking I'm okay, but then something happens and I'm dripping like a tap again." She blew her nose hard.

Erin hesitated, not sure that this was a good time, but then she jumped in with her idea. "I want to go to England to see what I can find out about your parents."

"Oh, Erin, no." Her mother looked stricken.

"Why don't we both go? It would be a change for you and—"

"No." Kate shook her head vehemently. "Definitely not. I'm getting much better, but I want to be on home ground. I feel safe here. I certainly wouldn't want to go all that way away from home."

"Okay, okay. It was just a thought." Erin reached across the table to touch her mother's agitated hands. "I'll stay here with you until you feel able to be by yourself."

"That's something I wanted to talk to *you* about. I am quite capable of being by myself now. It's time you went back to your apartment and got on with your own life."

"I'm perfectly happy being here with you, you know that."

"I do. You've been wonderful, but you need to get back to normal life, too, just as I do. I'm beginning to rely on you too much. That's not healthy."

"Maybe it's too soon."

"No. I've spoken to Dr. Prentice and she agrees. So, you can pack up your things this weekend and move out."

Erin smiled at her mother's mock severity. "Okay, I can tell when I'm not wanted. But we'll spend this weekend together, okay?"

"I'd like that, if you haven't any other plans."

"My only plan was to spend the holiday weekend with you."

They were silent for a moment, both occupied with thoughts of other May holiday weekends, the traditional coming together of the family to start the summer season.

Erin broke into the uneasy silence. "What about *my* going to England? I've got some holiday time due to me. I'm not too busy in June. I think I could take a couple of weeks off." She grinned. "I'll tell them I have to go to England to research a story with a Winnipeg connection."

"It won't lead you anywhere, Erin. You're doomed to disappointment. I'd feel much happier if you left it alone." Her mother's expression reminded Erin of a trapped animal, wary and afraid. The healthier her mother became, the more she seemed to be trying to sublimate those childhood memories that had resurfaced in the nightmares.

"There is a story in it," Erin insisted. "I know there is."

Her mother's lips formed into a thin line. "If there is, it's my story, not yours."

"I'm sorry, Mom, but your history is mine. These aren't just your parents. They're my grandparents as well. I have a right to find out about them, too."

"You've got a perfectly good grandmother in Winnipeg."

"Of course I have. Gran's great, but I want to know about your *real* parents."

"If these snippets of memory are fact, then my mother was probably some sort of servant and I was illegitimate."

"So?"

"I don't want you to have some romantic notion about my family, that's all."

"I haven't. I just want to find out the truth. That's why I work in the media."

"Ha! Since when was the media interested in the truth?"

"Oh, Mom." Erin shook her head. "I want to find out what I can. For your sake, mainly."

"I'm just fine as I am, thank you very much." Kate picked up a copy of *Chatelaine* and opened it, pretending to be intensely interested in something she was looking at.

"Dr. Prentice says that the more you're able to discover about your past," Erin continued, determined not to be put off, "the better it will be for you in the long run."

"I've told you what I think about Dr. Prentice."

Erin chose to ignore her mother's skepticism. "All the inquiries we've made from this end have drawn a blank. No one's been able to track down where you came from. Anyone who might have known is long gone by now. But if I go to England, I can do all my research at firsthand."

Her mother threw down the magazine and stood up. "Then go."

"I can't leave you alone."

"I won't be alone. I have plenty of friends, thank you. And if I don't like being by myself, Gran can come and stay with me. It would give her a little break as well."

"That's a great idea."

"She shouldn't really be on her own at her age."

Erin saw in her mother's eyes the same guilt and panic *she* had felt at the thought of being trapped with having to take care of her mother. "Gran prefers to be independent."

"I'm not sure she can manage by herself."

"Wait until you are sure she can't. Then we can find an alternative."

Her mother walked to the door, but then she turned back, her hand clutching the doorknob. "I feel guilty about Gran, now that I'm alone."

"I know. I do understand. I still think you should wait

a while, until Gran definitely can't manage by herself. She likes her independence."

"She's not the only one," her mother said.

As her mother went out into the hall, Erin wondered if she would ever really understand her. She got up and followed her into the kitchen, where she was briskly clearing the table.

Erin fetched the broom from the closet in the hall and began sweeping the floor. When she'd finished, she stood in the doorway. "If you don't want me to do this, you only have to say so. I'd understand."

Her mother turned from the sink. "Do what? Sweep the floor?"

"No, silly," Erin said, smiling. "I meant tracking down your past."

"I know you did." Kate drew the dish towel through her hands. "I admit I have extremely mixed feelings about all this," she said eventually. "Part of me really wants you to do it, but part of me is scared of what you'll find. After all, my mother was so desperate to get rid of me, she gave me a false name and address. She certainly won't want to be found, will she?"

"Maybe she'd feel differently now, after all these years."

"You realize, don't you, that she's probably dead by now? After all, I'm sixty, so she could be eighty. There's a good chance she won't be alive."

Erin's heart sank. Her mother was right. Somehow she'd been thinking of her mother's mother as the pretty woman in the photograph, forever young. Yet, still she felt this burning desire to discover the truth.

"Even if she is dead, we can try to find out what really happened, can't we? Are you telling me that you really don't want to know who your parents are? That you don't want to find out the meaning of all these dreams of yours?"

Her mother stood in the center of the kitchen, the damp dish towel dangling from her hand, tears filling her brown eyes. "Of course, I do," she whispered. "I'm just afraid of what you'll find."

Erin ran to her and hugged her. "Better to find out what really happened, even if it is the worst scenario possible. At least, you would realize how lucky you were to find Gran and Granddad."

"I realized that a long time ago." Her mother moved away to the sink. "All right, go . . . with my blessing. I couldn't stop you if I wanted to, anyway. Although where you'll start, I haven't a clue."

Erin grinned at her. "I've got several clues. I just have to put them together and find the pattern. After all, I've got a lot of facts to go on."

"Such as?"

"The stately home, the cherubs on the ceiling, the book, an Irish mother who was—"

"How do you know she was Irish?" her mother demanded.

"Oh, Mom, that's easy. You were called Kate. You named me Erin."

"I just liked the name Erin."

"Yes, but why did you like it? Then you sometimes talk of your mother as 'Mam.' "

"Do I? I hadn't realized that." Her mother turned away to empty the coffee grounds from the pot into the wastebin.

"Exactly. It just came out of your subconscious."

Her mother slapped the coffeepot down on the counter. "As far as I'm concerned, too damned much came out of my subconscious. I wish it would all go back and disappear forever."

"Too late now." Erin went into the hall and bounded up the stairs. "I'm going to ask Harry today if I can have a couple of weeks off in June," she shouted.

"You can't," her mother shouted back to her.

"Why not?"

"Because it's the weekend. Unless you intend to phone him at home."

"Damn! I forgot. Then I'll ask him on Tuesday."

Chapter Eight

It wasn't until Erin was actually on the flight to London that she realized how relieved she felt. The past few months had been a great strain. At the same time, she also felt guilty for having left her mother. Fortunately she wasn't going to be alone. Gran had agreed "to come and look after her" while Erin was away, and Pam Thiessen had assured Erin that she would make sure Kate was kept busy.

The final encouragement had come from Dr. Prentice, who told Erin that she was doing the right thing, for her own sake as well as her mother's. Kate must learn to cope by herself. Indeed, Dr. Prentice assured Erin, she was already doing so. Now, they were working on the avoidance. If Kate could learn to face the nightmares and the memories they evoked she might be able to resume her life with an enhanced understanding of herself.

In early June, a week before she was due to leave, Erin had been surprised to receive a telephone call from Rob in Toronto.

"What's all this I hear about you going to England on a story?" he'd said, without preamble.

"And hello to you, too, Rob Harris," Erin said, annoyed at his offhand manner, yet in a way glad to hear his voice again.

"Hi. How are you doing?"

"I'm fine."

"I miss you like hell."

Erin swallowed. She was tempted to say, "I'm too busy with other things to miss you," but it would sound too much like sour grapes. After all, it was she who'd decided not to go to Toronto with him.

"I take it that your being back in the apartment means your mother's okay now," Rob said.

"She's getting there. We both are."

"Yeah." Silence. Rob always found it hard to deal with emotions. "So, what's this story in England?"

"How did you hear about it?"

"Oh, you know the CBC grapevine. So what's the scoop?"

"It's not a story, really. It's something personal—about Mom." Erin gave him a capsule version.

"Yo! That sounds like quite a quest," Rob said, when she'd finished. "A potential cracker of a story, too. Specially if it does turn out that Hogarth's place is where your mother lived."

"Mom's not at all sure. She thinks Amberley Court looks like the house she remembers, that's all."

"Hogarth's hot news at the moment. The British Tories' great white hope to beat out Rutherford. Their only hope, I should think. Maybe the earl's little Irish kitchen maid was seduced by one of the royals sixty years ago and your mom was the result. Just think what a great story that would make. There hasn't been a royal scandal for at least a week."

"Why did you call me, Rob?" Erin asked him coldly. This call was reminding her of some of her reasons for having broken up with him.

"Have you lined up somewhere to stay in London?"

"Not yet. I've got a long list of addresses from friends, though. Why?"

"I've got a friend in London who could put you up. Samantha Wakeley. She's an executive with UTV now. Used to have her own show. Lives in Richmond."

"Richmond. Isn't that where Kew Gardens is? It's a bit far from central London, isn't it?"

"Perfect spot. On the tube and the Waterloo line, so you can get into the center of London in a few minutes. Samantha has a large house on Richmond Green. I've stayed there myself. Lovely place. Very fashionable area."

"I'm not really interested in fashionable areas. I just want to have easy access to information."

"That's why I thought of Samantha. She knows everyone who is anyone. Her husband's a movie producer."

"I can't see how that will help me find out about Amberley Court. Besides, how do you know this fashionable friend of yours will be willing to take a stranger into her house?"

"Still the confident old Erin, eh?" Rob said caustically. Before Erin could say anything, he added, "I've spoken to her already. It's all fixed, if you want it."

Erin wasn't sure she wanted to be beholden to Rob for anything.

"For God's sake, Erin, don't be so bloody stupid," Rob yelled down the phone, correctly interpreting her silence. "I'm not asking for anything in return. Just call it a favor for old time's sake, okay?"

"Okay," she told him, after a moment of hesitation. "Thanks, Rob."

"Don't mention it. Glad to help. Happy hunting."

"Rob . . ."

"Yeah?"

"I don't want anyone to know the real reason for my interest in Amberley Court. Not even your friend, Samantha."

"Understood. I'll use the Simon Hogarth story as an excuse, okay?"

"Fine."

When she reached Richmond, jet-lagged and frazzled from the long journey, Erin wasn't quite so sure she should have accepted Rob's offer. Maybe a nice, big impersonal hotel in London might have been better.

Samantha was fortyish, tall, reed-thin, her blond hair twisted into an untidy knot at the back. She was dressed in a long black-silk dressing gown and her feet were bare, with scarlet-painted toenails.

"Come in, come in," she said, waving her hands expansively, her smile displaying large, white teeth. "Rob tells me you're a television producer in Canada and you're onto some big story connected with Simon Hogarth. How exciting! We're Liberal Democrats, of course, but Simon is big news at the moment. Leave your luggage in the hall."

Erin lifted her suitcase over the step and set it down in the wide hall, feeling totally overwhelmed by the larger-than-life Samantha.

"That's right," Samantha said over her shoulder, as she led the way down the hall, through a door, and into a vast kitchen, which could be best described as a scene of organized chaos.

Every available surface was covered with piles of paper and stacks of magazines and newspapers. The large porcelain sink was filled to overflowing with dirty dishes, although there was a dishwasher under the counter, and the top of the Aga cooker seemed to have become an interim storage space, with saucepans and casserole dishes stacked on it.

"Excuse the mess. Our housecleaner comes tomorrow, God bless him. Sit down. Anywhere at all. Chuck those newspapers on the floor. That's it. Now, kick off your shoes and tell me all about it, while I pour us some wine."

Dazed, Erin sat down, well aware that anything she told Samantha would be broadcast to the world in a flash. She cleared her throat. "Would you mind if I had a cup of tea instead of wine?" she asked.

"Tea? Of course." Samantha glanced at the kitchen clock, which was in the form of a plastic black-and-white cat with eyes that clicked from side to side. It was a rather bizarre contrast to the golden oak cupboards and dark blue Aga. "I suppose it is only ten o'clock," she said. But this didn't deter her from pouring herself a large glass of white wine. She plugged in a streamlined kettle that looked more like a tall jug and made the tea in a chipped brown pot, grabbing two tea bags from a tea caddy on the counter.

Erin, who'd never stayed in a private home in England before, was vaguely disappointed to see that Samantha used plain old tea bags and not the loose tea leaves she'd thought all English people used.

"How about a few bickies?" Samantha asked.

Bickies? "I'm not that hungry, thanks."

"Oh, come on now. You can't be on a diet. You've got a super figure. What do you do to keep it? Treadmill, weights, aerobics, what? I'd love to know your secret."

All the time she talked, Samantha's ring-laden hands flashed from glass to kettle to tray to the old tin with the picture of an old thatched farmhouse on the lid, which was labeled Somerton's Country Biscuits. Now, as she watched Samantha put a handful of the cookies on a plate, Erin realized what bickies were.

She also gauged that it wouldn't be too difficult to steer Samantha away from the subject of the Hogarths. All she had to do was bring up another subject, and she'd be off and running in a new direction.

But there, Erin soon discovered, she was quite wrong. Her lack of sleep had made her forget that Samantha was also in television, albeit in an executive position. As soon as they'd moved into the front room, which was also cluttered, but sunny and beautifully decorated with Laura Ashley-style fabrics, Samantha was zeroing in on Simon Hogarth again. "What exactly is your angle? I mean, why would someone in the Canadian prairies be interested in the new British Tory leader?"

A good question. If Erin hadn't been quite so tired she might have had a good answer at the ready. She'd certainly been trying to concoct something on the flight over. Yet nothing sounding remotely credible had come to mind.

"People in Canada are fascinated by the angle of Simon Hogarth giving up a title and his inheritance for politics," she blurted out. "All this stuff about aristocracy and titles and heirs is a mystery to us western Canadians, so I thought I'd do a story about it."

"Oh, I see," said Samantha, looking as if she didn't really. "But . . . forgive me for saying so, darling, surely Winnipeg, Manitoba, isn't exactly . . ." Her words trailed away.

"Not the hub of the universe, you mean?" Erin was about to launch into her usual heated defense of her hometown—citing the fabulous Royal Winnipeg Ballet, the Manitoba Theatre Centre where Keanu Reeves had performed his first Hamlet, the home of the bear that had inspired Winnie-the-Pooh . . . but decided that, for once, she would let it go. "I'm hoping to get a scoop," she told Samantha in a conspiratorial tone, "so that I can be moved to Toronto, where the big money and opportunities are."

"Ah, now I understand. But with all the syndication we have nowadays, it would have to be a completely new angle to sell, wouldn't it?"

"Absolutely. There must have been dozens of interviews with Simon Hogarth, but I haven't seen any with his grandfather. My angle is to find out how the earl feels about his grandson giving up his title. Is he proud at the thought of his grandson possibly becoming Prime Minister of Great Britain? Or is he furious that he's going to give up the title?"

If only Rob could hear her now, Erin thought, he'd be proud of her. *Now that sounds more like a true investigative journalist,* he'd say. *Way to go!*

"I wish you the best of British luck, my dear." Samantha gave her a rather condescending smile. "You're one of dozens trying to get an interview with Lord Maybridge."

"I rather thought I might be," Erin said ruefully, realizing that she must sound rather naive.

"Unfortunately, so far no one has been able to get any response from him. He's locked himself up at Amberley and adamantly refuses to speak to the media, even though some of them have been camped at his gates ever since the announcement about the leadership was made."

"He's in his eighties, isn't he? The Earl of Maybridge, I mean." Erin had spent a great deal of time on research before she'd left Canada.

"I believe so. I saw him last at one of the royal weddings. Prince Andrew's, I believe. The old earl was very upright, very proud and military looking. I don't know Simon Hogarth personally, but my sister was at Oxford with his wife, Olivia. Clever woman. Knew what she was doing when she married Simon, I think. Except that now she won't become a countess, of course. She says—publicly, at least—that she doesn't mind at all, but one does wonder how she really feels about it."

"Yes, it would be interesting to know," murmured Erin, not one bit interested in Simon Hogarth's wife.

Samantha suddenly beamed at Erin, flashing her large

teeth. "I quite forgot. I *do* know someone with a connection to the Hogarth family. David Lennox."

"Who's David Lennox?"

"He's a distant relative of the Hogarths. A third cousin twice removed or something like that. David's an entertainment lawyer, so he's part of our world. The only problem is, though, that he might not be willing to discuss his connection with the family."

"Why not?"

"David's rather *persona non grata* with the old man."

"Why?"

"Because he was brought up in America. The old earl considers him some kind of alien from outer space, I believe."

Erin suddenly felt less tired. She'd been in England only a few hours and already she had a possible contact. "What are my chances of meeting him?" she asked.

"David? I was thinking of having a few people in for an informal lunch on Sunday, anyway. Couldn't get Dickie Attenborough and his wife, unfortunately."

"You mean Richard Attenborough? The man who was in *Jurassic Park*?" Erin couldn't hide the fact that she was impressed.

"Yes, my dear. *Sir* Richard." Samantha's amusement made Erin feel very gauche. "He lives a few doors down from us. But they're away filming at the moment. We could eat on the terrace if it doesn't rain. I'll ask David and his latest, whoever she is. Some actress or other."

"That would be great."

Samantha leaned over and placed her hand on Erin's knee. "One word of advice, darling, from an older and more experienced member of the business. It might be best to hide your interest in the Hogarths and Amberley Court at first. As I said, David usually steers clear of the subject. Between you and me, I think he's rather bitter about the old man."

"Of course. I won't mention my interest in the Hogarths at all." That suited Erin perfectly.

Samantha looked at Erin speculatively. "It's possible that an inexperienced girl from the prairies might be able to find out more than the ruthless hacks over here.

And you're very attractive in a fresh, rather down-homey sort of way."

Erin bristled. She objected to being treated like some country hick. But then she gave Samantha a good-natured smile, realizing that it was better to keep her as an ally. She'd probably get absolutely nowhere on her own.

"You never know," Samantha continued. "Although he usually goes for the more sophisticated type, you just might appeal to David. If you play your cards right, if you know what I mean, you could be onto an international scoop."

This was too much. Erin, who had no intention of sleeping with David Lennox—or anyone else, for that matter—to get her information, brushed the cookie crumbs from her lap and stood up. "If you don't mind, I really would like to take a rest. I didn't get a wink of sleep on the plane."

Samantha sprang to her feet, pulling her robe across her long bare legs. "Of course, darling. Here I am being utterly thoughtless and forgetting how far you've traveled today. Come on upstairs and I'll show you your room." She strode out to the hall, grabbed Erin's carry-on bag, and led the way up the wide staircase.

Erin followed her—and the trail of her exotic scent—upstairs.

The room she had given Erin was enchanting. Large and sunny, the bedroom was furnished with ivory-painted furniture, including a four-poster bed draped with a fabric of green ivy and pink roses. When Erin crossed the room to look out the sashed window, she saw a broad sweep of emerald lawn and the fast-flowing River Thames beyond it.

"Oh," she said, turning from the window, "this is absolutely lovely. I don't know how to thank you for your kindness," she told Samantha, and meant it, despite having been taken aback by Samantha's frankness. She was so grateful that she was almost tempted to tell her the true reason for her interest in Amberley. Fortunately, caution overruled instinct and she said nothing.

"It's my pleasure," Samantha said. "Rob's a dear friend."

Something in her expression prompted Erin to ask, "How often has Rob stayed here?"

"At least four times, I think . . . The first time he came, he was just a kid, about twenty-one or two. He'd come to London looking for adventure—and a job. I couldn't find him a job, but I like to think I gave him some adventure." Samantha smiled her she-wolf smile.

Bet you did, Erin thought, suddenly getting it. She was furious with Rob for having sent her here to this woman. She could just imagine Samantha creeping to Rob's room after her husband had fallen asleep. Erin had met her only a short time ago, but it was easy to see that Samantha was a woman who got her kicks from living on the edge.

"No need for that black look, darling," Samantha said. "There was nothing to it. Just fun. Besides, it all happened years ago, long before you and Rob were an item."

Erin felt her face grow stiff. "I take it that Rob told you that."

"Yes. He also told me that you'd split up. I'm sorry. It must have happened recently enough for you to still feel raw."

"I didn't realize it was quite that obvious," Erin said coldly. "No need to feel sorry for me. It was my decision to end it."

Samantha smiled. "I must be at least ten years older than you, darling. Would you mind if I said something personal to you?"

Erin had had just about enough personal talk from Samantha Wakeley. "I'm not sure I want to hear any more, thanks very much."

"Well, at least you're honest. That's always a refreshing aspect of North Americans. One gets so used to English people not saying what they actually feel. All I wanted to tell you was that, although I've only just met you, I think you did the right thing not to stay with Rob. He's not the right man for you."

"Why? Because I'm an inexperienced hick from Winnipeg?"

"Oh hell, I really did get off on the wrong foot with you, didn't I?" Samantha said, sweeping her hands through her long hair. "No, darling, because I think you deserve someone better than Rob. He's not a keeper, if you know what I mean. Charming as he is, I think it will be many years before he wants to settle down, if ever. You, on the other hand, strike me as someone who is looking for something secure in her life."

"I'm extremely career oriented," Erin said, bristling. "I don't need a man in my life to make me feel secure."

"I'm sure you don't. And as to the career, I'd say you were one of those tenacious journalists who won't let a story go until you've tracked it down and put it to bed. But we're talking about your personal life, aren't we?"

Erin was about to tell this woman who was, after all, a complete stranger to her, that she didn't remember giving her permission to talk about her personal life, but she didn't. Samantha knew someone who was related to the Hogarths. She needed her. "It appears that we are," she said.

"You're one of those people with high ideals, I imagine. Not that common nowadays. I just hope you find what you're looking for, that's all. Whatever it is, I don't think you would have found it in Rob."

Erin looked at her. Then the stiffness around her mouth dissolved into a rueful smile. "That's why I didn't go to Toronto with him."

"That must have been a tough decision for you. Rob's a very attractive man."

Erin turned away to stare out the window. "It was. But it was the right decision."

"Forget about Rob. He's not worth breaking your heart over. I'll do my best to help you with your story." Samantha went to the door. "I'd like to see you succeed with this."

Erin turned back, suddenly wishing she didn't have to deceive her. "Thanks, Samantha."

"We'll start with David and see what comes of that."

Chapter Nine

Sunday morning dawned with a mist that rolled in from the river, partly hiding the large old trees at the end of the garden. Erin was disappointed, but Samantha assured her over their morning coffee that it was the harbinger of a fine June day.

She was right. By eleven o'clock the mist had lifted and the sun was shining, the moisture shimmering on the leaves and grass.

Erin was tingling with excitement. She felt as if she were an actress in the wings, waiting to perform the most important role of her life. This meeting with David Lennox was her big chance to find out the relevance of Amberley and the Hogarth family to her mother.

She hoped he wasn't an absolute jerk. That would make her task doubly difficult, but she was determined to get to know him, whatever he was like.

When he arrived a few minutes before twelve-thirty, Erin was occupied in the kitchen helping Samantha's extremely efficient houseman, Max, prepare lunch. She heard Samantha's drawl in answer to another rather high-pitched voice, and then a man spoke, his voice an attractive contrast to the two women's overexuberant tones. His accent was predominantly British but, knowing David Lennox's background, Erin was also able to detect a strong hint of American plus a slight Scottish burr. It sounded very pleasant after the rather nasal English accents of Samantha and her friends.

Erin remained in the kitchen with Max. She was garnishing the salmon terrine when Samantha dashed in.

"What the hell are you doing in here, darling? Leave the rest to Max. Come and meet David and his woman. She's perfectly stunning," she hissed in a loud whisper, as she steered Erin down the hall, "but she speaks hardly any English."

Erin found herself propelled into the large sitting room that overlooked the river, before she even had time to dry her hands properly.

"This is Erin Benson, the famous television producer from Canada I've been telling you about," was Samantha's introduction. "Erin, meet Françoise Auber, and David Lennox."

Erin shook hands with the striking young woman, whose gleaming black hair hung straight almost to her waist. " 'ow do you do," Françoise said with a pronounced French accent.

Now David Lennox's hand was gripping hers. "Hi, famous producer," he said. "Glad to meet someone from my side of the world." He looked down at her with warm amusement in his eyes.

"Hi," was all Erin could think to say in reply. *Great,* she told herself. *You'll get far with that scintillating conversation!*

"Samantha tells me you're from Winnipeg," David said. "I thought the Canadian performance world gravitated around Toronto."

Erin's face felt warm under his scrutiny. He had unusual eyes, a warm mixture of green and brown, the colors of Scottish moorland. She responded to his smile. "I'm afraid Samantha exaggerated a little. I hope to move to Toronto soon. For now, I work at CBC Winnipeg on local shows."

"I'd be very interested to hear what a midwest city the size of Winnipeg is able to produce," he said.

Erin looked for irony in his expression, but found none. She was going to tell him about her latest project when she became aware of Françoise gazing at them and turned to her. "Are you working in England?" she asked. She looked like a supermodel with her lithe, boyish body and that wonderful hair.

"I am performing at the Royal Festival 'all next week," Françoise told her.

"Françoise is a violinist," David explained. "She's playing the Sibelius at the Festival Hall. I persuaded her to take a few hours off today." He frowned as if a thought had suddenly struck him. "How long are you going to be here?"

"A week or so. Why?"

"Would you like a couple of tickets for the concert?"

Erin was taken by surprise. "I—I don't know."

"Perhaps classical music isn't your thing."

"It certainly is. We have a terrific orchestra in Winnipeg." As soon as she said it, she realized how ridiculously defensive she sounded.

"I'm sure you have," David said, laughing. "I wasn't casting aspersions on your cultural facilities."

Erin felt decidedly foolish. "Sorry. Winnipeggers get so fed up with having to defend our city, because it's in the middle of nowhere, that we're all a bit supersensitive."

"That's okay. Anyway, there's nothing wrong with not liking classical music."

"*Mais certainement,* it is wrong not to like it," Françoise said with vigor, and they all laughed.

"I'd love a ticket for the concert," Erin said firmly. "Sibelius is a favorite of mine. His icy music is just right for our long, cold winters. I'm just not sure though . . . Perhaps Samantha would like to come with me."

"Samantha . . . sit still through a concert?" David said incredulously. "You've got to be kidding."

"What's this about me?" Samantha said, entering the room with several more people trailing behind her.

"Erin thought you might like to go to Françoise's concert at the Festival Hall."

"A concert? You must be joking."

"That's exactly what I told her."

The concert was forgotten as Samantha introduced her other guests. All of them were from the entertainment world. A set designer and a script writer, and the female star of a television series that had been an award-winning success on both sides of the Atlantic.

Erin tried to hold her own, but, despite Samantha's attempts to draw her into the conversation, she felt a little out of her depth. Apart from Françoise, everyone appeared to know everyone else. She caught sight of the young French woman standing alone by the open doors leading to the terrace, and realized that they were both outsiders here.

She made her way across the room. "Would you like some sherry?" she asked.

"I am drinking Perrier," Françoise replied, holding up her glass.

"Okay." Erin looked around. Everyone seemed to be occupied in their own conversations for the moment. "How long will you be in England?" she asked, this time speaking in French.

Françoise brightened noticeably. "I have three performances in London and then another four in Scotland."

They made small talk in French until David rejoined them. "Famous *and* bilingual," he said in an awed voice.

Erin had a childish urge to poke her tongue at him. They exchanged grins and then both began talking to Françoise in French.

"That was kind," David said in a low voice to Erin, when the script writer came over to engage Françoise in a rather one-sided conversation. "She understands English, but isn't that comfortable speaking it. I've told her she'll have to get used to speaking English now that she's doing international concerts."

Erin was puzzled. Somehow she didn't get the feeling that he and Françoise were a couple. "Are you acting as her manager?" she asked hesitantly. "Sorry, but I have to admit I'm not really quite sure what an entertainment lawyer does."

"You mean professionally?" he asked, laughter in his eyes.

"What else?" Erin found herself responding instinctively. She wouldn't have to pretend with this man. She liked people who laughed at life. And he was good to look at as well. Tall, with those gorgeous greeny-brown eyes and brown hair that curled a little at the nape of his neck.

"We're like any firm of solicitors except that we specialize in contracts in the entertainment business. We represent movie, television, and theatrical companies, and artists of all kinds. There are so many spinoffs nowadays—recording and movies and merchandising—it's become a highly specialized branch of law."

"Looks as if it could be fun as well." Erin raised her eyebrows in Françoise's direction.

"Sure can. But I'm just taking care of Françoise for her U.K. manager while she's away for the weekend. She seems quite happy at the moment, so I can stop being a nanny." He smiled down at Erin. "Tell me all about your television work in Winnipeg." He sounded genuinely interested.

Erin was about to tell him about the inner-city program she'd been working on, when Samantha announced that lunch was ready. As they all moved out onto the terrace, Erin felt a spasm of disappointment. She enjoyed speaking to David Lennox, which augured well for her investigation—if she could ever manage to get him on his own.

Samantha had set up tables end to end on the brick-paved terrace and covered them with leaf-green linen tablecloths and darker green napkins. The midday sun shone down on the silver and crystal, making them sparkle.

Although the conversation during lunch was confined to general small talk and entertainment gossip—most of which was about people Erin didn't know—she was acutely aware of David's bare arm brushing against hers. Once or twice she caught him looking at her with a rather quizzical expression, as if he couldn't quite make her out.

"Something wrong?" she asked him eventually, when she caught him looking at her again.

He looked startled. "Not at all. Sorry. Was I staring at you?"

"Not really." She smiled at him. "Well, maybe a bit."

"I must apologize. I was thinking how different you were from the rest of us here, and wondering if it was because you're from the Canadian midwest or just because you're different."

"Both, probably." She raised her eyebrows at him. "When you say different, do you mean less sophisticated?"

"God, I hope so. Sophistication to me means being

false and artificial. I don't know you very well, of course, but you strike me as being someone who tells it like it is. The Scottish part of me appreciates that in a person."

"I think lots of people from the midwest are like that. More straightforward, I mean."

"I wouldn't know. I grew up in Boston. My father was a Scottish businessman and my mother American," he added in explanation. "They divorced when I was six."

"I'm sorry."

David shrugged. "It's a common enough story nowadays. The difference was that when I was fourteen my mother married again and I was shunted back to my father in Scotland. He had remarried, too, so he sent me to a Scottish boarding school."

"Not Gordonstoun, I hope," Erin said quickly, remembering the stories she'd read about Prince Charles's miserable school days.

"Fortunately not, but even at my school my American accent was definitely not acceptable, so it was drilled out of me, and we had a heavy regimen of rugger—"

"Rugger?"

"Sorry. Rugby football, played in all weathers, including blizzards. Designed to toughen you up—or kill you."

"I take it that as you're still alive it toughened you up."

"Don't know about that, but it certainly put me off team sports for life." He frowned at her. "This is weird," he said in a low voice.

"What is?"

"That I'm telling you all this. I rarely talk about my school days."

"I'm not surprised. They sound awful."

"They were. Bloody awful. Mind you, that's nothing new in my family. Anyway, that's enough about me. Tell me about you."

She wanted to hear more about his family, but she knew she must be careful not to rush things. She told him about her early life in Winnipeg, skating and tobogganing in Assiniboine Park in the winter, the idyllic summers at the lake. "It all sounds pretty boring," she added.

"Not to me, it doesn't. No wonder you're so different.

You're one of those rare people who actually had a happy childhood."

"I suppose it was, in a way. I thought it was just a normal one. My mother and I didn't get along when I was a teenager, but I suppose that's nothing new, either. Dad and I always had a special relationship. We . . ."

Erin blinked and suddenly bent down, scrabbling for her bag beneath her chair. She drew out a tissue, dabbing at her eyes with it, and then blew her nose.

"Are you okay?" David asked, frowning.

She thrust the tissue into her pocket. "Sorry about that. My father was killed in a road accident just a few months ago. I guess it takes a while to adjust."

"God, that's awful. I'm so sorry." Beneath the table, his hand reached for hers and quickly squeezed it.

"More wine, Erin?" Samantha called down the table with such an obvious smirk that Erin felt as if everyone would suspect something was going on.

For a moment she hated both Samantha and herself, feeling that she was no better than the rest of them. Everyone here seemed to have some sort of hidden agenda: the script writer sweet-talking the producer, Samantha eyeing the handsome young actor . . . and Erin was using David Lennox for what she could gain from him.

"About the concert," David said.

"Concert?" Erin had been so lost in her thoughts that she couldn't think what he was talking about.

"Françoise's concert," he reminded her.

"Of course. Sibelius."

"Are you still interested in going?"

"Yes, I'd love to."

"With me?"

Erin barely hesitated. "That would be great," she said.

"You two seem to be getting on terribly well," Samantha said to her later, when Erin was helping her carry the dishes to the kitchen.

"I like him," Erin replied, her voice sharp.

"Of course you do."

"No, I mean it. I genuinely like him."

"Good. That makes it even easier, doesn't it?"

Actually, it made it more difficult, but Samantha wouldn't understand that.

"One word of warning, darling. Don't fall for David. He's rather like Rob. Doesn't believe in long-term relationships. He's been known to suddenly take off for New York or Boston if someone gets too close."

"That suits me fine. In fact, I'm glad to hear it. Don't forget that I'm going back to Canada in less than two weeks. Excuse me, while I fetch some more dishes."

Erin left the kitchen before Samantha could say any more.

Chapter Ten

Erin spent Monday at the Canadian High Commission and the Public Records Office, researching the evacuation of British children to Canada, but the only reference to her mother she could find was the same false name and address on a 1940 list of evacuees.

Before she had left Winnipeg, she'd spent hours poring over reports and lists in the Provincial Archives and read every book she could find on the subject.

Some of it had been harrowing reading. Not all of the thousands of children who'd been evacuated from Britain to Canada had been as fortunate as her mother. Some of the "guest children" had been treated as a source of free labor and put to work on farms or as servants in their hosts' homes.

At a few minutes past five o'clock on Monday, when all the government offices had closed, Erin stood outside the National Gallery, buffeted by the crowds, feeling dazed and extremely frustrated. She had learned absolutely nothing new about where her mother had come from. Nor had she been able to find a clue to her mother's true identity from the Registrar of Births, Deaths, and Marriages. Without the correct name or place of birth, she'd been told, her mother's birth certificate could not be traced.

As far as Britain was concerned, her mother didn't even exist.

Amberley Court was her only chance. It was a long shot, of course. Even her mother hadn't been sure that it *was* the house she had lived in as a young child. The pictures on the television might have triggered a memory of some other house. But Erin wasn't about to give up now. Tomorrow morning she would go to the library and find out everything she could about Amberley Court and the Hogarth family. That way she'd be well prepared.

She pushed away the insistent thought that there was little hope of getting inside Amberley, even with David Lennox's help. Not only was his relationship pretty remote, he also seemed extremely reluctant to discuss his Hogarth relations.

Someone had mentioned Simon Hogarth on Sunday afternoon and asked for David's opinion of Hogarth's chances at the next election. "You're a cousin of his, aren't you?" the man had said. "What's he really like?"

David's ready smile had faded. "I'm a very distant relative of the Hogarths. Apart from one visit a year to Amberley, I rarely see any of them," he'd said, and immediately changed the subject.

Hardly the person to help her gain an entry to Amberley, Erin had thought at the time, feeling extremely disappointed.

But she was determined not to dwell on negative thoughts. She had less than two weeks to discover her mother's background. To have any hope of achieving her goal, she must remain positive. If she got to know David better, she might at least be able to ask him questions about Amberley, however hostile his feelings about the place and the family.

The news hound in her was already wondering what had caused him to feel that way about the Hogarths.

The next morning, before she set off for London Library with Samantha's library ticket, she phoned her mother again.

"It's going well, Mom," she told her. "I not only met this David Lennox I told you about on Friday, but he's asked me to go to a concert with him."

"Oh, Erin, I hope you're not going to do anything silly just to pursue this wild-goose chase you're—"

"Not at all," Erin said firmly. "It won't be at all difficult to go out with him. He's very nice."

Nice was not how she would describe David to anyone else, but it was sufficient for her mother.

"Just don't do anything stupid, Erin," her mother warned. "I know you. Once you get an idea in your head you won't let it go. Don't take risks to get what you want, please."

"I promise to be careful."

"Did this David Lennox ask you why you were in England?"

"I just told him I was working on plans for a program about the Hudson's Bay Company and wanted to research the original documents from the seventeenth and eighteenth centuries."

"I thought most of them were here, in Canada, not in England."

"You know that. I know that. I just hope David doesn't know it. How are you feeling?" Erin asked, eager to change the subject. She didn't like lying to anyone, particularly David.

"I'm okay."

"Just okay? There's something wrong, isn't there? I can tell."

Her mother hesitated, then she said, "I just had another one of those damned nightmares again last night, that's all."

"Oh, no. I thought you were over them by now."

"So did I."

There was a long pause. Erin could tell that her mother was quietly crying. Her heart sank. "Oh, Mom, I'm so terribly sorry. Do you want me to come home? I could try to get a flight back tomorrow, if you want."

Her mother sniffed. "Of course not. You stay and enjoy yourself." There was an edge to her voice that annoyed Erin.

"I'm not here to enjoy myself. I'm here to try to find out about your family."

"Well, no one asked you to do so. I certainly didn't."

Erin took a deep breath. "I think it will help you, Mom."

"That remains to be seen. Did you have any luck in finding a birth registration?"

"None, I'm afraid. Without the right name it's useless. And you said you know only your mother's first name. Mary, right?"

"That's right." Another pause. "I'm sick of all this,"

Kate suddenly blurted out. "Why don't you just come home and forget all this nonsense?"

"Because it's not nonsense. It's your history and mine. And, if I ever have any children," Erin added heatedly, "it will be theirs as well."

Her mother said nothing.

"Mom, do something for me, will you?"

"What?"

"Please call Dr. Prentice and tell her about the nightmare. Remember, she said it was best if you discuss it with her while it's fresh in your mind."

"I thought I'd got rid of them," her mother said in a hollow voice. "I thought I was getting better." Erin hated to hear the old depressed tone back again.

"You *are* getting better, but you're still being plagued with these memories of your childhood. That's why I'm over here, Mom. I'm doing my damnedest to find out about your past, so that you can be at peace with it."

"I told you before. It's obvious my mother abandoned me. She didn't want me."

"And I don't think that's the way it happened. Just give me a chance to prove it, okay?"

"Okay."

"How's Gran?"

"She's fine." Her mother's voice dropped. "Driving me crazy with her fussing, but I suppose it's better than being alone."

When Erin finished the call, she stared down at the portable telephone in her hand. If she didn't find out about her mother's past, would she ever be truly well again? And, fast on the heels of that negative thought came another: even if she was able to find something, if it was bad news—like a mother abandoning her child—wouldn't it make her mother worse?

Erin began to wonder if she was doing the right thing, after all. She needed someone to assure her that she was, someone who'd give her an objective viewpoint, but the two people she might have been tempted to discuss it with—Samantha and David—were the last people she could talk to about it.

Chapter Eleven

By Wednesday, Erin was so anxious about her date with David that she wasted almost an hour trying to decide what clothes to wear. Trouble was, this was a very important date and she really didn't know David Lennox at all. Apart from the fact that she liked him.

Samantha didn't help. When asked for an opinion, she flatly rejected both dressy outfits Erin had brought with her, and suggested that Erin buy something new.

"What's wrong with this?" Erin demanded, holding the green linen dress with the long, slitted skirt against her.

Samantha leaned against the dressing table, waving a cigarette at her. "It's boring, darling. It's just not sexy enough."

"For heaven's sake. It's just a concert. Who says I want to look sexy?"

Samantha looked over the top of her glasses at Erin. "Are you telling me that you're making all this fuss about clothes because you *don't* want to look sexy?"

Erin had to grin. "No, I suppose not. So, what would you suggest?"

"With your great body . . . how do you do it, by the way?"

"Nothing special. I play tennis in the summer and cross-country ski in the winter."

"How can you bear to live with all that snow and the extreme cold?"

"It's fine if you dress for it. Anyway, I love the outdoors."

Samantha shivered. "Our terrace and garden is about as much of the outdoors as I like. How are you for money?"

"What do you mean?"

"I mean, what could you afford for a new dress? For instance, you could go to Robina's in Knightsbridge and get a lovely little dress for about four or five hundred."

"Five hundred *pounds*?" Erin screeched. "That's more than a thousand Canadian dollars."

"So?"

"There's no way I'd pay that for a dress, however gorgeous. I'll just wear this, thank you very much." She held up the green linen. "And if it doesn't meet with David Lennox's approval, that's just too bad."

Samantha shrugged. "Suit yourself, darling. You did ask me what I thought."

"And you told me. Thanks, Samantha. But if David doesn't like me the way I am—"

"You seem to have forgotten why you're wanting to spend time with him," Samantha reminded her. Her face visibly brightened. "Maybe you could charge a new dress up to business expenses?"

Erin had a sudden vision of Harry's expression if she presented CBC with a bill for a thousand bucks for a dress, and she started to laugh.

"What's so funny?" Samantha demanded.

"Nothing. This dress will be fine. Thanks for your help."

"I've got some fabulous earrings and bracelets that would brighten it up a little."

"That would be great," Erin said. Samantha's psychedelic jewelery wasn't exactly her thing, but she could always take them off after she left the house.

David had arranged to meet her at Waterloo Station and then they'd go for a "quick bite" before the concert. When she arrived at the huge station, she waited by the bookstore, stunned by the booming of unintelligible announcements and slamming of train doors, and the rush of people around her.

Although she tried to look in all directions at once, David appeared suddenly beside her without her noticing him approach. "You look a bit overwhelmed," he said.

"I am. This place is incredible. I don't think I've ever seen so many people at once."

"Welcome to Waterloo Station at the rush hour." He held out his hand. "Hi, Erin. You look great." As they shook hands, he gave her one of his warm smiles.

She smiled back. "Hi, David. So do you." He was dressed in an ecru lightweight suit with a casual knotted silk tie. "I wasn't quite sure what to wear for a London concert."

"You can wear anything in London. Most people go to the theater straight from work, so they don't dress up that much. It depends on the occasion."

"Samantha wanted me to buy a dress," Erin said impulsively, wanting to share the joke with him. "She suggested I go to some boutique where a dress could cost about a thousand dollars."

"She would!" David said, laughing. "What you're wearing is perfect."

He made her feel good. In fact, he made her feel like a million dollars. As he took her elbow to steer her through the crowd, her entire arm tingled at his touch. *Watch out,* she told herself. Despite the importance of getting to know David, she had no intention of becoming emotionally involved with him.

"We should really stay on the south side of the river to save time," David said as they left the station. "The Festival Hall is on this side," he explained. "You've been to London before, haven't you? Is there a special place you'd like to go for a meal?"

"The last time I was in London, I was a student and we ate at McDonald's or pubs. I was dying to eat in a Soho restaurant, but all we did was walk through the area. I never did get to eat there. Isn't that one of the things tourists should do, eat in a Soho restaurant?"

"Absolutely." David looked at his watch. "We haven't that much time, but the restaurants in Soho are used to people rushing off to the theater. We'll go to *L'Epicure* on Frith Street. It's not what you might call trendy, but the food is good. I think you'd like it there."

"I'm not quite sure how to take that," Erin said.

"It's popular with the theater crowd and it has old-fashioned comfort. I'll take comfortable over trendy any time," David said. "I must be getting old."

They took a taxi to Soho. Erin stared out the window,

fascinated by the sights and sounds and sheer mass of people in London. Although the taxi dashed along little side streets, trying to avoid traffic snarls, she was still able to catch glimpses of Trafalgar Square and Piccadilly Circus.

The taxi drew up at a corner restaurant with several flaming torches outside. "I love it already," Erin said.

"The burning torches are a bit incongruous in the sunshine," David said, "but it's quite striking when it gets dark."

The interior of the restaurant was intimate and cozy, all red velvet and white tablecloths and welcoming waiters in maroon jackets.

"Good evening," said one with a marked Italian accent. "A nice, quiet table for you?" He led them to a small round table for two in the corner.

Erin was handed a large menu and quickly scanned it. Pepper Steak, Sole Colbert . . . Everything looked marvelous, but there were no prices listed. She couldn't believe there were any restaurants left that still gave only the host a menu with prices.

"We're going to split the bill," she said.

"No, we're not."

"We certainly are. In fact, I would like to pay for the entire meal. After all, you're taking me to the concert. It's only fair that I pay for the dinner."

"A true North American woman."

"I should hope so. Let's not argue over it." She held out her menu. "Here, *you* take the one without the prices."

"I'm paying this time, as I asked you out. You can choose what we do next time and then you can pay. Okay?"

Erin looked at him.

"What does that funny look mean?" he asked. "Oh, God. I know. I've taken it for granted that you'd want to come out with me again, haven't I?" He struck his forehead with the palm of his hand. "What a monumental ego!"

Erin laughed. "Oh, stop kidding. Tell you what, I'll let you know at the end of this evening. Would that be okay?"

"You mean I'm on trial?"

"Something like that."

"I promise to be on my best behavior then. We'd better get a move on and order. What are you going to have?"

"Why don't you order for me? You know what's best here."

"Okay. We'll both start with sole *goujons*," David told the waiter, "and then Steak Diane with *courgettes* and *pommes frites.*"

"Sounds terrific," Erin said, when the waiter had gone. "But did I hear you order steak? Trust an American to order steak." She leaned forward. "I sometimes forget you're also a Brit, you know. I suppose we're alike, in that way."

"Alike how?"

Her heart thudded. Had she made a mistake in mentioning it? Of course not. Lots of Canadians had British backgrounds. "My mother was English. She came out to Canada as a child."

"Then you must have some relatives over here."

Erin's mouth felt dry. It *had* been a mistake to mention it. "No."

"What, no cousins or uncles or aunts?"

"None that we know of, anyway." That was true, at least. She didn't want to lie to him.

"What about your mother's parents?"

"Her mother—Gran—is still alive. Grandpa died many years ago." Erin crunched on a piece of homemade melba toast. That only made her mouth feel even more dry. She took a drink of mineral water.

"What part of England did they come from?"

Erin's eyes widened. "Who?"

"Your grandparents."

"Oh, my grandparents. Um . . . from the south somewhere, I believe. I don't really know. What about your grandparents? You said your mother was American and your father Scottish."

"That's right. My mother's parents were from Boston. My maternal grandfather was an attorney. He's dead now. My father's dad had a chemist's shop—a pharmacy—in Glasgow."

Erin was surprised. She'd thought David was upper-crust through and through. "Is he still alive?"

"Granddad? No. But my grandmother is." His face softened as he said it.

The waiter put a plate of little pieces of sole coated in crispy bread crumbs in front of Erin. "This looks delicious." She picked up her fork. "It sounds as if you really like her. Your paternal grandmother, I mean."

"I do. She's a very special person. A bit ditzy, but great fun."

"Is she Scottish, too?" Erin was beginning to wonder where on earth the connection with the Hogarths came in.

A shadow seemed to cross his face. "No, Lucy is English."

"Lucy?"

"My grandmother's name was Lucy Hogarth before she married."

Erin held her breath for a moment, and then let it out slowly. "I heard someone ask you about Simon Hogarth on Sunday. I thought I heard him say you were related to him."

"Lucy was the present Earl of Maybridge's cousin. He's Simon Hogarth's grandfather. Lucy was raised at Amberley Court, the family home."

Erin continued to eat her sole *goujons,* but they'd lost their flavor for her. She could sense David's tension, see it in the tightness of his jaw.

"Lucy's father had survived the first world war, only to succumb to the influenza epidemic that followed it. His wife, who was expecting Lucy at the time, caught it, too, and died a week after Lucy was born."

"How terrible."

"Lucy was brought up by her father's elder brother, Hugh, who was the twelfth Earl of Maybridge."

"What relation was he to the present earl?"

"His father. And a real bastard."

Erin was shocked at the acrimony in David's voice. "Why do you say that?"

"Because that's what he was. Lucy was a gifted designer. She had a hell of a job persuading her uncle to allow her to go away to study. But she managed it."

"I suppose this would have been in the thirties sometime, wouldn't it?"

"Right. Midthirties. When she went to the art school at Glasgow University, she met and fell in love with Ian Lennox and insisted on marrying him. Not only did her uncle throw her out of Amberley, he refused ever to let her visit the only home she'd known."

"Oh, David, why?"

"Because Ian Lennox came from a working-class family. If he'd been a wealthy industrialist, that would have been okay, but he was also poor. So they treated poor Lucy as if she didn't exist anymore and banned her from Amberley."

"What an awful thing to do. He must have been a horrible man."

"He was. One of those Victorian-style despots." He picked up his knife and fork. "My food's getting cold. How on earth did we get on to talking about my disreputable family?"

"You were asking about mine," Erin said lightly, "so, naturally, I asked about yours. Do you see Lucy, your grandmother, much nowadays?"

"Enough about families. Let's confine ourselves to each other for the rest of the meal, okay? Tell me about your day. How did the Hudson's Bay research go?"

Erin had to dig into her scanty knowledge about the Hudson's Bay Company to answer him. Then she managed to steer the conversation to the safer subject of her quick visit to the National Gallery that afternoon.

They ended the delicious meal with cognac and Turkish Delight and potent thick coffee in little heated carafes.

Erin leaned back and released a sigh. "I am so full I couldn't eat again for a week. I hope I don't fall asleep at the concert."

"If you do, I'll pinch you." David looked at his watch. "We must go. I promised to look in on Françoise before the concert."

Erin was reluctant to leave the restaurant. Not only had she enjoyed the meal and David's company, but she'd managed to steer him into talking about the Hogarth family. Although she'd sensed his uneasiness when he talked about the Hogarths, it had been frustrating to have their conversation about his grandmother cut off midstream, just when she was learning so much.

The concert was superb. As the violin was climbing to its climax in the last movement of the Sibelius, David's hand slid over hers. They sat, hands clasped, for the rest of the concert, Erin pushing everything from her mind except the soaring music and the nearness of David.

Later, very much later, after the reception and after David had driven her back to Richmond in his Porsche, he drew up outside Samantha's house.

"The lights are still on," Erin said. "Samantha must still be up. Will you come in for a drink?"

"I think not. I don't want to break the spell, if you know what I mean."

Erin knew exactly what he meant. He extended his arm across the back of her seat and she leant her head against it. His face was very close to hers. One little move and they'd be touching.

"So," he said, "what's the verdict?"

"About tonight, you mean? It's been absolutely great. All of it."

"I agree. But I meant, do we do it again? You said you'd let me know at the end of the evening, remember?"

"I'd like to," she said hesitantly, "if you would."

His eyes looked into hers. His face seemed even closer than before, his mouth hovering above hers, so that she could feel his breath warm on her cheek. "I would."

"Perhaps we could do something at the weekend?" she suggested.

"I'm afraid I'm all booked up this weekend."

"Oh." Erin was disappointed. She'd envisioned a day at the seaside, dinner at an old country inn, or a picnic on the downs, or something similarly English.

"I have to go to Amberley."

Erin's heart quickened. She willed herself not to tense up. "Oh, really? I got the idea you didn't go there much at all."

"I don't. But this is a sort of royal command. The whole family is summoned for the earl's birthday each year. So, obedient to the command, we all troop down to spend the weekend nearest to his birthday at Amberley, and have a thoroughly miserable time."

"Why do you go, when you dislike it so much?"

"There are two reasons. Firstly, Lucy won't go without me and I know how much it means to her."

"Oh, you mean your grandmother can go there now?"

"She's invited for the birthday bash, that's all. Although she and Giles—the present earl—spent their early childhood years together at Amberley, he's not keen on her unaristocratic connections, particularly the American ones, meaning me. And Lucy's not a great fan of his, either."

"He sounds as if he's as rotten as his father."

"No, not really. I've not much time for him or any of his kind, but Giles is more eccentric than rotten, I think."

"What was your other reason for wanting to go for this birthday weekend?"

He gave her a wry grin. "For some bizarre reason, I have a thing about Amberley Court itself. For that reason alone, I wish I could go there more frequently. Both the house and the grounds are truly beautiful. The oldest part of the house is Elizabethan, all rosy brick and wood beams, with some Jacobean additions, but it was modernized in the Victorian era to make it more comfortable. The gardens are especially beautiful at this time of year, with all the roses and rhododendrons blooming."

"It sounds wonderful."

"It is, or it would be, if it weren't for the Hogarths." David sighed. "I'd really rather spend the weekend with you, especially when you're in England for such a short time, but I can't disappoint Lucy."

"No, of course you can't," Erin said briskly. "What about another evening instead?"

He didn't reply for a moment. Then his hand tightened on her upper arm. "I've just had an idea."

"What?"

"I'm not sure that it's fair to ask you, though."

"Ask me what?" Erin asked, her heart pounding.

"If you'd like to come to Amberley with me and my grandmother."

Erin lifted her head to look straight into his eyes. "I couldn't possibly intrude in a family party."

"Why not? I'd love you to meet Lucy and as long as we obey the command to come to Amberley, no one gives a damn whom we bring with us. It's such a huge place you could smuggle in a dozen people and no one would be the wiser."

"Do you intend to smuggle me in?"

"Only if I could keep you entirely to myself, and I can't. But it would make a hell of a difference to me if you could come with us. Instead of dreading it, I'd be looking forward to it." His arm was warm across her shoulders.

No amount of telling herself that she should accept because David wanted her to could make Erin feel less guilty about deceiving him. But she also knew that she couldn't possibly pass up this heaven-sent opportunity to get inside Amberley. After all, that was why she was in England, wasn't it?

"I'd love to come to Amberley with you," she said.

Chapter Twelve

"Well?" said Samantha, when she let Erin in. "How did it go?" She peered out the door as David drove away. "Didn't you ask David in?"

"He apologized for not coming in. He has an eight o'clock appointment in the morning with a client who's flying to New York tomorrow."

"How was the concert?"

"Absolutely great."

"And everything else?"

"Just fine."

"Bloody hell! This is like pulling teeth."

"Sorry. Give me a moment to get these shoes off and I'll tell you more."

Before Samantha could ask any more questions, Erin slipped past her and ran upstairs. She was extremely reluctant to discuss David with her. After only one date, their relationship was at a precarious juncture. When David had kissed her in the car, Erin had turned what might have been a pretty heavy embrace into a light *thank you* kiss.

She wasn't sure which one of them had been the more disappointed by it, her or David.

As soon as she was in the comparative safety of her room Erin took off her dress, hung it on a hanger, and then pulled on her cotton robe. She sat on the stool, staring at herself in the dressing-table mirror. She didn't like what she saw. It wasn't just the blurred lipstick and the mussed dark hair. Behind the familiar face with her mother's rather sharp-boned nose, which she hated, she fancied she saw a hard, conniving witch.

Good fortune and good chemistry between her and David had enabled her to achieve her goal with remarkable ease. But she was left with such a load of guilt that she felt nauseous.

One thing was certain. She wouldn't make a very good news reporter. She hadn't the stomach for it. Maybe she should forget her ambitions to make it big. Better to stay in Winnipeg and continue to make good local documentaries. After all, they probably had more lasting social value than a story gained by lying and wheedling one's way into other people's private lives.

The one redeeming factor was that this was her mother's story. If Amberley held the key to her mother's background, then it was her duty to use any means possible to gain entry to it.

Even if she did have to con David to do so.

"Erin! Have you fallen asleep up there?"

Samantha's voice penetrated the closed bedroom door.

Reluctantly, Erin got up and opened the door. "Just coming," she shouted down.

Samantha was in the library. A rather grand name for a room that held not only many bookshelves crammed with books, but also the largest television Erin had ever seen inside a home, and a super stereo system with all kinds of technical equipment.

Samantha handed Erin a cognac in a balloon glass.

"I don't really need it, thanks," Erin said.

"Sit . . . and tell," was Samantha's command.

Erin perched on the forest-green leather couch and took the glass from Samantha. "David asked me to come to Amberley with him for the weekend."

"What!" Samantha screeched.

Erin raised her shoulders and smiled. "It was as easy as that. Apparently it's the earl's birthday and the entire family—even distant relatives like David—always spends the weekend at Amberley for it. It's an old family tradition."

"My God, Erin, I have to hand it to you. You're a sharp operator."

Erin's cheeks grew warm. "I feel like a confidence trickster. I hate lying to him." The fact that she was also lying to Samantha about her true reason for wanting to get into Amberley made it even worse.

"Who cares? You've managed to do what no other journalist has done, get inside Amberley."

"I haven't managed it yet."

"You will."

The knowing smile Samantha gave her was one of admiration, but it made Erin feel even more uncomfortable. She had an uneasy sense that the camaraderie between them had gone, replaced by professional envy.

"I hope you'll give me first British rights to your story," Samantha said. "After all, darling, I was the one who brought you and David together."

"Yes, you were." Erin swirled the amber liquid around in her glass. "If you don't mind, I'd rather not discuss it before it happens. I'm a bit superstitious about talking about a story as if it's a definite."

"Well, you're not going to come away empty-handed, are you? Whatever happens, you'll be able to concoct some sort of story. I can just see it now. *My Weekend with Simon Hogarth.*"

"For heaven's sake," Erin said, suddenly angry at both herself and Samantha. "Anything could happen between now and Friday evening. David or I could get ill. Or, even more likely, Lucy could."

"Who's Lucy?"

"David's grandmother. She's the reason he's going to Amberley. She wants to go to Amberley and she won't go without him."

"And the whole damned family, Simon Hogarth and all, will be there?"

"I imagine so." Erin put down the glass of untouched brandy with a sharp rap on the marble-topped table.

"You really are a miracle worker." Samantha's eyes narrowed. "What did you do to David to get him to invite you? Must have been something good."

Erin stood up. "Excuse me, I'm going to bed. Thanks for the brandy."

"Aww, shame. Now you're being a prairie prude." Samantha picked up Erin's glass. "If you're not going to drink this, I will. It's too good to waste."

"Go ahead." Erin would have liked to make a cup of tea, but nothing would make her stay downstairs with

Samantha. In fact, she was dreading having to spend the next couple of days with her.

"Oh, I forgot to tell you," Samantha shouted after her, as she started up the stairs. "Adam's coming home at some godforsaken hour in the morning, just in case you encounter him in the hallway and wonder who the hell he is."

"That's great," Erin said automatically.

"Don't you believe it." Samantha took another drink of Erin's brandy and went into the kitchen.

Erin was glad Samantha had warned her when she was woken the next morning by a male voice roaring, "Sam! What the shit have you done with my razor?"

Erin sat up with a start and glanced at her alarm clock. Ten minutes past seven.

A yelling match ensued between Samantha, who was presumably downstairs and her husband, who seemed to be all over the place upstairs. He paced from his bedroom to the hall to the bathroom, shouting as he did so. In fact, for one horrible moment, when he yelled outside Erin's door, she thought he was about to burst in.

Then the pandemonium ceased. She didn't know whether she should stay in her room until one or both of them had left for work.

When, eventually, she went down, she found Samantha's husband in the kitchen. He was quite unlike what she'd expected. Short, overweight, he looked like an ex-boxer gone to seed, but his expression was intelligent, and he smiled when he saw her. A smile of great charm.

"Good morning. You must be Erin." He held out his hand. "I'm Adam Friedman."

"Hello. Samantha told me you were coming home."

"Good thing she did, eh? Rude awakening. Sorry about that." It was strange to hear the clipped English tones coming from someone who looked as if he should speak with a New York Bronx accent.

"That's okay."

"I'm always bad-tempered when I miss a night's sleep."

"Most people are."

"Can I get you anything? No, I don't need to, do I?

You must know your way about the kitchen. Ignore me." He waved a hand and returned to reading the pile of mail in front of him.

Erin made herself coffee and toast and poured muesli into a cereal bowl. Dishes were piled up on the countertop and in the sink. Samantha had obviously left in a hurry.

"Samantha tells me you're a friend of Rob Harris."

Erin stiffened. "Yes, that's right." She wondered how much Adam knew about Samantha and Rob.

"Bright guy."

"Yes, I suppose he is."

"Bit of a bastard though, eh?"

She met Adam Friedman's gaze with a rueful smile. "Yes, I think you could say that."

He gave a satisfied grunt and returned to his mail. Nothing more was said, but Erin was thinking that if Rob was bright, Adam was brighter.

Adam's return seemed to make Samantha edgy, less relaxed, so that Erin began to feel that she was in the way. Their constant bickering disturbed her, although Samantha assured her it meant nothing. Whether it did or not, Erin was glad when Saturday came.

When David ushered her into the car, she sank into the back seat with a heavy sigh.

"That sounds suspiciously like relief," he said. "Don't tell me that living with Samantha is getting to you? Nice, quiet Samantha!"

"It's ten times worse since her husband came home."

David chuckled. "The shy and reticent Adam, too. Lucky you."

"Who are you talking about?" demanded a shaky but imperious voice from the front.

"Sorry, dearest," David said. "This is my friend from Canada, Erin Benson. Erin, this is my grandmama, Lucy Lennox."

Erin leaned forward. "Hello, Mrs. Lennox. I'd shake hands, but I think you'd rather not have to twist around."

"Quite right. David should have brought you to the front of the car before you got in."

"That was my fault, I'm afraid," Erin said. "I was so eager to get away, I just jumped in without thinking."

"Hmm. I hope you remembered to bring your suitcase?"

David smiled at Erin in the rearview mirror. "Yes, it's in the boot," he told his grandmother. "The trunk," he explained to Erin.

"She brought a trunk?" Lucy said.

"No," David shouted, as he started up the car. "I was telling Erin that her suitcase was in the trunk."

"Why in heaven's name would she put her suitcase inside a trunk? What a strange thing to do! Wouldn't that make it very heavy for you to lift?"

David glanced into the mirror again, raising his eyebrows at Erin. She was finding it very hard not to burst out laughing.

She leaned forward so that she could shout into Lucy's ear. "North Americans call the car boot a trunk, Mrs. Lennox."

"Do they, indeed. How very odd. By the way, young lady, there is no need for you to shout at me. I am not deaf, you know."

Erin couldn't even look at David. Her lips quirking, she sat back in her seat. Whatever happened when they arrived at Amberley, this was going to be quite an interesting drive.

"How long will it take to get there?" she asked at last, when she felt it was safe for her to speak again.

"Not long. An hour or so."

Erin's stomach muscles cramped. An hour wasn't long enough. She'd thought she had more time than that to relax before she had to face the Hogarth family. If Lucy was anything to go by, they'd be a formidable bunch. And David had told her that Lucy was a sweetheart.

"Anything wrong?" David asked.

"I'm a bit nervous, that's all."

"What about? My driving?"

"Of course not. Amberley. Meeting Lord Maybridge."

"No need to be nervous. Just be yourself."

"I'm not used to stately homes. All I know about them comes from the movies. *Little Lord Fauntleroy* and *Howards End*, and *The Remains of the Day*."

"Oh, things have completely changed since those days."

"You mean there isn't a butler at Amberley?"

"Well, actually there is, but it's one of the few places left that has one. Harrington's a relic of the older days in more ways than one."

"Who's a relic of the older days?" Lucy demanded. "I hope you're not talking about me."

This time David laughed openly. "Of course not. You're as modern as they come. We were talking about Harrington."

"Oh, that old idiot. You're right. He is a relic. Spilled a cup of tea all over my new silk dress last year. Silly old fool. I never got the stain out."

"What a shame," Erin said.

"Giles should get rid of him, but he kisses up to Giles, does Harrington. Knows what Giles likes."

Erin was growing to thoroughly dislike the Earl of Maybridge, and she hadn't even met him yet.

It was a pleasant relief to leave the M25, the motorway ring road around London, with its alternate bursts of high speed and long traffic holdups, and turn into a narrow tree-lined road that wound its way through the rolling countryside of Kent.

"It's hard to believe this is so near London," Erin said, as they drove through a lovely little village, complete with village green and a duck pond. "Oh, what a lovely old inn!"

"That's a pub, not an inn," Lucy said. "Nigel used to get soused in there."

"Who?"

"Nigel Hogarth, Simon's father," David explained. "He died several years ago." He turned to Lucy. "You promised me you wouldn't mention Nigel while you're at Amberley. It could upset everyone."

"Who cares?" Lucy said with a loud sniff.

"You do. You'd care very much if Giles didn't invite you to his next birthday party, so no mention of Nigel, please."

Erin liked the way David dealt with his grandmother. Firm, but kind.

"Almost there," David announced, when they came

to a small crossroads and turned down an even narrower lane.

The hedges closed in on them, so that in places there was room for only a single lane. Then the road widened and forked. They turned left and drove up the lane that ran parallel to a very high brick wall topped with vicious-looking iron spikes.

To Erin's surprise, there were cars and vans parked along the wall and, as they drove up to the closed gates, the group of people waiting there broke away and clustered around the car, cameras whirring and clicking.

Erin automatically shrank back as a camera was pressed against her window.

"It's okay," David said wearily. "It's just the press. They must be waiting for Simon to arrive. He's still a big news item." He rolled down his window.

"Who are you?" demanded a reporter, thrusting a tape recorder in his face.

"A friend of Mrs. Lucy Lennox, who is visiting her cousin Lord Maybridge for the weekend," David said calmly, but Erin could see the tension in his jaw. He opened the door and got out, locking it behind him, and made his way through the crowd of reporters to the gate.

"Disgraceful behavior!" Lucy shouted. She picked up her umbrella and pounded on the window at the grinning cameramen. "Get away from there. Get away!"

"I think it would be best if we just sat still until David came back," Erin suggested.

"Sit still? I've a good mind to get out and bash them with my umbrella."

"No, that wouldn't be a good idea at all." Erin leaned forward and took the umbrella from Lucy's hand. The indignant old lady looked so furious that Erin thought it very likely she would have struck her had she been able to reach back.

Now two security guards were opening the gates. David came back to the car, unlocked it, and jumped in. The car started off and the gates closed again behind them.

"That was awful," Erin said. She was surprised to find that she was shaking.

"The price of fame. Besides, I'm surprised to hear you say that, considering you're in the business yourself."

"You mean she's a reporter?" Lucy shrieked.

"No, no. I'm just teasing her." He grimaced at Erin in the mirror. "Erin's a television producer. She makes interesting documentaries."

"Oh, that's all right then. For a moment I thought she was a scorpion in our midst."

Erin swallowed. Lucy might well be right, she thought. She suddenly realized that plying Lucy with questions about the past at Amberley might be much more difficult than she'd thought.

In fact none of this was going to be easy. She might be getting inside Amberley, but where did she go from there? Even if it *was* the right house, who was left in the house to give her the information she needed? And Lucy's reaction was a warning of how she would be viewed if she began asking questions.

If her mother was somehow connected with the Hogarth family itself, rather than their servants, every member of the family would surely close ranks against her once they discovered her true reason for coming to Amberley.

All she had to go on was the photograph. She'd had a copy of it made before she came away. It was in her wallet. Instinctively, she pulled her leather bag closer to her side.

They were driving down a wide avenue lined by large trees that looked as if they'd stood there forever, their trunks wide and solid as stone pillars. And there, on a slight rise, was Amberley Court itself, spread out before them, looking more like a palace than a house.

"Oh, my goodness," Erin breathed. "I had no idea it was this big. The pictures—"

"Don't do it justice, do they?" David said. "You'd need one of those panoramic photographs to get it all in."

Amberley Court seemed far larger than the house she'd seen on television. As they drove around the fountain courtyard and up to the stone steps, Erin felt rather overwhelmed.

But as she stood waiting for David to help his grandmother from the car, she was also struck by the beauty of the place. There was a sense of harmony between the mellow rosy-red brick walls of the old house and the gardens and parkland that surrounded it.

David smiled at her. "Okay?" he asked softly.

"I'll be fine."

As she followed him and Lucy up the broad steps, the door opened and a woman came out. She was dressed in navy with touches of white.

"Welcome to Amberley, Mrs. Lennox, Mr. Lennox." She sounded as crisp and businesslike as her suit.

"Thank you, Mrs. Edwards. This is our friend, Erin Benson. Mrs. Edwards is the housekeeper at Amberley," David explained.

Erin was surprised. Mrs. Edwards looked more like an upwardly mobile executive than a housekeeper.

"Welcome to Amberley, Miss Benson."

Erin held out her hand. "Thank you, Mrs. Edwards." Then, remembering the faux pas made by Mrs. De Winter in *Rebecca*, she wondered for a moment if she, too, had made a mistake.

But Mrs. Edwards took her hand and shook it firmly. "I hope you enjoy your stay with us," she said with a pleasant smile.

"Are we the first to arrive?" David asked.

"Yes, you are. Mr. Simon and his family haven't arrived yet."

Lucy tapped David on the arm with her umbrella. "Are we going to stand outside in the cold blethering all day," asked Lucy, "or are we going inside?"

"Oh, sorry about that." David gallantly held out his arm.

Erin hid her smile. It was certainly not cold. The warmth of the June day had created a heat haze, making the stretch of parkland before her seem like a shimmering mirage.

She followed the others inside and found herself in a hall with a high, molded ceiling.

"This is the great hall," David told her over his shoulder. "The oldest part of the house."

The long hall had a carved wooden screen at one end, brightly colored coats of arms set into its paneling. There was a large stone fireplace in the main long wall, flanked by polished fire irons, with old pewter dishes on the mantelshelf above it.

Erin was about to follow the others when her eye was caught by a full-length painting at the head of the wide flight of stairs. It was a portrait of a young man dressed in the formal evening costume of black tailcoat and white tie. He was tall and strikingly handsome, with a lean face and bright blue eyes that stared out from the canvas with all the assurance of the wellborn and wealthy aristocrat.

Erin recognized the face immediately. It was the man in her mother's photograph.

Chapter Thirteen

Erin remained at the foot of the stairs, staring up at the painting, her heart pounding.

"Anything wrong?" David asked, his voice echoing in the vast hall.

Erin steeled herself to appear normal, determined not to give herself away. "I was just looking at this painting. It's very good. Is it someone famous?"

Lucy giggled. "He likes to think he is. That's Giles, when he was young. Come along, David. I'm dying for a drink." Grabbing David's arm, she dragged him through a doorway across the hall.

"The portrait is of the present Earl of Maybridge," said a dry voice.

Erin spun around, to find an elderly man dressed in a crumpled gray linen jacket behind her. He was thin and stooped, his wrinkled face suggesting a man of eighty, at least.

"I am Harrington, butler of Amberley Court," he announced, making it sound as important a position as King of England.

"I'm Erin Benson, Mr. Lennox's friend." This time Erin did not hold out her hand.

"Ah, yes, Miss Benson. Would it be your preference to take tea in the red room or to have Mrs. Edwards show you to your room?"

"I'd like to join the others, whatever they're doing."

"The others? Ah, you mean Mrs. Lennox and Mr. Lennox. Kindly follow me."

As Erin knew exactly which room David and his grandmother had entered, she didn't really need Harrington's assistance, but before she could say so, he took off, shuffling across the polished parquet floor.

She was able to gain only a vague impression of the rest of the beautiful old hall as she crossed it. The lower half of the stone walls was covered with wood paneling. Huge tapestries of hunting scenes covered the upper half, their colors still vibrant in places, but there were also many threadbare patches denoting their age.

Harrington opened the door at the same time as David was about to come out.

"Ah, there you are, Erin. Sorry, I didn't mean to neglect you," David said. "I was coming to find you."

The sound of car wheels crunching on the gravel outside and then children's excited voices heralded new arrivals.

"That must be Mr. Simon," Harrington said. "Excuse me." He hurried back across the hall.

David drew Erin into the room. "Let's have a drink before everyone comes in. What would you like?"

"What are you having?"

"A scotch. Lucy's having one as well."

"I'd rather have a cup of tea, if you don't mind."

The shock of finding the portrait had set Erin's mind spinning. A drink might help relax her tension, but she must keep her head as clear as possible. Now that she knew she was in the right place, who knew what clues to her mother's past she might find here.

"Mrs. Edwards will be pleased," David was saying. "She offered us tea to go with this huge spread of food she's laid on here, and we both turned our noses up at it. Come on in and sit down. This is the red drawing room, by the way."

It struck Erin that David was talking a little faster than usual. And when he sat down, he sat on the edge of his seat as if ready to spring up at any moment. He was almost as tense as she was.

She smiled at him as she chose a gilded chair covered with the red damask that had given the room its name. When she'd sat down, she glanced up at the ceiling, with its ornate plaster moldings picked out in gold. No cherubs here. "What a striking room!"

"It is striking, isn't it?" David looked around, the rather hunted look fading from his eyes. "A little too formal for my liking, though."

"May I pour you some tea, Miss Benson?" Lucy asked, setting her glass down.

"Please. And I wish you would call me Erin."

"Very well. Milk or lemon with your tea, Erin?"

"Milk, please. I—"

The door opened. All three of them turned expectantly. Erin saw David's expression relax a little when two little girls entered, followed by a strikingly beautiful woman with a willowy figure and ash-blond hair coiled into a French knot. She was dressed in an informal silk pantsuit the color of terra-cotta.

She came forward, hands extended. "Cousin Lucy, how lovely to see you again." She bent to kiss Lucy. "And David." Another kiss. A perfunctory brush on the cheek this time, though.

Now, it was Erin's turn. As the woman looked at her, a slight questioning smile on her lips, Erin knew that she was being thoroughly sized up.

David came to her side. "Olivia, this is my friend, Erin Benson. She's from Canada. Erin, meet Olivia Hogarth, Simon's wife. Oh, and we mustn't forget the Misses Hogarth, Nicola and Perdita. Hi, girls."

As the girls responded warmly to David, chattering to him about their dog having been sick in the car, Erin felt her hand taken lightly in Olivia Hogarth's cool hand, and then released.

"Canada? Are you one of David's visiting performers?"

"No. I produce documentaries."

"Oh, really." Olivia's tone suggested surprise. "What kind of documentaries?"

"I make television documentaries."

"Television?" Olivia frowned, her pale-blue eyes wary. "David, you didn't tell me that Miss Benson worked in television." The way she emphasized the word gave it a wealth of meaning.

"I haven't had the chance yet, have I? Don't worry, Olivia. Erin makes social documentaries in midwest Canada. There are important things happening other than the election of the great Simon Hogarth. And other places in the world besides this little island of ours, you know."

Erin tried to smile, but found that her face had become too tight to do so.

Olivia turned away. "Now, girls, don't bother David."

David had produced two tubes of Smarties from his pocket. "Yummie," the younger child said.

"They're only allowed sweets after meals, David."

"This is after a meal, surely? They had lunch, didn't they?"

The girls giggled. "He's right, Mummy," Nicola said. "This is after lunch."

"Come on, Olivia. Give a little," David said. "How often do I see them to be able to give them sweets?"

"Oh, very well." Olivia sat down on the sofa beside Lucy. "Off you go, children. Go and play in the garden. Take Trixie with you. The fresh air will take away that awful smell."

"Where's Simon?" Lucy asked, as the girls ran from the room.

"Seeing to the car. The wretched dog was sick, that's why we're late. We had to stop for a while to give her a pill and air the car out." The door opened. "Here he is now."

Erin was watching David. His face had grown tense again as he waited for the man who had entered to come forward into the room. "Hello, Simon."

"David, good to see you. Cousin Lucy, you're looking younger than ever."

Erin had the impression of a strong force of energy entering the room. Simon Hogarth was not a large man, but, despite his medium height and slender build, he was one of those people who seemed to take up a large amount of space. Like all those with star quality, he drew your eyes to him and yet seemed quite oblivious to his effect upon people.

In one swift movement, he bent to kiss Lucy's cheek, shook David's hand—all accompanied by suitable greetings—and then turned to look at Erin. As he came nearer, she saw that his eyes were gray with a slight touch of blue, which could be a legacy from his grandfather, if the portrait was anything to go by.

"This must be Miss Benson. Harrington was telling

me that we had a special guest staying with us." He held out his hand to her. "Welcome to Amberley."

The warmth of his greeting took Erin by surprise. He really seemed to mean it. "Thank you, Mr. Hogarth. It's lovely to be here."

"What do you think of Amberley?"

"What I've seen is very beautiful. We only arrived a short time ago. I'm looking forward to seeing more of the house and gardens."

"You must allow me to be your guide. When I was younger, I used to go around with the tours, so I'm quite an expert."

"Oh, I didn't realize there were tours of Amberley."

"The house and gardens are usually open to the public on Sundays in the summer, but we've closed it this year, for obvious reasons." Simon raised dark eyebrows at Erin. "You saw the reporters at the gates. They'd love an opportunity to get inside Amberley. It wasn't an easy decision to make. We like to share our beautiful home with the public."

The remark of a true politician, thought Erin. She wasn't quite sure what to make of Simon Hogarth. He had an angular face, dark—almost black—hair, and a charismatic smile. Very attractive to women. She herself had felt the pull of attraction immediately. She had also sensed his wife's gaze upon her as she talked to Simon, as if Olivia were still assessing her.

Simon and David were talking together now, but it was the small talk of comparative strangers, not the warm exchange of reunited family members.

There was a wariness between the two men that surprised Erin. Considering Simon's position, she would have thought that it would have been easy for him to be relaxed and friendly with David. What had he to lose? Yet she had the impression that this meeting was as much a strain for Simon as it was for David.

The door opened again. Harrington pushed it fully ajar and stood back. This time everyone except Lucy stood. Erin felt as if there should be trumpets blowing a fanfare or at the very least an announcement, but the Earl of Maybridge entered with no pomp other than that inherent in his own person.

He was tall and remarkably upright for a man of his age. Both face and body were lean—almost gaunt—as was the hand that leaned on the stick as he crossed the room slowly. Erin noticed that the brilliant blue of his eyes had faded in comparison with his portrait in the hall, but everyone felt their piercing quality as he took up his stance before the marble fireplace and surveyed them.

"Her Majesty's leader of the opposition and his wife. My cousin Lucy. Her grandson, David Lennox." He listed them slowly in an autocratic voice. "And our guest, Miss Benson."

Erin had a ridiculous urge to curtsy.

"Welcome to Amberley, Miss Benson."

"Thank you, my lord."

He smiled at her. Immediately, she saw from whom Simon Hogarth had inherited his charm. "Harrington tells me that you're a Canadian."

"Yes. From Winnipeg, Manitoba."

"I had Canadians under my command in the war. Damned fine fellows. Unassuming quiet lads, unlike the noisy Yanks, but also excellent fighters."

"That's good," Erin said. She avoided meeting David's eyes in case she had a fit of giggling. Canadians, it seemed, were okay, even if Americans weren't.

Again, Lord Maybridge surveyed the others in the room. "Well, well, well. All my loving family gathered under my roof for one more time." There was no mistaking the acid in his voice.

"Let us hope that there will be many more such occasions," Olivia said.

"Thank you, my dear. That was very nicely said."

"I meant it," Olivia protested.

"I know you did." He limped over to the large leather armchair and lowered himself into it, stretching his long legs out before him. His dogs, a brown-and-white spaniel and an Airedale, settled at his feet.

"Where are the others?" Simon asked his grandfather.

"What others? Do you mean my other dog? Hector's out in the fields somewhere, chasing rabbits."

Simon smiled. "No, not Hector. I meant Basil and Cecily."

"Oh, them. They've called off. Said they had the flu and didn't want to expose me to their germs. It's more likely Cecily got cold feet because Basil made such an ass of himself last year."

Erin was dying to know who Basil and Cecily were and exactly what Basil had done last year to disgrace himself.

As the stilted conversation rose and fell behind her, she sat and watched this famous family in action. Part of her job as a producer was to observe people as they interacted. As an outsider at this family gathering she was in the unique position of being able to do so without being accused of being antisocial.

It wasn't difficult to gauge, for instance, that the earl was at odds with everyone there, except Olivia, with whom he remained reasonably civil. He was a grouchy old devil with a vitriolic tongue, but for some reason Erin admired him. The inveterate military man, he would no doubt fight to the bitter end for what he believed in.

As she sat there, listening to him bait Lucy—who missed half of his barbs because of her deafness—Erin thought of the portrait in the hall. That brought her to the photograph again. She wondered what would happen if she were to take it from her wallet and show it to everyone.

The thought gave her a feeling of power. That *I know something you don't know* feeling.

But what did she know? She knew who the man in the photo was. But why had it been put into her mother's book? If the woman in the photo had been her mother's mother, did it mean that the earl was merely her lover or . . .

"You're very quiet."

Erin jumped. David had moved behind her chair and whispered in her ear.

She turned to face him. "I was just listening to you all talk."

"Let's get out of here," he whispered.

"David," the earl said, raising his voice. "I haven't asked you how your mother is. Not married again, has she?"

Erin saw David's hand tighten on the back of her chair so that the knuckles gleamed white against his tan. "Not yet," he answered lightly.

"So she's still with husband number three, eh?"

"No, they were divorced two years ago, as you know very well, sir. Excuse me. I think it's time I took Erin out for some fresh air."

"What a good idea," Erin said brightly and stood up.

As she passed by the earl's chair, to her great surprise he grasped her hand. "It's a pleasure to have a pretty young face about the place again. Come and have a chat with me later, Miss Benson."

"I'd like that."

"Dinner's at eight. Drinks at seven-thirty. Come down at seven. You'll find me in the library. Harrington will show you where it is."

"I'll be there. Thank you."

"Only you, mind," he said, frowning over her shoulder at David. "I need a break from my family."

"But they only just arrived," she reminded him.

"I'll have to put up with them for the rest of the evening."

"You should be glad to have a family who cares about you."

She heard a sharp intake of breath from the middle of the room, too far away to be David. It was followed by a cackle of laughter from Lucy.

Lord Maybridge glared at Erin. "The only thing my family cares about, young lady, is what they're going to get out of me when I die."

"I don't know about that. But I'm sure—" She felt a sharp nudge in her back from David. "We'll talk later," she said hurriedly and followed David from the room.

"The old man has really taken to you," David said. He sounded half admiring, half annoyed.

"Is that bad?"

"Olivia wasn't too happy. She likes to be the old man's darling. The only one. Talk of the devil," he said, lowering his voice, "here she comes. From the look of her, we're in for stormy weather."

"Miss Benson," Olivia said, her voice crystal-cold. "I hope you won't mind me saying this, but my husband's grandfather has serious heart problems. He must not be upset in any way. It is better not to argue with him, or he might have another seizure."

Erin blinked rapidly. "I am sorry. I hadn't been aware that I had argued with him."

Olivia smiled. "We are used to him saying disagreeable things that might upset an outsider. It doesn't bother us, you see."

"Speak for yourself," David said.

"I wasn't speaking to you, David. I was speaking to Miss Benson."

"You were speaking about how Giles's rudeness doesn't bother you. It bloody well bothers me."

"Ah, but then you have to deal with it only once a year, David. Simon and I must face it more often. We are used to it. We consider it merely a manifestation of growing old."

"I'm sorry," Erin said. "I certainly didn't mean to upset him. But I can't agree with you that rudeness has to be part of growing old. If he's allowed to get away with it, it becomes a habit. I get the feeling he actually enjoys it."

"Quite right. He does." This time it was Simon who came out into the hall. "How very perceptive of you, Miss Benson. My grandfather really likes you, by the way. He said it was a pleasure to meet someone who stood up to him for a change."

Erin didn't know what to say in response to that, especially with Olivia standing stone-faced opposite her.

"But my wife is also right. We all have to be very careful not to upset him. That's why we put up with his bad tempers. I know you won't mind us mentioning it." Simon's mouth slid into a warm smile.

"I promise to be more careful."

"That's all we ask. Coming, Olivia?" He spoke softly, but Olivia responded as if it had been a command, and followed him back into the drawing room.

David led Erin out to a flagstoned terrace at the rear of the house and down rough stone steps to the green lawn.

"I'd hate to have to cut this every weekend," Erin

said. "I thought our lawn was bad enough, but this is unbelievable."

David laughed. "It's quite something, isn't it? And this is only a small part of the gardens." He led her across the lawn to a walled rose garden that was filled with all types and colors of roses, the beds edged with paths of close-cut green lawn. How Mom would love to see this! Erin thought. She adored flowers of all kinds, particularly roses.

There were floribundas covered with flowers, standard rose trees pruned into ball-shapes, and tea roses, their blooms of every imaginable hue, large and brilliant. At the foot of the garden, there was a trellised arbor, covered with climbing roses, yellow and creamy-white.

"Oh, this is absolute heaven. I don't think I've ever seen so many roses all in one place." Erin breathed in the amalgam of scents that filled the air.

David sat down beside her on the wooden bench fashioned from a tree trunk. "It certainly beats the atmosphere inside the house, anyway." He dug angrily at a daisy clump in the grass with his toe.

Erin put her hand on his arm. "He really gets to you, doesn't he?"

"Giles?" He gave her a rueful smile. "He really does. And he knows it."

"I take it that he meant to get your goat with the question about your mother?"

He nodded, his gaze fixed on the grass. "When my father and mother got divorced he used to say to my father, *What else did you expect, when you married a Yank?* God, how I hate the way he uses that word."

"And now he gets at you instead of your father." She hesitated and then said, "Would you mind me if I gave you a word of advice?"

"Not at all. But I know what it's going to be."

"What?"

"Don't let him get to me."

"Right. He'll stop doing it if he thinks it doesn't bother you. I did a documentary about old people in a nursing home once. Some of them were absolute horrors. Deliberately peeing on the ground, knocking over their trays of food. When I questioned one of the nurses, she said that this was their way of showing they were still alive. Maybe that's what Lord Maybridge is doing."

"Maybe. But I'd rather he practiced his affirmation of life on someone else."

Erin laughed and David's face relaxed into a smile. He reached for her hand. "God, you're good for me. I'm glad you came to Amberley with us."

"I'm glad I did, too." She hesitated. Maybe she wouldn't get the chance to be on her own with David again this weekend. "David, just out of interest, whom did Lord Maybridge marry?"

"Do we have to talk about him?"

"Sorry. I was just interested. He was such a good-looking man when he was young, he probably had his pick of beautiful women."

"His wife was Lady Cynthia Hazlehurst, daughter of a marquess. Suitably upper-crust for the heir to the Maybridge title."

"Was she his only wife?"

"Yes. She died in 1980."

"Was it a happy marriage?"

"I doubt it. How should I know?" David frowned at her. "You're asking a hell of a lot of questions. Not thinking of doing a show about the Hogarth family, are you?"

Erin's heart beat uncomfortably fast. "Of course not."

At least *this* time she was telling David the truth.

Chapter Fourteen

When Giles had changed into his dinner jacket for dinner, he made his way slowly down the stairs to the library. He had no idea why he'd invited David's young woman—what was her name? Erin something or other—to meet him there. Perhaps it was the sight of a fresh, young face. Perhaps the fact that she stood up to him and appeared unafraid of upsetting him. Whatever it was, something about her had stirred him.

Now, as he settled himself slowly in his chair, he was wishing he hadn't acted on impulse. He'd spent half an hour playing with his two great-granddaughters after they'd had their supper and he was feeling bone tired. Yet the evening had barely begun.

These reunions were becoming more of a strain each year. He couldn't abide David Lennox, with his un-English accent and manner, and his lack of deference to him. As for Lucy . . . Well, the less said or thought about Lucy the better. She was more gaga every time he saw her. Impossible to guess what she was going to say next.

Lucy's presence at Amberley made him feel so nervous that it took away his appetite.

At least Cynthia's rackety cousin Basil and his empty-headed wife wouldn't be coming. Thank God for small mercies!

He drew out the gold pocket watch that had been his father's. Four minutes to seven. Sliding it back into his pocket, he sighed and closed his eyes. Perhaps this young woman would help him, just for a few minutes, to forget why he dreaded these birthday visits so much.

The longcase clock in the hall was striking seven as Erin came downstairs. She hesitated at the foot of the stairs, gazing around. Then she saw Harrington outside a door across the hall. He raised his hand in a little gesture that indicated she was to come across the hall and opened the door for her.

"Miss Benson, my lord," he announced and stepped back to allow Erin to enter.

"Please don't get up," she said hurriedly, when she saw the earl struggling to lever himself from the chair.

Both hands clutching the arms of the chair, he hovered in an uncomfortable half-standing position, and then lowered himself again. "Good evening, Miss Benson. Won't you sit down?"

As she was already doing so, his suggestion made her feel that she'd been a little too quick. But, determined not to be intimidated by him, she made herself comfortable in the wing chair across the hearth from him. The golden retriever, whom she gathered was the missing Hector they'd been talking about earlier, came to sniff at her and she shrank back.

"Don't tell me you're afraid of dogs," the earl said scornfully.

She gave him a rueful smile. "Sorry, but I am. My mother was bitten on her leg by a large dog when she was a young child. She must have passed her fear of dogs on to me."

He stared at her, frowning, so that the heavy eyebrows met over the bridge of his nose. Then he cleared his throat. "That's all nonsense. You'll have to get used to them. We've several dogs at Amberley."

She grimaced. "So I noticed."

"Show them you're afraid and they'll sense it. Fear is catching, you know. It makes dogs nervous and more inclined to bite."

"Thank you so much for that reassurance," Erin said caustically.

To her surprise, he leaned his head back against the cushion and laughed. "You're very refreshing, Miss Benson."

"Could you possibly call me Erin? I find it disconcerting being called 'Miss Benson' all the time, especially when I'm staying in your home."

"While we're on that subject, I'm not sure that I actually invited you to stay here, did I?"

Erin tensed for a moment, but then relaxed. His out-and-out rudeness was easier to take than, say, Olivia's frosty hospitality. "I believe David spoke to Miss Edwards about it, and she said it would be fine. I'm sure she must have cleared it with you."

"Perhaps she did. Perhaps I thought it would be interesting to meet David Lennox's young woman for myself. I take it that his intentions towards you must be serious, considering you are the first woman he has brought to Amberley."

Yikes! Erin thought. What should she tell him? That she and David had met less than a week ago? That he'd asked her to come with him to Amberley on the spur of the moment?

"I like David very much," she said, feeling her way. "We seem to get on well together."

The earl grunted. "That doesn't sound like much of a basis for marriage."

Erin swallowed. "Well, we—"

"Don't tell me you don't believe in marriage, like most of the immoral young people of this generation."

"I would very much like to debate this generation's immorality with you," Erin said indignantly. "But, as a matter of fact, I do believe in marriage. My parents had a wonderful marriage—" She stopped short, overcome by her feelings, and fumbled in her bag for a tissue.

"I'm sorry. I seem to have upset you."

Erin blew her nose. "That's not your fault. My father died unexpectedly only a few months ago. It was a terrible shock for me and my mother. I still get choked up when I think about him."

"I am sorry." Giles Hogarth leaned forward. "Was he ill for a long time?"

"He wasn't sick at all. He was killed by a motorist who was going too fast. He skidded on the ice and crashed right into my father's car." She began to shred the tissue in her lap.

The earl patted the seat of the sofa beside his chair. "Come and sit here," he said.

Erin threw the bits of tissue into the blazing fire and moved across to sit beside him.

"You obviously loved your father a great deal," he said softly.

"Yes," she whispered.

"Tell me about him."

She hesitated. But then, meeting nothing but sympathy in the old blue eyes, she began to talk about her father, something she had been unable to do since his death, even to close friends. She found herself telling this comparative stranger all about those shared times at the lake, about how her father had been the one to teach her how to swim and ski, how to drive first a boat and then a car, how to change oil and build a fence . . . The list was endless and, in the telling of those shared moments to someone who was not emotionally involved, she was able to relive them. As she spoke about him, she began to realize that her father was still alive, in her memory.

Lord Maybridge remained silent while she spoke, not even interrupting her with a grunt or a slight comment. So that when the clock on the mantelshelf struck seven-thirty, she started, only then realizing how long she had been talking.

The blood rushed into her cheeks. "I'm so sorry. I hadn't realized I'd been going on for so long. You must have been bored to tears."

"Not at all." He leaned forward to pat her hand. "I was fascinated by the tales about you and your father. He was a fortunate man to have such a loving daughter."

"I was the one who was fortunate. You didn't have any daughters?" Erin asked impulsively . . . and then froze.

He looked directly into her eyes, and opened his mouth as if to say something, but then closed it again. He turned his head away to gaze into the fire. "Lady Maybridge and I had only one child, Simon's father. And he was a great disappointment to us."

As if on cue, the door opened and Simon entered.

"I don't recall sending for you," his grandfather said brusquely.

Simon appeared entirely unruffled by this greeting.

"No. But you asked us to join you here for a drink before dinner at seven-thirty." He looked at his watch, shooting back the cuff of his black dinner jacket to reveal the shirt cuff white against the tan of his wrist. "It is now seven thirty-two."

Lord Maybridge grunted and dragged himself to an upright position in his chair. "Very well. Bring 'em all in." He turned to Erin. "I regret that our peaceful time together is at an end. We shall talk again before you leave."

Erin saw Simon dart a quick frowning glance at both of them before he turned away to summon the rest of the family into the library.

When David entered, behind Lucy, he sent her an inquiring look across the room. She grinned back at him and quickly stood up to make room for the members of the earl's family.

As she glanced around for a place to sit that was sufficiently far away for her not to feel that she was being intrusive, she happened to look upward and saw, for the first time, the library ceiling. It was divided into large panels with a circular section in the center of the room. Each section was painted with a mythical scene in bright colors.

In every scene there were clouds bearing cherubs with gossamer wings and pastel garments. Erin heard her mother's voice in her head, as if she were standing right beside her.

"There was a painted ceiling with pictures of fat babies with wings floating in the sky."

Chapter Fifteen

Erin stood there, frozen, gazing up at the ceiling.

"You are admiring the ceiling, Miss Benson?" Lord Maybridge's voice broke into her thoughts.

"I rather doubt that she's admiring it," Simon said dryly.

"Yes, Simon. We all know that you intend to whitewash it when I'm dead," his grandfather said.

"I never said that I intended to whitewash it," Simon told him, smiling indulgently. "That was mere conjecture on your part, Grandfather."

During the ensuing argument, Erin was forgotten, giving her time to collect her thoughts. This surely must be the library her mother remembered. Her description of the cherubs on the ceiling had been too vivid for it not to be.

Which meant that Amberley was indeed the house where her mother lived before she was sent away to Canada.

"Are there other houses with ceilings like this?"

The words came from her spontaneously, her voice cutting through the ongoing argument like a scythe through dead grass, stilling them all.

"I beg your pardon," Simon said, frowning.

"Sorry. I didn't mean to interrupt. I was just asking if there were any other stately homes with painted ceilings like yours. Ceilings with cherubs on them, I mean."

"I should imagine there are hundreds of them," Lord Maybridge said. "It was a very common theme, particularly in the eighteenth century."

"In bedchambers and drawing rooms, perhaps. But not in libraries," Simon said. "It's totally incongruous in here, with all the leather and dark oak furniture. This is a very masculine room. Pastel cherubs are feminine."

Olivia laughed. "Perhaps it was deliberately painted that way. One of the Hogarth wives decided she had a right to sit and read or write in the library and decided to make the room more feminine accordingly."

"My uncle wouldn't allow me in here when I was a girl." Lucy's querulous voice came from the sofa.

"Why on earth not?" asked Olivia.

"He said there were books in here that weren't suitable for girls. Of course that made me even more keen to get in here and look for the forbidden books."

Lord Maybridge snorted and began to make some disparaging remark, but David cut through him. "And did you find them, Grandmama?"

"No, they were locked away. But my aunt found me in the library and she gave me a thrashing with her horsewhip."

"Quite right, too," growled Lord Maybridge. "You disobeyed an order."

"I shall never forget it. She made me bleed. I couldn't sit down for a week."

To Erin's horror, the old lady began to cry, the tears streaking mascara down her raddled cheeks. Erin moved forward, but David was already beside his grandmother, his arm around her shoulders. "Shush, Grandmama, that's all in the past. No one's going to hurt you now."

Lucy pulled away from him and staggered to her feet to confront her cousin, who glowered up at her from his chair. "It was all your fault, Giles Hogarth. It was you who dared me to go into the library."

"For God's sake, Lucy," Giles said, his voice taut with anger. "We're talking about something that happened about seventy years ago. You'd better take her to her room, Lennox, if she's going to carry on this way."

"She'll be fine," David assured him. "Let's go and show Erin some of the other rooms, shall we, Grandmama?"

Lucy shrugged David's arm away. "She beat me with her horsewhip. I couldn't ride my lovely Topsy for a week. Your parents were wicked people, Giles Hogarth, and they did wicked, wicked things. I swear that one day I'll tell the world about their wickedness."

She stood over him like a small baleful witch, her hair tangled and clothing all awry.

Lord Maybridge got to his feet, towering above his cousin. For one heart-stopping moment Erin thought he was going to strike her. "If someone doesn't take this woman from my sight," he roared. "I swear I'll send the pack of you away this very moment and shut the doors on you all, forever."

"Take her upstairs, Olivia, would you?" Simon said. He was obviously concerned for his grandfather, whose face had turned puce with anger.

"I won't go upstairs," Lucy screamed. "I won't. I want my dinner."

Erin took her arm. "Lucy, it would make me very happy if you would show me some of the rooms. I'm sure that no one else knows as much as you do about the history of the house."

She expected to be pushed aside, as David had been, but Lucy turned to her, her eyes wide with surprise. "Who are you?"

"I'm Erin. Remember, we drove down in David's car together?"

"Erin." Lucy frowned, struggling to remember. Then she shook her head. "I can't remember." She put a trembling hand to her forehead. "I'm sorry, I don't remember you. This keeps happening to me."

"That's all right. It doesn't matter. But you did promise me that you would show me the other rooms. Shall we go now? We don't want to miss dinner, do we?"

"No, we don't want to miss dinner," Lucy repeated like a small child. "Can David come, too?"

"I'm right here," David said. He gave Erin a grateful look as they both led Lucy out.

Simon followed behind them and mouthed "Thank you" to Erin as he closed the door behind them. It wasn't quite closed when she heard Lord Maybridge say, "That's the very last time that woman comes to Amberley."

Fortunately, Lucy had not heard him, but Erin could tell by David's grim expression that he had. She smiled at him over Lucy's head, wrinkling her nose sympathetically at him.

"Where are we going?" Lucy asked, walking between them, her hands clinging to theirs.

"Why don't we go into the powder room or cloakroom or whatever it's called and tidy up for dinner?" Erin suggested.

"David, too?"

"No," David said. "I'll wait outside for you girls."

Lucy looked at him for reassurance.

"It's okay. You'll be fine with Erin," he told her. He led them down a corridor and down three steps and opened a door. Inside was a comfortably modern washroom with a wide well-lit mirror and several padded-velvet chairs. Lucy sat down on one of them and opened her sequined evening bag.

"Okay?" David asked Erin at the door.

She nodded. "We'll be fine. That was awful."

"Yes, it was. I'm sorry. Amberley always brings out the worst in her," he said in a low voice. "All those miserable memories, I suppose. She seems to revert to her childhood whenever she comes here. And Giles doesn't help."

"Poor David. No wonder you loathe coming to Amberley."

Impulsively, she touched his tense face, brushing his cheek with her fingers. He caught hold of her hand before she could take it away, and turned to press his lips to her palm. The moment seemed to last forever. Then, still holding her hand to his face, he drew her to him.

"Are you coming in or not?" demanded Lucy. "You can't leave the loo door open like that, so everyone can see inside."

Guiltily, they sprang apart and then both burst out laughing.

"What's so funny?" Lucy asked.

"I'll see you in a few minutes," Erin whispered to David, and shut the door on him.

By the time she had managed to tidy Lucy it was almost eight o'clock. She had soon realized that the tangled hair had probably not been brushed properly for ages and there was little chance of repairing the ravaged layers of makeup, but she did what she could and was quite proud of the results.

"Do I look all right?" Lucy asked, patting her perm-frizzled hair anxiously.

"You look terrific." Erin pulled a stool over and sat in front of her. "Now, Lucy, I think you'll agree that we are friends."

Lucy looked bewildered. "I sincerely hope so. You are David's friend, after all."

Erin breathed a sigh of relief. This short respite from her relatives seemed to have restored Lucy's sanity. "That's right." She took Lucy's hands in hers. "As your friend, I want to give you a little word of advice."

Lucy frowned. "What is it?"

"I think it would be best if you didn't talk about the past to your cousin Giles. It seems to upset him."

"So it should. They didn't treat him well, either."

"I'm sure they didn't. That's why you should avoid the subject. After all, he hasn't been well recently, has he?"

"So I believe. Looks fit as a carthorse to me, though."

Erin stifled a smile. "Looks can be deceptive. I've been told it's best not to upset him."

"He has his father's temper."

"I'm sure he does. All the more reason to avoid upsetting him."

Lucy's red lips grinned at her. "I'll do my best. But he can be extremely annoying."

"Of course he can, but you want to stay on his good side. You know how much you want to come to Amberley again."

Erin could have kicked herself when she saw Lucy's eyes filled with tears again. But this time Lucy merely sniffed and said, "Although I was very unhappy here, it is the home of my childhood and there were some happy moments. I used to ride Topsy for hours."

"Was Topsy your pony?"

Lucy looked at her as if she were crazy. "Of course not. She was my rocking horse. I used to ride her for ages in the nursery."

The rocking horse in the nursery.

That decided it. Erin knew now that Amberley was

definitely the house where her mother had spent her early childhood.

She drew in a deep breath to calm her racing heart and was about to speak when Lucy said, "Andrew had a rocking horse, too."

"Who was Andrew?"

"The boy who lived nearby at Mallow House. His horse was all brown. Topsy was far nicer. She was shiny black with a red leather saddle."

"I suppose most nurseries had rocking horses in the old days, didn't they?"

"I don't know. The only other one I ever saw was Andrew's, but you're probably right. These old toys were handed down through the generations, until they fell apart."

So the rocking horse wasn't such a definite clue after all. Erin was beginning to feel light-headed with all the jags of adrenaline she was getting.

The door began to open. "Come on in, David. We're all ready," Erin said. But it wasn't David who entered, it was Olivia.

"I was sent to look for you. Lord Maybridge is growing rather impatient." Olivia's slight smile remained about her mouth, without touching her eyes. "We are all in the dining room, waiting to begin dinner."

"Well, you can wait," Lucy said, snapping her evening bag shut.

"I am sorry," Erin said to Olivia in an undertone. "It took a while to get things settled, if you know what I mean."

Olivia did not respond to her friendly smile. Well, damn her, thought Erin. At least she knew where she stood with Mrs. Simon Hogarth.

She felt even more sorry for both David and Lucy. The Hogarths certainly appeared to have a propensity for lining up in separate camps, with only Simon Hogarth bothering to make any attempt at courtesy.

When Erin entered the dining room, she was glad she had worn her long gold-silk slip dress. Only her dressiest outfit would be suitable for this jewel of a room, with its white-painted paneled walls picked out in gold. The most notable pieces of furniture were the huge serving buffet against the long wall and the massive dining table in the center of the room, both fashioned of some kind of rich, red-hued wood. Mahogany perhaps.

Although there were only six of them dining tonight, Erin gauged that the table would seat thirty people at least.

Lord Maybridge sat at the head of the table, with Olivia as his hostess at the other end. Erin was at the earl's right, with David beside her. Simon sat opposite, next to Lucy. Thus, Erin thought, ensuring that the earl had neither David nor Lucy beside him.

She could understand his exasperation with Lucy. She could be very annoying. It would be hard for someone of Lord Maybridge's age to be patient with her swings between autocrat and child. But Erin felt that more than mere impatience caused his hostility to both Lucy and her grandson. Class, xenophobia . . . who knew what it was?

As she watched the Hogarths interact, Erin was fascinated. If, indeed, she had been here to get an international political story, she could have gained some terrific material just from listening to Simon Hogarth discussing current national and international problems with his grandfather.

How strange to think that she could be sitting directly opposite the future Prime Minister of Great Britain!

As she cut into the poached sole with lobster mousse, David—who had been making stilted polite conversation with Olivia—turned to her. "Okay?" he asked softly.

"Just fine. The food is fabulous."

"We have an excellent chef," Lord Maybridge said. "A brilliant young Scotsman. Miss Edwards stole him from the Savoy."

"Ah," said David. "So you don't object to the Scots as servants, merely as relatives."

Erin winced inwardly. She loved David's courage in standing up to his formidable relative, but she wished he hadn't chosen such a public setting to goad the earl. The last thing they needed was Lucy to get upset again. Perhaps Lord Maybridge felt the same way, for he turned to speak to Erin.

"You may inform your boyfriend that I admire anyone who maintains high standards, whatever his nationality."

"I think we all feel that way," she said, seeking to

quieten things down. At the same time, she reached for David's hand beneath the table and squeezed it. "In the newer countries like Canada, people of all nationalities have to work together. I think it helps to make us more tolerant of other people's differences."

"What about the English-French problem?" Lord Maybridge demanded. "Not so much tolerance there, eh?"

"Have you addressed the Quebec problem on one of your television programs, Miss Benson?" Olivia's clear voice sliced through the air.

"No, I don't—"

"Television? What's this about television?" Lord Maybridge was visibly agitated.

"Oh, didn't David tell you?" Olivia said, all surprised innocence. "Miss Benson is a television producer."

The shaggy eyebrows lowered at Erin. "Is that correct?"

"I work with the CBC in Winnipeg."

Lord Maybridge slammed his hand down on the table, jangling crystal and cutlery. "By God, Lennox, you have a bloody nerve smuggling someone from the media inside Amberley."

"I didn't smuggle Erin in. I would remind you that Erin works in Canada, not Britain. And she's not a news reporter."

"Did you know about this?" the earl demanded of Simon.

"As a matter of fact, I did not," Simon said, frowning at his wife. "Olivia omitted to tell me."

"I intended to, but—"

"That is neither here nor there," Simon said curtly, cutting her short. "What matters is Miss Benson's motives for coming here. We all thought that she was here because David wished the family to meet her, that she was someone special to him."

Heat rushed into Erin's face. But, before she could speak, David jumped in. "You're absolutely right there," he said. "She *is* special. Anyone who could survive the onslaught of a weekend at Amberley has to be pretty bloody special."

The ironic smile he gave Erin helped to compensate

for her embarrassment. Then a rush of guilt swamped her. If David knew her real reason for being here, he wouldn't be half so supportive.

"Am I right in thinking that you sweet-talked David into bringing you to Amberley?" Lord Maybridge asked her.

"No, she did not," David said. "I asked her to come with me. I should have known better."

"You certainly should have. You know how I feel about the media."

"I meant that I should have known better than to expect this family to make anyone feel at home, least of all a friend of mine."

Erin stood up, pushing back her chair. "I don't want to upset your family weekend. I'll leave now."

David sprang up, but it was Lucy who spoke next. "I think you are all behaving abominably to David's friend. What happened to the famous Hogarth hospitality? Your parents might have been cruel people, Giles, but they never treated a guest in such a shabby manner. Shame on you."

Before his grandfather could reply to this, Simon spoke. "Lucy is quite right. I think we're all in agreement that it was a mistake for David to invite not only a stranger, but also a member of the media to Amberley. But having said that, I want to assure Miss Benson that we shall be happy to treat her with the courtesy due to a friend of David, so long as she, in turn, can assure us that she has no hidden agenda."

Erin met Simon's penetrating gaze across the width of the table. "Perhaps you would explain what you mean by hidden agenda, Mr. Hogarth."

"I mean that, in coming here, it was not your intention to amass information about our family to be used in the news media."

Erin's mouth felt as dry as dust. "I have no intention of using any knowledge that I may gain about your family in the media." The words came slowly, carefully. She had told enough lies already. "Nor will I pass on anything I learn here to any other member of the media." She bent to pick up her bag. "Perhaps you'd like me to sign an affidavit to that effect before I leave."

"Sit down, young woman," Lord Maybridge said.

"I'd rather not, thank you. I'm leaving."

David pushed back his chair. "I'll come with you."

"No, please don't. You can't leave Lucy. We passed a train station, didn't we? I can get a train into London."

"I asked you to be seated, Miss Benson," Lord Maybridge said in a peremptory tone.

"And I told you that I'm leaving," Erin said, her eyes blazing at him.

To her amazement a slow smile twitched the corners of his mouth. "You have an Irish temper to go with your Irish name. I like that."

"Am I supposed to feel flattered?"

His smile broadened. "I apologize for my rudeness, Miss Benson. Please give me a chance to make amends. Stay the night and then David can drive you home tomorrow morning, if you wish to leave then."

She hated to go back on her decision to leave, but how could she go, when she felt so close to verifying that this had been her mother's home? If she left now, she knew that she would never be able to return.

"You have to stay," Lucy said. "If you go, David will go, too."

That did it. "All right. I'll stay until the morning." Erin avoided looking at Olivia, knowing what she would see in that ivory-skinned perfect oval face.

When she looked across the table at Simon she saw exactly what she expected to see, inscrutability.

Chapter Sixteen

As soon as dinner was finished, Lucy announced that she was going to bed. Once David had made sure she was in the care of Mrs. Edwards, he quietly suggested to Erin that they "Get the hell out of here."

She didn't need a second invitation. "Where?" she whispered.

"Who cares, as long as we can get away." David looked at his watch. "It's still early. Let's go find a decent pub and lose ourselves in a pint or two of Fremlin's."

Not even pausing to ask what Fremlin's was, Erin got to her feet.

"I'm taking Erin off to a good old-fashioned country pub." Before anyone could say anything David had ushered Erin ahead of him across the room to the door. "Anyone want to join us?" he asked, his hand on the door handle.

Erin smiled to herself. David's tone of voice suggested that anyone who did would not be welcome.

"It's Saturday night," Lord Maybridge said. "Every pub in the area will be packed to overflowing with Londoners."

"That's okay. I'm a Londoner, too. Besides, it's a lovely warm night. We can sit on a tree stump or something." Taking Erin's hand in his, David drew her from the room and shut the door.

Standing out in the hall, they grinned at each other, and then burst out laughing. "I feel like I used to when I was a kid being taken away from boarding school for an outing," David said. "Do you need a coat or anything?"

Erin glanced down at her gold silk dress. "Shouldn't I change?"

"No need. People can wear anything in a pub."

"Okay. I'll get a sweater then, in case it gets chilly."

"Be careful," David warned as she took off up the stairs. "Don't let anyone stop you on the way or you might never escape."

Erin knew exactly what he meant. She'd been in the house only a few hours, but already she was feeling its tensions and the undercurrents of past and present conflicts.

Pausing only to spray on a little more of her new citrus summer perfume and run lipstick over her mouth, she grabbed her mohair sweater and ran downstairs again.

Just as they were about to go out the garden door, Harrington appeared behind them.

"Damn! almost made it, but not quite," David said quietly in a hollow tone to Erin.

"Are you planning on leaving, Mr. David?" the butler asked.

"Just going out for an hour or so. I'm taking Miss Benson out for a drink."

"We have an ample selection of drinks here," Harrington said in a sepulchral tone of rebuke.

"I know you do, Harrington. You keep an excellent drinks cupboard and cellar, but I thought Miss Benson might enjoy seeing a country pub, being a foreigner, you know."

Erin whispered a suitable protest.

"Which would be the best to take her to, do you think, Harrington? I thought of somewhere where we could get some good local ale."

Harrington's face brightened. "Of course. Yes, that would be an excellent idea." Obviously Harrington was something of a connoisseur of local ales for he rattled off several strange-sounding pub names, all of which sounded to Erin like titles to the books of Martha Grimes.

David decided on the easiest to understand. "Yes, the Wheatsheaf. That'll be perfect. Thanks, Harrington."

"Would you like your car brought around to the front, Mr. David?"

"No, I can get it myself. See you later."

"I don't think I shall still be up when you return, but young Jim will be here to let you in."

"Young Jim is about fifty," David told Erin as they walked to the garages at the rear of the house.

As David sped along the narrow lanes, the branches of the trees on both sides almost touching above them, Erin began to relax. There was a high silvery moon in the night sky, sailing in and out of moody clouds. When they paused at a crossroads, the hooting of a night owl came in the open window.

"I never realized that Kent was so lovely. I thought it was just a suburb of London."

"Parts of it are, but it has remained remarkably rural despite being so close to the city." He glanced across at her. "Feeling better now?"

"Much. Your family can be pretty overpowering."

David's hands tightened on the steering wheel. "I try not to think of them as my family. They certainly don't want me to be."

"Why is that? I know you told me all that stuff about being Scottish and American, but there must be more to it. Lord Maybridge is positively rude to you."

"I don't let it get to me anymore." He looked at her. Erin had the feeling that he was about to tell her something, but then decided against it. "He was pretty rude to you, too. That was inexcusable."

"I can understand how he feels. I'm sure it's hard for them all to escape from the media. They can't even go in and out their gate without everyone pouncing on them."

David had avoided the media camp by driving out of the grounds by an unpaved back lane. Even there, he'd been stopped by a couple of more enterprising journalists. When he told them who he was, they'd let him go.

"You come from midwest Canada, for God's sake. What on earth did Giles think you'd do? You haven't even brought a camera."

"Actually, I have." Erin's heartbeat quickened. "I was hoping to take a few pictures of Amberley to show my mother." The absolute truth.

"A word of advice. If you do take any pictures, do it when you're alone or they'll blow a gasket." He looked at her speculatively. "A picture of the inside of Amberley, with Simon or even Olivia or Giles in it, would fetch a pretty penny if you sold it to one of the scandal sheets."

Erin turned away to look out the window at the dark hedges sweeping by, but she was acutely aware that David was still frowning, as if some new idea had struck him and he was trying to work it out.

As Giles had warned them, the pub was full to overflowing, but it was also delightful. Set in a floodlit clearing in the abundant Kent woodland and surrounded by massive beeches and horse-chestnut trees, the pub was an old wood-beamed building with a red-tiled roof. It was so filled with people that Erin had the impression that it might just burst any minute, disgorging its contents all over the wood.

In fact, many people were outside in the gardens at the front and rear of the pub, enjoying the warmth of the night. They sat on wooden benches, their glasses and mugs and plates of food set on plain wooden tables.

The noise was deafening. Music blaring from inside the pub. People laughing and shouting to one another. The honking of car horns and revving of engines as a couple of cars left, and more came to replace them.

At first Erin was taken aback by the sheer volume, but then she was swept up in the exuberance of it all.

"Quite something, isn't it?" David shouted in her ear. "A summer Saturday night at an English country pub. Let's try to find a seat somewhere."

He led the way around to the rear of the building, where they found a sunken garden. It was lit by carriage lamp standards on the terrace along the rear of the pub and little fairy lights twinkling on the trees.

"Cheers," a man said, as they approached. "We're just leaving."

"Thanks," David said, quickly sitting down at the small table the man and woman were vacating, before someone else could grab it. Erin sat across from him. "Guard this chair with your life," he said, getting up again. "If you take your eyes off it for a minute, someone will whip it away. What'll you have to drink?"

"You said something about Fremlin's? Is that an English ale?"

"It is. I'm not sure which make of ale they have here. Would you like to try? It's not fizzy like lager, you know."

"I know that, at least. Yes, I'd like to try."

"Tell you what. I'll get you a half of ale and something else you know you like. What will you have? Brandy? G and T?"

"A brandy would be fine."

"One brandy and real ale coming up," he said loudly. "You Canadians have a very strange taste in drinks." As he strode away, Erin grinned, knowing that people were giving her funny looks.

The hour and a half before closing time sped by. Erin was aware that it had been a very long time since she had enjoyed herself so much. She and David seemed to talk about every subject under the sun, jumping from one topic to the next without a break. They agreed on many subjects and violently disagreed on a few, but always ended up laughing and joking, as if they had known each other for a lifetime.

Never before had Erin felt herself quite so at ease with a man. It was like being with a close girlfriend, except for one difference. She was strongly attracted to David sexually. Every time he touched her hand or put an arm around her or, at one point, when he leaned forward and gave her a swift kiss, she felt her skin tingle and a frisson of delight run along her nerve endings.

She knew she should pull back, set a distance between them, but somehow in this place of pleasure and fun she could not, would not, listen to her head. Time for that later. For now, she would enjoy the wonderful feeling of strong attraction, without dwelling on the fact that there was no future in it at all.

When they drove back, David drove very slowly, as if reluctant to return to the reality of Amberley. On a hill high above Amberley's grounds, he pulled the car over and parked it facing the house.

The clouds scudded above Amberley, so that its walls

were alternately bathed in the eerie silver of the moonlight or almost hidden from view.

"I love this place. God knows why, but I do. Each year when I come here for the family get-together I vow it will be the last time. Yet somehow I can't resist it." David's arm tightened around Erin's shoulder. "Does that sound crazy to you?"

"No. It has a magic all its own, doesn't it? It's as if the people don't really matter. People come and people go, but Amberley remains."

He looked down at her in wonderment. "That's incredible. You've caught my feelings about Amberley perfectly." His eyes gleamed in the moonlight. Then his head moved closer, so that she could no longer see his eyes. "God, Erin, I think I'm falling for you."

When he kissed her, all other thoughts vanished. She was acutely aware of his mouth and his hands—and his body striving to come closer to hers, despite the steering wheel and the gear shift.

In fact, it was the pressure of the gear shift against her knee that brought Erin back to reality.

"What's wrong?" David asked, sensing her coldness.

Erin pulled away from him. "Sorry," she said with a light laugh. "The gear shift was sticking into my knee."

He looked relieved. "Sorry about that." He hesitated, and then said, "Want to get out of the car?"

She looked away from him and checked her watch. "It's quite late. If you don't mind, I think we should call it a day."

He studied her face. "It's okay, you know. I wasn't asking you to go any further, if you didn't want to. I just thought you might like to stretch your legs, go for a walk . . . whatever." Although his face was half hidden, Erin could tell by his voice that he was hurt by her withdrawal. "I know it sounds crazy but I want to stay here alone with you for as long as possible. I feel I shall lose you once we get back to my overpowering relatives."

How right he was! Tears stung Erin's eyes. Thank God for the semidarkness.

"I have to go back to Canada soon," she said slowly. "We live on opposite sides of the Atlantic. I think it would be best if we didn't become too involved, don't you?"

He drew his arm away and shifted his seat forward again. "How eminently practical of you! I thought lawyers were supposed to be the cold, analytical ones, but you have us beat."

"Is that what you think, that I'm cold and analytical just because I face the truth?"

He shook his head. "Let's go back."

He turned the key in the ignition and the engine revved into life. As the car swung around Erin caught a last glimpse of Amberley from the hilltop. The moon had disappeared behind the gray clouds and the house now looked dark and sad, like a widow in mourning.

Chapter Seventeen

Erin slept fitfully all night, and then sank into a heavy sleep just before dawn. She awoke with a start to the sound of children laughing below her window and sunlight streaming in through the half-open shutters.

She sat up in bed, feeling disoriented. She'd been dreaming. The dream was still remarkably vivid, so that she wondered whether this waking was a dream and the nightmare the reality. Something had been chasing her through a dark tunnel, which had only a tiny circle of light at its far end. As she ran, she saw her father standing at the end of the tunnel, half in shadow, half in the light that shone behind him. His arms were outstretched to catch her, but she couldn't reach him. She could sense the hot breath of the monster on her body, so close was it behind her. She was running, running, running . . . but never coming closer to her father. Indeed, he seemed to be receding, diminishing in size. "Daddy!" she'd cried despairingly, but he grew smaller and smaller, until he was a mere speck in the center of the blinding light that dazzled her eyes.

Erin put up a hand to shade her eyes from the sun, to find that her eyes were wet, as if she'd been weeping in her sleep. For a moment, she buried her face in the pillow. "Oh, Daddy," she cried. Then, rubbing her eyes with the top of the sheet, she sat up.

A soft breeze riffled the curtains. She felt it cool and gentle on her breasts and shoulders, like a balm. She leaned forward, hugging her knees. *This* was the reality, not the nightmare. Her father was gone, but the memory of him would remain forever, soothing her.

In a way, the nightmare had strengthened her resolve. She had come to Amberley for one purpose: to discover the facts about her mother's birth and childhood. She could not let her feelings for David stand in her way. They were to drive back to London after lunch. Therefore, she had only this morning left.

"What on earth can I do in one morning?" she asked herself aloud. She glanced at the clock and groaned. Nine-fifteen! She didn't even have a full morning left.

There was little chance of gaining any information from Lord Maybridge subtly. He was too suspicious of her now to give anything away inadvertently. Despite his age, he was a canny old devil, likely to guess when she was pumping him for information. She had hoped that she might try Harrington, but no doubt he would have been warned against her, as well.

She felt like screaming. To be so near and yet so far from finding out about her mother's parentage was extremely frustrating.

Enough of this sitting around feeling miserable! She sprang out of bed and stalked across the room to the bathroom. The direct approach was the only way.

When she'd had her shower, Erin pulled on oatmeal linen pants and a crimson cotton sweater and went downstairs. She was directed to the dining room, which adjoined the terrace.

"Ah, there you are, Miss Benson," cried Simon, when he saw her. "It's such a glorious day, we decided to take our breakfast out onto the terrace."

"What a lovely idea." Erin glanced at the array of dishes set out on warming trays on the long sideboard. "Do I just help myself?"

"That's right. Take a plateful of food and then come out and join us. There are tea and coffee and orange juice outside. We had breakfast a while ago, but we're having some coffee now."

"Thank you." Erin turned to the sideboard and helped herself to fried egg, tomatoes, and back bacon, wishing she felt more hungry. Then, aware that Simon was still there, watching her, she asked him, over her shoulder, "Is Lord Maybridge joining us?"

"No. He takes his breakfast in his room. Why?"

This was Simon. All polish and charm, lulling you into

a false sense of security, and then the direct, stabbing question. No wonder he'd reached the top so fast.

Erin shrugged. "I just wanted to make sure I would see him before I left, that's all."

"Oh, you will, certainly." Simon gave her his enigmatic smile and walked out to the terrace.

Erin loaded her breakfast onto a tray and went outside. To her dismay, she saw that she was to be alone with Olivia and Simon. Neither David nor Lucy were there.

"Looking for David?" Olivia asked, her expression not particularly friendly.

"Has he eaten already?"

"No, he hasn't been down yet. You must have had a good night." Olivia's mouth curved into a knowing smile.

"Why's that?" Erin set her tray down with a distinct rap on a nearby wrought-iron table.

"Simon said he heard David drive in at about two o'clock this morning."

"Two o'clock? Was it that late?" Erin tried not to show her surprise. David must have gone out again after he'd driven her home.

"Yes. I must say we're rather surprised to see you up this early, all things considered."

"I don't call nine forty-five early," Erin said, her mind still on David. "The sunshine woke me up."

"And the children shouting, no doubt, as well," Simon said. "Your bedroom is above the terrace."

"Yes, I know." She watched the two little girls playing with an assortment of dogs on the lawn. "I'm glad they woke me. I wouldn't want to have missed this."

She looked out across the green lawn to the walled rose garden beyond, remembering her walk there with David yesterday. How beautiful this place was! It saddened her to think that she had seen so little of it and that she probably would never see it again after this morning.

As if by some preconceived arrangement, Olivia rose from her chair and summoned the children. "Come along, girls. It's time for you to change into your dresses."

Dresses? Erin wondered if they were all going to church.

"Oh, Mummy, do we have to?" moaned Nicola.

"Yes, of course we do."

Olivia departed with the children, leaving Erin alone with Simon on the terrace.

He moved over to sit across the table from her. His aquiline face was unsmiling. "Exactly why are you here, Miss Benson?"

She met the gray eyes directly. For a moment she was tempted to tell him the truth, but immediately she knew it would be a mistake. Simon would act as a shield between her and his grandfather. She wouldn't have a hope of getting to Giles Hogarth, once Simon knew why she was here.

She spread butter on a half slice of toast, and then added thick honey. "I'm here because David asked me to come with him." She bit into the toast, the honey sweet against her tongue and palate.

"After you had suggested it." It wasn't a question.

"No. It came quite out of the blue."

"Why would he bring a stranger to Amberley? You are the first woman he has brought here, you know."

"Yes, I know that. I can understand why."

The dark eyebrows arched. "Oh, really? And why is that?"

"Because you're a formidable bunch, that's why. I should imagine David thought you might frighten a girlfriend off."

"But you, he brought here." He spoke in a low voice. "Because you weren't really his girlfriend at all, were you?"

"David and I like each other very much."

"I'm sure you do. How long have you been in England, Miss Benson? Don't lie to me," he added, his voice sharp. "I can easily run a check on it."

Erin lifted her chin. "Just over a week."

"So I thought." Simon sat back in the chair with a satisfied smile. "And you work for CBC television."

"I'm a television producer, not a roving journalist, Mr. Hogarth." Erin took a sip of orange juice to moisten her lips.

"But a very ambitious television producer, I'm sure. *My weekend at Amberley with Simon Hogarth*."

Erin started. He had used the very words Samantha had used. "I told you last night that I had no intention of using or selling anything I've learned this weekend."

"Oh, come now. I'm not as naive as my grandfather. I didn't get where I am today by believing what members of the media say. I find it suits me best to use the media to my advantage, not the other way around." Simon leaned forward, his eyes cold and hard as slate. "As leader of the opposition, I am in a position of considerable power, Miss Benson. That power, I assure you, can extend well beyond the boundaries of Great Britain. If you want to continue your television work in Canada—or anywhere else, for that matter—I'd advise you to—"

"That sounds distinctly like a threat to me."

Both Simon and Erin started, not having heard David come out behind them onto the terrace.

Erin felt she'd been holding her own with Simon, but still she experienced a wave of relief when she saw David.

Then she saw Simon's expression as it rested on David, and she shivered involuntarily.

"Miss Benson's position, I can understand. She is a journalist. But yours is beneath contempt, Lennox. As a member of this family—"

"Ah, an acknowledgment at last," David said, giving Simon a mock bow.

"You have brought a member of the media into Amberley at a time of great sensitivity for both me, personally, and the nation as a whole."

David sat down and munched on an apple. "Forgive me, Simon," he said between bites, "but there's something I don't quite understand. What is it exactly that you're trying to hide from the media?"

If the half smile on David's face annoyed Simon it wasn't at all obvious. Not by a flicker did he show his feelings. "I have nothing whatsoever to hide."

"That's what I thought. The gorgeous Olivia and you seem blissfully happy together. You have two great kids. Why the paranoia?"

Simon shot him a look. This time David had got to him. "I prefer to call it a dislike of having my privacy invaded. And of using my grandfather and his home for that invasion."

"And if I swear again to you that I am not here for media or political reasons," Erin said, "you will wouldn't believe me?"

"What other reasons could there be for you to infiltrate Amberley?"

David stood up. "I've had enough of this. Come on, Erin. Let's get out of here."

Erin pushed back her chair, iron grating on the flagstones.

"You can't go before the presents." Simon looked at his watch. "He'll be down at ten o'clock. Exactly seven minutes from now."

"Presents?" Erin asked.

Simon's lips slid into a cold smile. "Yes, Miss Benson. It seems to have slipped your memory that this weekend was for the private family celebration of my grandfather's eighty-first birthday. Today is, in fact, his birthday. The members of his family will be presenting him with gifts to commemorate the day of his birth. A quaint tradition that perhaps you don't have in North America."

"Quit being such a bastard," David said and, taking Erin by the arm, led her into the house. Erin could feel the tension in him as he pressed her arm against his side.

The confrontation with Simon left her feeling as fragile as spun glass.

"I'm sorry about this," David said, as they stood in the hall. "If it weren't for Lucy, I'd leave with you now. The gift-giving won't take long."

From upstairs came the sound of the earl's voice.

Erin groaned. "Oh, David, I'm such an idiot. I completely forgot to bring a gift for him."

"For God's sake, who cares?"

"I'm sure you and Lucy brought something for him."

"Yes, but we're relatives, God help us. He won't expect anything from you."

"I can't believe I'd be so rude as to come to a birthday celebration and not bring a present."

Everything seemed to be falling apart. Her visit was a dead loss as far as her mother was concerned. She was going to lose David. And there was a chance she might lose her job as well, if Simon were to put his threat into action. To Erin's horror, tears filled her eyes.

"Hey, hold on now. It's certainly not worth crying over." David put his arms around her.

She stood tense within the warmth of his embrace. "Why did you go out again last night?"

"Who told you I did?"

"Simon or Olivia. I can't remember which."

"That figures." He released her. "I went out again because I couldn't face sleep. I had too much to think about, so I went for a long drive."

"Were you mad at me?"

"No, not mad. Disappointed, I suppose. It wasn't your fault, anyway. Just fate."

They couldn't talk anymore. Lord Maybridge was being assisted downstairs by Harrington and another one of the housemen, with Olivia behind him, holding the children's hands. Behind them, all alone, came Lucy.

It was like a royal entrance.

"Good morning, Miss Benson." Lord Maybridge was dressed in a smoking jacket of burgundy velvet.

Once again, Erin felt like curtsying. "Good morning, my lord. May I wish—"

He swept by her before she could say any more. David was ignored completely. As Simon joined Olivia and their children, David and Erin tagged on behind, with Lucy.

The procession moved into the library, which seemed to be Lord Maybridge's favorite room at Amberley. For Erin, it was an uncomfortable reminder of the scene between Lucy and Lord Maybridge the previous night.

She glanced up at the ceiling, the sight of those damned cherubs twitching her conscience.

The earl sat down beside the fire, his dogs settling on the hearth rug in front of him. Harrington wheeled in a trolley laden with wrapped gifts and set it to the earl's left.

Olivia produced a camera. "Go and stand beside your great-grandpapa, girls, and I'll take your picture."

Several pictures were taken of the family, even one with Lucy and David flanking the old man. Then Olivia set down the camera. "Now it's time to open your presents, Great-grandpapa," she cried. "Simon, don't forget the champagne!"

"I would like to have a picture of myself with Miss Benson."

For a fleeting moment, everything stilled and everyone's eyes turned to Erin. Then, as if the pause button on a VCR had been clicked off, everything moved again.

"Of course," Olivia said brightly. "Why didn't I think of that? Go and stand by Lord Maybridge, would you, please, Miss Benson?"

Erin did so, her face feeling as if it were on fire.

"Sit on the arm of my chair," Lord Maybridge said. Erin did as she was told. The camera flashed, and it was over. "Thank you, my dear," he said, patting her hand.

Erin felt like an utter Judas.

She quickly moved to the other side of the room to perch on the edge of a buttoned gold-velvet chair.

"Now for the presents," squealed Perdita. "You'll love mine."

"Yes, open your presents," said the more sedate Nicola, giving her exuberant sister a warning frown.

Erin watched as the earl opened his presents. They were modest gifts, suitable for a man who was no longer active and who probably already had everything he needed. Gloves of the finest kid leather, books of history and gardening and hunting, a silk paisley scarf lined with wool, a velour dressing gown in a warm burgundy color.

David's gift was the last. He gave him a book. "*The American War of Independence*," Lord Maybridge read out loud. Olivia stiffened and shot an angry glance at David, but the earl smiled. "I shall enjoy reading this," he said, his large hand spread on the open pages of the book. He reached out to shake David's hand. "Thank you, my boy."

A lump formed in Erin's throat when she saw David's expression as he returned from the earl's side. Heart pulsing hard, she bent down to pick up her handbag.

"Is that all?" Perdita asked. "Aren't there any more presents for Great-grandpapa?"

Erin stood up, her legs feeling like wooden fence posts. She clutched the envelope in her left hand, the index finger of her right hand running up and down the top of the flap.

"I have something for Lord Maybridge," she said.

Chapter Eighteen

Lord Maybridge beamed at Erin. "How very kind of you."

Erin handed him the envelope, watching him intently as he opened it and drew out the photograph.

"What on earth can this be?" he asked before he had looked at the picture in his hand.

Erin said nothing, but stood there intently watching his face.

The earl adjusted his glasses to peer at the photograph. Slowly the excited color in his cheeks drained, leaving his face deathly pale. "Where did you get this?" he asked in a harsh whisper, blue eyes blazing in the suddenly haggard face.

"From my mother."

"Your mother?" His body slumped in the chair. For a horrible moment, Erin thought he was having a heart attack. She started forward, but Simon was there ahead of her, pushing her side.

"What is it, Grandfather?" The earl's eyes were closed, his body lax. Simon turned to Erin. "What the hell are you up to?"

"Get out!" Lord Maybridge had opened his eyes again. Pushing Simon away from him, he hauled himself up in the chair. "Out! The lot of you!"

"Grandfather, I don't think—"

"I don't give a damn what you think. This is between Miss Benson and me alone."

Perdita began to cry and Nicola asked her mother, "Why is Great-grandpapa so angry with us?"

"Hush, darling. He's not angry with us. He's angry with Miss Benson."

Erin could tell how furious Olivia was from the contained rage in her voice.

"Very well, Grandfather. We shall leave you to speak to Miss Benson." Simon turned to look at Erin. His expression appeared bland. Then, for a split second, she felt the malevolence in his eyes strike her like a laser beam. She blinked . . . and his expression had become inscrutable again.

She turned for a moment, her gaze seeking David's. He was standing beside Lucy, who was whispering insistently to him, but he wasn't answering her. When he looked at Erin, he tilted his head in a small gesture of inquiry laced with suspicion.

Later, she mouthed to him across the room.

He looked at her, unsmiling, and then took Lucy's arm, leading her from the room. Erin could hear Lucy's voice demanding to know what was happening. "What did Erin give to Giles? Tell me. No, I won't be quiet." And then, fading away down the hall, "What's all this secrecy about?"

"A very good question," Olivia said from the doorway, having hustled the children from the room. "May I ask what it was that Miss Benson gave you that has upset you so much, Giles?"

"No, you may not," he replied. "I want you and Simon to leave us alone."

"The children are very upset, Giles. This is your birthday party, after all." Although Olivia spoke to Lord Maybridge, Erin could feel her anger directed at her.

He shook his head, not able to speak.

"You're not well," Simon said. "I don't want to leave you like this."

"Have to," the earl whispered. "Please go."

For the first time in ages, Erin spoke. "I'll come and get you as soon as he's ready," she told Simon.

Simon made no response until he reached the door. Then he turned and said, "On your head be it," before going out and pulling the door closed.

"Sit down, Miss Benson." Giles Hogarth still held the photograph in his hand. He looked down at it again, perhaps hoping that it might have changed since he last looked at it. "Now, tell me again where this came from."

"From my mother. Actually, from a book of hers. *The Secret Garden.*"

He put a trembling hand to his forehead. "A book? I don't understand."

"The photograph was hidden in the lining inside the back of the book."

"This book, did your mother buy it in a book sale, perhaps?"

Erin sat on the edge of her seat, her hands clasped tightly on her knees. "No, it was her book, given to her by her mother."

"*Her* mother? I don't understand," he said again.

Erin felt sorry for him. He looked like a lost, bewildered old man, not at all the stately aristocrat. "That is you in the photograph, isn't it?" she asked gently. "You, as a young man? I realized it was you as soon as I saw the portrait of you in the hall."

"What do you mean, you realized it? Surely you knew before you came to Amberley who was in the photograph. Don't tell me it was a bizarre coincidence that you came here with David," he said harshly, "and that you just happened to have the picture in your handbag."

"No, it wasn't a coincidence." Erin swallowed hard. "But I wasn't absolutely sure that Amberley was the right place until I saw the portrait."

"So Simon was right. You *did* trick David into bringing you here."

She gave him a faint smile. "No. Actually, that was a bizarre coincidence. David asked me to come on the spur of the moment. Although I was desperate to find out all I could about Amberley and the family from him, I never dreamed that he'd ask me down here."

"I'm sure he'll be delighted when he finds out that you conned him into it?"

Erin blinked. "I didn't con him. But, you're right, he won't forgive me for not telling him the truth."

"And what is the truth, young lady? I take it that you just happened to find this photograph and thought it would tie in nicely with my grandson's renunciation of the Maybridge title to become leader of the Tory party? You were hoping to track down some big, juicy story. Am I right?"

Erin sat up very straight. "No, not at all. You seem to have forgotten that I told you I found it in a book given to my mother by her mother. I think it was a farewell present."

"Farewell?"

"Yes. My mother was evacuated from England to Canada in 1940. She never saw her mother again."

A fine tremor shook the grand old head and the age-spotted hands. "What was your mother's name?" The words came slowly as if they were dragged from a place hidden deep within him.

"Kate. Katie, she called herself when she first arrived in Canada."

He shook his head vehemently, tears spurting from his eyes. "She died. They both died."

"Both?"

"The child. Katie. And her mother. They both died. Torpedoed. They were on *The City of Benares.* It was torpedoed." The tears ran freely down his cheeks.

Erin found herself weeping with him. "No," she cried. "My mother, Katie, was on a boat that sailed before that one." She paused, trying hard to swallow down tears. "She was sent to Winnipeg," she told him.

"With her mother?"

"No. Her mother didn't sail with her. She never saw her again." She looked directly at him, amber eyes clashing with blue. "My mother thinks she saw the war and the evacuation as a good chance to get rid of her child."

He stared at her, not comprehending.

Erin leaned over and took the photograph from him. "This is Katie's mother, right?"

His gaze met hers. "You actually have no proof of that, do you?" he said carefully, his canniness returning.

"No, none at all. Apart from your reaction to the photograph and my story."

"That is no proof, young lady."

"I know it's not." She leaned forward and touched his hand. "I told you about my father's death. Kate, my mother, was hit very hard by it. She began having nightmares about being parted from her mother and going on the boat to Canada. Posttraumatic stress, the doctor called it, rising from my father's sudden death. She's starting to get better, but we think she will never fully recover until she learns the truth about why she was abandoned by her parents."

"Abandoned?"

"Yes. That's what I said. She was given false papers. The names and address were made up. There she was, a little girl of only five, all alone in a vast new country."

"Oh, my God!"

" 'Oh, my God' is right. I ask you again, is the woman in the photograph Katie's mother?"

His hesitation was barely perceptible. "Yes," he whispered.

"And were you Katie's father?"

This time the answer didn't come quite so easily. "I'm not so sure I should answer that question," he said, after a pause. "There may be . . . repercussions."

"We're not looking for money, if that's what you mean," Erin said, anger flushing her cheeks. "We want the truth, that's all. And it appears that you're the only one left to give it to us."

"But what happened to her?"

"To whom?"

"To Mary. Mary Foley."

"Was that her name? Then I was right," Erin said triumphantly. "She *was* Irish."

A smile spread across his face. "My Irish rose. Mary Foley was the loveliest, most natural woman I ever knew." He seemed to be lost in his memories for a moment and then said, "At times, you have the look of her, you know. Isn't that surprising?"

"Hardly," Erin said softly. "Considering she was my grandmother."

He looked at her in wonderment. "So she was. It hardly seems possible. Mary's grandchild."

"And yours?" she asked delicately.

He looked at her. Erin could sense the struggle within. "I need to know," she told him. "More important, my mother needs to know, to be able to heal."

"When was your mother born?"

"Nineteen-thirty-five. She was five when she was sent to Canada."

He released a small sigh. "That was the year Mary's child was born."

"What did you do, send her and her child away to some little hovel?" Erin demanded. Then she suddenly remembered. "No, you didn't, did you? You kept her at Amberley."

"How do you know that?"

"Because that's how I traced you. Ever since my mother started having these nightmares we've been trying to piece the story together. From her description of the dreams, we realized it was a stately home of some sort. The cherubs on the ceiling were another big clue."

"She remembered the cherubs?"

Erin glanced up at the ceiling. "Yes, she remembered them."

"But she was hardly ever in here. My mother didn't allow her—" He stopped abruptly.

"Well, these cherubs must have made a big impression on a little girl, because my mother recalled them quite vividly. But it was her recognition of Amberley that did it."

"She saw Amberley?"

"On the television. When your grandson was appointed leader of the Conservative party. She felt quite strongly that she recognized the house. I was determined to get to the bottom of this. So, armed with all the clues—and the photograph—I came to England to look for my mother's parents. And the truth."

"The truth?"

"Yes. The reason why you both abandoned your child."

"I haven't said she was my child."

"You haven't denied it, either. It had to be the only reason for Mary putting the photograph in the book. Even if she was getting rid of her child, no mother would put a photograph of herself and her lover in a child's book unless there was a good reason for it."

"Perhaps it was the only photograph of herself that she had?"

"That's what my mother said, but I told her that her mother—Mary Foley—would have cut the man out of the photo."

He looked away from her into the fireplace with its still-glowing fire. His hand went to his forehead again, the long fingers trembling. "I don't understand at all. What happened to her?"

"To my mother? She was adopted by two wonderful people who had little money but plenty of kindness and love."

"No, no, not the child. Mary! What happened to Mary?" He turned his ravaged face to her. "There must be some mistake. They told me that she had died on the ship that was torpedoed. That both she and Katie had died on the ship."

"Who told you?"

"My parents. My mother, actually."

"I don't understand. Weren't you around to be told directly?"

"Of course, I wasn't," he said in an exasperated tone. "We were at war, remember? I was in my twenties then. Off fighting for my country in North Africa."

"You mean you were away from England when Mary and Katie were evacuated?" Erin stared at him open-mouthed.

"That's what I said. You can imagine the terrible shock when I got home, to discover that they'd been killed."

"Did you know they were going to be evacuated to Canada?"

"No, I knew nothing about it." His lips trembled. "I thought they'd be perfectly safe at Amberley. But my mother told me there'd been several raids over Kent, prior to the Battle of Britain. They considered it best to send them away."

Erin thought for a moment. "Wasn't it strange for a man to keep his mistress at his parents' home?"

His jaw tightened. "Mary lived in a cottage on the estate. I wouldn't allow them to send her away."

Erin suddenly recalled Lucy's tales about Giles's parents. "That must have caused quite an uproar with your parents. But when you went off to fight in the war, it would have been a heaven-sent opportunity to get rid of Mary and Katie, wouldn't it? They must have been quite an embarrassment to your parents." Erin's voice hardened deliberately. "I can just imagine how they felt. Their son's whore and bastard, living on their estate."

Fire blazed in the blue eyes. "How dare you call them that! Mary was no whore. I was the first man to love her. And I loved her child. I told them when Katie was born that if they sent them away, I'd go with them."

"But what about your wife?"

He started. "What do you mean?"

"The Lady Cynthia. Surely she didn't accept this rather strange arrangement?"

"I didn't marry Cynthia until 1942. Eighteen months after Mary and Katie died."

"It might have been difficult for an eligible woman to accept this rather bizarre arrangement, though," Erin suggested. "If it were me, I certainly wouldn't have. Especially when you obviously intended to continue the relationship."

The gaunt cheeks flushed. "None of your business," he muttered.

"Oh, yes it is! That's the point, Lord Maybridge. I told you, I came here to find the truth. What I seem to be finding is a pretty nasty tale of deception."

"I haven't deceived you."

"No, I don't think you have. In fact, I think *you* were the one who was deceived."

She could tell from his expression that he was beginning to understand. "Are you suggesting that my parents sent Katie away to Canada and deliberately provided her with false papers?"

"That's exactly what I'm suggesting."

"But what about Mary? They told me she was with Katie."

"From what we can gather from my mother's dreams, Mary was sent away from Amberley before Katie left, but she was allowed to say good-bye to her."

"What makes you say that?"

"My mother remembers being put in an attic with a servant. She also remembers that her mother wasn't there on the day the boat sailed, that she'd said good-bye a while before then."

"You mean they had been separated beforehand?"

"Yes. Perhaps your mother told Mary it was safer for

Katie to be sent to Canada and she agreed to it, thinking that it would only be for a year or so. After all, many mothers did the same, thinking the Germans might be invading England."

"What would you know about it?" he asked scornfully. "You were born years afterwards."

"I researched it. Don't forget I'm a newshound," she added, with a hint of a smile. "Thousands of children were sent away by loving parents. Some parents accompanied their children, but many did not."

"But what happened to Mary, then? She must have been killed soon after Katie left for Canada."

"Why?"

"Because she would have made inquiries about her child. Mary adored Katie. I can recall her going berserk when one of my dogs bit Katie. Yes," he said, nodding his head, as he met Erin's eyes. "She *was* bitten by a dog. Mary thought the world of her little girl. She would never have just left her in Canada."

"Katie had been given false papers, remember? It would have been difficult to find her."

Lord Maybridge shook his head vehemently. "If Mary had still been alive, she would have come to me."

"Perhaps you were still away, fighting. And then you were married. Were you and Lady Cynthia engaged for a long period of time?"

"A year." Again, his cheeks flushed when he saw Erin's expression. "You're thinking Mary wouldn't have come to me once she knew I was going to be married."

"Exactly."

"I think perhaps that you are right," he whispered. His large hands curled round the carved ends of his armchair. "So my parents lied to me."

"I'm afraid it does look like it, doesn't it?"

"They planned it all and then told me that Mary and her child had been killed, God damn their bloody souls!" His cry rose to the ceiling, reverberating around the paneled walls, filling the room with anguish.

The door burst open. "What the devil's going on in here?" Simon demanded.

Chapter Nineteen

Simon had been standing calmly outside the door, while Olivia paced about the hall. Every other minute, she admonished him for not having insisted that this woman leave Amberley immediately. But Simon knew that his grandfather would not permit him to usurp his authority.

For now, he must bide his time. He would deal with Miss Benson once her discussion with his grandfather was over. Whatever it was about, Simon would make sure that Erin Benson would be left with no professional credibility on either side of the Atlantic. As he leaned his back against the wall by the paneled door, arms crossed, he cursed the fact that these old walls were so solid that nothing could be heard from behind them.

But he heard that terrible cry, all right.

"Dear God!" Olivia cried and came running across the hall, but Simon was already inside the room.

As he flung open the door, he saw his grandfather, the leonine head bent, fingers grasping the long gray hair, as if he would wrench it from his scalp. Erin was kneeling on the floor at his side, one hand on his left arm, the other on his bent head. Simon was shocked by the unexpected intimacy of their posture.

He strode forward and grabbed Erin by the arm. "What the hell do you think you're doing?" he demanded. He twisted her arm, so that she gave a small cry of pain as she was forced to her feet.

His grandfather lifted his head. The eyes were bloodshot, still filled with moisture, but they also contained such fury that Simon recoiled from him. "Take your hands off her."

Simon released Erin. She stood between them, rubbing at her arm, her face contorted. "I think you owe me an explanation," Simon told her.

"She owes you nothing," his grandfather said. "How dare you burst into the room! I told you we were to be left alone."

"I am hardly likely to do so when I hear you cry out like that, am I?" Simon said, his voice caustic. "For all I knew, she might have been attacking you."

His grandfather released an exasperated sigh. "I never knew you were prone to melodrama, Simon. Be assured, Miss Benson was not attacking me." His gaze rested on Erin for a moment. The warmth of his expression gave Simon a sharp stab of foreboding.

What the devil was going on here?

Olivia came in. Simon frowned at her. He would have preferred to deal with this by himself. Her chin lifted as she intercepted the look. "I was worried about Giles," she said. "Are you all right?" she asked Giles, advancing into the room.

"I was all right until you all barged into the room."

Erin had moved away to the window. Now she spoke. "I think it's time I left Amberley."

"Amen to that." Simon nodded his head in agreement.

"You seem to have caused a general upset in this house, Miss Benson," Olivia said. "You had no right to impose yourself on a private family weekend."

Giles struggled to his feet, angrily pushing Olivia's helping hand from him. "Miss Benson . . . Erin had every right to be here." He leaned both hands on his gold-topped cane, glaring from beneath bushy gray eyebrows at Simon and Olivia.

Simon looked from his grandfather to Erin and back again, a small half smile on his lips. "Are we to receive some sort of explanation about this meeting you have just had?" he asked in a controlled voice. "Or are you intending to keep us completely in the dark?"

"It was a private matter," Erin said. She turned to Giles. "I really should go, you know," she said in a low voice. "Your grandson is right. I shouldn't have broken into a private family party."

"You had every right to be here," Giles said again. "Every right."

Although the sunlight was still streaming in the tall windows, Simon suddenly felt very cold.

Erin went to his grandfather and laid her hand on his arm. Simon had to strain to hear what she was saying. "Please don't say anything now. It's too soon. Give yourself time to think about it."

Before Giles had time to reply she had walked away and was about to leave the room, but the entrance of Lucy followed by David barred her way.

"So this is where you all are," Lucy trilled. "I thought Giles wanted to be left alone with Erin."

"For once, Lucy, you are right. I did wish to be left alone with Erin, but Simon and Olivia decided that I needed rescuing from her, so here we are, one big, happy family once again. Come in, come in, all of you." Giles waved his hands at everyone in an exaggerated fashion.

Lucy took him at his word and came forward, but David did not follow her. He stood by the open door, his back to the rest of the family.

Erin hesitated, her hand on the doorknob. She desperately wanted to leave. Simon's arrival had come at a most inopportune moment, before there was any time to discuss what was the best move for both her and Lord Maybridge.

My grandfather, she thought, and felt a rush of warmth. Then she looked up . . . and found herself looking directly into David's eyes, and the warmth became an arctic coldness, chilling her through and through.

"What's going on?" he asked quietly.

"I'll explain later. I'm sorry it had to happen like this. I wanted to be able to tell you first." Seeing his obvious distrust made her even more desperate to leave. "I must go." Suddenly, she wished she had never come to Amberley. Never come to England at all.

"Erin!" Lord Maybridge's voice exploded through the room like a gunshot.

David moved aside, so that Erin could see across the room.

Lord Maybridge held his hand out to her. "I want you to stay. Please."

Lucy's wavering voice penetrated the silence. "I don't

know what's happening. Would someone tell me what's going on? Why is everyone so upset?"

Lucy's voice seemed to startle Lord Maybridge. "For heaven's sake, will someone take that woman away from here," he said.

"I'll take her," Erin said.

"No, not you."

"Then I will," David said. He crossed the room to fetch Lucy.

"I don't want to go," she cried in a plaintive voice. "Why can't I stay when everyone else is?" She slapped at David's restraining hand. "No, I'm not going." She promptly sat down on the sofa, her little hands gripping the beaded bag, which had shed so many of its glass beads it was almost threadbare.

"I'm leaving now," David told her gently. "It's time to go home."

"This is my home. I grew up at Amberley. It's my home, too." She turned to Giles, who was glowering at her. "You promised me I'd always be able to visit my old home whenever I wanted. You promised me. But you broke your promise."

"For the love of God, Lucy. You're here now, aren't you?"

"Only because it's your birthday. You never let me come at other times. You broke your promise, Giles. That means I don't have to keep my promise, doesn't it?"

"For God's sake! Will someone send for Mrs. Edwards to take her away?"

"No need," David said. "I'm leaving. Lucy and I are leaving."

"No, you must stay," Giles said. "As the—" He hesitated. Erin saw a strange look pass between him and Simon. "I want you to stay, David. Mrs. Edwards can look after your grandmother until we've finished here. Then you can all go."

Olivia must have slipped out, although Erin hadn't noticed her leave. Now she returned with Mrs. Edwards in tow.

"Mrs. Lennox, would you be so kind as to help me sort through that box of old linen before you go?" said the ever-efficient housekeeper. "You are the only one who is able to tell me if something is valuable or important to the family."

Lucy looked at her, her head cocked to one side. "Linen?" she said with a frown.

"Yes. You may remember I was asking you about it when you were here last year and you promised to help me sort it."

"Ah, yes. That was when I saw you about to throw out the tablecloth that had been hand embroidered by my—and Giles's—grandmother."

"Exactly. I have ordered some tea and cakes. We can sit in the morning room and go through the box together."

"I'd rather have a glass of whiskey."

Mrs. Edwards' lips twitched. "That can be arranged, too." She guided Lucy gently across the room, but just before she reached the door Lucy turned back.

"You broke your promise, Giles," she said, wagging her forefinger at him. "I haven't forgotten, you know. I shall never forget." Then she was gone.

"That woman is completely crazed," Lord Maybridge said, looking distinctly troubled. He mopped his face with a checked handkerchief. "It's time she was put into a nursing home."

"Over my dead body," David said. "She may be a bit doddery, but my grandmother still has all her marbles. Unfortunately, Amberley seems to bring the worst out in her."

"There's a remedy to that," Giles said.

"Are you asking me to break the family tradition? I'd be delighted not to attend at this delightful annual family ritual, but you know how much it means to Lucy."

"Yes, yes, you're right," Lord Maybridge muttered, "but she's definitely growing senile. Half the time she doesn't make sense or she imagines things that never happened."

David sighed impatiently. "You asked me to stay. Why?"

"I have something to tell you all."

"Connected with Erin?" David asked. His gaze zeroed

in on Erin, but there was no warmth in it when their eyes met.

"Yes." Lord Maybridge lowered himself into his chair again. "Sit down, all of you."

Only Erin remained standing. "I think it would be better if you were to wait before you tell people," she said. "You need time to think this out." She tried to pick her words carefully. "There's no point in—in upsetting people unnecessarily, is there?"

"Sit down. There, beside David." It was an order.

Erin sat down beside David, trying to put as much distance as possible between them. Although she didn't look at him, she was very much aware of him. He sat very stiffly on the edge of the sofa, tension emanating from him.

As she watched his hands rolling and unrolling an old copy of *The Field* Erin had a sudden memory of those hands touching her, holding her face between their palms before he bent his head to kiss her. The thought that she might never again feel their touch was almost unbearable. Was it possible to have fallen in love with someone she'd known just one week?

She blinked rapidly, trying to erase the fine film of moisture that blurred her sight. She had succeeded in her quest to find her mother's father, but at what cost?

She looked up . . . to find Simon watching her from his place behind Olivia, who sat in the wing chair opposite Lord Maybridge. As Erin exchanged looks with Simon, he raised his dark eyebrows, his thin lips sliding into a mocking half smile. Simon Hogarth was prepared for whatever his grandfather had to tell him. The look told her that whatever it was, he could deal with it.

His wife was not smiling. She glared at Erin with unconcealed loathing.

Lord Maybridge cleared his throat and leaned forward in his chair. "What I am about to tell you is extremely painful for me to divulge, but it must be told." He looked at Erin. "I would ask, however, that it not go beyond this room."

"You may ask," Olivia said, "but I doubt that Miss Benson will undertake that promise." She shrugged. "Of course she might, knowing that it will be broken."

"I am not asking Erin to do so. There is someone else she must tell. Perhaps, more than one person. Whoever she chooses to tell is up to her."

"I don't understand," Olivia said.

"If you keep quiet, you will. You thought that Erin was here under false pretenses, didn't you, Olivia?"

Olivia sat bolt upright in her chair. "Yes, I did. I do. I didn't trust her from the very beginning. And you," she said, turning to David, "were the one who brought her here. I can't believe you would do such a thing!"

David made no response, but Erin could see his knuckles white as his hands gripped the rolled magazine.

"What you did not know," Giles continued, "was that although Erin is a television producer she had not come to Amberley in her professional capacity. In other words, contrary to your expectations, she wasn't here to get a story on the great Simon Hogarth." There was no mistaking the sarcasm in his voice.

Erin was watching Simon. As he leaned his arms on the back of his wife's chair, he did not respond with even an extra blink to his grandfather's baiting.

"Of course, Olivia, you were, in a way, correct in your assumption that Miss Benson hadn't come to Amberley merely as a friend of David Lennox," Giles continued. He glanced at David. "I have not yet learned the full extent of your part in this matter, Lennox."

David set the magazine down on the table. For the first time since she had sat beside him, he glanced at Erin. In that fleeting look, Erin saw anger and hurt . . . and something approaching contempt. But if David had been about to say something to Giles, he decided against it, turning a stony profile to Erin again.

"Miss Benson was here to do some highly personal detective work," Giles said. "She came to Amberley to verify her very strong suspicion that I was her mother's father."

Chapter Twenty

Everyone looked at Erin. Then Olivia and David spoke at the same time.

"What on earth do you mean, her mother's father?" Olivia demanded.

"So you *were* using me," David said to Erin in a low voice.

Only Simon was silent. He barely moved from his former position, contemplating Erin through narrowed eyes. Then his gaze moved to his grandfather. "And are you?"

"Am I what?"

"Her mother's father?"

"It appears that I very well could be."

"Which means that Miss Benson could be your granddaughter?"

"We hadn't even got to that when you all barged in here uninvited," Giles said. "Bloody infuriating."

"I think you owe us some sort of explanation," Simon said.

"I *what*?" Giles spluttered. "Who the hell do you think you are, addressing me in that superior tone of yours? I would remind you, laddy, that I owe you nothing. Absolutely nothing."

Erin was surprised by the venom in Lord Maybridge's voice. She suspected that there was something else going on between these two, other than her own involvement with the family.

Simon inclined his dark head to his grandfather. "Forgive me. I intended my remark for Miss Benson."

"She bloody well owes you even less than I do." Giles's face was beet-red.

David stirred. "I tend to agree with Simon." As if he

could no longer bear to be near her, he got up and went to stand by the wall, leaning his back against the bookshelves. "I'd like Erin to tell us why she came here *and* why she kept her big secret—whatever it is—to herself."

"You don't have to answer them," Giles told Erin in a gruff voice.

"No, I want to. I just wish we'd been allowed more time alone together, that's all. Why don't you and I talk this out alone first?" she pleaded with Giles. "Wouldn't that be much better?"

"Better to get it all out in the open," he said. "Have it all over and done with."

Better for him, thought Erin, but not for her. Apart from David, these people were strangers to her. And now David was behaving like a stranger, too. But who could blame him?

As she tried to arrange her thoughts into some semblance of order, she was glad that David was behind her, out of sight. She sat forward, hands clasped, staring directly into the fireplace.

"I'll just give you the bare bones for now. Please feel free to ask me questions when I've finished." She told them about her father's death, her mother's nightmares, the discovery of the photograph, and the effect that seeing Amberley on the television had on her mother.

As she spoke, Giles Hogarth turned his face away from them all, shielding it with one hand.

"I was so worried about my mother's health that I was determined to try to discover the truth about her background." Erin looked directly at Giles, willing him to look at her. "I needed to know for myself, as well. My mother's family history is also mine."

"I take it that Samantha was in on your little plan," David said. "Or are you going to tell me that fate just happened to arrange for me to be there in Samantha's house last week?"

Erin twisted around to face him. She wasn't about to let Samantha down. After all, she'd deceived her as well. "I told Samantha I wanted to find out as much as I could about Amberley. Naturally, she thought I was after the Simon Hogarth story. She told me you were related to the Hogarth family and that she'd be happy to invite you to lunch, so we could meet. The rest was up to me."

"You both conned me nicely. Nice work, Erin."

Erin's face flared. "I'm not making excuses, but I would remind you that it was actually your idea to bring me to Amberley. I never suggested it."

David shook his head, his mouth twisting into a smile. "You're right. I don't know how you did it, but you obviously got what you wanted from me."

Erin blinked back tears. She swallowed and turned from him, knowing that nothing she could say would alter his present perception of her.

As she turned, Erin saw that Simon was watching her intently. She had been surprised by his silence, but she knew that his mind was working full-time. Now he spoke.

"I take it from what you said, Grandfather, that you are acquainted with Miss Benson's story. I mean the facts that pertain to her mother."

"I knew nothing about her mother's history other than what she has told me."

Simon frowned. "But I thought you said . . . Does that mean you are denying any relationship to Miss Benson, to her mother?"

"Not at all. From what she has told me, I think it is highly likely that her mother is my child."

"But you said that you knew nothing about her mother," Olivia said in a strident tone.

Simon placed a warning hand on his wife's shoulder and then came around her chair to sit on a corner of the sofa, next to his grandfather. "We don't want you to be stampeded into anything that you might regret later on, Grandfather. Please think very carefully before you speak."

Giles shoved him away with his left elbow. "I'm not a child that you have to tell me what to say. I will tell you what I know. And, as that damn fool television program used to say, *Listen very carefully, I shall say this only once.*"

Erin hid a smile. She was growing more and more to like this irascible, independent old man. He reminded her very much of the feistiness of her mother even during her worst days, when she was battling the debilitating mood swings of her depression.

The comparison made her catch her breath. After all, if this was Kate Benson's father, she *would* be like him, wouldn't she?

He was talking now of his love for Mary Foley. "It was long before I married your grandmother, Simon, so you don't need to sit there scowling at me."

"I take it from the name that she was Irish," Olivia said. "What was she, a housekeeper, a secretary?"

"No, my dear Olivia, she was not. You will be shocked to hear that she was a mere chambermaid."

"Oh, my God!"

Erin could have struck Olivia when she saw the look of horror that crossed her beautiful, sleek face. It was obvious that she found the entire tale extremely unsavory. Her head was tilted back in an unnatural position, as if she were trying to avoid an unpleasant smell.

"We had a child," Giles continued, "a daughter. Mary named her Kate, after her own mother, who lived in Ireland. She was born in 1935. Mary and her daughter then went to live in the small cottage on the edges of the hazelwood."

Simon's mouth tightened almost imperceptibly. "You mean the cottage that was all boarded up, the one you forbade me to go into as a boy?"

Giles ignored him as if he hadn't heard. "When the war began I had to go to North Africa with my regiment. There was talk of evacuating both Mary and the child because of the Battle of Britain. When I returned, the Christmas of 1940, my mother told me that they had both died en route to Canada. Their boat had been torpedoed in the Atlantic."

Simon frowned. "Then how on earth—"

Giles impatiently shook his head. "Don't ask me to explain all that now. Some official idiot made an error, I suppose. All I knew was that they were dead. At least, that's what I thought until Miss Benson here landed her bombshell with that photograph."

"May I see it?" Simon asked.

"Ask Erin. It's hers. Or I should say it's her mother's." The sad smile he gave Erin turned her heart in her breast.

"I think you put it in your inside pocket," she told him.

His fingers fumbled at the pocket of his velvet jacket. "So I did." He drew out the picture and, leaning across Simon, handed it to Erin.

She looked down at the smiling young couple and then handed the creased photograph to Simon.

"That was the old Lagonda," Giles told him. "My father bought it for me as a twenty-first birthday present. I had it for years afterwards."

"So this *is* you?"

"Of course it is. Can't you see that?"

Simon was silent.

"As soon as I saw the portrait in the hall," Erin said, "I knew I had come to the right place."

"May I see?" Hand outstretched, Olivia rudely leaned across Erin as if she didn't exist. Simon gave her the picture. "Oh, you can tell she's Irish, can't you? As if she's just come from the—"

"Bog?" Erin suggested in honey-sweet tones.

"No. I was going to say the country."

"That was Mary, as I remembered her. She was a lovely girl." Giles's voice cracked as he spoke. He cleared his throat and then took out his large white handkerchief and loudly blew his nose.

"Just how do we know that this young woman was Miss Benson's grandmother?" Simon asked.

"I told you about my mother's nightmares."

"Please, Miss Benson," Simon said in his most patronizing tone. "Nightmares are hardly concrete proof, are they?"

"My mother was under the care of a clinical psychologist. She still is, as a matter of fact. All the facts will be in her file."

"Dreams are hardly facts, Miss Benson."

"There's the photograph." David had been quiet for so long that everyone looked surprised when he spoke.

"I beg your pardon?" Simon said.

"The photo was in her mother's possession, wasn't it? How would it get to Canada unless all this was true?"

Erin couldn't believe that David appeared to be supporting her. "It was in her book," she said eagerly. "The copy of *The Secret Garden* that her mother gave her to take with her to Canada. It was a sort of parting gift, I suppose."

Olivia turned to Giles. "But didn't you say they both went to Canada? Mother and daughter?"

"Apparently not. It seems they were separated. The mother died, possibly in the blitz."

Erin was about to intervene, but his look of appeal stopped her. Perhaps he was right. What was the point of divulging the secret of his parents' despicable deception after so many years had passed?

"Katie grew up in Canada, unaware of her parentage," she said. "The kind people who took her in as an evacuee eventually adopted her. I knew nothing of this story until after my father's death this year."

"So you decided to come to Amberley and meet your long-lost relatives, eh?"

Erin bridled at Simon's cynical tone. "Not exactly. When I first came here, I had no idea who my mother's parents were. I just knew she recalled a stately home and the painted cherubs on the ceiling in the library. She distinctly remembered that. I wrote it down exactly as she recalled it."

Giles let out a crack of laughter. "I knew those bloody cherubs would come in useful some time or other. Told you so, Simon!"

Because she knew she was up against a potent adversary, Erin had been studying Simon closely. His face was expressionless, but a small pulse was throbbing in his lean cheek. For some reason he was intensely annoyed by his grandfather's remark.

"I believe we need a great deal more tangible proof before we are prepared to believe this rather far-fetched story," he said in a calm voice.

"Who the devil are you to decide what or what not we need?" his grandfather demanded. "This is my business entirely. Keep your nose out of it. I thought it best to tell you the facts before they get all garbled."

The pulse quickened. "By the press, you mean?" Simon said.

"God knows what I mean. I just thought that, as family members, you should know. Trust you to be worrying about the press." Giles leaned his head wearily against the chair back and closed his eyes. "I am extremely tired. Would you all go now, please?"

"But—" Olivia's words were cut off by a warning frown and a tiny shake of the head from Simon.

"I'm afraid I have to get back to London in time for tomorrow's debate in the House," he told his grandfather, "but Olivia can stay with you."

Giles opened his eyes. "Aren't the children still in school?"

"Well, yes, actually they are," Olivia said, "but I'm sure they'd love to have a day off to be with their grandfather."

"Their grandfather has had enough of his family," Giles said. "I'd like you all to go and leave me in peace." His eyes opened. "Except for Erin. You'll stay, won't you?"

Erin could feel three pairs of eyes boring into her like laser beams, two in front, one from behind. "I think not, if you don't mind. What I would like to do is have just a little more time with you now, before I leave. There is something special I'd like to discuss with you, if you don't mind."

He nodded. "Very well, child." He drew his gold watch from his pocket. "Time for my medicine. Give me a few minutes to rest. Then we'll talk."

Simon stood up. "We'll wait until you've finished, so that we can all leave together."

"No need. I've said all I want to say to you." Giles frowned. "Did you drive Erin here? If you did, you'll have to wait for her."

"I drove her." David came forward.

"And are you intending to drive her back again?" Giles asked him.

"No need," Erin said quickly, seeing David's hesitation. "I can get a bus or train or something."

"Nonsense!" Giles said. "Someone will wait for you and drive you back to . . . wherever it is you came from. Can't remember."

"Richmond. I brought Erin here," David said quietly. "I shall drive her back."

"There's no need," Erin said. She suddenly felt very frail emotionally. Everything had happened so fast and she was very much aware of the fact that she was in a hostile situation. She turned away, searching for tissues in her bag, but finding none.

"Here." David grabbed a handful of tissues from the box on the small table beside Giles's chair and pushed them into her hand. He grasped Erin's elbow. "You need some fresh air. Let's get out of here."

"Will you be all right?" Giles asked her.

"She'll be fine," David answered. "I'll bring her back in fifteen minutes, okay?"

Giles nodded an assent.

David steered Erin to the door and then turned. " 'Bye, Olivia, Simon. See you next year." He was out in the hall before they could reply.

"I'm so sorry, David," Erin whispered, tears coming fast now.

"So am I." Now he was openly furious. "Why the hell didn't you tell me about all this from the start?"

"Because I . . . I don't really know why I didn't. I thought that telling anyone in the family would put an end to my chances of finding out. Once I saw the portrait I had a strong suspicion that Lord Maybridge could be my mother's father, but I knew the family would block me from getting to him, if they knew why I wanted to see him."

"You are right there, Miss Benson. We certainly would have done so." Simon closed the door softly behind him and came across the hall to them. It occurred to Erin that Simon Hogarth had a nasty habit of silently sneaking up on people.

Olivia followed him from the drawing room. "I'm going to fetch the children," she told Simon, ignoring Erin and David. She went down the passageway to the garden exit, her heels tapping on the polished oak floor.

"Tell me, Miss Benson, exactly what is your object in all this?" Simon asked Erin.

"I don't know what you mean," Erin said, but she had a damn good idea what he meant.

"Is it your intention to sell the story to the highest bidder? Or do you intend to use that threat to screw as much money as you can from us?"

"Shove off, Simon." David looked so belligerent that Erin was afraid he was going to hit Simon.

"It's okay, David. I can fight for myself. My answer, Mr. Hogarth, is neither of the above. I came here merely to find out as much as I could about my mother's parents. Thanks to the generosity of Lord Maybridge, I have done what I set out to do."

"No doubt you are hoping for more tangible generosity from him."

"That's enough!" David's hands clenched at his sides. "We'd better get out of here, Erin, before I forget my good manners and smash my cousin's handsome face in. He'd have trouble explaining that to the House of Commons, wouldn't he? The honorable leader of the opposition brawling with his cousin at Amberley."

Simon smiled. "It would be interesting to know what part you had to play in this, David. What was it to be, an even split down the middle on the profits? Or were you to get just twenty-five percent, considering all you had to do was get her inside Amberley?"

"You bastard!" David leaned across Erin to grab Simon by the front of his shirt. He was taller than Simon by several inches and looked as if he were about to strangle him with just one hand.

"Let him alone, please," Erin shouted. "I don't want to be the cause of fighting in this family. *Please*, David. Let him go."

David released Simon, who looked distinctly rumpled, his maroon silk tie askew, the white collar of his pristine maroon-and-white-striped shirt creased.

"You might say the gloves are now off," Simon told David with an unpleasant smile, as he straightened his tie. "You have shown yourself in your true colors today, Lennox."

"Just for the record," David said, through clenched teeth, "I knew absolutely nothing about Erin's connection with the family. I invited her here because I liked her and because I wanted her to see Amberley. Strange as it may seem, much as I dislike the Hogarth family, I happen to love Amberley. Which, considering the circumstances, is a bloody good thing, isn't it?"

"I'm sure you do love Amberley. I must say I admire your style. Nothing like allying yourself with a supposed long-lost illegitimate daughter—"

"Granddaughter."

"Granddaughter, then. Whatever. But I warn you that I intend to make sure you never get your hands on Amberley, Lennox. Amberley is mine and my children's."

"Who said it wasn't?" David sighed exaggeratedly. "Chill out, Simon. Politics are making you paranoid. Let's go, Erin. We've got ten minutes." He led Erin away, leaving Simon standing in the center of the hall.

"Thank you for standing up for me," she said, as they walked out onto the stone terrace.

"That's okay. I enjoy riling Simon. Trouble is, he's not easily riled, so it makes me feel good when I do get to him."

"I didn't understand half of what went on between you."

"Good." David turned to look out at the great expanse of velvety green lawn. "None of your business."

"You're right. Except in one way."

His face was still averted. "What?"

"I do feel very responsible for Simon blaming you for bringing me here. How can I make them believe that you weren't in on it?"

"You can't. So don't even try."

"That makes me feel terrible."

"So it should. Let's face it, Erin. You used me to get into Amberley."

"But you asked me to come here. I didn't ask you to bring me."

"You know damn well what I mean. You knew I was attracted to you." A line of red flared along his cheekbones. "You strung me along to get what you wanted."

Erin held back a hasty denial. How amazingly sensitive even a self-confident man could be when it came to the apparent abuse of his emotions. "I was very attracted to you, too," she said slowly, carefully feeling for the right words. "You know that. I had come to England for the sole purpose of finding out about my mother's childhood. I do admit that when Samantha said she knew you, I jumped at the chance to get close to the Hogarth family. But I soon realized that I—I was growing a bit too personally involved as well."

"That's when you should have told me."

"I know that now. It's easy to say in retrospect, isn't it? But how was I to know how you'd react? I felt terribly guilty for deceiving you, but I was so concerned about my mother. . . ."

"You could have told me that."

"How could I be sure? Can't you see, David? It was like a quest. To have come so near and then throw it away because I didn't want to deceive you would have been a disaster." Erin turned away. "Hell! I'm not explaining myself very well, am I? I feel totally screwed up."

"You're not the only one. What it comes down to is that you didn't trust me enough to tell me your secret, right?"

"I didn't know you well enough to know if I *could* trust you."

"Oh, great. That makes it even better. You didn't know me well enough to tell me the truth, but you did know me well enough to kiss me. Tell me, Miss Benson, where would you have drawn the line in this deception? Would you have gone to bed with me? Don't tell me I missed out on a great opportunity."

Erin felt like hitting him. "That's pretty nasty."

"Answer the question."

"No, I won't. I never used sex to gain entrance to Amberley. If you don't want to believe me, that's your prerogative. But it's the truth."

"Well, when it comes to truth, we shall never know, shall we?" He looked at his watch. "Time for your next interview with your granddaddy."

"Don't wait for me. I can find my own way home."

"Oh, for God's sake stop putting on the martyr act. I'll drive you back to Richmond."

"You don't need to," Erin said, her voice like ice.

"Yes, I do need to. British trains are practically nonexistent on a Sunday." He gave her a wry smile. "Don't worry, I won't bark at you all the way back. After all, we'll have Lucy with us. Knowing her, we'll probably spend the time dishing the Hogarths. What are you going to tell her, by the way?"

"Lucy? I don't know. I'll play it by ear."

Mrs. Edwards came out on the terrace. "Lord Maybridge will see you now, Miss Benson. I have been asked to warn you not to tire him."

No doubt on Simon or Olivia's orders, Erin thought. "I'll spend only a few minutes with him."

"Good. He isn't strong, you know. Mr. Hogarth is deeply concerned about what effect all this upset will have on him," Mrs. Edwards said accusingly.

"I promise I'll do my best to keep him as calm as possible." She wanted to add that his grandson seemed to upset Lord Maybridge more than anyone else.

"Have the children left yet?" David asked.

"They are about to leave. Mr. Simon was just getting the dog into the back of the car."

"Right. I'll just go and say good-bye to the girls," he told Erin. "Then I'll fetch Lucy. Has she been good?" he asked Mrs. Edwards.

"Very." A ghost of a smile lit her rather stern features. "I gave her rather a strong measure of whiskey, I'm afraid. She fell asleep on the morning room couch and only just awoke."

David grinned. "Good for you. I must remember that trick next time I want to quieten her down."

Mrs. Edwards looked shocked. "I can assure you it wasn't intentional, Mr. David."

"Of course it wasn't."

Erin watched him as he loped down the terrace steps two at a time, then she blinked and squeezed her eyes closed for a moment. "Well, I mustn't keep Lord Maybridge waiting, must I?" she said after a moment, with an attempt at a smile.

Mrs. Edwards did not respond. Silently she led the way back into the house, across the hall to the door of the library, and knocked on it.

Harrington opened the door. He looked at Erin, suspicion in his rheumy eyes. "Miss Benson is here again to see you, my lord," he announced.

"Good. Come in, come in, my dear." Lord Maybridge waved his hand at the sofa. "Push that animal off and make yourself comfortable." He, himself, looked remarkably comfortable in his old leather chair, his feet on the footstool, and two dogs lying on the hearth beside him.

"Thank you." Erin lifted up the tabby cat, setting it down beside her, and sat in its place on the sofa.

"Fetch a drink for Miss Benson, Harrington. What will you have, my dear?"

"Nothing, thank you. I won't stay more than a few minutes. You must be very tired." He looked drained and more frail.

"Nonsense! It's just that Simon infuriates me. I'm fond of the boy, but he likes to be in control of everything. Can't think where he gets that from."

Erin hid a smile. She could hazard a guess. "I'm afraid my coming here . . . and the photograph . . . It all must have been a great shock to you."

He put a trembling hand to his forehead. "It was. I must admit it was. I thought they were dead, you see. I thought they'd both died more than fifty years ago. It was a shock." He gazed at her, moisture in his eyes. "You have a look of her, you know. I can see it now. The brown eyes and the dark hair. Although both are lighter than hers."

"I'm like Mary, you mean?"

"Yes. Couldn't you see it, from the photograph? Where is it, by the way?"

"I put it away in my wallet."

"Oh." He looked disappointed.

"Would you like me to send you a copy? I can have one made."

"Yes. Yes, I'd like that. I don't have any pictures of her." He smiled, stroking his long fingers across his forehead. "Only the ones up here."

"I wanted to ask a favor of you."

"Anything, my dear. Ask away. Do you need money?"

Erin recoiled as if she'd been stung. "Definitely not. Your family already suspect that I'm up to no good."

"They would. Afraid they'll lose some. Well, it's not theirs yet."

Erin wanted to steer him away from the topic of money. It made her very uneasy. "The favor is to do with my mother."

"Ah, yes. Little Katie. Have you a picture of her as she is now?"

"Yes, I have." Erin brought out a picture of her mother and father taken at Banff last year, when they'd been there for a skiing holiday. "It's not terribly clear, I'm afraid."

He peered at it. "She's an old woman." He was obviously disappointed.

Erin smiled. "Well, not really old. She's just sixty."

"My God, sixty. It doesn't seem possible."

"The thing is, would you like to meet her?"

"Your mother?"

"Yes, your daughter." He seemed to have difficulty in realizing that the sixty-year-old woman and Katie were one and the same. "I'm not sure if she'll feel up to flying over yet, but if she did, would you be prepared to meet her, to have her come here to Amberley?"

He thought for a moment. "Why not? Nobody left to hurt by it, is there? Simon's too far removed to worry." He seemed to be persuading himself that this would be the correct thing to do.

"I doubt if Simon would be happy about it," Erin said.

"None of his business whom I have to visit at Amberley. But would your mother want to come all this way just to see a doddery old man?"

"You are her father," Erin said softly. "I think it would be very good for her to meet her father and to see the house of her dreams in reality."

"She hasn't been well, you say."

"No. The shock of my father's death affected her badly. It brought back all the terrible memories of losing her mother and leaving England when she was only five."

"Poor little girl," he murmured. He suddenly slapped both palms on his knee, making the dog at his feet jump up and yip. "Quiet!" Giles told it. "Of course Katie must come to Amberley. It was her birthplace."

"I'm not sure she'll be well enough yet," Erin reminded him. "It may be a while before she can come."

"That doesn't matter. It will give me time to have the cottage opened up and cleaned out. I'd like to show her the cottage." His eyes twinkled at her. "That was where she began."

For a moment Erin didn't comprehend, then she got it. "Oh, I see. A sort of trysting place, eh?"

"Exactly so." He beamed at her, his weariness suddenly gone. "Yes, I'd like to meet Mary's child again."

"*Your* child," Erin reminded him.

"Yes, indeed. My child."

Erin stood up. "I really must be going. David and Lucy are waiting for me."

"Is David driving you back to London?"

"Yes."

"He's an American, you know." He made it sound like some dread disease.

"I'm a Canadian."

"Ah, but you have good Hogarth blood in your veins."

"So has David."

"Lucy's blood is full of bubbles. So is her head. A bubblehead, that's what Lucy is. Talks a lot of nonsense. Can't believe a thing she says."

Erin said nothing, not wanting to upset him by arguing with him. She stood looking down at him for a moment. "May I write to you or perhaps phone you once I speak to my mother?"

"Of course. I shall be expecting to hear from you this week. If you don't telephone me, I shall be forced to ring you, which I hate. Leave your number with Harrington." He looked up at her face, warmth in the old blue eyes. "And you must come down to Amberley again, even if your mother cannot."

"Thank you. I should like that." Erin held out her hand. "Well, good-bye, then."

"Is that all I get, a handshake?"

Erin tilted her head, smiling, not quite knowing what to do. He took her hand and, to her surprise, kissed it. Then he drew her down and kissed her cheek, his mustache bristly against her skin.

"God bless you for coming here. It took courage to do so. You have made me very happy."

Tears filled Erin's eyes. "That's exactly how I feel, too."

"Good-bye, my dear child."

"Good-bye . . . Grandfather."

She took the memory of his expression with her, to warm her against the chill of David's rejection.

Chapter Twenty-one

When David drove into the driveway of Samantha's house, Erin felt only a minor sense of relief. She wished she were staying at some comfortable but impersonal hotel where she could be left alone to think for the next twenty-four hours.

Instead, she'd have to face the barrage of Samantha's questions.

For most of the journey she'd sat with her eyes closed, pretending to doze, while Lucy chattered away to David about that "cold bitch Olivia" and about how unkind Giles was.

Strangely enough, it wasn't until she was about to get out of the car that Lucy turned around to her and asked, "What were you and Giles talking about?"

Erin intercepted David's quick frown. "When?" she asked.

"Mrs. Edwards told me that something strange was going on between you two and that Simon wasn't at all pleased about it." Lucy twisted farther around in her seat. "What was it?"

Erin wasn't sure what to tell Lucy. She sent a silent plea for help to David.

"Erin was telling Giles that she thinks she is related to the Hogarths in some way, that was all," he said.

Lucy's eyes were round with excitement. "Oh, really? What branch of the family do you come from, my dear? Is it—"

"Here's Samantha," David said quickly. He turned his head to speak in a low voice to Erin. "She'll probably ask us in."

"Oh, no."

"I agree. I'll say Lucy's too tired."

"Too tired for what?" Lucy demanded. "I could do with a good stiff drink, I know that. A nice cold G and T would go down very well." She leaned out the window. "Hello, dear," she said to Samantha. "I hope you're going to ask us in."

There was no way to avoid it. As Erin sat in the sitting room, which seemed minuscule after the vast rooms of Amberley, she felt as if she were sleepwalking. Everything that was going on around her took on a dreamlike quality. She answered Samantha's eager questions about how she'd enjoyed Amberley in monosyllables, knowing that the tough questions would come later, once Lucy and David had left. She was also aware of Samantha's keen gaze going from her to David, noting the obvious coolness between them.

She wanted David and Lucy to go, but at the same time she dreaded it, knowing that it was highly unlikely she would ever see David again. Eventually she couldn't stand the strain a moment longer.

"I hope you'll excuse me," she said, standing up. "But I promised to call my mother today. If I leave it any longer she'll have left to go to church."

Lucy looked at the gold watch that hung loosely on her bony wrist. "Church? But it's a quarter past four," she protested.

"That's a quarter past ten in the morning, Winnipeg time," Erin explained.

"Oh, is it? How strange. I didn't know. Who is your mother? Do I know her?"

"No, you've never . . ." Erin stopped short, her heart skipping a beat. "You've never met."

But they could have met, couldn't they? When her mother was a small child. After all, Mary Foley had lived in a cottage on the Amberley estate after Kate's birth. Erin's heart pounded.

Although she'd hoped to ask Lucy questions about the family, until she had discovered more facts about the Hogarths' history it had never occurred to her that Lucy could actually have *known* both Mary Foley and Kate.

She felt the room swimming around her. From a long way away she heard David's voice ask, "Are you okay?"

Erin tried to focus on the faces that had turned to look at her. "I'm feeling a bit tired, that's all."

"You look ghastly, darling," Samantha said. "Perhaps you're coming down with the flu or something. Go and lie down at once."

"I think I will. But first I must phone my mother." Erin got up and walked on shaky legs to the door.

"Take the portable up to your room. Help her up, would you David? She looks as if she's about to pass out."

Erin tried to smile. Dear Samantha. Trying to patch things up between them. Unfortunately it would take more than a visit to her bedroom to reconcile her and David. "Thanks, Samantha."

"Good-bye, Erin." Lucy's voice held an edge of rebuke.

"I am sorry." Erin turned back and went to Lucy. "I must be half asleep. Good-bye, Mrs. Lennox. It's been a great pleasure meeting you."

"Good-bye, my dear. Perhaps we shall see each other again. David said he didn't think so, when I asked him, but one never knows."

Erin felt the heat rising in her face. She could imagine that David was feeling as embarrassed as she was. "You're right, one never knows." On an impulse, she bent to kiss the old lady's dry cheek. "Good-bye."

She stumbled from the room, past David, before anything more could be said.

He followed her, closing the door behind him. "Here's the phone," he said, taking it from its stand on the hall table.

"You don't need to come with me," Erin said. "I can manage."

"I had no intention of coming upstairs with you."

Their eyes met. Then Erin glanced away. "I didn't want you to. I just don't want . . . I don't want it to end this way, with you hating me."

"I don't hate you."

"You look like you do."

"I just don't like being used, that's all."

What was the point of denying it again? They'd been through it all before. "Could we talk about it again, another time, do you think? When you're less angry with me?"

He shrugged. A small gesture that denoted so much. "What's the point?"

Her lips trembled. "I'm not very coherent at the moment, but I would like to try to explain to you what it meant to me, what it will mean to my mother, to find her parents."

"You've already done that."

"No, I haven't," she cried. "Not properly. I did it in front of several people, most of them—including you—hostile to me. Can't you imagine how it felt to go through what I went through today?"

For the very first time since they'd left Amberley he looked at her as if he was really seeing her. "I'm trying to, but I guess all the stuff about you playing me along is getting in the way."

"You still believe that I don't care about you, that I pretended to so I could get into Amberley, right?"

"Right."

"That's not true, David."

He looked down at the telephone in his hands. "Well, that's the way it seems to me. Let's just drop it now, shall we? You need to call your mother. I need to get Lucy home."

Erin was desperate. She was about to lose them both, David *and* Lucy.

"I think Lucy might have known Mary Foley."

"Who? Oh, right. Your mother's mother. What makes you say that?"

"She grew up with Giles, didn't she? She probably knew Mary when she worked at Amberley." David still looked blank. "Mary was a chambermaid in the house, remember?" Erin said, her voice rising.

David glanced at the closed door. "If you're going to get all excited, we'd better move outside." He took her by the arm and led her out the front door. "Now, what were you trying to say?"

"That Lucy probably knew Mary Foley, my grandmother."

"So?"

"I want to find out more about her, that's all. Lucy

might even know if she did die in the blitz or not. I don't know why I didn't think of that before."

"Probably because, much as I love her, Lucy's a bit wandered, at times. Even if she did know your grandmother, I'm not sure you could believe what she tells you. You heard what Giles said about her. It may be unkind to say so, but unfortunately she *is* a bubblehead."

"But she often makes sense, too. You never know. She might remember something that would help."

"What exactly are you looking for now? Aren't you satisfied with an earl for a grandfather?"

Erin bit back an angry retort. "He's only one half of the equation. My mother's mother is the other half. Lucy is probably the only person left who could help me find out what happened to her."

He looked down at her with sudden suspicion. "Ah, now I see why you want to stay friends with me. That way you can get to Lucy, right?"

She stared at him, feeling numb. "No," she whispered. "That wasn't it at all."

He kicked at a stone in the driveway. "Well, you can forget it. I'm not getting involved in this anymore. I owe allegiance to the Hogarth family, not to some fortune-hunting journalist."

"Now you sound exactly like Simon. And I thought you preferred not to ally yourself with the Hogarths."

He drew himself up, standing tall and straight before her, suddenly very British. "I am part of the Hogarth family," he said coldly. "And, as such, I deeply resent your using me to infiltrate Amberley, however important your reason for doing so. End of conversation."

He walked to his car and unlocked it. Climbing into the driver's seat, he slammed the door and turned on the radio, which blared out Stravinsky's *Firebird*, suitably discordant for the occasion.

End of conversation, indeed. Erin stood watching the car for a moment, in case he might change his mind. Then she turned and went inside the house again, wearily climbing the stairs to her room.

The elation she'd felt at solving the riddle of Amberley and finding the painted ceiling *and* her mother's father had disappeared ages ago. Now all she wanted was to lie down, pull the covers over her head, and sleep for twelve hours. But first she must call her mother.

She locked her door, refusing to give in to the temptation to stand on the landing and listen for Lucy and David's departure. She dragged off her sweater and went into the bathroom to brush her teeth and splash cold water on her face. Then she closed both windows, lay down on the bed, and punched out her mother's number.

Chapter Twenty-two

Kate Benson was also lying on her bed. She had been rereading Carol Shields's novel *The Republic of Love*, with its affectionate depiction of Winnipeg as well as of love itself. She wasn't sure that love was what she should be thinking about at present. It was surprising how many young people believed that older people never thought about sex, let alone engaged in it. But, even during the last few years, she and Jim had an active sex life, augmented by a great deal of touching and cuddling and other physical manifestations of their affection. She missed that terribly.

Although she was eating much better now, Kate felt as if she were being starved of the vital nutrients of life. She missed the shared laughter, the stimulating—sometimes heated—conversation, the cozy winter evenings in front of the television with a large bag of caramel popcorn, the discussions on such important matters as whether or not they should plant zinnias or snapdragons in the flower bed under the living-room window.

She was seeing Dr. Prentice only once a week now and had taken on some of her volunteer work at Grace Hospital again, but Kate knew that even if she worked twenty-four hours a day, she still couldn't fill the gaping hole in her life.

Sighing, she threw back the bedclothes and got up. She felt restless, bored. *If only I'd been able to travel,* she thought as she put on her slippers and tied the belt of her robe.

She had two friends who'd also been widowed in the past couple of years. Both of them had gone traveling when their husbands had died. One to Europe, the other to Hawaii. Later, they'd recognized their traveling for what it was, an escape, a postponement of their mourning, but both said it had helped them over those wretched weeks after the funeral, when friends had ceased calling to see how they were doing.

Kate envied her two friends their travels. Her panic attacks had tied her to the house, emphasizing the emptiness within and without. Still, she'd been so lucky to have had Erin with her . . . until she'd left on this fool's errand to England. What on earth did she think she could achieve, with nothing but an old photograph and a few weird snatches of memory from her mother's nightmares to go on?

Perhaps Erin was also traveling to escape. Kate hadn't thought of that before. Poor girl, she and her father had always been very close. And she hadn't really adjusted yet to the break with Rob last year. It had been the right decision, there was no doubt about that, but she'd been left feeling vulnerable and lonely, and her father's death had only increased her loneliness.

Well, if traveling to England helped Erin, then good luck to her.

Kate was about to go downstairs to make herself some tea when the telephone rang. She lifted the receiver after the first ring.

"Hi, Mom. How's it going?"

Kate smiled when she heard Erin's voice. "Hi, sweetie. I'm fine. I was just thinking about you."

"I wanted to catch you before you left for church."

"I'm not going. I'm ashamed to say I slept in this morning."

"That's a good sign. No more nightmares, I hope."

"Not for the past few nights, thank heavens."

"I am glad. Is Gran okay?"

"She's great. Itching to get back home, though. She doesn't say so, of course, but I can tell. I've told her I'll be just fine, but she insists on staying."

"Oh, no. I am sorry. Is she driving you nuts?"

"No, but having her here makes me realize that I should be looking after *her*, not the other way around. She's getting very frail."

There was a moment of silence, as if they'd been cut off, then Erin spoke again. "I've got news for you."

There was an edge of suppressed excitement in her voice that made Kate's heart pound.

"What?" She wasn't sure she wanted to hear this.

"You're not going to believe it," Erin warned her.

"I'm certainly not if you don't tell me what it is."

"Are you sitting down?"

"For heaven's sake, Erin," Kate said impatiently. "Don't keep me in suspense."

She could hear Erin take a deep breath at the other end of the line. "I've found your father."

"You've what?"

"Found your father. You'll never guess who he is."

"Someone rich and famous, I trust." Kate's light-hearted tone belied the sudden tremor in her hands.

"Got it in one!" Erin said triumphantly. "Take a guess."

Suddenly Kate didn't want to hear any more. Her hand was slippery on the receiver. She licked her dry lips. "I can't," she whispered. "Tell me."

"You should have a big fanfare playing. I wish I could be there to see your face."

"For heaven's sake quit playing games, Erin, and tell me." Erin had always had an inflated sense of the theatrical.

"Okay, okay. I feel like the master of ceremonies in that old show *This Is Your Life*."

And Kate felt like screaming.

"Sorry, Mom," Erin said, obviously sensing her mother's annoyance. "You remember the Earl of Maybridge? He was the elderly man they showed at the beginning of the video we got from the BBC."

"Yes."

"He's your father."

"I don't believe it," Kate said flatly.

"Well you'd better, because it's true. I've spoken to him—"

"When?"

"Today. This very morning. We had a long talk."

"Where?"

"At Amberley. That was the house you recognized, the ones with the cherubs painted on the ceiling." Erin's voice rose with excitement. "They're there, Mom. Those cherubs are there on the library ceiling, just like you remembered. I can't tell you how excited I was when I saw them."

"There must be several places with painted ceilings," Kate said, not wanting to believe what she was hearing.

"Maybe so, but everything else fits. The house, the photograph—"

"Who were they, the people in the picture?"

"They were your parents, as we thought. The earl—before he became an earl—and your mother, Mary Foley."

Kate repeated the name. "Mary Foley?"

"That's right. Does it sound at all familiar?"

Kate's lips moved in a silent repetition of the name. *Mary Foley. Mary Foley, Mary Foley.* Then, like an echo of church bells ringing in the distance, it came back to her. *That's Mary Foley's little girl. You know who her father is, don't you?* And the sound of girls giggling.

"Do you recognize the name?" Erin asked again.

"Yes, I—I think I do," Kate said hesitantly. "Is she alive, too? My . . . Mary Foley, I mean."

"We don't know. Lord Maybridge swears she can't be. He says she would never have left you in Canada if she was."

Kate felt tears forming. She sniffed. "What happened to her?"

"He thinks she must have been killed in the London blitz the same year you were evacuated to Canada."

"Erin, I'm sorry but I'm not understanding much of this." Kate brushed a trembling hand across her mouth. "There are so many questions. . . . Why did they give me a false name and address, for instance? Oh, that's a stupid question, isn't it? Obviously an earl wouldn't want an illegitimate daughter hanging around."

"Actually, it's far more complicated than that. Too much so to tell you everything now. I could fax you all the details, if you like. But better still . . ." Erin paused.

Kate wasn't sure she wanted to hear what Erin was about to say. "What?"

"Why don't you fly over?"

"When?"

"Right away. This week, anyway."

"I couldn't possibly do that." Kate's voice sharpened. "You know how difficult it's been for me since . . ." She was ashamed of her whining tone. It wasn't like her at all. "Since your father died."

"I do know, but this might help. Lord Maybridge said he'd like to meet his daughter."

"I doubt that very much. God knows how you managed to see him, Erin. Knowing you, you probably wheedled your way in."

"In a way, I did. That and fate, I suppose."

Even over the phone Kate could recognize a hint of dejection in her daughter's voice. "I hope you didn't do anything illegal."

"No, not illegal. Anyway, Mom, that's not important. What is important is that I've found your father for you."

"Yes."

"Is that all you can say? *Yes*?"

"Sorry. Thank you, darling. I'm still sort of stunned. It's hard to believe."

"He's old, Mom. And he has heart trouble. I don't think he's expected to live very long."

Erin, don't do this to me, Kate wanted to shout. She said nothing.

"I think it would help you to meet him."

"I don't want to make that long journey." Two journeys: one to England, the other into her hidden past.

"Why don't you talk about it with Dr. Prentice?"

"Good idea."

"When do you see her next?"

"Wednesday."

"How about giving her a call tomorrow?"

"Okay." Kate ran her hand through her short hair. She hadn't even brushed it yet. "What is he like?"

"The earl? Oh, just what you'd imagine an earl to be like. Tall, still handsome, piercing blue eyes, domineering, very impatient. Reminds me of you at times, Mom," Erin added, laughing.

"Thanks a lot," Kate said, but she, too, was smiling. Then her smile faded. "You don't make him sound very attractive."

"That's because that's what you see on the outside.

The most important thing you need to know, Mom, is that he adored your mother and, from the sound of it, he loved you very much as well."

"So much so that he abandoned me."

"No, he didn't. He—"

"No. Don't tell me. I'm too shaken up to talk about it anymore."

"I bet you are. It is a shock, isn't it? Even I felt that way. I'll call you again tomorrow, sometime in the afternoon, after you've spoken to Dr. Prentice. Why not speak to Jean Wainwright as well? After all, she's not only your doctor. You've been friends for years. Why don't you speak to her, see what she thinks."

That was Erin. She never let a thing go once she'd got her teeth into it.

When she'd said good-bye to Erin, Kate went downstairs and made herself a pot of tea. Then she took out the photograph Erin had found in *The Secret Garden* and sat gazing at it.

My mother and father, she thought. And then she said it aloud, "My mother and father." Then she grimaced, hoping that Anna hadn't overheard her. The last thing she wanted to do was upset her. After all, she and Jo Bartley had been her *true* parents, the ones who'd been there for her during those all-important growing-up years. She doubted that these two strangers in the photograph could have had a sufficiently plausible excuse to justify sending a five-year-old child to a vast new country all by herself, and then abandoning her.

That night, Kate lay awake for a long time, her overactive mind filled with images of ships and painted ceilings and stately homes. When she faced the fact that her birth mother had probably died half a century ago she wept silently, realizing that, deep down, she'd been harboring the hope that they might be reunited.

Then she fixed her thoughts on the tall, aristocratic man with blue eyes who, Erin said, was definitely her father.

How could she be so sure? Erin could be so tenacious. Maybe the man had admitted it just to get rid of her. But that was hardly likely, was it?

Kate began to wish she'd asked Erin more questions, instead of cutting her short.

Eventually, she fell into a heavy sleep which, to her great relief, was untroubled by dreams of any kind.

On Monday morning, she called Dr. Prentice, telling her answering service that it was urgent. Dr. Prentice called her back at ten-fifteen.

"You sound a little frantic," she said in her calm, slow voice that sometimes annoyed Kate intensely. "What's wrong?"

"Nothing wrong, really," Kate said. She told her about Erin's call.

"My goodness," was the psychologist's reaction. "I think we'd better have you in as soon as possible. Can you make it before lunch?"

Kate could, but she didn't want to. Somehow she knew what Dr. Prentice would advise—what *both* her doctors would advise, in fact—and the thought of it made her break out in a cold sweat.

Chapter Twenty-three

Throughout the journey home to Hampstead, Simon was very quiet. The girls had fallen asleep in the back seat, Perdita with her pillow clutched tightly to her skinny body, Nicola sitting upright, trying, as always, to avoid touching her sister, her head awkwardly flopping to one side, like a drooping flower on a slim stalk.

Olivia was wide awake, but she spent most of the journey listening to her portable CD player.

"Soon be home," Simon said cheerfully, not wanting her to think he was worrying.

"Good." She gave him a wan smile. "Once the children are in bed we can talk."

Simon nodded and glanced at her with a reassuring smile. "Of course."

He didn't want to talk about it. Not now. Not later. He had to rally his thoughts. What had happened today at Amberley could have enormous repercussions. This woman, Erin Benson, was like a loose cannon. She was a threat to him in many ways, both personally and professionally.

Since the public announcement about his intention to give up the title, his grandfather had no time for him. Giles was old and vulnerable, easily flattered. Simon had seen his expression when he had looked at Erin Benson. How easy it would be for this woman, this utter stranger, to wheedle her way into Amberley, to usurp his place as Giles's grandchild.

His hands tightened on the steering wheel.

"Darling, you're going over eighty," Olivia quietly reminded him.

Simon glanced at the speedometer. She was right.

Eighty-three miles an hour. He eased his foot off the accelerator. "Sorry about that."

She said nothing more, merely giving him a sympathetic glance and then switching on her opera disk again. Simon preferred to drive with nothing to distract him, so Olivia listened to music if the children were asleep.

Obviously this time he had too much to distract him, he thought.

If this story got out it could be a disaster. There was a new puritanism in politics nowadays, a reaction to the scandals that had riven the Tories for so long. The electorate wanted their politicians to be squeaky clean. "Not a hint of scandal can be attached to my name or that of any member of my family," he had told Ransome.

Now that was no longer true. Even if he, himself, were clean, who knew how much of this story would rub off on him. The aristocrat seducing the little Irish chambermaid, the family sending their child away to Canada, and then that child's daughter turning up at Amberley almost sixty years later. Had this happened sixty years ago nothing might have been made of it, but today it would hit the headlines of every newspaper in the country, especially with Simon's bid to become the next Prime Minister of Britain.

He had threatened Erin Benson with repercussions if she published a story about the Hogarth family, but that was when he'd thought he was dealing only with the infiltration of a journalist looking for a story about Simon Hogarth.

Before he'd learned about her relationship to his grandfather.

How in God's name was he going to stop her from telling her story to all and sundry? Even worse, she herself was a member of the media. Surely her instinct would be to use what she had to her best advantage.

He could see it now. *Family secret discovered. Earl finds long-lost daughter. "I thought she was dead," Lord Maybridge says.*

"Christ!" he muttered.

"What?" Olivia asked.

"Sorry. That idiot pulled in front of me without any warning."

He could feel her gazing at him, knowing that he'd made that up. Her hand went out to cover his on the gearshift. "It will all work out," she said. "You'll find a way to get rid of her."

He glanced in the mirror to make sure the children were still sleeping. "Other than sending her a box of poisoned chocolates, I'm not so sure."

Their eyes met. For one horrible moment Olivia thought he was serious.

Simon shook his head. "Don't look so worried, darling. I'm not about to do anything quite so drastic."

"I suppose it is true, all this stuff about his mistress—"

Simon's mouth hardened. "The word is hardly appropriate for some little Irish chambermaid he seduced in his lusty youth, is it?"

"I don't understand why the family didn't just bundle her off back to Ireland, before she had the child."

"I agree. That's usually what happened in those days."

"Perhaps Giles really loved her."

"Knowing what I do about his parents, I doubt that Giles's protestations of love would have swayed them in any way. They were absolute tartars, from what I've heard, particularly my great-grandmama, Alice. She had my great-grandpapa wrapped around her proverbial little finger." He slowed down and pulled into the inner lane to turn off the motorway.

"Do you think it happened the way Giles said it did?"

"I doubt it," Simon replied, as he waited for his turn to enter the roundabout. He glanced over his shoulder. "I believe someone's stirring in the back there," he warned her.

Olivia turned around. "Hello there," she said to Perdita, who was sitting up, her hair like a furze bush. "Did you have a good sleep?"

Any further discussion on the subject had to be postponed until the girls had gone to bed. While Olivia was making mugs of cocoa for them, Simon sat in his office staring at the blank computer screen.

Usually when he had problems to solve he put himself in the shoes of the person causing them. But he was finding that singularly difficult this time. Hard to imagine yourself as a young Canadian woman who has just discovered that her mother's long-lost father is an English peer with a vast amount of land and property.

What would I do in those circumstances? Simon wondered. Probably milk it for all it's worth, he thought gloomily. He supposed it depended on the Benson woman's background. Who would have all the facts on her? David?

If David was to be believed he knew nothing about Erin Benson's background. He'd certainly appeared surprised when Giles had made his big announcement. And the icy wall between him and Miss Benson had seemed genuine enough.

Where was she staying while she was in England? Now David *would* know that. Simon drew his minuscule recorder from the pocket of his linen jacket and spoke into it.

"Phone David re E.B. address."

He'd phone David tonight, while he was still feeling raw from having been deceived. That way he might spill a few more particulars in the process.

He spoke again into the recorder. "Get Pat to check with CBC about E.B. Discreetly."

Once he'd got more information about Erin Benson he would know what to do. But for now his main objectives lay at Amberley. Again he spoke. This time with no hesitancy.

"Phone Dr. Alexander and Mrs. Edwards."

He switched on his computer, watching as his screensaver spread across the screen. Then he spoke into the recorder again. "Deal with Harrington."

Olivia knocked on the office door and announced, "The girls are ready for their bedtime story."

"Right. I'll be there in five minutes. Just have to make one phone call."

A pause ... and then Olivia opened the door and came in. "To whom?"

"David." He picked up the black telephone receiver, pointedly waiting for her to go before he made his call.

Olivia showed no signs of leaving. "David? Is that wise?"

"I want to find out where she's staying."

"What if he refuses to tell you?"

"David's not a fool, darling. He knows I can find out easily enough. No doubt she's given her address to Giles."

He held the receiver up, tilting his head in a gesture that suggested she leave. "I promise this won't take long."

"The girls are waiting," was all she said, but this time she went out, closing the door behind her.

David picked up the phone on the second ring, as if he'd been standing beside it, or actually had it in his hand.

"David?"

"Yes."

"This is Simon."

Silence. Then a cold, "What can I do for you?"

"Can you tell me how I can get in touch with Miss . . . with Erin Benson?"

"Why?"

"Because I think we need to talk, that's why."

"About what?"

Simon gritted his teeth. Then he took a deep breath and smiled, watching himself in the mirror above the white fireplace. "As she is obviously related in some way to the Hogarth family, I thought it would be a good idea for us to get to know each other a little better."

"I've a feeling she can't be bought, Simon."

"How crass of you to suggest such a thing." Simon's voice hardened. "My main consideration is the welfare of my grandfather."

"I think he proved to us all today that he's still perfectly capable of looking after himself."

"Certainly, he is." He must remember that David was no fool. Although he was only a solicitor, not a barrister, he was a highly successful solicitor and certainly made more money than Simon did. "I just want to clarify your friend's intentions."

Simon wondered for a moment whether David would deny that she was his friend.

"You also want to clarify my involvement in the whole thing, right?" David said.

"You gave us your word that you knew nothing of

her personal involvement with the family. That was enough for me."

"Good. Then I need say no more about it. Erin is staying with Samantha Wakeley in Richmond."

"The name sounds familiar. Should I know her?"

"I don't know if you *should*, Simon, but you might. Samantha used to have her own show on UTV. She's now an executive there. She lives on Richmond Green." David gave Simon the address and phone number.

"Thank you." Simon wrote it down in his small black notebook, adding *Samantha Wakeley* and *UTV*.

"I suggest you leave it until tomorrow," David said. "Erin was pretty shattered by all this. When I dropped her off in Richmond, she was going to call her mother to tell her the news and then she was going to bed."

"I won't bother her tonight, I assure you." Simon took up a red pen and underlined Samantha's name. Then he put three thick red strokes beneath UTV.

"Anything else?"

"I hope you don't think me too curious, but just how well do you know her?"

"Erin or Samantha?"

"Erin."

"As I told you, I met her a week ago. She'd just come over from Canada. I took her to a concert at the Festival Hall."

"That's all?"

"Just about."

"I find it hard to believe that you would bring a woman with you to Amberley after such a short time of knowing her." Simon chuckled. "She must be pretty hot stuff."

"Go stuff yourself, Simon." David slammed the receiver down in his ear.

Simon glanced into the mirror and saw that he was smiling again. So . . . David was still smarting from what had happened. That meant he still cared about the woman. The telephone call had been most productive.

Simon checked his black notebook before locking it in his briefcase. Then he went upstairs to read to the children. They were still in the middle of *Charlie and the Chocolate Factory*. This was the fourth reading. The girls loved Roald Dahl's books. So did he. There was something delightfully subversive in the writing that appealed to him.

Chapter Twenty-four

It was past ten o'clock when Erin awoke the next morning. She had hoped to speak to Samantha before she left for the studio, but by the time she made it downstairs the house was empty. Well, it would have to wait until Samantha got home that evening.

Unfortunately, Simon made his move long before then.

Samantha came home early. Her Lancia streaked up the road and into the driveway with a screech of brakes so that Erin could hear it from the kitchen. First the car door crashed shut and then the front door.

As Erin came out of the kitchen into the hall Samantha confronted her. "What the fucking hell is going on?" she demanded, hands on her hips. She was a formidable figure in her scarlet, mini-skirted suit.

"What do you mean?"

"I was called into the director's office this afternoon and charged with unprofessional conduct."

Erin's eyes widened. "What on earth for?"

"What for?" Samantha echoed. "Don't you go playing Miss Innocent with me. You know damned well what for. I should have known not to take one of Rob Harris's discards into my house. What a bloody fool I was!"

Erin slammed down the glass she was drying. "Hey! Hold on a minute. What the hell are you talking about?"

"You and the bloody Hogarths, that's what I'm talking about. I was threatened with losing my position, that's what I'm talking about. Treated like some junior run-around." Angry tears filled Samantha's eyes and rolled down her cheeks.

"Oh, my God. Simon."

"That's right, sweetie. Simon bloody Hogarth got to

the big boss. I was accused of working in collusion with you to get you inside Amberley so that I could get a juicy story out of it."

Erin was puzzled. The last thing she'd expected was for Simon to go public on this. Surely he would want everything kept under wraps. "I can't believe it."

"Well, you'd better believe it, honey. You certainly screwed me up."

"God, Samantha, I am so sorry."

"Fat lot of good that'll do me. I need a drink."

"I'll get you one. What do you want?"

"A straight vodka."

"No, seriously."

"Yes. Seriously. I'll do it myself, thank you." Samantha barged past her and went into the kitchen. There followed much crashing of doors and drawers, accompanied by violent curses.

Erin went into the kitchen and stood in the doorway, half expecting to have a jug of ice cubes thrown at her. "What exactly did Simon tell them?"

"He said that you and I had hoodwinked David—"

"Oh, that's just great. David will be thrilled to be dragged into this."

"Can I finish?"

"Sorry."

"We'd hoodwinked David into taking you to Amberley so you could get a story about Simon Hogarth and—"

"About *Simon*?"

"Yes, of course. What else would you be there for?"

"I'll tell you in a moment. Go on."

Samantha pushed past her and walked into the sitting room, throwing herself down on a couch and kicking off her high-heeled shoes. "There was talk of dirty tactics and trespass and all sorts of other nasty legal terms. The Tories may be only the opposition at the moment, but with Simon leading them there's a good chance they'll get in next time. He's got clout. He also has a point. I tell you, everyone at the studio was running scared."

"The whole country should be running scared if that man gets in as Prime Minister," Erin said. "Talk about underhanded tactics." She wished she had Simon here. Her fists clenched at the thought.

"Don't start blaming him. You were the one who did this. I can't believe you spilled the beans to Simon. Talk about ham-fisted! That's what happens when you send some inexperienced hick into the battle zone."

"Hold on a minute! Just cut out the name-calling, okay? If you'd let me get a word in, I might be able to explain before you get me so mad I'll just walk out. Then you'll never hear the truth."

But it seemed that nothing Erin said was going to stem Samantha's tide. "I hope it was worth it. You'd better get a bloody good story out of it. Unfortunately, UTV won't be carrying it."

UTV might not be, but Erin wouldn't put it past Samantha to sell this story to the highest bidder. And she could imagine there'd be some high bidding for what would be a very hot story.

Samantha launched into more bitter complaints against Simon, the director of her company, and everyone in general, but Erin tuned her out.

She'd been feeling so guilt-ridden about lying to Samantha that she had intended to tell her the entire truth. Now she realized that would be insane. Samantha couldn't be trusted to keep a secret. She was so ambitious that she'd likely break even a solemn promise if it meant she could get a good story out of it.

Erin decided she would have to give Samantha a diluted version of the truth. Her mother might be coming to England soon. Giles Hogarth's privacy must be protected. There was too much at stake to risk the truth coming to light at this point.

She cut into Samantha's flow of complaints. "Will you just shut up for a minute, so I can tell you what really happened?"

"It's not going to help. I can't use it."

"No, you can't, but there's something you should know." Erin waited a minute, expecting more invective.

To her amazement, Samantha suddenly stopped talking. She stood up, wiggled out of her panty hose, pushed them under a cushion, and then sank back on the couch, her long, bare legs tucked beneath her. "Okay, I'm listening. Fire away."

"I'm afraid I didn't tell you the truth about my reason for wanting to get into Amberley."

"Well, you might not have spelled it out, but we both knew why, didn't we?"

"Actually, no, *you* didn't."

"Come on, darling. I'm not a bloody fool."

"Of course you're not. You see, I wasn't one bit interested in a political story about Simon Hogarth."

Samantha rolled her eyes. "Come on, let's get real. Don't act stupid with me."

"I'm not. I think it's fair that I tell you why I wanted to get into Amberley, considering you were the one who helped me do so."

"Yes, to my cost."

"I am truly sorry about that, but I had a good reason for it. You see, my mother was born there."

"Your mother?" Samantha repeated incredulously.

"Yes. She was a daughter of one of the housemaids there. She left Amberley when she was evacuated to Canada during the second world war. *That* was my real reason for wanting to get inside Amberley."

Samantha's mouth fell open. "But why on earth didn't you tell me this from the beginning?"

"I don't know. It was stupid of me not to, I know. I was just so excited at the thought of finding out about Amberley. My mother didn't know anything about her background, you see, so we've had to do a lot of detective work. She just happened to recognize Amberley Court when she saw it on the television."

"How amazing!" Samantha looked speculatively at Erin. "I suppose I should have known you weren't really the type of journalist who'd stalk Simon Hogarth into his own lair."

Erin wasn't sure if she should take that as a compliment or put-down. Knowing Samantha, it was probably the latter.

"Of course," Samantha continued, "if your mother had found her parents—or at least one of them—that would have made a great human-interest story."

Erin didn't move a muscle. "You're right."

"But merely finding your birthplace isn't that exciting, is it? I'm sure it is for your mother, but it wouldn't mean much to the viewers."

Erin breathed a sigh of relief. She'd gambled by telling Samantha this much, but at least now she'd partly told her the truth. "Of course Simon Hogarth didn't believe my story. He was convinced I was there to get a story on him. That's why he was so annoyed."

Samantha went to pour herself another drink. "Annoyed isn't quite the word I'd use."

"Did he actually come into the studio, do you know?"

"Oh, yes. I was called in just before his meeting with the boss ended. I found him very . . . I'm not sure how I'd describe it. He's not really tall enough for me, of course, but . . . Dynamic's the work I'd use. He has that aura of power that can be extremely sexy. He was quite charming. Shook my hand. Said, 'So this is Samantha Wakeley,' as if he'd been waiting to meet me for ages. It wasn't until he'd left that I found out what his visit was all about. As you can imagine, darling, I swiftly changed my first impression of Simon Hogarth and decided he was as sexy as a snake."

Erin couldn't help smiling. Samantha had a way with words.

"I take it that I can quote you to my director, about your real reason for being at Amberley, I mean. It might help. Of course the best way to help would be for me to find some fantastic human-interest story that would garner heaps of viewers."

Knowing that she had that very story locked inside her at this very minute made Erin feel a twinge of guilt. "You can tell him about my mother being born at Amberley," she said.

"So, what's next for you?" Samantha asked. "Flying back home to Winnipeg, are you?" She emphasized the name, making it sound like some backwoods shantytown.

"No, I'm not. Not yet, anyway. But don't worry, Samantha, I am moving out."

"I wasn't worrying," Samantha said enigmatically.

"I've a feeling my mother may fly over and join me.

Now that I've confirmed that she was born at Amberley, I think she'd like to go and see it."

Samantha laughed. "I don't think you've much chance of getting back inside Amberley."

"We could go when it's open to the public." Erin hoped Samantha didn't know that Amberley had been temporarily closed to the public.

"You can stay on here, of course," Samantha said.

Erin was extremely surprised. "No, I can't. Apart from the fact that I've caused you so much trouble, I've taken advantage of your hospitality enough."

"Nonsense! I have to go to Paris next week for some research into the fashion industry there for a special I'm planning. I'd be glad to have someone here to care for the house while I'm away. We've been burgled twice in the past year."

"What about Adam?"

"Adam? Oh, he's gone to L.A. Won't be back for at least ten days. So you'd have the house to yourself. And if your mother does come over, there'll be plenty of room for you both."

Now Erin was swamped with guilt. Samantha's generosity made her sincerely hope that the story about her mother's parentage would never leak out.

The telephone rang. *Saved by the bell*, she thought.

Samantha got it. "It's for you," she said, handing the portable to Erin.

"Hello," Erin said into the phone.

"Hi, Erin," said her mother's voice. "It's me."

"Hi, Mom. Just a minute, okay? It's my mother," Erin told Samantha. "I'll take it upstairs." Then she realized that Samantha could listen in on the other phone. God, she really was getting absolutely paranoid!

"No need. I'm going up to have a bath." Samantha gathered up her shoes and panty hose and left the room.

Erin uncovered the receiver. "Hi, Mom. I'm still here."

"I thought I'd lost you," her mother said sharply.

"Samantha was just leaving. How's it going?"

"I'm not sure how it's going. I've spoken to Jean and Dr. Prentice."

"And?"

"They both think I should come over, if I feel able to."

"And do you?"

"I wish I could say I do. Flying never worried me before, but now . . ." Her mother's voice trailed away.

For once Erin didn't try to reassure her. Her mother had plenty of friends and two doctors to do that. "I think you should come. Don't take time to think about it. That'll only make it more difficult."

"It'll be very expensive."

"For God's sake, Mother, this is your father we're talking about. Your own flesh and blood. He's eighty-one and has a heart problem. You *must* come over."

"I suppose so." A long period of silence followed.

"Are you okay?" Erin asked.

"I'm . . . I'm just fine." A new, more positive, tone entered her mother's voice. "You're right. I should come over. I'll book the flight today. Then I'll let you know when I'll be arriving. It will take me a few days to get organized, though."

"That's okay. Samantha's going to be away next week. She says it's fine for us to stay here."

"How kind. She sounds like a very nice person."

Erin grinned to herself. *Nice* was not exactly the word she'd use to describe Samantha Wakeley. She wondered what her mother would think of Samantha if they were to meet. Madame Exotica meets prairie doctor's wife.

Then her smile faded. They must not meet. Her mother was a stickler for the truth. She would never agree to lie about her relationship to the Hogarths.

"Erin! Are you still there?"

"Sorry, Mom, You were saying?"

"I asked you what clothes I should bring to go to Amberley. Casual or dressy."

"Lord Maybridge likes to dress up for the evenings. At least he did when we were there. But casual for daytime. You always look smart, Mom, whatever you wear. We can talk about all that once you've got your flight booked. Give me a call as soon as you know. I'll be here all evening."

As soon as she'd put the phone down, Erin went out into the hall to make sure that Samantha was still in the bathroom. Above the noise of running water, Erin could hear her belting out something from *Cats* in a wincingly off-key voice.

She went back into the sitting room and dialed the number at Amberley, smiling to herself as she thought of Lord Maybridge's pleasure when he heard that his daughter was coming to England to see him.

Chapter Twenty-five

Giles could hear the telephone ringing somewhere in the house. Automatically his hand reached out for the portable that was usually at his side, but it wasn't there. Come to think of it, it hadn't been there since the morning.

Damn Harrington! He must have moved it somewhere. He tried to think where it could be, but his mind felt like a ball of cotton wool. Must be the pills his doctor had given him this morning. Fool! Yapping on about high blood pressure and essential that he rest.

"I'm warning you," Alexander had said. "No more excitement for a while. This birthday weekend of yours has been a little too much for you. I've given you a mild sedative and I am leaving you in Mrs. Edwards's capable hands. She will make sure that you take all your medication regularly."

It was Simon who'd called in Alexander, of course. Interfering young pup! He'd be damned if he'd take orders from a quack his grandson had chosen for him when his old doctor, Burroughs, had died. Oh, young Alexander was competent enough, he supposed, but he had a nasty habit of speaking to Simon about Giles's medical condition. When Giles had challenged him about it, Dr. Alexander had informed him in his wordy Scottish manner that "Mr. Hogarth is your next of kin, Lord Maybridge. I consider it my duty to inform him when I have concerns about your health. Particularly when I'm concerned that you are not taking—or not being given—your necessary medication."

That, of course, was a dig at Harrington. Did they really expect the poor old chap to force him to take those bloody pills against his will?

Giles frowned. He was concerned about Harrington. He hadn't seen him at all today. It was Mrs. Edwards who'd served him his morning coffee and then his lunch and tea. "Mr. Harrington is a little under the weather," she'd explained. "Possibly too much work over the weekend. He isn't as able as he used to be, you know."

Giles picked up the intercom. "Who was that on the phone?" he demanded when Mrs. Edwards answered.

"Mr. Simon rang to see how you were. I told him you were resting. He said he'd ring later."

"You had no right to tell him that when I'm wide awake." He wished he *were* wide awake. That pill she'd given him with his tea was making him feel extremely woozy.

"Dr. Alexander said you must rest, my lord," she said firmly. "And I know that speaking to Mr. Simon will get you all excited again. Why don't you let Collins take you upstairs, so that you can lie down and be comfortable? I can bring you your supper and you can have it in your room."

"I have never had a meal in my bedroom in my life and I don't intend to start doing so now. And what's all this about *supper*? I expect my usual dinner, Mrs. Edwards."

"A light meal of poached fish, Dr. Alexander suggested. Nothing more."

"Who pays your salary, Mrs. Edwards?"

"You do, my lord. That is why I have your best interests at heart."

Damn the woman! She had an answer to everything. "I will eat in my dining room tonight, Mrs. Edwards. Tonight and every night until the day I die."

He slammed down the intercom, hoping it hurt her ear, and sank back against the worn leather cushions of his chair.

Of course she was right about Simon. He would get excited if he spoke to him. The mere sound of Simon's smooth voice enraged him. The thought of what he had done made Giles's heart beat faster. To throw away the title that had been in the family for hundreds of years, as if it meant nothing more than, say, a packet of cigarettes!

But, for once, it hadn't been Simon who'd sent his

blood pressure up. He'd lain awake most of the night thinking about what had happened yesterday, his mood swinging between exhilaration and fear. It had been a marvelous surprise, of course, knowing that his daughter—Mary's and his—was alive, but it was also a bombshell. One that had untold repercussions.

Not only was his daughter alive. She could be coming here, to Maybridge.

No wonder his blood pressure was soaring.

Kate was to arrive at Heathrow next Monday morning.

Erin had been trying to call Giles for three days. The first and second times she had spoken to Mrs. Edwards and been fobbed off. "Lord Maybridge is unwell and in the care of his physician," Mrs. Edwards had said.

"May I have his doctor's name?" Erin had asked when she'd called the second time.

"Certainly not." Mrs. Edwards had seemed astounded at the suggestion. "If you have any inquiries about Lord Maybridge's health, I would suggest that you ring Mr. Hogarth."

Simon was the last person Erin wanted to call.

The third time she called Amberley, she was greeted by an answering machine, with Mrs. Edwards's voice asking the caller to "kindly leave a message."

"I am trying to get in touch with Lord Maybridge about his daughter's proposed visit to see him," was the message Erin left.

By Wednesday evening, when she hadn't had a response, she knew that something was definitely wrong. Was Lord Maybridge genuinely sick or was there something else going on?

She couldn't phone Simon. There was only one person who could help her, but she wasn't sure how David would respond. It was entirely likely that he, too, would have his answering machine on and ignore her calls.

Despite—or, rather, because of—her newly discovered relationship to the Hogarth family she seemed to be *persona non grata* with all of them.

She dialed David's home number. To her surprise, and instant embarrassment, David answered on the second ring.

"I wasn't expecting you to answer," Erin said hesitantly. "I didn't think you'd be home this early." Then, realizing how stupid that sounded, she blurted out, "This is Erin. I didn't know who else to call."

"Hi, Erin." She expected to feel the chill all along the air waves, but he sounded . . . okay. Not elated, but not totally freezing her out, either. "I'm still in my office, but I had my home calls switched here. What can I do for you?"

"I—I don't really want to talk over the phone. Could we possibly meet? I mean, just for a drink somewhere?"

"This week, you mean?" He didn't sound particularly enthusiastic.

"I was hoping . . . tonight."

"Sorry. I'm all booked up tonight."

She felt tears of disappointment forming at the back of her throat. "Of course you are," she said brightly. "Sorry to have bothered you. Maybe some other time."

"Erin."

"Yes?"

"It sounds important."

She swallowed down the lump in her throat. "You can say that again."

"I can be in Richmond by, say, just after ten, if that's okay."

For a moment, Erin couldn't speak. The thought of actually seeing him again, of being able to share all her concerns about Giles with him, rushed over her like a tidal wave. "Thanks, David," was all she could say.

"If you don't mind, I don't feel like a session with Samantha and Adam, so I won't come in. I'll meet you outside the house at ten-fifteen. Then we can walk across the green to the White Swan or some other pub by the river. Okay?"

"Perfect." She hesitated. "Thank you."

"See you at ten-fifteen."

Thank God Samantha was out or she would surely have driven her nuts, advising her on what to wear and what to say. Since Erin had spoken to her about her real reason for having wanted to go to Amberley, Samantha had been commiserating with her on losing David and kept making suggestions as to how to go about achieving a reconciliation with him. "You won't get anywhere just sitting around being miserable, you know," she'd said just that morning.

Although Samantha would probably not have agreed, Erin decided that casual wear was the best for a drink at a local pub. It was a cool night with a hint of rain in the air. She pulled on the linen pants and scarlet sweater she'd worn on Sunday morning. The morning she had found a grandfather and lost her chance of developing a relationship with David.

She gazed at herself in the white-and-gilt oval mirror that stood in a corner of the bedroom. The red sweater looked good on her, enhancing her dark hair and amber eyes. The eyes themselves were not so good: the eyelids puffy and pink. The last few days had been an emotional roller-coaster.

The hair wasn't that great, either. Damp weather always tightened it up, making it go curly. "Let's face it, Erin Benson, you're a mess," she told her reflection.

But, what the heck? This meeting with David was about Giles, not her. About her grandfather.

When she went out to the driveway at ten minutes past ten, she could see that David was already there, waiting for her outside the wrought-iron gate, his umbrella open. It was raining quite hard now.

"You'll need a coat or an umbrella," he said when he looked up and saw her standing in the driveway.

She was about to say, "That's okay. We can share your umbrella," but decided against it. If he'd wanted to do that, he would have made the suggestion himself. She went back inside to grab her rain jacket from the wooden coat stand in the hall and a black umbrella from the huge blue-and-white Chinese vase that acted as an umbrella stand.

It was only when she'd locked the front door again and wrestled the umbrella open that she discovered it was broken. Four ribs were bent and the fabric torn, so that only half the umbrella gave her protection. The other half dangled precariously close to her face, threatening to poke out an eye.

She opened the gate. "Hello," she said, feeling as embarrassed as a teenager on her first date. "Oh! You're all dressed up." Beneath his open raincoat, David was wearing a formal dark suit with a striped shirt and green silk tie.

"I came straight from a meeting," he explained. "No time to change."

The formality of his clothes was matched by the tone of his voice. All crisp and businesslike.

"Should I change?" Erin asked.

"Why? You look fine as you are. Let's go before the pubs close." As they started off across the large expanse of green, he glanced at her umbrella, noting the dead half flapping against her face. "Maybe we should change umbrellas," he suggested.

"No, I'm fine," Erin said. "You're the one who needs the good umbrella."

"Very well."

They marched across Richmond Green—their umbrellas touching every now and then—and then turned down a narrow lane that led to the river. When they reached the low white walls surrounding the old, timber-framed inn, they could see it wasn't going to do. It was so crowded that there were people actually perched on the walls, holding their glasses.

Only the English would sit and drink outside in the pouring rain, Erin thought.

"This is bloody ridiculous," David said.

Erin's heart sank. She had wanted so much for their meeting to be a friendly one, free of any fraught emotions, but David was growing increasingly annoyed.

"Wait here," he told her. "I'm going to get the car."

"The rain doesn't bother me," Erin insisted.

"Well, it bothers me. See if you can get inside in the dry. I'm parked just a few minutes away from here." He walked away before she could say any more. She watched him until he had disappeared around a bend in the lane.

She didn't want to go inside. She stood beneath the low eaves of the pub, which seemed to afford more water than shelter, listening to the sounds of exuberant talking and laughter from inside. The conviviality of the brightly lit interior was a stark contrast to the darkness outside, with its dismal patter of rain, the constant gurgle of water in the gutters, and the knowledge that her new red suede sandals were going to be ruined.

When she saw David rounding the corner, she had an impulse to run to him and throw her arms around him.

"I've parked at the top of the lane in a no-parking zone. I hope to God I don't get a ticket."

He started off again before he reached her, striding ahead of her up the lane, so that Erin almost had to break into a run to keep pace with him. "Okay," he said with a whistle of relief, when he reached his car. He opened the passenger door for her. Then he went around to the driver's side, jumping in and hurriedly driving off before she had time even to fasten her seat belt.

"Are they that sticky about parking here?" she asked, aware of the edge in her voice.

"They certainly are. It's the wheel-clamping that's a real pain."

"Wheel-clamping?"

"Yes. They put a device on the car-wheel. Not only does it mean you can't drive the car, but you have to try and find the place where you pay the fine . . . and then wait, sometimes for hours, for them to come and take the clamp off."

"Oh. No wonder you were worried about parking."

"Parking in a no-parking zone is breaking the law," he said in a somber voice.

For a moment Erin thought he was joking, but when she glanced at him she could see he wasn't.

It struck her that she was seeing the other side of David, entertainment lawyer, tonight. Last week she'd seen the entertainment half of him. Tonight she was seeing the lawyer half.

As he drove away from the green, she sat in silence, the water from the sodden umbrella she was still holding soaking into her legs and forming a puddle at her feet. Without any warning, tears began rolling down her cheeks.

Don't worry, she told herself. *Your face is so wet, he won't notice.* He probably wouldn't notice even if her face wasn't wet.

But he did. As they drove up to the top of Richmond

Hill he said, very quietly, "Don't cry, Erin. It can't be that bad."

"It is," she sobbed, furious with herself for breaking down like this. "It damn well is."

He drew over to the side of the road and stopped.

"Are you sure you won't get a parking ticket here?" she asked, her voice heavy with sarcasm.

"Yes. " He put out his left hand to touch her shoulder. "God! You're absolutely soaked."

"I know. It's gone right through my jacket."

"No wonder, with that light nylon thing. That's no use in this sort of rain." He thought for a moment. "We'd better go back to Samantha's."

"No, I don't want to." The thought of not being able to share her concern about Giles with him made her feel panicky.

"Why not? You're soaking wet."

"I don't want to go back. I have to talk to you."

"Okay, okay. But we must get in somewhere warm, so you can dry out. Are you hungry?"

"Not very. Why?"

"There's a cozy little Italian restaurant halfway down the hill. Why don't we go there? What you need is a bottle of vino rossi and a plate of pasta."

As soon as he said it, Erin knew that was exactly what she needed. A warm restaurant, pasta, wine ... and David. As she shivered inside the car, it sounded like heaven. "That sounds good. But with our luck, it'll be closed."

"I never took you for a pessimist."

"I'm not usually."

The restaurant wasn't closed. As David opened the door for her, the warmth—and the fragrance of basil and tomato, with a hint of garlic—enfolded her.

"Ah," she breathed. "This *is* heaven."

A little man bustled forward, the tight black waistcoat emphasizing his rotund figure. *"Buona sera, signor, signorina. Come sta?"*

"Very wet," was David's reply.

The man made sympathetic sounds as he removed Erin's jacket and David's raincoat. David put his umbrella into the stand at the door. Then he took Erin's umbrella, which she was holding away from her. "This is for the rubbish bin," he told the man, who appeared to be the proprietor.

"I throw it away for you, signor."

"We'd like a table for two in a warm, quiet corner, please."

"I 'ave the perfect place for you."

He did, too. Tucked away in the warmest place, near the kitchen, but in a cozy corner, partly hidden by green climbing plants. Real ones, too, Erin noted with approval, when she pressed her fingers into the planter.

As she sank onto the padded chair she released her breath in a long sigh.

"You look as if you're half drowned," David said.

"Thanks a lot. That makes me feel really great." Erin ran her hands through her wet hair. It was a mess of tight curls. "Oh yuck," she said.

For the first time since they'd met that evening he smiled. "I like it like that." He put his hand out as if he was about to touch her arm, and then stopped, his face slightly flushed. "Your sweater must be damp."

Erin shrugged. "It's not too bad. It's just that my hair is dripping down my neck."

"Let's see if we can get a towel."

Within a minute David had summoned the proprietor and procured a towel to dry her hair. Erin went through the door marked *Donne*. When she looked at herself in the mirror she rolled her eyes. David was right. She did look half drowned. Moreover, her mascara had run in streaks down her face and she hadn't a scrap of lipstick left on.

Good thing they weren't interested in each other, romantically speaking, anymore. If they had been, David might have thought twice when he saw her looking like this.

She scrubbed her hair ruthlessly until her scalp hurt and then dragged her comb through the tangles, making her eyes water. Then she washed off the mascara and applied just a touch of lipstick.

Suddenly she was ravenously hungry. Whatever she had lost with David, at least she knew that she could trust him and that he would share her concern about Giles.

Taking one last look at her scrubbed face and glistening hair, she pushed open the door and went back to their table.

Chapter Twenty-six

"Feel better?" David asked.

Erin nodded.

"I went ahead and ordered some wine," he said. "Bardolino. Hope that's okay."

"That's great."

"Let's wait until we've ordered before we talk, okay?"

Erin nodded again. She felt as if she were floating comfortably, suspended in limbo. The rain seemed to have washed away all the stress, leaving her interested in only the basic needs: warmth and food . . . and love.

David gave her a quizzical look. "I'm not sure you'd be capable of talking, anyway. Are you still with me?"

"Just about. Sorry if I'm not very good company."

David didn't respond to that. He picked up the menu. "So, what are you going to have?"

"Spaghetti Bolognese."

"Is that it? They've got two pages of things here. Some lemon veal, perhaps? Maybe start with minestrone to warm you up?"

"I have a yearning for spaghetti. Comfort food."

Again, he made no comment, but scanned the menu. Erin noticed how the light shining down on him turned his brown hair to the color of ripe chestnuts. She felt a pang of deep sadness around her heart. So much to learn about this man and no time left to do so.

Once the food came, the conversation was very general on David's part, desultory on hers. But as soon as her appetite was satisfied, her concerns seeped back. By the time she was sipping her cappuccino and nibbling the almond biscotti that came with it, she was impatient to share her worries with David.

He sat now with his long legs stretched out beside the

table, one arm dangling over the chair back. The wine and warmth had relaxed him, which made it easier for Erin to turn to the subject that was again uppermost in her mind.

"Before I tell you what's worrying me, will you let me just say one thing about what happened at Amberley? *Please*," she added when she saw closure in his expression.

He shrugged. "If you must."

"I'll keep it brief." She looked down at the chocolate shavings floating in her cappuccino. "I never meant to use you to get into Amberley. I had just hoped you might give me information about the family." She shot him a quick glance and then looked down again. "You know why now. When you invited me to Amberley it seemed like, literally, a heaven-sent opportunity. I felt it was meant to be. Preordained." She gave a wry, embarrassed grin. "Sounds stupid, I know. But that's how I felt. My father's death, followed by my mother's breakdown had really affected me . . ."

He frowned down at his small cup of espresso.

"Sorry. That's dirty tactics, making you feel sorry for me. You get the picture, anyway."

"I do. I understand why you did it, but not why you didn't tell me. But we've been through all that before."

Erin felt like screaming. A typical male. No wish to talk it out until the puzzle was solved.

"Obviously something new has occurred," David said. "What?"

"Simon." Erin told him about his visit to Samantha's boss. "I was amazed. I thought he'd want everything kept quiet."

"He obviously believes that the best defense lies in attack. That way he takes away your credibility before you spread the truth." David's lips twitched into an ironic smile. "That's why Simon is where he is today. He knows exactly how to play these games."

"There's more."

"I thought there might me."

Erin flared. "This isn't funny."

"I didn't think it was."

"I'm worried about Lord Maybridge."

"Giles?" David frowned.

"Before we said good-bye on Sunday, I asked him if my mother could come and see him."

"I thought your mother was still in Canada?"

"Yes, but she's planning to fly over." Erin clasped her hands together and leaned across the table. "I've been trying to contact Giles since Monday, David. First Mrs. Edwards answered me and told me he was resting. The second time she told me that he was sick and that I must speak to Simon if I wanted to know any more. The third time I called, this morning, they had the answering machine turned on and—"

"They don't have an answering machine at Amberley. Giles loathes the things."

"They do now," Erin said grimly. "Am I being paranoid?"

"No, I don't think you are, really. Either Giles is genuinely ill or you're being blocked from speaking to him."

A relieved smile spread across Erin's face. "How wonderful to hear my two fears put so concisely. I thought lawyers were supposed to be wordy."

"I've had to learn not to be. Many of my clients don't understand words of more than one syllable."

"Oh, David, you're so good for me," Erin said spontaneously, with a gurgle of laughter. Then, for an instant, she squeezed her eyes shut, remembering.

"Have you spoken to Simon?" David asked.

"No. Frankly, I wouldn't know what to say to him."

"You could ask him how Giles is. Tell him that Mrs. Edwards had told you he was ill. It would be natural for you to want to find out how he is."

"He'd tell me it was none of my business. Oh, very smoothly, of course. Samantha said she found him charming. It wasn't until he'd gone that she discovered what he'd done."

David folded his red gingham napkin into a neat triangle and then unfolded it again.

"I—I thought that as you know Simon so well you might try to find out what's happening," Erin said, the words coming in little jerks of hesitation. "I mean, I'd engage you professionally, as my legal representative, of course."

David looked down at his wineglass. "I'm sorry, Erin. I can't act for you."

"Because you're related to the Hogarths, you mean?"

"Exactly. It would be unethical for me to act against my own family."

"Ha! Some family! I mean yours is a pretty remote connection, isn't it?"

His face tightened, so that his strong jawline became more prominent, and she caught a glimpse of a resemblance to Giles. "Not so remote that I would act against them."

Erin was suddenly furious. "If you're so worried about your family, then you should be concerned about Giles."

"I am concerned. I intend to inquire into it first thing tomorrow."

"Good."

"But I'm afraid that doesn't necessarily mean that I shall pass on any information I receive to you."

Erin felt as if she'd been punched in the stomach. "I see."

Frowning, he leaned forward. "No, I don't think you do see. I'm glad that you told me about all this. It's important that I find out whether Giles is genuinely ill or not."

"Have you considered that if Giles isn't sick, things are being done without his knowledge?" Erin hotly demanded.

"And have you considered that, after you left, Giles might have regretted his decision to accept his illegitimate daughter at Amberley?" David's coolness was the very antithesis of Erin's heat. "And that it's on his orders that you're being prevented from speaking to him?"

Erin was about to blurt something out, but the words never came. Their eyes met. Slowly, she shook her head. "No, I hadn't thought of that at all. He—he seemed so glad to hear that his daughter was alive, after believing she'd died fifty years ago." Her eyes filled with tears. "Oh, David, could that be it, that he's had second thoughts and he doesn't want to see me again—or my mother?"

"I'm afraid that's a possibility you must consider," he said gently.

"Oh, God," she said, suddenly remembering. "What am I going to do? My mother's arriving on Monday. I can't tell you what an effort she's made, how courageous it is for someone who's been battling agoraphobia to make a transatlantic flight on her own. If her father were to reject her before he'd even met her, it could be a huge setback for her."

The restaurant proprietor was hovering anxiously near them. "Something wrong? Would you like more cappuccino?"

"No, thank you," Erin said, her face averted from him.

"I give you a Sambuca, *sí*? On the house." He bustled away before they could reply.

"I'd rather know the truth than have my mother fly over and Giles refuse to see her. I *must* know before she leaves Winnipeg on Sunday. Will you call Simon for me, David? Please."

A mixture of emotions seemed to be vying for expression. "I'm sorry, Erin," he said, at last. "I'll call Simon, but I can't do it primarily for you. In other words, whatever I find out, my loyalty has to be to the family first."

"I see." Erin sat staring at him. "Well, at least I know exactly where I stand, don't I?" She pushed back the chair and stood up.

"Surely you understand, Erin," David protested. "It's a question of ethics."

"Oh, I understand, all right." She took her jacket from the coat stand and pulled it on, her skin shrinking against the chill wetness. "The Hogarths all stick together, whatever dirty business one of them is involved in." Her eyes blazed at him. "That's why my mother was sent to Canada alone at the age of five with a false name and address."

David was on his feet. "You don't understand."

"Oh, I understand, all right!" Erin said, marching to the door.

"Hang on," he shouted after her. "I have to pay the bill."

The proprietor came bustling back, carrying a lacquered tray with two narrow glasses of Sambuca, blue flame leaping on the surface of the liquid.

"You haven't had your Sambuca," he cried.

"I'm sorry," David said. "We have to go. Just the bill, please."

The man shrugged and went away muttering beneath his breath. Erin came back to the table. Without saying a word, she opened her bag and took her credit card from her wallet.

"Put that away," David said.

"No, I asked you to meet me, so I pay."

"The restaurant was my idea. Don't insult me, please." David spoke in a low, taut voice as the owner returned.

As soon as David had paid the bill, they left, walking along the rain-slick sidewalk as far apart as possible.

"I can walk back to the house," Erin said when they reached David's car. "It's only a few minutes away."

"Just get in," David said, flinging open the door.

Erin did as she was told, knowing that he wouldn't let her walk back to the house on her own. He drove down the road to Richmond Green like a maniac. Where was the law-abiding lawyer now? Erin thought, but she wasn't smiling. She felt sick at heart. They were further apart than ever.

David pulled the car up a short way from Samantha's house. Erin felt even more sick when she saw Samantha's Lancia in the driveway.

"Samantha's home," David said.

"So I see." The thought of having to face Samantha's questions and another tirade about Simon's visit was too much. She turned in panic to David. "I'm sorry. I just can't go in yet."

His answer was to gather her in his arms and crush her against him. For a moment she thought she was about to break into a thousand pieces. Then, as his mouth came down on hers, she relaxed and her body changed from brittle glass to molten liquidity.

"Oh, Erin," he whispered against her mouth. "My sweet, darling Erin. Please forgive me." He kissed her feverishly, his mouth moving down her neck to the hollow in her throat. She cradled his head in her hands, pressing him closer. His hand found the zipper of her jacket and he tugged at it. She helped him open it. Then his hands were on her breasts, inflaming her with delight, his head bending to kiss them—

An arc of brilliant light ran over the interior of the car, illuminating it.

"Christ!" David exclaimed and they sprang apart, Erin ramming her elbow against the dashboard as she struggled to drag down her sweater.

Chapter Twenty-seven

Flashlight in hand, a policeman stood grinning at them, jerking his thumb in a motion that indicated they should get the hell out of there, and then resumed his beat.

Erin clamped her hand over her mouth. "Oh, my God!" she said, and promptly dissolved into a paroxysm of giggles.

"I'm glad you find it so amusing," David said, himself trying not to laugh. "I hope to God he didn't take my number."

"Oh, for heaven's sake, David. Who cares? Lawyers can have their fun as well, can't they?"

"Yes, but not out in public." He grinned at her. "You're bad for me, Erin Benson, that's what you are."

"Am I?" She gazed at him, her expression suddenly serious. "Can you forgive me for what happened?"

"Just now, you mean? I'm not sure. My reputation may be completely shot."

Erin wasn't sure whether she should take him seriously or not. "No, you idiot. What happened at Amberley, I mean."

"Oh, I see. I guess I can. I suppose I must have."

She grinned. "Oh, I don't know. Perhaps what happened now was just the heat of the moment."

"You can say that again. All I know is that I can't bear to have you mad at me." He took her face between his hands and kissed her, his lips moving gently over hers.

Erin's eyes fluttered closed and, for a moment, everything else was forgotten. "Better watch it or the cop will give us a ticket,' she said eventually, when she needed to breathe.

"You're right. I hate to leave you, though."

She drew away from him. "What's going to happen to us, David?"

"What do you mean?"

"I'm not sure I know what I mean, really." She gazed into his eyes, which were like deep highland pools in the light of the street lamp. "Yes, I am. If Giles doesn't want to have anything to do with us, I'll have to tell my mother. If that happens, I must fly back to Winnipeg as soon as possible to explain everything to her properly."

"When?"

"I'm booked to go home on Friday. I haven't changed that flight yet. I was waiting to make sure my mother was definitely coming."

"I'll call Simon." David glanced at his watch. "I'm afraid it's too late to call tonight. I'll call him first thing tomorrow morning."

"Thank you. I know you can't communicate everything to me," she added hurriedly. "But I am genuinely worried about Giles, just in case he really is sick."

"I understand that. I'll do my best to get the truth from Simon." He hesitated, and then said, "I'm in the devil of a position there."

"So you keep telling me. I know, I know," she added, before he could chime in. "The family honor and all that."

"Family honor dictates also that I make sure Giles isn't being manipulated by Simon." Again, he hesitated.

"There's something else, isn't there?" Erin said.

"Yes. Something that anyone could know if they wished to, but which I prefer to be kept quiet."

"That sounds very mysterious. Am I to know what this other family secret is?"

"It's not really a secret, but I'd prefer that it not be discussed with others."

"Like Samantha, for instance?"

"Particularly Samantha. Actually, I'm surprised it wasn't brought up by the media when Simon made his announcement about giving up the title when Giles dies."

"You have me bursting with curiosity. Tell me." Then, catching that wary look in his eyes, "Okay, okay. I promise not to mention it to anyone else. Cross my heart."

"The main reason for my reluctance to make inquiries into what's going on at Amberley is that I am Simon's heir."

Erin stared at him. "What do you mean, Simon's heir?"

"I mean that, after Simon, I'm the next in line to the Maybridge title."

"But . . . I don't understand. Simon has two children."

"Both daughters. The title and all the estates that go with it are entailed so that only male heirs can inherit."

"How disgustingly sexist! You mean that when Giles dies, Simon inherits the title—"

"Which he intends to renounce."

"So I understand. Can he actually do that?"

"He can, once Giles is dead, but he can only say he *intends* to give it up until then. Hence the big announcement to the media."

"He couldn't become Prime Minister if he were an earl?"

"He couldn't even sit in the House of Commons. Only in the House of Lords. So he definitely couldn't be the Prime Minister."

"I'm sorry if I'm being a bit dense, but why are you Simon's heir, when you're such a remote relative?"

"Because I'm the only male who's directly descended from a previous earl. Although Lucy's father was a second son, *his* father—Lucy's grandfather—was the twelfth Earl of Maybridge. As her grandson, therefore, I am a direct descendant."

"You mean you could become an earl?"

"Yes. Amazing, isn't it? My American ancestors would turn in their graves."

"But if Simon gives up the title, doesn't that mean you get it when Giles dies?"

"No. I can only inherit the title if Simon dies before me and doesn't leave a son."

"Oh, I see. If Simon has a son—"

"Simon's son will inherit on Simon's death."

"Even if Simon has given up the title."

"Right. He can only give the title up for himself, not for his heirs."

"Ah, now I understand. I think." Her lips flickered

into a little smile. "I also understand why you were so reluctant to get involved in my problems."

"It makes it a trifle awkward, to say the least."

"Hey! Hang on a minute. Why didn't you tell me this before?"

"What?"

"That you were the heir, that's what! You accuse me of keeping secrets from you. What about you? This one's a pretty big one, I would have thought."

"The windows are getting all misted up," David said.

"Don't change the subject."

"That policeman will be coming back soon. I'd rather be out of here when he does." He raised his hands in mock defense. "Okay, okay. You're right. We both kept secrets from each other. No doubt for the same reason: that we didn't know each other well enough to know if we could trust each other, right?"

"Exactly."

"Well, now we're quits."

Erin gazed at him. "I can't tell you how much better it makes me feel to hear you say that," she said softly. Suddenly she shot up in her seat. "Wow!"

"What?"

"I've just realized that you could inherit Amberley. Lucky you!"

"Not necessarily."

"I thought all the estates went with the title."

"No, only those that were part of the title when it was bestowed on the first earl."

"Wasn't Amberley part of them?"

"No, it wasn't even built at that time. It came into the family in the seventeenth century. Some wealthy bride brought it into the family as her dowry. It's highly probable that it will be part of the inherited estate, but if Giles wanted to he could leave it to, say, one of Simon's daughters. But, knowing Giles, that's highly unlikely. He wouldn't want to break up the estate. Particularly as he knows that the property attached to the title is worthless. A rackety old castle in Yorkshire and a few houses on the castle estate that cost more for upkeep than they are worth."

Erin thought for a minute, trying to digest all that

David had told her. "Do you realize that we're related?" she said suddenly.

"The thought had occurred to me."

"It's not a close relationship, though, is it?"

David smiled. "I haven't had time to work it out precisely. But we must be very distant cousins, I should think."

"Good." Through the rain-streaked windows she caught sight of a figure coming toward them. "Oh, God! Here's that policeman again."

David hurriedly started the engine and drove off. "I'll drive right round the green and then I'll drop you off. I'll do my best to get hold of Simon tomorrow. As soon as I speak to him, I'll call you."

Erin noticed he made no mention of family loyalty this time. "David, would you do one more thing for me?"

"What?"

"In all this worry about Giles, I've totally forgotten the real reason I came to England."

"Oh, no," David groaned. "What now?"

"What I really came to England for was to find my mother's *mother*. Her father was a sort of secondary quest. Giles is convinced that she died in the blitz. Would you do something for me?"

"I'll try, but a search for a missing person takes a long time, you know."

"I think I know a shortcut. Would you ask you grandmother if she knew Mary Foley and her daughter, Kate?"

"I'm not sure Lucy would have been at Amberley when—"

"I'm sure she was. After all, Mary must have been working there for a while before she and Giles became lovers, and then she stayed on at Amberley—or, at least, in a cottage on the estate—for five years after Katie was born. Your grandmother must surely have known them for some of that time."

"I'll ask her, but you know Lucy. She's not particularly reliable when it comes to memory, sad to say."

"You never know. She might come up with something that would help."

"What exactly are you looking for? I thought that

you'd be satisfied with finding your mother's father and her birthplace."

"I won't be satisfied until I discover what happened to her mother. After all, there's a chance she might still be alive."

"Only a very slim one, considering no one's ever heard from her." David peered through the windshield. "Once more around the block?" he asked.

"No, I think we'd better stop or that policeman will get really suspicious. Will you ask Lucy for me? *Please*, David?"

"How can I resist when you ask me so nicely? Okay. I'll ask her. Mary Foley, right?"

"And her little girl Kate or Katie. That was my mother."

"Right. Will do." David drew up once more outside Samantha's house. "Good night." He smiled at her, a slow, warm smile that spread across his face. "I'm glad you called me."

"I'm glad I did, too." Erin leaned toward him and kissed him, his lips infinitely warm beneath hers. Despite the rain and the policeman—and all her worries about Giles—she felt quite zingy with happiness.

David suddenly pulled away from her. "Uh-oh! Here he is again. You'd better get out fast." The policeman halted, flashlight at the ready, as Erin hopped out of the car.

David leaned from his window. "Good evening, officer."

"Evening, sir, miss. Rather a damp night, eh?" The officer grinned at them both through the pouring rain. "You live here, miss?" he asked, as Erin walked to Samantha's gate.

"Yes, I'm staying with friends," she told him, trying to look him straight in the eye without showing any embarrassment. Fortunately, the rain would help to hide her face.

"And their name would be?"

"Samantha Wakeley and her husband Adam Friedman," David supplied.

"Right. She's a famous television interviewer, isn't she? My missus and I really liked that program of hers that was on a couple of years ago. What was it called? *The Best of British Luck.* Something like that."

"Good night officer," David said, starting up his engine again. Then, to Erin, "Better get inside quickly or you'll get soaked again."

Taking the hint, Erin pushed open the gate and dashed up the driveway, aware that the policeman stood there, stolidly watching her, until she had opened the door and stepped inside.

Chapter Twenty-eight

Next day, Erin stayed at home the entire morning, waiting for David to call her. Fortunately, the rain had ceased, so she was able to sit at the end of the garden, with the portable telephone beside her. She found that watching the waters of the Thames flowing past soothed her. The heavy rain had caused the wide river to overflow its banks and flood the towpath, so that no one could walk along it. For once, she felt she had the river all to herself.

Each time the telephone rang she answered it after the first ring, her heartbeat increasing. So far, all the calls had been for Samantha or Adam. After taking down several messages for them, many of them from different European countries—with occasional difficulties in communication—she began to think she should switch on the answering machine and sit in the office beside it, monitoring the calls.

She had gone inside to prepare lunch for herself when David called. "Hang on a minute," she told him. "I'll take this through to the sitting room so I can sit down."

Her heart raced as she hurried into the other room. She wasn't sure if it was excitement at the anticipation of his news or the mere sound of his voice. A combination of both, she suspected. She made herself comfortable on the sofa, stretching out with two cushions behind her head, and then picked up the sitting room telephone receiver. "Okay, I'm ready."

"What did you do, go and wash you hair or something?"

"No," she said indignantly. "I didn't want to stand in the kitchen with a chopping knife in one hand and the phone in the other. Besides, that portable phone crackles. Any news?"

"I'm afraid I'm not getting very far with Giles. It's hard to get by an answering machine. I left a message with Simon's secretary, but he said he might be tied up until tomorrow afternoon."

"I wish he *was* tied up!" Erin was deeply disappointed. She'd thought that getting David involved would bring quick results. "What are we going to do about Giles? I mean if he's really sick, I'd like to know."

"Frankly, so would I. The old man and I don't get on that well, but I'd still like to find out if there's anything the matter with him. I tried Olivia at home, but I got her answering machine, too. I'll try her again later."

"You're not likely to get anything from her. If Simon's up to something, she's not likely to tell you, is she?"

"That depends. I think she would tell me if Giles were genuinely ill. I'm also going to try his doctor. He won't give me personal details, of course, but, again, he might be willing to tell me if he wasn't well."

"So we're not any further than we were before, are we?"

"I'm afraid not. But I'm sure we'll hear something soon. By the way, I have to go to Knightsbridge this afternoon, so I'm going to drop in on Lucy after lunch."

"Oh, great. Would you let me know if she comes up with anything promising?"

"I will. You haven't phoned your mother yet, have you?"

"No. I don't want to. Not until I'm absolutely certain that Giles won't see her."

"The day's not over yet. I may get some information back this afternoon. Will you be around?"

"I'm staying in all day, just in case."

"Okay." There was a moment of hesitation. Then he said in a voice that was far less businesslike and infinitely warmer, "I'm glad we're friends again."

Erin cradled the phone against her. "So am I. Thanks for being so understanding."

"Thank *you*. Speak to you later. Hang in there."

"I will. 'Bye." Erin put down the phone, hating to be cut off from him. She wanted to talk to him for hours, ask him all sorts of questions about himself and his family, his likes and dislikes. She wanted to get to know the real David Lennox.

While she was waiting to hear from him again, she tried to fill the time by preparing a salad for dinner and then trying to tidy the house a little, but *that* was a daunting task. No wonder Samantha had to pay Max so much. Every surface seemed to be covered with glossy magazines: *Options, Tatler, Harpers & Queen* . . . and all kinds of newspapers, and open books piled on top of one another.

Eventually she gave up and went for a long walk up Richmond Hill to the terrace gardens and then walked down the other side of the hill, and back to Richmond across Petersham Meadows. She was surprised at how rural the scene was, with cows grazing in the lush grass by the river, and hens scratching in a farmyard nearby. Hard to believe that this was actually part of Greater London.

When she got back, pleasantly tired from the long walk, she switched on the television in the library. She was watching a rerun of *Absolutely Fabulous* when David rang again.

"Are you free this evening?" was his greeting.

"Yes. Why? What's happened?"

"Regarding Giles, nothing much. Olivia's still out. I got the au pair or nanny or whatever you want to call her. She said Olivia was at some committee meeting. And I'm waiting for Giles's doctor to call me back."

"How disappointing!"

"Yes, it is. Back to tonight, though. I thought you might like to have a quick meal somewhere and then go and visit Lucy."

Erin sensed a hint of mystery in his voice. "Your grandmother's told you something, hasn't she?" she said, her voice rising with excitement.

"I'm not sure, really," said David, the ever-cautious lawyer. "I don't want you to get your hopes up, only to find that Lucy's making up a complete fairy story."

"I was right," Erin said triumphantly. "She did know Mary Foley, didn't she?"

"She *says* she did. She says she also knew little Katie.

But, knowing Lucy, she may be saying that just for the hell of it. She told me a great many things that sound extremely far-fetched to me. I'd prefer it if you asked her the questions. That way you can judge which is truth and which fantasy."

"Oh, David! I can't believe I might be close to finding out what happened to Mom's mother."

"Just so long as you take everything she says with a pinch of salt, okay?"

"Okay." As David was telling her which train to catch from Richmond Station and where exactly he would meet her, Erin kept grinning to herself. Nothing could mar her optimism, not even her concern about Giles.

Lucy lived in the first-floor flat of a slightly decayed but still elegant Georgian house in Kensington.

She greeted them at the door, dressed in a blue-and-white chiffon dress, which would have been eminently suitable for a royal garden party at Buckingham Palace. "Come in, come in," she said, peering past them to look into the hallway. "No one else with you, is there?" She shut the door even before David had said, "No. Just Erin and me."

She frowned at Erin, her eyelashes, which bore clumps of mascara, fluttering. "I'm not sure I should be doing this," she muttered. She slapped David on the hand. "It's all your fault, you naughty boy. You shouldn't have forced me into it."

"No one's forcing you into anything." David put his arm around her shoulders. "Why don't you take Erin into your lovely front room and show her the view?"

"Don't try to change the subject, David Lennox," she told him. Grumbling beneath her breath, she led them into the sitting room. "David wants you to see the view," she said, moving to the tall sash window and pulling back the faded green velvet curtain.

Erin looked down and saw, across the curving street, a little park surrounded by wrought-iron railings. It looked very peaceful, the leafy trees shading the lawns and flower beds. With its wooden benches and little pathways it would be a lovely oasis on hot summer days. "How lovely. Is it a public park?"

"Certainly not," Lucy said, glaring at her. "If it were, it would be full of druggies and bag-snatchers. It's a private park for only those people who live on the crescent."

"How do you get into it?"

"With a key, of course. There's a gate farther down." Lucy turned abruptly. "You can serve the drinks, David. I'll have my usual scotch and water. What about you, Miss Benson?"

"I don't suppose you have a lager, do you?"

"Of course I do. Mabel bought some at the off-license for David. By the way, David, bring in the plate that's in the fridge. Mabel made some canapés. Sardine and tomato, I think. But I'm not sure if they came from the tin we opened for the cats. They don't look very appetizing."

"We've just eaten," Erin said hurriedly. She caught David's amused glance as he passed her to go to the kitchen, and found it hard to keep a straight face.

"Still have to eat them or you'll hurt Mabel's feelings." Lucy sank into a high-backed chair, draping her layers of chiffon about her. She lifted her legs, which were remarkably shapely, onto a footstool covered with needlepoint. "Don't hover, girl. Sit down."

Erin sat in the nearest chair, a love seat covered in cotton chintz and an abundance of cat hair. "What a lovely footstool," she said. "Did you make it yourself?"

"I did. Years ago. Needlepoint was one of the useless things I was taught by my governess at Amberley. My eyes aren't as good now as they used to be. But you didn't come here to talk about my needlework, did you?"

Erin gave her a rueful smile. "I suppose not."

David came back with a tray of drinks and the plate of canapés. Lucy was right. They didn't look at all appetizing.

"David has told me quite an incredible story," Lucy said, when she'd taken a large gulp of her drink. "He says that you are Mary Foley's daughter."

"Her granddaughter. My mother was—"

"Yes, yes, yes." Lucy waved her hand impatiently. "That's what I meant. What proof have you?"

"A photograph." Erin took it from her wallet and handed it to Lucy, who peered at it.

"Hmm! So this is what you gave Giles, eh?"

Erin nodded.

"Foolish girl. He could have had a heart attack on the spot."

"In retrospect, I agree with you. But I didn't know how else to approach him."

"After some of his money, are you?"

David spoke before Erin had time to respond. "That's not very nice, Grandmama."

"Nice or not, it's what everyone will think." Lucy turned to Erin. "Are you?"

"After Lord Maybridge's money? No. In fact, I never thought of that at all until Simon asked me the same question."

"He would, of course. Why did you come to Amberley, then? It's going to cause a lot of trouble, you know."

"Do you think so?"

"Oh, yes. Bound to."

Erin looked at David. "Did you tell your grandmother that I can't get through to Giles?"

"He did," Lucy said. "Can't say I'm surprised."

"Well, I certainly was," Erin said. "Do you think that Giles doesn't want to speak to me or see me?"

"Of course."

Erin swallowed hard. "I am sorry," she said, when she felt it was safe to speak. "I just don't understand. He seemed to be so pleased when I told him who I was. Of course, it must have been quite a surprise, considering he'd always thought that Mary and Katie had been killed in 1940."

"Yes, well we know who was responsible for that little story, don't we? That cow of a mother of his. She certainly spun him a fine tale of woe, didn't she?"

Erin's eyes widened. "Did David tell you about that?"

"He didn't need to. I knew already."

"You knew? But . . . why didn't you tell Giles the truth when he came back from the war?"

"Because I didn't know then, did I?" Lucy put a

trembling hand to her forehead. "All these questions are making me very tired."

Erin darted a dismayed look at David.

David leaned forward. "Erin wants you to tell her about Mary and her daughter," he said to Lucy.

"Mary who?"

"Mary Foley. She was a housemaid at Amberley, right?" David prompted. "Was she pretty?"

Lucy tapped at the photograph on the table in front of her. "You can see she was. Fresh-faced. Glossy black hair and great brown eyes. But I don't care how pretty she was. Giles was still a fool," she said, her voice full of scorn.

"Why?" Erin asked.

"You don't set a maidservant up in a cottage on the family estate, do you?"

Erin lifted her chin. "You might, if you loved her."

"Stuff and nonsense. Caused all kinds of trouble, just like you're doing, missy."

"I didn't come to Amberley to cause trouble, Mrs. Lennox." Erin was fighting to hold back her anger. "I came to right a wrong. My mother was abandoned by her parents, sent to Canada with a false address."

"Giles and Mary knew nothing about that. Giles was the heir. He had to make a decent marriage. They had to send his mistress and child away."

"You mean Giles's parents had to get rid of Mary and Katie, right?"

Lucy frowned, peering at her through the clotted eyelashes. "Does Giles know you're here?"

"No, he doesn't. I told you, I've been trying—"

"He'd never forgive me if he knew I was speaking of this to you. I promised him I wouldn't tell anyone. He said I'd never be able to see Amberley and Topsy again if I told." Her hands clutched at her skirt, twisting the filmy chiffon of her skirt tightly between her fingers.

Impulsively, Erin went to kneel beside her, loosening the crumpled fabric from the agitated fingers and trying to smooth it out. Then she took Lucy's hands in hers. "You haven't told me anything I didn't know before," she said softly, "apart from the fact that you knew Mary and Katie, and I guessed that you probably did know them."

Tears began to roll down the old lady's cheeks, moisture trapped in the wrinkles. "And she'd never forgive me, either."

"*Who* wouldn't?"

"She's my only friend from the old days. I promised her I'd never tell anyone, not even Giles, poor fellow. But how could I tell him, anyway? Think of what would happen if I did."

Erin looked up at David, who had risen from his chair. "That's why I wanted you to come and see Lucy tonight," he said. "I didn't want to say anything until you'd spoken to her yourself." His expression was so solemn it scared Erin. "Ask her who this friend is."

Erin gave him a puzzled look. Then her breath caught in her throat. She turned to look at Lucy again, her heart pounding. "Who is your old friend, Mrs. Lennox?"

"I told you," Lucy said, her voice fraught with impatience. "Mary. Mary Foley. She's Mary Callahan now, of course. We only write to each other once a year, at Christmas time. She gives me all her news and I tell her all about Giles and Amberley."

Chapter Twenty-nine

Erin felt as if the entire world had made several hectic revolutions within a few seconds. "You mean that not only is Mary alive, but you're in communication with her?"

"If that is some sort of jargon to mean I write letters to her at Christmas, the answer is yes."

Erin turned to David, a mute appeal in her eyes.

"My grandmother says she has the letters and cards in her bureau drawer," he told her.

"But I'm certainly not going to show them to you. They are *my* letters. My private and personal correspondence." The old lady clamped her lips together and the hands on her lap formed into fists, as if she would fight for her right to keep the letters private. "Mary's my friend. She's the only friend I had at Amberley."

Again, Erin knelt at her side. "Of course she is." She tried to swallow down the tears that were choking her. "But she is also my mother's mother. My grandmother." She took one of the age-spotted hands in hers. "Imagine how you and David would feel if you didn't have each other."

"Mary has plenty of grandchildren. And great-grandchildren, too. She sent me the family photograph."

Erin held her breath for a moment. Then, exhaling, she said, "I suppose you wouldn't like to show us the picture of Mary with her family, would you?"

Lucy withdrew her hand. "I certainly will not. It is *my* picture, not yours."

David sent Erin a warning glance. "Of course it is. I expect it was taken for some special occasion, wasn't it?" he said quite casually.

"It was Mary's golden wedding anniversary."

"I thought it would be something special," David said. He gave Erin a quick shake of the head to suggest that she leave the rest to him. Erin resumed her seat.

"That's quite enough about Mary Foley," Lucy said, patently relieved that Erin had moved away. "It's time I started thinking about my bed."

"I don't think Erin believes you know Mary at all," David said in a hard voice, completely taking Erin by surprise.

"Of course I—" Erin began to protest.

David gave her a quick frown. "Erin thinks you made it all up," he told Lucy.

Lucy lifted her feet from the footstool and sat up very straight, her eyes darting fire at Erin. "Well, Erin is very much mistaken. She's also very impertinent to think such a thing."

Erin felt extremely uncomfortable, but she knew that David had his reasons for using such aggressive tactics.

"If you were to show her some proof," he told his grandmother, "she would have to apologize, wouldn't she?"

"She certainly would." Lucy levered herself out of her chair. "And I *will* show her that I'm not making this up." She went to the large bureau by the window. It had three wide drawers below, each with two tarnished brass handles. Above the drawers was a writing shelf and then four shelves, displaying delicate and rare-looking china behind glass doors. "Help me with this drawer," she ordered David.

He swiftly crossed the room and pulled out the top drawer for her. Lucy reached into the very back of the drawer and drew out a battered old biscuit tin decorated with what looked like Constable's *Hay Wain*.

Erin had to stand up. She was so anxious and excited that she couldn't remain still a moment longer.

Refusing David's offer to help her open the tin, Lucy tried to ease the lid off, but it wouldn't budge. It was obviously rusty.

Erin felt as if she was about to burst with impatience.

"Damn the thing," Lucy said, slamming the tin back in the front of the drawer. "It's not going to open."

Erin opened her mouth in a silent scream behind

Lucy's back. Before Lucy could close the drawer again, David had snatched the tin from the drawer and opened it.

"There. All it needed was a man's touch," he said, smiling over Lucy's head at Erin, who mouthed a silent "Thank you," to him.

From where she was standing she could see several bundles of letters tied up with faded ribbons or bits of string.

Lucy picked up one of the bundles and untied the pink ribbon around it. She drew out a card with a picture of a horse-drawn coach beside a snow-covered inn. "There you are, doubting Thomas," she said triumphantly, holding out the card to Erin.

Barely breathing, Erin took the card, holding it reverently in her hands. Then she opened it.

To my dear, dear friend Lucy, the inscription read. *May you receive the blessings of the holy family at Christmastime. From your ever-loving friend, Mary (Callahan).*

The writing was in the same childish hand—albeit a little more shaky—as the inscription in her mother's copy of *The Secret Garden.*

Erin clamped a hand to her mouth, tears swelling in her throat. David went to her and drew her into his arms. She could feel his heart beating against her cheek as her face pressed against his shirtfront.

After a moment or so, she drew in a sobbing breath and eased away from him. She returned the card to Lucy, whose eyes were wide in wonder as she gazed at them both.

"I am very sorry that I doubted you," Erin told her. "I can't tell you how happy you have made me." She bent to kiss Lucy's wrinkled cheek. It felt like soft leather beneath her lips.

"Don't expect me to let you read the letters," Lucy said, drawing away from her.

"I don't need to read them. They're your letters."

"She's my best friend."

"It makes me very happy to hear you say that," Erin told her.

Lucy carefully inserted the card back into the bundle and replaced it inside the tin. David was about to close the lid for her, but she stopped him. "No, I think I'll read some of her letters before I go to bed." Lucy ran her fingers over the bundles as if just touching them gave her pleasure.

"It must be a long time since you saw her," David said. "You've never visited her in Ireland, have you?"

"No. She made me promise not to come. Her family there know nothing about her past life at Amberley."

"Of course they don't."

Lucy looked directly at Erin. "That's why you must go back to Canada now and forget everything I have told you tonight. Mary is happy in Ireland with her family. It would be disastrous if you were to seek her out. She thinks her daughter died aboard the ship that was torpedoed."

Erin released her breath in a long sigh. "So that's why she returned to Ireland. She thought that Katie was dead. Another lie told by Giles's parents." Erin didn't even try to hide her bitterness.

"I didn't discover the truth until about three years later," Lucy said. "By that time, Giles had married Cynthia and Mary had married an Irish schoolteacher in her village and was expecting a child. What was the point of telling them what I knew?"

"You were forgetting about her daughter, Katie. She was all alone in Canada. Just a little girl, cut off from her home and her mother and father. Surely they should have been told that their daughter was alive."

Lucy turned abruptly away from her. "I'm tired, David. I want to rest. Take her away, please."

Erin felt as if she'd been slapped in the face. Yet she understood. The burden of the secrets Lucy had harbored for so long must have been an unbearable strain at times. No wonder she didn't want to discuss it.

"Just one more question, Grandmama," David said, "and then we'll leave you in peace."

"What is it?"

"Did Mary stay in her own village or did she move elsewhere with her husband?"

"Oh, no, you don't, you clever dick lawyer, you. You're not going to catch me that way."

David carried on as if he hadn't heard her. "She didn't

come from Adare originally, though, did she? I wondered if she had moved there with her husband. Adare's a beautiful place. I was there a few years ago when I had a holiday in the west of Ireland."

"In Adare? How very strange. Just think, you might have met Mary and never known—" Lucy stopped suddenly and slapped David's arm. "I'm not saying one more word. It's very bad of you to keep on at me like this."

"Sorry, darling. Erin and I will get out of your hair now." He took Lucy in his arms and hugged her, kissing her on both cheeks. "I love you."

"And I love you, too, even though you've been very naughty." She patted his shoulder.

"Don't come to the door," David said. "I know the way out."

"The day I don't show my guests out is the day I've been carried out myself in a coffin. I just want a plain box, remember, David. No expensive wood or fancy brass handles."

"I remember. I've got it all in writing."

"Good." Lucy turned to Erin. "I hope you don't think I'm being a stubborn old woman," she said. "But I really think it would be for the best if you were to go home and tell your mother that both her parents are dead." For once Lucy sounded utterly rational. "Better for everyone that way."

"For everyone except my mother," Erin reminded her.

"She must be an old woman herself by now. Just tell her that her parents adored each other and her . . . and they did, I can assure you, otherwise Giles would never have done what he did. That's all she really needs to know, isn't it?"

"But if Mary is still alive, how can it be right not to tell her that her daughter was never killed in 1940? And what about Giles? Shouldn't he know that the woman he loved is alive, not dead, as he thought? I think it's cruel not to tell him."

Beneath the heavy makeup Lucy's face was haggard. She gripped Erin urgently, her fingers digging like talons into her arm. "If you tell Giles that Mary Foley is alive, it will be the end of him. The shock will kill him. Leave things alone, girl. That's not just mere advice. I'm begging you not to stir up trouble. Now, please go, before I say more than I should. I've said far too much as it is."

With indecent haste, she bustled them out the door and slammed it to behind them. They could hear various locks turning and bolts being shot into place.

As Erin stood beside David in the old-fashioned cage elevator she remained silent, her mind occupied with all that she had learned tonight.

"Penny for your thoughts," David said.

"I was wondering if Lucy was right about not going any further. I feel as if I've opened up a can of worms and I can't get it closed again."

"Knee-deep in worms."

"Exactly." She searched his face. "My mother accused me of the same thing. She said that once I got my teeth into a story I couldn't let go. Yet I was doing this for her, dammit."

The lift shuddered to a halt and David opened the gate. "I'm sure you were. But I think you were doing it for yourself as well." He went to the front door and looked out. "It's raining quite hard. Let's wait a moment to see if it eases off."

"Okay. What do you mean, doing it for myself?"

"I'm no psychologist, but I imagine that your father's death was a horrible shock to you. You've told me yourself how close you were. Perhaps, subconsciously, you were trying to find more family to replace him. Is that possible or does it sound like pop-psychobabble?"

She gazed at him, seeing the genuine concern in his eyes. "I must admit that I miss him terribly."

"Of course you do. And, as you told me, you'd also ended a relationship fairly recently. I'm sure that didn't help, either."

Erin had to smile. "Rob and I were never right for each other," she said ruefully. "To him, work always came first. I love my work, but family and the people I love are just as important, if not more so."

"That's because you're a woman."

Erin felt as if an icy Manitoba wind had just swept over her. "That's rather a sexist statement, isn't it?"

"I didn't intend it to be. It's just that some men are not interested in the family thing."

Erin had to bite her lip to stop herself asking if David included himself among them. What was it Samantha had said? Something about David not being into the commitment thing.

"And some women shouldn't be, either," David added.

This time there was no mistaking the bitterness in his tone.

"Do you mean me, by any chance?" Erin demanded, ready to do battle with him.

David's hazel-green eyes opened wide in amazement. "*You*? Good God, no. Whatever made you think I was talking about you?"

Erin shrugged. "I've no idea. I think we've gone off the subject a bit, haven't we? I was merely saying that family was important to me. I suppose that's why I'm still living and working in Winnipeg and not in the big T O."

"T O?"

"That's what Canadians call Toronto." She stood on the blue-tiled floor, contemplating him. "Do you think I should back off, return to Canada, and forget all about Mary Foley?"

"Not at all. I think you've gone too far now to turn back. You said that your mother's doctor thinks this is a good thing for her."

"So you think I should go and see Mary, despite what Lucy said?"

"Yes, I do."

"But we don't know where she is, do we? Unless . . . What was all that stuff about some Irish village you'd seen on holiday? What was it called?"

"Adare. It's one of Ireland's loveliest villages. In County Limerick."

"What made you mention it to Lucy?"

"There was a postcard on top of the bundle of letters and cards. I recognized the picture. It was Adare."

"Oh, wow!" Erin was all admiration. "We two should start up a detective agency."

"At the rate I'm going, I'll need to."

"Oh, David. I am sorry. I've really got you involved in this, haven't I? Are you sure you don't mind?"

"I'm sure."

"You really think I should stay and track Mary down?"

"Yes, I do." A slow smile spread like a sunrise across his face. "But I'm probably not the right person to ask. When it comes to advising you, I don't think I'm capable of being totally objective. All I know is that I don't want to see you returning to Canada without achieving what you set out to do, when you're so near your goal."

They were very close. Erin breathed in his cologne, the fragrance of something vaguely evergreen, like pine. She had an overwhelming longing to move into his arms and just be held, as he'd held her when she'd seen Mary's writing on Lucy's Christmas card.

"Thanks for being so understanding," she told him.

"My pleasure." He pushed open the heavy door. "The rain's eased off a little. I'll go fetch the car. Wait inside until you see me."

"Okay."

While she waited for him, Erin concentrated her mind on David for the first time in ages. What did she really know about David Lennox? Nothing much, apart from the fact that he was from a broken home, with a mother who'd been married three times, and had spent most of his childhood and adolescence in boarding schools.

Not a very promising start for a child. Compared to her childhood David's sounded like hell. Yet he could be amazingly sensitive. His response to her emotional reaction to Mary's handwriting had been exactly what she needed, as if he was perfectly attuned to her feelings.

She wished she had the time to get to know him better, to explore her own feelings for him—and his for her—but she knew that her personal life had to be shelved for now. At least until she found Mary Foley.

Besides, there was still the Hogarth Family barrier between her and David. She represented the bastard interloper side. He the legitimate heir to the title side. That could be a source of considerable conflict between them.

She was brought back to the present by the blast of

David's car horn. Pushing open the door, she dashed out and climbed into his car.

"David," she said, after they'd driven in silence along Kensington Road for a minute or so.

"What?"

"How difficult will it be to find her, do you think?"

"Mary? Dead easy. Adare's quite a small place. Besides, in Ireland everyone knows everyone else. I bet if you were to walk into the local tourist office they'd be able to tell you where she lives."

"As easy as that? Wow!" Erin thought for a moment. "I don't think I should contact Mary before I go over to Ireland. What do you think?"

"I agree with you. If you were to speak to her first, I'm sure she wouldn't be willing to see you."

"That's what I thought. However much I promised her that I'd keep everything a secret, I'm sure she'd never believe me. I can understand that."

"It's an extremely sensitive issue, when you think about it. We're talking about having an illegitimate child in the days when that was an absolute taboo."

"Exactly. I'm going to have to be very careful."

Erin turned her head to look out at the Royal Albert Hall, which David had pointed out to her earlier. "Here's my plan," she announced after thinking for a few minutes. "As soon as my mother arrives and has a couple of days to get over jet lag, we'll go to Ireland."

"Sounds good."

Erin waited for him to say more, but he remained silent. She hesitated and then said, "I feel awful for asking this of you, after all you've done already, but . . . I don't suppose you'd consider coming to Ireland with us, would you? I'd pay all the expenses, of course."

David grinned at her. "I thought you'd never ask."

Chapter Thirty

Later that night, as David was driving home to his flat in Highgate, he decided to make a detour and stop at Simon's house in Hampstead.

As he'd told Erin over their meal in Chelsea, Giles's doctor had called him back just before he'd left the office to pick her up. Dr. Alexander had told him only that Lord Maybridge was suffering from his usual hypertension, aggravated by the effects of what had been, apparently, a stressful weekend.

"I have advocated a good deal of rest and a mild sedative. If you wish to know any more about his lordship, you must ask his grandson."

With his Scottish burr and careful Highland speech, Dr. Alexander had sounded to David like an actor who'd escaped from *Dr. Finlay's Casebook*.

With Giles inaccessible and his doctor noncommittal, David had decided to confront Simon. And if Simon wasn't home, Olivia would have to do. In fact, Olivia might be better. She didn't lie quite so convincingly as Simon did.

Some of the lights were still on in the Hogarths' elegant Regency house near Hampstead Heath. David mounted the steps and was about to ring the bell when he became aware of a dark figure behind him.

A policewoman this time. He seemed to be dogged by the force lately. Of course, as the leader of the opposition Simon would have to be carefully watched by the boys and girls in blue. "Good evening, officer."

"Evening, sir."

David smiled at her as he waited for the door to open. "I'm family," he said.

"I see, sir. Mind if I wait?"

"Not at all. Good idea."

The au pair opened the door, poking her head around it. "Yes?"

"Is Mrs. Hogarth in? Or Mr. Hogarth?" David asked.

"Ah . . . I will see. Who is it, please?"

"David Lennox. Their cousin."

Several minutes later, Olivia came to the door. Her face was shiny in the light from the lamp above the doorway. It was the first time David had seen her without makeup.

"David?" Somehow she looked more pale and fragile without the darkened eyelashes and the artifice of natural-looking makeup. "Is something wrong?"

"I'd like to speak to you and Simon. Is he home?" Then, recalling the policewoman at his back, "Vouch for me, would you?"

"I'm not sure I should at this time," Olivia said, sounding like a strict schoolteacher. "It's half past eleven, you know."

"Sorry about that," David said breezily, "but I've been trying to get hold of you and Simon since Monday."

"Mr. Lennox is a friend, officer. Thank you."

"Said he was family, Mrs. Hogarth. Told your girl he was your cousin," the policewoman said, a wealth of suspicion in her voice.

"He's my husband's cousin." Olivia sounded as if she'd just eaten an ice cube. "Good night, officer."

She went ahead of David, leaving him to close the door, and led him into the front room. "You must have something pretty important to discuss, coming here at this time of night," she said. "What's the problem?" She perched on the arm of the sofa, making no suggestion that David should sit down.

"I take it Simon's still at the House."

"He should be home soon." Then, realizing that she shouldn't have revealed that fact, Olivia hastily added, "But there's no guarantee that he will be, of course. There never is. What is it you want, David?"

Years ago, when David had first met Olivia, he'd found her strangely attractive in a kind of ice-maiden way, sensing that hidden beneath that aloof exterior was a passionate woman. He'd soon come to realize that Olivia's one and only passion was Simon. He was convinced that she would do anything for him: lie, steal, cheat. Perhaps even murder, if it ever came to that.

"What's happened to Giles?"

She bit her bottom lip between small white teeth. "Giles? Nothing as far as I know. What makes you ask?"

"I've been trying to get him on the telephone. Mrs. Edwards is blocking me from speaking to him. Is he ill?"

"He . . . he hasn't been well since the weekend. That episode with your friend really upset him."

"I can imagine it would." David's mouth twisted into a wry smile. "It's not every day you discover that the daughter you thought had been dead for fifty-five years is, in fact, alive."

Olivia waved a coral-tipped hand in the air. "Heavens, you read about these things every day in the newspaper, don't you?"

"Not about the Hogarth family, you don't. Must have given old Simon quite a shock. Especially when he's trying to paint his new regime gleaming white for its purity."

Olivia's eyes were the color of a northern glacier lake. She stood up. "You must excuse me now, David. I'm going to bed. I have to drive the girls to school first thing in the morning."

"If you don't mind, I'll wait for Simon." David enforced his words by sitting down on the leather couch.

"But it could be hours before he gets home," Olivia protested.

"I don't mean to be rude, Olivia, but Simon has been avoiding me. There's something going on at Amberley and I want to find out from Simon exactly what it is. If it means sitting here until dawn, then I will do so."

The glare she gave him made her face look tight and pinched. "I consider it extremely rude of you. I could call that constable and have you thrown out, you know."

"I'm sure you could, but it wouldn't look very good in tomorrow morning's *Mirror,* would it? *Simon Hogarth's cousin tossed out of house by wife at midnight.*"

"That sounds suspiciously like blackmail."

"Must run in the family. May I help myself to a drink?"

"Do as you please." Olivia turned on her heel and marched from the room, the blue satin robe clinging to her body.

David wasn't even vaguely turned on. Now that he was older, he found Olivia far too cold to his liking. And too thin. She probably spent any spare time she had, after all her committee work, in working out to make sure she kept slim. No spaghetti bolognese for her, he imagined. Smiling to himself, he thought of Erin tucking into her pasta, expertly twirling and then slurping it up like a true Italian, her tongue coming out to lick the excess tomato sauce from her lips. Now *that* for him was sexy!

He got up to pour himself a very weak whiskey. The ice bucket, he noticed, was full. Waiting for the lord and master to come home. As, no doubt, was Olivia. Hence the satin robe.

Glass in hand, he sat down again, surveying the room of the house that Simon had bought and his wife had decorated in her impeccable good taste. He raised his glass to the portrait of Simon that hung on the wall. "Here's to you, cousin," he said softly. "May your good fortune last for exactly as long as you deserve."

He picked up a copy of the *Financial Times* and leafed through it, but images of Erin kept intruding. He had never met anyone quite like her before. If she felt an emotion, she didn't hide it, she showed it. Perhaps that was because, at the moment, she was caught up in a series of vitally important events in her life, undergoing so many conflicting emotions that she couldn't hide them. She didn't button up and hide her feelings behind a bland exterior, as many Englishwomen did, so that you never knew how you stood with them.

Perhaps Erin was more open because she was Canadian. But he knew several Canadians, and he wouldn't say that they were particularly demonstrative. Of course, most of them were men involved in high finance, a breed that was notoriously poker-faced. It could be that mid-westerners were different. Or perhaps it was Erin's Irish blood. Whatever it was, David found it both overwhelmingly attractive and downright disconcerting.

His Scottish father, who'd died from a heart attack three years ago, had taught him by example to be sparing with his emotions or, at least, to keep them well hidden. Life at David's spartan boarding school had reinforced that teaching.

And when he'd lived with his mother as a boy or, later, visited her in Boston, her volatile nature and emotional outbursts had been so embarrassing and frightening that they'd served to underline the importance of controlling one's feelings. As a consequence, he'd learned to steer clear of women who openly displayed their emotions.

Erin not only displayed them, she also forced him to feel, as well. Witness his passionate outburst in the car last evening. That loss of control had been bloody frightening. It had also been bloody exciting. It was as if Erin Benson held the key to some secret room inside him. He wanted her to use the key, yet at the same time he was terrified of what he might find inside if she did.

Erin, the excavator of secrets, he thought, smiling to himself.

The sound of a taxi drawing up put an end to his reverie. He heard Simon's voice saying good-night to the driver and then his light footsteps on the steps up to the door.

As Simon's key turned in the lock, David drew in a long, deep breath. He was preparing for what he was sure was going to be an uncomfortable encounter. You had to keep your wits about you, dealing with Simon.

The front door opened and then clicked softly shut. David heard footsteps padding down the carpeted stairs.

"Hello, darling," Olivia said softly. There then ensued a whispered conversation—about him, no doubt—which culminated in Simon saying, "Don't worry, darling. I'll deal with it. It won't take long. I'll let you know when he's gone."

The door to the front room opened and Simon came in, closing the door carefully behind him. He leaned his back against it. "I don't want to wake the children, so let's keep it quiet. What brings you here at this late hour?"

"I want to know what's wrong with Giles."

"I see that Olivia gave you a drink."

"She told me to help myself."

"Good. Excuse me while I do the same." Simon crossed the room to go to the drinks trolley in the corner and poured himself a sparkling mineral water, adding a dash of lime juice and several ice cubes. Then he sat down opposite David. "So you're concerned about Giles."

"Is he ill? I've been trying to reach him, but Mrs. Edwards seems to have set up some sort of blockade."

"His doctor has advised that he be kept free of any source of stress."

"Which includes me, of course. And Erin Benson."

Simon looked into his glass and slowly swirled the liquid around, the ice cubes tinkling against the glass. "Particularly Miss Benson. And as you two appear to be working in tandem, I regret that you also must be included in the list of prohibited callers."

David felt a rush of anger, but pushed it down, aware that he could never deal successfully with Simon if he lost his temper. "Working in tandem? You make it sound like some sort of conspiracy."

"Precisely, my dear cousin. I could not have used a better word myself."

"Perhaps you'd tell me what I would gain by conspiring with Miss Benson?"

Simon's blue eyes locked with David's. "You're an intelligent man. You will have guessed from observing us that my grandfather and I are at odds over my renunciation of the title. What a perfect opportunity for you to wheedle yourself into his affections."

David laughed. "I'd never thought you capable of such a vivid imagination, Simon. Affection is certainly not the word I'd use to describe the feeling Giles has for me."

"Ah, but the introduction of a long-lost daughter—and a granddaughter—could change all that, couldn't it?"

David's eyes narrowed. "How many times must I tell you that I met Erin Benson about twelve days ago at—"

"At Samantha Wakeley's. Yes, I know all that."

"Of course you do. I've heard about your visit to UTV. Such open blackmail is not quite your usual style, is it?"

"That woman was part of the conspiracy. It was she who arranged the meeting between you and Miss Benson. Once you heard her incredible story, you must have realized its potential."

David set his glass down on the bookshelf at his side. "Do you believe that Erin Benson is Giles's granddaughter?"

"Of course not. She hasn't an ounce of proof."

"Except for Giles's own acceptance of her story. How do you explain that?"

"Emotion. Bewilderment. Stress of the moment." Simon raised his shoulders and slowly lowered them again. "He's an old man, easily swayed."

"I've never thought of Giles as someone who was easily swayed by anyone, let alone a perfect stranger. His explanation seemed very clear to me. Are you suggesting that your grandfather is senile?"

David was watching Simon very carefully. He caught an almost imperceptible hollowing of his cheeks, as if he'd sucked them in against his teeth.

"Certainly not," Simon said. "Obviously the emotion of the moment overcame him."

"Knowing what I do of Giles—"

"Ah, but how little that is. An annual visit hardly makes you an expert on Giles, does it?"

"Certainly enough to know that he believed that Erin was his granddaughter. You're not denying the fact that there must have been some liaison in the past that resulted in a daughter, are you?"

Simon hesitated, obviously wishing he could deny it. "No, I admit that there probably was, but—"

"Because if you are, my grandmother will vouch for that fact. She knew Mary Foley and her daughter, Kate."

"Lucy?" Simon's eyebrows lifted in astonishment. "Forgive me, David, but Lucy's as scatty as a squirrel. Can you imagine her in a witness box?"

David stared at Simon until he looked away to glance at his watch. "How did we get to a courtroom, Simon? Of course, you're right, it could come to that. Nasty public places, courtrooms. The media love them, particularly when there's a case involving someone famous."

"Don't threaten me, David. If you want to employ dirty tactics, you'll find that I have far more clout than a solicitor who acts for rock groups and movie starlets."

"Ever heard of DNA testing?"

Simon glanced at his watch again, stifling a sigh of impatience. "This is all growing very tedious. Of course I've heard of DNA testing."

"Erin's mother is arriving in London next Monday. We could have her and Giles tested. That would settle the question of whether or not she's his daughter."

"I don't think you quite understand. I'm not permitting you or any of your cohorts to come near my grandfather. His personal physician has advised me that his heart couldn't withstand any further stress or excitement. Daughter or not, that is sufficient reason for me to refuse you access to him."

"I hadn't realized that you'd been authorized to act as Giles's spokesman. Has he given you power of attorney, also?"

Simon stood up. "It's time you left, Lennox. I've listened to all you have to say." To David's amazement, Simon smiled and held out his hand. "Despite our differences, I must thank you for your concern for my grandfather. I assure you he is being well cared for."

"Bet he is," David said, ignoring the outstretched hand. He strode to the door. Once he reached the hallway, he turned to confront Simon, who had followed him. A rustle of fabric told him that Olivia was listening from the landing above.

"One more question and then I'll go."

"Ask away," Simon said, his buoyant smile restored now that David was leaving.

"Where is Harrington?"

The smile faded a little and then was resurrected. "Harrington's taking a well-earned rest. Poor old chap, he badly needed a holiday. You can imagine what it's like being at Giles's beck and call all the time."

"I can, indeed." David walked to the door and opened it, before Simon could. He stepped out onto the red-tiled porch and looked up at the ornate glass fanlight above the glossy black door. "So Harrington's not at Amberley?"

"No, he's away on vacation."

David nodded slowly. "That's exactly what I was afraid of," he said, and turned to walk down the steps, fully aware that Simon was standing in the doorway watching him until he'd turned the corner and was out of sight.

Chapter Thirty-one

When Erin met her mother at Heathrow on Monday morning, she was prepared to find her exhausted from the flight and overwhelmed by all the people. What she wasn't prepared for was the bright-eyed, excited woman who abandoned her luggage cart and came rushing forward as soon as she saw her.

"You look as if you had a good flight," Erin said, hugging her mother. It was good to feel the plump body against hers, smell the familiar crisp scent of *Miss Dior,* her mother's favorite perfume since she was a teenager.

"I had a wonderful flight. I sat next to the nicest young man and we chatted all the way over. The film was one of those stupid comedies, so we just kept talking through it. Oh, there he is. I must say good-bye to him."

Kate hailed a young man with long hair tied in a ponytail, wearing rumpled beige shorts, a T-shirt that read *Be Good To Everyone, Especially Yourself,* and leather sandals. To Erin's amazement they hugged each other before they parted.

"He's given me his phone number. Such a nice fellow," Kate said, watching him carry his oversized nylon bag through the crowds. "I wouldn't have minded a son like him."

"He . . . he didn't quite look like your sort, Mom," Erin said, grinning.

"I've always told you, Erin, you can't go by appearances. He's taking archeology at the University of Toronto, and he's in England to visit his grandfather."

"Well, I'm glad he helped to pass the time."

"He certainly did. He was extremely interesting to talk to. Now, where's this David you've been dropping hints about?"

As Erin weaved the luggage cart through the hordes of people and baggage, she wondered whether her mother was on jet-lag adrenaline or was she really returning to her old exuberant self again. The latter, she sincerely hoped. Time would tell.

David was waiting by the exit to the car-park. He'd insisted that Erin go and meet her mother by herself, to give them a few minutes alone together.

"Is that him?" Kate asked, as they approached him.

"Yes. The tall one in the obligatory legal gray suit."

"Hmm, very nice," Kate said. "I hope he's as good as he looks."

"I think so," Erin said, "but it's early days yet." Her caution was addressed to herself as well as to her mother. "There are certain complications I'll explain later."

To her great relief, David and her mother seemed to hit it off immediately. Of course it helped that Mom was in such an upbeat mood. No amount of David's charm would have worked on the woman who'd hidden herself away in a darkened room. A shiver ran over Erin as she remembered those times, which hadn't been so long ago. *Please God,* she prayed, *may she never go back to being that way again.*

When they reached Richmond, David carried in Kate's bags and then held out his hand to her as they stood in the hall. "Good-bye, Mrs. Benson."

She looked disappointed. "Oh, are you leaving us already?"

"I have to get back to work. Don't worry, you'll be seeing more than enough of me. Erin's invited me for dinner this evening."

"Good, I'm glad." This time Kate took the hand he'd proffered.

Erin went to the door with him. "In a way I wish you were staying," she said in a low voice, "for moral support."

"You said yourself this morning that this was something you should tell your mother when you were alone together. I agree."

"Wish me luck."

"I do." He bent to kiss her, a brief kiss suitable for the occasion. The kiss gave her courage.

"Thank you. See you tonight." She watched as David crunched across the gravel and climbed into his car. Then she closed the door.

"What a lovely house!" Kate said, standing in the hall and looking around. "I like David. At least, I like what I see. No one knows what someone's really like until they've known them for a while."

"Sounds like a motherly warning," Erin said.

"No, dear. Just a reminder, that's all. But he seems very down-to-earth, which I like, as you know."

"Yes, he's that, all right."

Mom certainly hadn't liked Rob much, but then Rob had never put himself out enough to try to get her to like him. When Erin had told him how much she wished he and her mother got along better, he couldn't understand why it mattered so much to her. Another example of Rob's disinterest in family.

Erin felt a surge of panic. Now that David had gone, she could no longer postpone her mother's questions about Giles. "Shall I take you up to your room first, Mom?" she asked, thinking that might buy her some time.

"In a minute. I'd love a cup of tea first."

"Great. I'll make a pot for us both. Come and see the kitchen." Erin led her mother down the hall and into the kitchen. It looked even more tornado-stricken than usual. "Excuse the mess. Samantha's not very tidy."

Her mother looked around the kitchen. "You can say that again."

"She left at the crack of dawn this morning to take the Eurostar train to Paris, and I didn't have time to clear up before I left for the airport. Oh, well, never mind. Max should be here soon. He'll soon have it gleaming."

"Max?"

"Samantha's houseman. Her cleaner," Erin hurriedly added, in case her mother might get the wrong idea. "He's a gem."

Her mother sank into the Windsor chair by the Aga stove and groaned. "I must sit down. My ankles have swollen to twice their size. They always do that when I fly."

Erin shoved the step stool over. "Here. Put them up on this."

"What a marvelous kitchen! You know what it reminds me of?"

"No, what?"

"The kitchens you read about in those lovely Joanna Trollope books. Particularly the Aga stove. It is an Aga, isn't it?" Kate put on her glasses to peer at the name on the front of the stove.

"Yes. But I don't think those kitchens are quite so cluttered as this one is."

"It gives it atmosphere."

Erin turned from the sink to grin at her mother. "You'd have a fit if your kitchen were this untidy."

"But it's not mine, so it doesn't matter, does it?" Kate said.

Erin was pleased with her mother's relaxed mood. It would make it a great deal easier when she told her the astounding news she had for her.

When the tea had steeped for a few minutes, she set cups and saucers on a tray, added a plate of mixed biscuits, and carried it out to the patio—or terrace, as Samantha called it.

"Come on out, Mom. It's a bit windy, but at least it's not raining today. Samantha said it's going to be hot this week, so you've come at the right time."

Somehow Erin had thought that the outdoors would be a good place to talk to her mother, less claustrophobic, but she soon realized that the constant passing of people on the towpath beyond the hedge—now that the water level had dropped—was a distraction.

"Perhaps we should go inside," she said, when they'd finished their tea. "We need to talk and it's too noisy out here."

"I think we should or you're going to burst. I've never known you to be so edgy." Kate's face suddenly looked drawn. "Is it bad news?"

"No." Erin stood up abruptly. "I'll take this into the sitting room," she said and walked back into the house.

This time her mother made no comment on the room,

but sat on the edge of the sofa, her eyes fixed on Erin's face. "Let's hear it."

"More tea?"

"Not until you've told me what's going on."

"It's mostly good news, but maybe you should have something stronger than tea ready."

"Tell me."

Erin told her the bad news first, but a diluted version. That Giles was sick and they were unable to see him at present.

"Then what am I doing here?" her mother demanded, color rushing into her cheeks. "It cost me a lot of money to fly over. You should have told me, Erin."

"Calm down. There's more news. Something that makes your coming here more than worthwhile." She couldn't stop the grin that was spreading across her face. "Are you ready for this?"

"How can I be when I don't know what it is?"

Erin took a deep breath and then, as she released it, said, "Your mother's alive."

Kate's hand went to her throat, her trembling fingers spread across her mouth. "Oh, my God," she whispered. "When did you find this out?"

"Just a few days ago. I didn't want to tell you until you got here." Erin beamed at her. "I wanted to see your reaction for myself. I've found her, Mom. I've actually found your mother."

"Where is she?"

"She's in Ireland. In the west of Ireland."

"How did you find her? Did you use a detective agency or what?"

"Actually, the knowledge has been right under our noses, but we didn't know it. David's grandmother, Lucy Lennox, has kept in touch with Mary Foley—your mother—all these years. It's all a big secret, as Giles thought that Mary was dead. As far as he's concerned, he *still* thinks she's dead. Lucy feels, and I think she's probably right, that the shock would be too much for him. What do you think?"

"Me? I'm far too befuddled to know what to think." Her mother looked utterly shell-shocked.

"I can imagine. Poor Mom. I'm sorry to come out with all this when you've been traveling all night."

Her mother gave her a faint smile. "That's okay. It couldn't have waited. You were saying about Lucy?"

"Oh, yes. Lucy didn't want to give us Mary's address, but David found out which town in Ireland she lived in. The rest will be easy. We plan to go to Ireland on Wednesday, as long as you feel rested enough by then to travel."

Her mother's face was ash-pale. "Does she know we're coming?"

Erin went to sit beside her, gathering her hands in hers. Her mother's hands were soft but very cold. "No. There's a problem, you see."

Kate's hands drew away to clench into fists. "What?"

"Lucy says that Mary hasn't told her family about . . . about Giles and you."

"Her family?"

"Yes." Erin picked her words delicately. "You see, she thought you had died, so she went back to Ireland and later married. She had several children, then grandchildren, and even great-grandchildren, Lucy said."

Her mother sat up very straight. "What do you mean, she thought I'd died? She knew very well that I'd gone to Canada."

"She thought your boat had been torpedoed." Erin's breath caught in her throat as she saw her mother's face go chalk-white.

"What would make her think that?" Kate asked in a voice as harsh as sandpaper. "That was what she wanted to think, because she'd sent me off to Canada with false papers. She never even made inquiries about how I was." Her voice rose. "She didn't care."

Erin's hands gripped her mother's again, stilling their agitation. "She made no inquiries because she was told your boat had been torpedoed and that you'd been among the many children who were killed."

"Who would tell her such a thing?"

"Someone she thought wouldn't lie to her. You must remember that your mother was still a young, inexperienced woman. She was probably too trusting."

"Who told her?"

"Giles's mother, the Countess of Maybridge."

"What a load of garbage!" her mother said, with cutting scorn. "Where did you get that from?"

"From Lucy. But I also got it from someone even closer to the situation. Your father. He was away fighting in the second world war at the time this all happened. He returned to find both Mary and you gone. His mother told him that Mary had been on the boat with you and that *both* of you had been killed. You can imagine how devastated he was."

"So devastated that he won't see me, even though I'm alive." Kate's tone was growing increasingly caustic. Erin knew that it was her way of hiding the deep sense of hurt she was feeling.

"No, Mom, that's not true. There's a lot more going on, but I won't burden you with that until later, when all I'm telling you now has sunk in properly."

"When did my . . . Lord Maybridge find out that I hadn't been killed?"

"You won't believe this—"

"Probably not."

"Giles didn't know you were alive until I told him a week ago on Sunday."

"That's what he *told* you."

"No, Mom. I know it was true. He was like a wounded animal when he heard what his parents had done."

"Then why doesn't he want to see me?"

"I'm not sure that's the case. The rest of the family—particularly his grandson, Simon Hogarth—isn't too happy about us, as you can imagine. David and I are trying to discover whether Giles is genuinely sick or Simon is just trying to keep us from seeing him."

"So, I'm not really welcome at Amberley Court, am I?"

"I wouldn't say that at all. When we parted, Lord Maybridge said he wanted me to bring you there to meet him."

Kate eyed her speculatively. "Perhaps in the heat of the moment you coerced the poor man into saying that, because it was what you wanted to hear. You can be very persuasive when you're enthusiastic about something, you know."

Erin was stung by the suggestion, particularly as she was beginning to worry that there might be a modicum of truth in it. "When you meet Giles, you'll soon see how difficult it would be to coerce him into anything."

"Perhaps he's reluctant to meet me because he's afraid that I'll accuse him of not having taken proper care of me and my mother."

This time Erin was not so dismissive. "That's possible, I suppose. We shall find out when we get to see him."

"*If* we ever do." Seeing Erin's crestfallen expression, Kate patted her knee. "Never mind, sweetie, you've worked miracles in finding my parents. It was far more than I ever expected."

"I get the feeling that I'm even more excited about it than you are." Erin couldn't hide her disappointment.

"I think you are. Perhaps that's because, from the sound of it, I'm not sure that my parents wanted to be found. And I'd rather never meet them than be greeted with ill-concealed dismay. Can you understand that?"

"Of course I can." Erin met her mother's brown eyes and saw a well of sadness there. "Have I done the wrong thing, Mom?" she whispered.

"No, Erin. You have not. Even if neither of them wants to see me, at least I know now that they didn't deliberately abandon me."

"Lucy said that they both adored you."

Her mother's lips tilted into a smile. "That's nice to know," she said, her voice soft as eiderdown. "How many children can say that nowadays?"

"I can." Erin found herself enfolded in her mother's arms. "Oh, Mom," she murmured against her mother's soft cheek, "I did so hope that it would all turn out well."

"I know you did. That in itself means more than anything to me, the fact that you did all this for me."

"I wanted to help you get better. I couldn't bear to see you so cut off from the world . . . from me."

Erin felt her mother's lips warm on her forehead. "It must have been awful for you, my sweetie, to lose your father and then to think that you were losing your mother as well."

Erin nodded, tears squeezing from her eyes. "I was so afraid," she said. "I felt as if I were totally alone."

"I know, darling. I felt so helpless and I hated myself for abandoning you at a time when you most needed me. Dr. Prentice tells me that those feelings of self-loathing were actually hindering me from getting well." Kate lifted Erin's chin so that she could look into her eyes. "But I am better now and growing stronger every day, so you needn't worry that I'm going to fall apart on you again. I've seen the abyss and I've crossed it. I may come to it again, but it will never again hold such terror for me. Okay?"

"Okay." Erin nodded, feeling like her six-year-old self being consoled for a skinned knee by her mother.

They eased apart. "So," Kate said briskly, "instead of seeing my father in rural England, I'm off to see my mother in rural Ireland, is that right?"

Erin nodded, blowing her nose in the tissue her mother had taken from the pack she always carried in her bag. Then she looked up to see that her mother was smiling her wry smile, and she couldn't help grinning.

"It is a bit farcical, isn't it?"

Her mother nodded. "It certainly is. Something like a Monty Python sketch. I 'aven't got a father at the moment, would a mother do?" Her imitation of a John Cleese accent was so right that Erin burst out laughing.

"Oh, Mom," she said, hugging her again, "I've missed you so much."

"Well, you don't need to miss me anymore, because I'm right here. Now, before I fall asleep—because I'm about to, I warn you—I'd like to hear some more about the Hogarth family, including David. After all, even if I come from the wrong side of the blanket, I suppose I do have Hogarth blood in my veins."

Chapter Thirty-two

To David's surprise, when he told his grandmother that Mary Foley's daughter Kate was in England, not only did she appear interested, she also said that she'd like to meet her. It was as if she had forgotten all the dark warnings she'd given Erin.

"But I want to be alone with her," Lucy told David. "I don't want you and Erin hanging around. I'm sure you two young things can find something nice to do together," she'd added, with a huge wink.

"She asked if you'd come for sherry early tomorrow evening," David told Kate that evening, when he came back for dinner. "Would you mind being left alone with her?"

"Not at all," Kate said. "Erin tells me that your grandmother remembers me, so it's not as if we were total strangers."

"There's just one thing," Erin said, exchanging glances with David. "I don't think you should tell Lucy about our trip to Ireland."

"Why on earth not?"

"Because she—" Erin hesitated, searching for the right words. "She doesn't think we should be going to see your mother."

"Why not?"

Erin sucked in her breath. Honestly, her mother could be annoyingly obtuse when she wanted to be. "Because Mary hasn't told her family about you or about Giles. Don't forget that, as far as Mary Callahan—that's your mother's married name—is concerned, you are dead. Your sudden resurrection, as it were, could be a terrible shock to her. A happy shock, of course," she hastily added, "but, nevertheless, it could cause her a great deal of stress."

"I see." Kate lifted her chin and looked down her long nose at Erin. For a fleeting moment Erin caught such a strong resemblance to Giles that her breath caught in her throat. "Are you asking me to lie to Mrs. Lennox?"

"Of course not, but—"

"Because I won't."

"The problem is, Mrs. Benson," David said, trying to explain, "that if Lucy knows we're going to Ireland to see Mary, she might phone Mary to warn her."

"That's her business, not mine. And if my mother chooses not to see me, that is *her* business. Now that I understand what has happened, I can see how difficult it might be for a woman of—what is she, nearing eighty, perhaps—to accept that a daughter who died fifty-five years ago is suddenly alive and standing there in front of her. Mary Callahan may deny she ever had a daughter. She may refuse to see me. That is between her and me. But I will not tell lies so that I can inveigle myself into an old woman's home. Whatever will be, will be."

Realizing that they weren't going to get anywhere with her, Erin and David quickly changed the subject.

Remembering Kate's determination not to avoid the truth, it was with extreme apprehension that they left her and Lucy together the following evening.

"We'll be back in an hour. Will that be okay?" David asked.

"Quite sufficient," Lucy said, eyeing Kate.

"I wish I'd been able to set up a surveillance bug in Lucy's sitting room," David said to Erin, as they made their way to the elevator.

Erin rolled her eyes in reply.

If there had been someone listening in to the conversation between the two women, they would have heard nothing at first. For what seemed to Kate like several minutes, Lucy Lennox stared at her over the top of her glasses without saying a word.

"You have Giles's nose," she said at last.

"Ah, so he's the one responsible for it," Kate said. "Too big, eh?"

"I'm afraid so. It probably looks good on him, though."

"It does. Would you like to see a picture of him?"

"Yes, I would." Kate said nothing about the picture Erin had found in her book.

Lucy had obviously sorted some photographs ahead of time, for she handed Kate a box with a picture of wildflowers on it, which had once contained notepaper and now held several faded and crumpled photographs. Some of them had corners missing, suggesting that she'd torn them out of photograph albums.

All the photographs were of Giles Hogarth. Giles on his horse, erect and handsome. Giles with his parents, his father tall and autocratic, his mother also tall, with an expression of hauteur on her patrician face. Then Giles as a youth with a very pretty Lucy, who was gazing up at her cousin with adoring eyes.

"He was my hero then," Lucy said, her cheeks turning pink when she peered at the photograph. "I absolutely adored him." She gossiped away about her escapades with Giles when they were children, and about nannies and tutors and cooks and grooms, but Kate heard only half of what she said, as she examined the photographs.

So this is my father, she thought as she looked again at the photograph of him seated at the wheel of his open sports car. His world was so alien to her that he might as well have been from Mars. The clothing, the obvious wealth, the cars, the horses, Amberley itself . . . all were a world apart from the north end of Winnipeg with its railways tracks and goods yards and ethnic mix of emigrants. It was hard to believe that the small house on Redwood Avenue where Kate had grown up was on the same planet as Amberley Court.

Yet both had been her homes. And didn't they say that the first four years of a child's life were the most important formative ones? Certainly that had been one of the arguments Dr. Prentice had employed to persuade her to fly to England to confront her past.

But, looking at these pictures, she saw no evidence whatsoever that this *was* her past.

She looked up at Lucy, who had risen to fetch something from the large bureau. "I don't suppose anyone ever thought to take a photograph of me, did they?" As soon as she said it Kate realized how accusatory it sounded.

Lucy smiled, so that Kate could see the gap between the bright pink of her dentures and her gum. From behind her back she brought a small snapshot, only about three inches square. She held it out to Kate.

Kate held her breath for a moment, before looking down at the picture. Black and white, it showed Giles sitting on a swing hanging from the branches of a huge tree. Beside him, holding onto one of the ropes, was the pretty, dark-haired woman of Kate's own picture. Her mother.

Giles held a small child on his knee. A child of, perhaps, two, who laughed up at him and was reaching out her hand to his face, with all the assurance of a child with a well-loved father, the moment caught forever on this small square of celluloid.

Tears blurred Kate's eyes so that, for a moment, she couldn't see the picture. "Was this me?" she asked in a whisper.

"That was you. You were such a pretty little thing and quite opinionated, if I remember. You had your mother's prettiness and your father's stubbornness." Lucy touched the photograph with a chipped nail painted fuchsia pink. "My aunt, Giles's mother, ordered me to destroy any pictures I had of you or Mary, but I hid this one from her. I've kept it all these years."

Kate ran her fingers over the photograph with great delicacy, not wanting to smear its surface, and then held it carefully between thumb and forefinger. "This is me as a child with my mother and father."

She hadn't realized that she'd spoken aloud until Lucy said, "Yes, that's right. Your mother gave it to me before she went to Ireland."

"Didn't she want it?" Kate asked, feeling a pang of deep sadness tinged with bitterness.

"No. She couldn't bear to look at anything that reminded her of you."

"Why not?" Kate asked, anger surging inside her.

"You forget. She'd been told you were dead. Her world as she knew it ended at that moment."

"Oh, God," Kate breathed. "But . . . why didn't she wait for Giles to come home? If he loved her, surely she would have wanted to be with him, even if she did think her child was dead?"

"Not once his parents explained to her that Giles's duty as heir to the earldom of Maybridge was to make a suitable marriage to someone of his own class, preferably someone who'd come with a fortune for a dowry."

"I would have told them to go to hell," Kate said, her eyes flashing with anger.

"Would you, now?" Lucy glared at her. "You make me sick, you young people. You've no idea what life was like then. Your mother was the most courageous person I ever knew. She'd put up with all the slurs and insults from Giles's parents because she wanted to be with him."

"When Erin told me about that I thought it must have taken great courage to stay there, on the estate, against his parents' wishes."

"It did. They were horrible, cruel people. Even Giles was afraid of them. Yet he stood up to them and told them he'd relinquish the title if they didn't allow Mary and you to stay. But then the war came and the world was in turmoil. Giles wasn't there to protect Mary against them anymore. She'd been a servant since she was a child, a menial who was trained to take orders without question. How could she demand to stay at Amberley—especially as she'd already been sent from there when you were evacuated—when the earl and countess were handing her a one-way ticket to Ireland? She did what she did for Giles's sake. They told her his life would be ruined if he stayed with her. She believed them."

"She must have loved him very much to have forfeited her chance of a future with him."

"She adored him. She worshiped him. She was too bloody good for him, that's what. Poor girl. Many years later, she wrote and told me about that journey. There were precious few boats over to Ireland at that time. She had to go through northern Ireland and make the long journey south with great hardship. A young girl all on her own, who had just lost her child and her lover.

Can you imagine how she felt? Pah!" Lucy spat. "You've no idea how women lived in those days, how we were treated. Fifty-five years ago we lived in another world, particularly in upper-class England. I didn't fare much better than Mary myself, but when it was my turn to be tossed out of Amberley at least I had an education and a good man who stood by me."

As she recalled those times, Lucy's hands—the arthritic fingers like bent twigs—twisted together. Kate laid her hand gently over them. "My aunt told me I must not mix with servants," Lucy said. "But Mary was my friend. My only friend. When she left, there was no one left at Amberley, not one solitary soul, who cared about me."

Kate felt Lucy's tears moist on her hand. Seeing a woman in her late seventies weeping for the loss of a friend she hadn't seen for over fifty years made Kate feel her own loss even more keenly.

For a long time they sat side by side, Kate's hand on Lucy's. Then Lucy snatched hers away to gather up the photographs. "Don't want them to see us weeping like a couple of babies over a lot of old snapshots, do we? How about a wee drinky, eh?"

They exchanged smiles. "I'd love one," Kate said.

"Thought you might."

"This has all been a bit of a strain, hasn't it?"

"You can say that again. My brain's spinning like a Catherine wheel. Do you remember those fireworks on Guy Fawkes night, spinning fire and sparks? I'll get Mabel to sort out the drinks for us."

"Mabel?" Kate was surprised. She hadn't realized there was anyone else in the apartment.

"Yes. She's my housekeeper, but she thinks she's my keeper." Lucy cackled. "I have to make sure I keep her in her place."

When Lucy left the room, Kate gazed down at the photograph of her and her parents. She was still holding it when Lucy returned.

"Mabel's bringing the drinks in," she said.

Kate held out the photograph. "Thank you for showing this to me. I can't tell you what it means to me to have seen it."

"Keep it."

"Oh, no, I couldn't."

"Why on earth not? It's yours. That's what Mary would want. You going to see her?"

At first Kate didn't quite understand what she meant. "See her?" she repeated.

"Mary," Lucy shouted, as if Kate were deaf. "Are you going to see her?"

Remembering the warning David and Erin had given her, Kate didn't reply at once. Then she said, "I'd like to. After all, she is my mother, isn't she?"

Lucy sighed. "True. But she thinks you're dead."

"Yes, I know. Do you think it would be too much of a shock for her?"

Lucy's uneven shoulders hunched. "No idea."

"I wouldn't want to be the cause of any harm coming to her."

"You'd have to be careful. Her family knows nothing about her past life with Giles."

"So Erin said." Kate thought for a moment. "If only we could go and see her without her knowing who I am. That way I could judge what was the best thing to do, once I was there."

"That's it!" Lucy shrieked so hard that she startled Kate. "Well done," she said, slapping Kate on the knee. "We can say that my grandson's coming to Ireland with his girlfriend and her mother for a few days. They'd love to pop in for a quick visit if they're anywhere near Adare. That way you could see your mother and decide for yourself how much you should tell her. Perfect!" Lucy jiggled with excitement as if she were a teenager.

"But surely she won't want anyone connected with Amberley to know where she is, will she?"

"I know where she is," Lucy shouted, "and I'm connected to Amberley, aren't I?"

"Yes, but you've kept her whereabouts a secret for over fifty years," Kate reminded her patiently. At times it was hard to follow Lucy's rather haphazard logic.

"That's true." Lucy's mouth turned down at the corners with disappointment. "Maybe it wouldn't work."

"Oh, I think we can work out something on those lines," Kate said.

Lucy immediately brightened again. "Oh, good. I wish I could be there, too. I'd love to see Mary again."

"Then why don't you come with us?"

"No, no, no. I don't like traveling. It makes me nervous to be away from my home. I like my own things about me. And I don't like leaving my cats." Lucy stretched out her hand to stroke the marmalade long-haired cat that was curled up, nose to tail, beside her. "Besides, I don't want Mary to see how old and dotty I've become."

"Mary will be old, too, don't forget. And you're not dotty."

"Oh, I am you know. Sometimes I get all mixed up."

"Don't we all."

"No, not like this," Lucy said. "There are some days when the past appears more real than the present to me and the two seem to blend, so that I'm not quite sure where I am."

This time Kate didn't protest. She'd worked with too many older people at the Grace Hospital not to know that what Lucy had described was fairly common.

"I feel safer, more comfortable when I stay here with Mabel," Lucy said. The door opened, as if on cue. "And here she is. About time, too."

A woman of about fifty lumbered in, bearing a tray. She was both tall and wide, dressed in a floral cotton dress that was stretched to its fullest capacity across her stomach. "Sorry. I couldn't find the lemon for the G and T," she said in a rich, fruity voice. She set the tray down on the table and then stuck her plump hand out to Kate. "Hello, Mrs. Benson, I'm Mabel."

"Hello, Mabel."

"Anything else you need, dear?" Mabel asked Lucy.

"No. Nothing. Thank you."

Mabel loomed over them for a moment.

"I suppose you want to join us for a drink," Lucy said ungraciously.

"No, thanks. I'm watching *Roseanne*."

Lucy gave an exaggerated shudder. "Then kindly go back to it. *Roseanne!* What deplorable taste that woman has."

Kate frowned, fearing that Mabel would have heard

Lucy. Indeed, she had, but Mabel was laughing a deep plummy laugh as she closed the door behind her.

Lucy grabbed for her drink and took a great gulp of it. Kate inadvertently wrinkled her nose. She had never liked the smell of scotch. "Are you on any medication?"

"Pills, you mean? A few."

"You shouldn't really mix them with alcohol," Kate said.

"Of course I shouldn't, but what other pleasures do I have in life, eh?"

Kate shook her head, but she smiled as well. "True, but the combination might be causing some of the forgetfulness that's bothering you."

"Oh, it's not forgetting I'm worried about, it's remembering too many things all at the same time." Lucy took another large gulp of her drink. "For instance, all this talk of Mary has made me remember the day she got married, but that's all mixed up with the day my aunt told her that you had been killed, so the two are all muddled up together."

Kate had lifted her glass. Now her hand froze halfway to her mouth. "But I thought you'd never met Mary's other family."

"I haven't. I've never been to Ireland. David has, though. He tells me it's a beautiful country. Very unspoiled in the west. Not like England. England's been raped by the developers and the road-builders. It's disgraceful what's happened here."

Kate's mind was beginning to reel. "You were talking about Mary's wedding. If you were there, you must have met her husband."

"Where?"

"In Ireland."

"In Ireland?" Lucy stared at Kate as if she were crazy. "I told you, I've never been to Ireland."

"But you said you were at Mary's wedding."

"Now it's you who's getting all muddled up. That was the first wedding, not the second. I told you, I've never met Mary's husband. Besides, he's dead now."

"Who is?"

"Mary's husband. Not Giles. You know that *Giles* isn't dead," Lucy added, frowning over her glasses at Kate.

Kate's stomach seemed to be doing somersaults. Now her brain was following suit. She was afraid to ask the question that hovered on her lips. But she knew that she must or she might never again have the chance.

"Mary was married twice?"

"Well, of course she was. Once to Giles, once to her other husband."

Kate had heard of striking thunderbolts. Now she knew how they felt.

"You knew that already, though, didn't you?" Lucy grinned at her, her bright-pink lipstick smeared down the side of her mouth. "After all, you were there."

"I was?" Kate murmured.

"Yes." Lucy gave a cackle of laughter. "You were in your mother's belly."

"Of course I was," Kate said lightly. "And you were there, too, you said."

"That's what I said. I was one of the witnesses at the wedding."

This time Kate was afraid to ask more questions in case Lucy suddenly realized what she was saying.

"Harrington was the other witness. A handsome young man he was then, too. Not the old dodderer he is now. He and Giles wore green velvet. The wedding took place in Westminster Abbey and the Queen was there with Prince Philip. She was dressed in red satin and she wore her coronation crown. Prince Charles was the best man. We all went to the Fox and Hounds for drinks and sandwiches afterwards."

Kate was totally stunned. She had no idea what was fantasy and what wasn't. For a moment she'd believed Lucy was telling the truth, that Mary and Giles had, indeed, been married. But now she realized that there was no way of telling whether *any* part of Lucy's story was true.

"Do you have any pictures?" she asked very quietly.

"Of what?" Lucy demanded, slopping the remaining liquid from her glass onto her skirt. "Damn, I've spilled my drink. Go and ask Mabel to bring the bottle of whiskey in, would you?"

Never had Kate been more tempted. But she resisted.

"I think we've both had enough," she said. "I'm almost asleep. That's jet lag, I suppose."

"Jet lag? What's that?"

"What you get when you fly long distances across several time zones."

"Oh, did you fly here?" Lucy looked into her empty glass and then set it down with an unsteady hand. "I'm feeling very tired all of a sudden. I don't really like having visitors. Where's David?" she asked, sounding like a querulous child. "You should go home now."

"Yes, I should." Kate checked her watch. Ten minutes before David and Erin were coming back. She picked up the photograph to put it away in her wallet.

"That's my picture you're taking," Lucy said.

Kate drew in a deep breath and slowly released it. "You gave it to me as a present, remember?"

"Did I? I shouldn't have. Mary wouldn't like it."

"Yes, she would," Kate said, her voice very firm. "Mary would think you did the right thing in giving it to her daughter." She put the picture in her wallet and then stood up. "I'm just going to ask Mabel for a glass of water."

"Tell her to bring in the bottle of whiskey," Lucy shouted.

The door opened and Mabel appeared in the doorway. "I heard that," Mabel said. "You know very well what Dr. Chester said. No more than one drink at night. Even that knocks her squiffy," she added in an undertone to Kate.

Kate smiled at her. "I wasn't sure what to do."

"Just you leave her to me. I can deal with her. Is she turning difficult?"

"I wouldn't say that, but she isn't quite making sense, although she was fine earlier on."

"Her brain gets tired and then she gets all mixed up. One drink makes it worse, I'm afraid. But if I didn't give her one she'd get it herself and take a lot more besides."

"You can just stop talking about me over there," Lucy shouted. "I can hear everything you're saying."

To Kate's great relief, she heard the rattle and wheeze of the elevator and then Erin's voice outside the front door.

Mabel went out into the hallway to let them in. Kate followed her.

"You okay, Mom?" Erin asked. "You look a little frazzled.

"I am, a bit."

"Lucy can have that effect on you," David said.

"She was fine for a while, but then—" Kate found herself shaking when she thought of what Lucy had said.

"Oh, poor Mom. I'd never have left you for so long if I'd known." Erin put her arm around Kate's waist.

"I'm okay. It was all a bit emotional, that's all. Very worthwhile, though," Kate assured them.

"That's good," Erin said.

Mabel closed the door. "Come in for a moment and say good night to her before you go, would you? Then I'll give her her cocoa and get her off to bed. She'll be right as rain in the morning once she's had a good rest."

Although Kate showed the photograph to both Erin and David when they returned to Richmond, she said nothing about Lucy's story of Mary's marriage to Giles. What was the point? It was bound to be an invention of Lucy's overheated brain.

And if it was true, then the possible consequences were too overwhelming for her even to think about. At least, for now, anyway.

Chapter Thirty-three

On Wednesday, Erin, Kate and David flew to Shannon Airport, arriving in the midmorning to a fine rain that shrouded the green fields in a fluid mist.

Erin stood beside her mother outside the airport with their bags, waiting for David to bring the car they'd rented. Neither of them said a word, but Erin was sure that her mother was thinking the same thing as she was. *This is where my maternal roots lie. This damp, green country with air as soft as the accents of its people.*

She gripped her mother's arm and squeezed it. Kate turned with a start. Erin saw that her eyes were moist.

It had been agreed that they would stay at a hotel near Shannon, rather than one in Adare. That way they would avoid any chance meetings with members of Mary's family either before or after they had contacted her.

The hotel was only a few minutes drive away from the airport on the main Ennis to Limerick road. As David drove the rented Nissan into the driveway, Erin surveyed the long low modern building fronted by banks of bright-green grass and beds of flowering rosebushes.

Kate released a long breath like a sigh. "It really is emerald green in Ireland," she said. "I thought it might all be tourist hype, but it isn't."

The green of the grass was repeated inside the hotel with the emerald carpet. They had booked two rooms. One for Erin and Kate, one for David. Erin let Kate check in for them. As she watched her speak to the pink-cheeked reception clerk, she could see how much her mother's confidence was returning.

There had been many times in the days before her father's death that Erin had resented her mother's take-over style, but now she delighted in seeing her deal with the soft-spoken young woman at the desk with her old self-assurance.

The rooms were modern, with low beds in the Scandinavian style and green bedcovers and chair cushions. Everything was tasteful and comfortable.

"Thank God the beds are firm," her mother said, testing one out by bouncing up and down on it. "That was one of the things I hated about going to England with your father. The soggy mattresses."

"I think that's probably all changed now." Erin sat on the tub chair, facing her. "You okay, Mom?"

"I'm fine. Stop worrying about me. I sometimes wonder which of us is the mother and which the child."

Erin laughed, ignoring the urge to shout, *I'm not a child any longer, Mother!* "While you were checking in, David suggested we meet and make plans over coffee in the lounge. Is that okay? Or would you rather just discuss it here, just the two of us?"

Kate hesitated, wondering if it was wise to include David in their discussion. After all, he was not only a Hogarth but also, as Erin had told her, a possible heir to the title and all its estates. Erin was so attracted to him that she would hotly deny any suggestion that David Lennox had the potential of being a spy in their camp.

"He's not coming with us to see Mary, if that's what you're worried about," Erin said, seeing her mother's hesitation. "He just wanted to be in on our general plans, as he's going to be our chauffeur for the next two days."

"Great idea," Kate said, standing up. "I could do with a cup of coffee. I'll just unpack a sweater in case we're going out. It's a bit cool here, isn't it?"

"I think it's your rain jacket you'll need," Erin said, peering out the window.

"It's not heavy rain. I'll take my umbrella."

As they walked along the corridor to the lounge, Kate's heart was pounding. *This is the home of my ancestors,* she told herself, feeling a rush of excitement at the thought. She had always known that she'd originally come from England, but when she'd first visited England many years ago with Jim she had been disappointed to feel no sense of belonging.

This time was very different. This time she was in her mother country. Literally.

"I want to make it clear that I'm here mainly as your chauffeur," David said, when they'd been served pots of coffee with both hot and cold milk and a plate of sweet biscuits. "You tell me what you want to do and when you want to do it. I'll get you there. Okay?"

Erin gave him a grateful smile. She'd sensed that her mother was anxious about David's involvement in this excursion. Although Erin had assured her that David was on their side, she could understand her misgivings.

"As you know," David said, when no one seemed to want to set the ball rolling, "my grandmother provided me with Mary's address. I've no idea why." He smiled at Kate. "It must have been your visit."

Erin leaned forward to take another ginger crunch. "Yes, Mom. You were right about telling her you were coming to Ireland. We were wrong."

"She asked if I was going to see her. I said I'd like to." Kate gave a little grimace. "She didn't seem surprised. But I didn't think she'd actually hand out her address."

"It certainly makes it easier."

"Does it?" Kate said in a low voice. "For you, perhaps. Not for me."

David blinked. "I'm sorry, Mrs. Benson. I didn't mean it that way."

"Of course you didn't. David meant that it would take less time—"

"You needn't be so defensive, Erin. I know exactly what David meant and he understood me. No need to interpret for me."

Erin's neck and cheeks grew warm. She felt like her twelve-year-old self being publicly rebuked by her mother. Then she felt David's hand take hers and squeeze it. She was grateful for his sensitivity.

"Anyway, as I told you," David said quickly, "Mary doesn't live right in Adare, but in a small village nearby. It's about an hour's drive from here."

"As much as that?" Erin asked.

"It's south of Limerick. Knowing Irish roads, even on the main ones I doubt we'll average much more than thirty miles an hour, forty at the most. Let's allow an hour, anyway. The question is, do you want to go there today or tomorrow?"

Both Erin and David looked to Kate for an answer. She didn't reply right away. Then she said, "I'm not sure. What do you think, Erin?"

Still smarting from her mother's put-down, Erin was tempted to put the ball right back in her court and say "It's up to you," but she knew that would be childish. "I know you said you'd like to do a little sightseeing, too, while we were here," she said, her words coming slowly as she thought this through, "but I should imagine you're going to find it very hard to enjoy anything else until you've seen Mary."

"She may not be there. She could even be dead," Kate said, suddenly insecure again.

"We know that, Mom," Erin said gently. "We've talked about those possibilities. She might not believe you're her daughter. Or she could be sick, in hospital, senile . . . I know that you're prepared for anything, including the worst: that she might have died. After all, it's six months since she last wrote to Lucy. What I'm saying is that it might be better to go to see Mary as soon as possible, as that's what we're really here for, isn't it? The rest—seeing Bunratty Castle and Limerick and the countryside and so on—is really just an extra. We can enjoy the sightseeing after we've been to see Mary, can't we?"

"Or not enjoy it," her mother said gloomily. "I can't see us enjoying anything if I find that my mother died a few weeks ago or that she's totally senile, can you?"

"True."

"I'm sorry," Kate said. "I'm being a pain in the neck, I know."

"Not at all," David said. "We can appreciate what you're going through."

"The truth is," she whispered, "I'm dreading this." She looked down, her eyes hidden from them, and brushed biscuit crumbs from her linen pants. "What if she tells me to get lost? What if she's not interested at all in seeing me? That would be worse than any of the other possibilities we've discussed."

Erin sprang up to hug her mother, pressing her cheek against hers. "If that happened, Mom," she said, "You've still got me."

Her mother sniffed. "You're right, darling. I have. Thank God for that," she added, pressing a kiss on her daughter's cheek. "Sorry, David. I'm being a silly old woman."

David shook his head. "Not at all."

"Poor David," Erin said, straightening up. "He won't know what's hit him, stuck with two super-emotional women. You're going to learn a whole lot of new stuff about women these next two days."

"I'm doing so already." His eyes sparkled with warm light as he looked at Erin.

Kate looked from one to the other of them. "I've decided," she said in a firm voice. "I'd like to do it today."

"Good for you." Erin turned to David. "Should we have lunch first?"

"I think so. How about—"

"I doubt if I'll feel like eating," Kate said.

"I'm sure you won't," Erin said. "But I don't think it would be a good idea to land in on Mary at lunchtime. There's bound to be someone with her then, I should think."

"Particularly as rural people usually have their main meal in the middle of the day," David added.

"You're right," Kate said. "Besides, I'm being selfish. You and Erin will want to eat."

Erin gave a wry grin. "I'm not sure I'll be hungry, either."

"Okay," David said. "Both of you can watch me eat. There's a good dining room in the Dunraven Arms in Adare. Why don't we go there?"

"Is it a pub?" Erin asked.

"It's an inn, really. A lovely old place with timbered walls."

"Sounds great."

It was great. Although neither Erin nor Kate ate everything on their plate, they both enjoyed the meal of tender roast lamb with new potatoes, fresh peas, and mint sauce. Erin even went for the sherry trifle for dessert. David had cheese and biscuits. Kate said she couldn't eat another bite, but she didn't decline David's suggestion that she have a cognac with her coffee.

"French courage," she said with a smile as she sipped the amber liquid from the balloon glass.

The tiny village was just a few minutes' drive from Adare. It consisted of a stone-built church, a school, one post office and shop combined, and a handful of houses.

They parked by the church and planned everything meticulously. Once they found the house, David would drop them off, watch to see if they got inside, and then he'd wait for them in the car right beside the church.

"I've armed myself with some CDs and a couple of books," he told them.

It didn't take long to find the house. It was a small detached bungalow built of brick, with a low brick wall around the front garden. Gleaming white paint surrounded the windows and the door was painted a cheery bright yellow.

"Oh, God," Kate breathed, "here we go."

"Are you certain you want me to come with you?" Erin asked.

"Are you kidding?" her mother said. "I wouldn't dare do this on my own. Besides, Erin Benson, I'd like to remind you that you're the one who's responsible for all this. At this very moment, I feel like wringing your neck."

They were both smiling as they got out of the car.

"See you soon," Erin said to David.

"Not too soon, I hope." David held up both hands, to show them his crossed fingers.

Erin pushed open the little wooden gate and walked down the paved path that was bordered by a neat green lawn and flowerbeds. The front garden was divided from the back by a hedge of fuchsia covered with rosy flowers.

Kate's heart was pounding like a jackhammer. "You push the bell," she told Erin.

Erin did so. They heard the bell ring. From somewhere in the house a dog barked, but that was all. No voices, no footsteps.

They looked at each other. "It doesn't look as if there's anyone in," Erin said eventually.

Her mother squeezed her eyes shut for a moment.

"We can come back again," Erin hurriedly added.

"Hello, hello," a voice suddenly said from behind the tall hedge. "Is someone there?"

"Yes."

"I thought I heard old Toby barking. If you wait a moment I'll be right there with you. I was clipping the hedge. It's growing like a weed, sure it is, with all this sunshine we've been having."

The speaker spoke in the soft voice that was typical of the western Irish, but she spoke so quickly, her words all seeming to run together, that it was difficult to understand her.

Kate looked at Erin.

"Her daughter, perhaps?" Erin said.

Kate nodded. She'd prepared herself for some relative to be there looking after Mary.

The door opened. A diminutive woman in a large battered straw hat stood in the doorway. She was wearing a light rain jacket and gardening gloves, and still held a pair of wooden-handled hedge clippers in her left hand.

"I'm sorry I didn't hear the bell till Toby started barking. I was out in the garden cutting the hedge." She tilted her head in an unspoken question. There was a smudge of earth across her wrinkled brown cheek.

The pounding of Kate's heart echoed in her ears. She felt as if her entire body was a drum being beaten. She opened her mouth to speak, but nothing came out.

"We were looking for Mary Callahan," Erin said.

The woman smiled delightedly. "Well then, you've found her," she said, her brown eyes sparkling. "I'm Mary Callahan. Come in, the both of you."

Chapter Thirty-four

Erin stepped back to allow her mother to go in ahead of her. They both stood in the narrow hall as Mary closed the front door. On the wall opposite them hung a large picture of Jesus, pointing to his crimson heart, from which emanated golden rays.

Mary put down her garden shears and hung up her jacket in the hall closet. "Now where shall we go?" she muttered to herself. She smiled at them. " 'Tis a little too wet for sitting in the garden. I think we'll go into the parlor."

She led them into the front room. A peat fire glowed a welcome in the tiled fireplace.

"You'll have to forgive the mess," she said, pointing to the sewing machine sitting on the table in the bay window. "I'm making my great-granddaughter a dress for her first communion."

"How lovely!" Kate said, going to the table. She touched the soft white satin. "I'm sure it will be beautiful."

Mary stared at her. "You're not from hereabouts, are you?"

"No."

"Sit down. Sit down." Mary indicated the small sofa covered in a brown tweed.

Kate and Erin sat side by side, upright, tense, both breathing fast.

Mary sat in the modern rocker by the fireplace, her feet barely touching the floor. "Is it England you're from?" she asked.

"We flew in from England today," Erin said, when her mother didn't reply.

"We're from Canada." This time it was Kate who spoke.

"Canada?"

Was it merely Kate's imagination or did a flicker of sadness cross Mary's weathered face when she repeated the name?

There was a little statue of the Virgin Mary on the mantelshelf, her hands pressed together in prayer. Kate fixed her eyes on it as she said, "My name is Kate. Kate Benson. And this is my daughter, Erin Benson."

"Kate . . . and Erin. You must have Irish ancestry to have Christian names like that."

"Yes," Kate said. "My mother was Irish."

"Was she now? And was she from these parts?"

"Yes."

"Ah," Mary said, with a relieved smile. "So that's why you came to call on me. I must say I was wondering about it. Now I understand. We have many people coming here from America, looking for their ancestors."

"I don't think many of them would have such a strange story as mine to tell."

"Oh, they have all kinds of stories. Father O'Malley—he's our parish priest—was just telling me this morning when I was at mass that he'd had a fellow from Texas come into the church. He asked Father O'Malley if he could help him find the ancestors of someone who'd gone to America in the time of the great famine. 'His name was Paddy Fitzgerald,' said he to Father O'Malley. 'Then he was one of hundreds with that name,' says the good father to the man." Mary chuckled at her story.

Erin and Kate conjured up weak smiles.

"But you were telling me about your story, Mrs. . . . I'm sorry, my memory's like a sieve nowadays."

"Benson."

"Ah, yes. Mrs. Benson. Would you be wanting a cup of tea? I've everything ready for my own tea. It wouldn't take me a minute to get it."

"Maybe in a few minutes?"

Erin could sense her mother's tension as she tried to find a way to tell Mary who she was. She knew that she didn't want to shock her, that this slow preamble was the right way to do it, but she felt like screaming with impatience. Any minute now someone could come in and their chance would be gone.

Kate must have felt the same way, because she leaned forward and said to Mary, "Would you mind if I told you my story? I'll try not to make it too long."

Mary nodded, but there was a small frown between her eyebrows, as if she was beginning to regret letting these two strange women into her house.

"My name is Kate, but my mother used to call me Katie," Kate began. "My mother was a servant in a big house in England."

Mary gave a tiny gasp, her brown eyes widening. "You did say she was Irish, your mother."

"She was. She'd come from Ireland to serve in this big house. The master of the house had a handsome son. He fell in love with the servant-girl and they had a child. The child was me."

"Holy Mother of God," Mary whispered. The quiet hands became agitated, twisting the gold crucifix that hung from a chain about her neck. She began to rock her chair, back and forth, back and forth, her eyes never leaving Kate's face.

"Then the war began. The second world war. The young man went away to fight. Most of the children near London were being sent away."

"Evacuated," Mary whispered. And still she rocked, her chair squeaking as it moved back and forth, back and forth.

"That's right. Evacuated. It was suggested that the child—me—should be evacuated, too. Some children were going to Canada. That was the safest place, the lady of the house told my mother. Canada was far away from all the bombing and, if Hitler invaded England, I would be safe from all harm."

"That's what *she* told me," Mary said.

Kate continued as if Mary hadn't spoken. "But even the ships bearing innocent children weren't safe from attack. One of them was torpedoed and dozens of children died."

Mary stopped rocking. Her face was contorted. Her lips pursed together as she struggled to keep her composure. "She was killed. My darling Katie was killed."

Tears began rolling down her cheeks. "I sent her to her death."

Kate was on her feet. She dropped to her knees beside the rocking chair. "No, you didn't. You didn't. I'm here."

Mary shrank from her, her chin trembling. "I don't understand. You're not making sense. Bridget will be in soon to make me my tea. You'd best speak to her."

Kate sank back on her heels. "Don't be afraid of me. Please, don't be afraid. I'm your daughter Katie."

"Katie's dead."

"You thought she was. They told you a terrible lie to get rid of you. When I arrived in Canada, I had false papers. No one could trace my parents or my original address. All I knew was that I was Katie. I never really knew my surname because everyone always called you Mary, of course."

Erin broke in. "We didn't know your surname until Giles told me."

Mary went so white that Kate was afraid she was about to faint. "Giles? What does he know about this?"

"He knows that I'm alive," Kate said. "My daughter Erin told him. It was she who found all this out for me."

"Did Giles know about the lie?"

"No," Erin said. "He was horrified. What's more, his mother told him that you had been on the ship with your daughter and that you were dead, too."

Mary reared up in her chair, her hands pressing down on the armrests. "God in heaven! That lying bitch!"

Kate recoiled at the venom in Mary's voice.

"May her soul be damned to everlasting fires for what she did."

Kate was tempted to say "Amen" to that.

Mary sank back into her chair again, her lips pursed tightly together as if she were desperately trying to hold back tears. She drew in several deep breaths. "Was it Lucy told you where to find me?" she asked eventually.

Erin answered, knowing that her mother might have trouble with that question. "She told us you were alive. Her grandson found out where you lived."

Mary's lips twitched. "Young David. She's so proud

of him. He sounds like a good boy." The fresh color left her cheeks again. "Does Giles know I'm alive?"

"No," Kate said.

"Thank God." Mary clutched at Kate's shoulder. "He must never know. You must never tell him." Her grip tightened. "Promise me in the name of Jesus and His Holy Mother."

"I promise," Kate said.

"You, too." Mary nodded at Erin.

"I promise."

"He mustn't know. Giles must never know," Mary murmured. Her head sank back against the chair cushion. Then she sat bolt upright again as if she had just realized something extremely important. She peered down at Kate, who was still on her knees beside her chair.

"Are you really my Katie? You look far too old to be my little Kate."

"I'm sixty."

"Sixty? Ah, to be sure," Mary said with a long sigh. "That would be right, I suppose. To me you'll always be a child with long pigtails down to her waist. Tell me what you remember of me?"

"I remember the song you sang to me. *Toora, loora, loora.* And I still have the book you gave me. *The Secret Garden.* And the photograph inside it of you and my father. That's what started all this. I'd forgotten everything, you see. Then . . . then my husband was killed and I started having nightmares about being sent away."

"You poor child." Mary's hand strayed over her daughter's bent head. Then she looked up at Erin. "Erin."

"Yes?"

"Your mother's knees will be sore from kneeling on the floor beside me. Will you come and sit here in my chair, so that your mother and I can sit together on the sofa?"

"Of course." Erin stood up.

" 'Tis a tall girl you are, compared with us shorties, isn't that so, Katie?"

"Erin takes after her father," Kate said. She waited

for Mary to take her place on the sofa and then sat beside her.

Mary turned to Erin, as if she was afraid to look at her daughter. "So you are my granddaughter, Erin?"

"Yes, I am."

"And have you any children of your own?"

"Not yet. One day, I hope. I would like a family."

"Don't leave it too long. Your family is God's best gift to you. Any young man?"

Erin hesitated.

"She's going out with David," Kate said.

"David who?"

"Lucy's grandson."

"Jesus, Mary and Joseph! Is she really? Fancy that. Isn't it a strange world we live in? My granddaughter going out with Lucy's grandson. Does Lucy know about this?"

"Yes."

"Well, well, well." Mary glanced at the clock on the mantelshelf. "I should be making the tea for you, but Bridget comes in at half three, so we haven't much time to talk." She took Kate's hand in hers. "Katie, my child, let me be looking at you. You were such a pretty little thing when you were small. Now I see you have your father's nose." She ran her forefinger down Kate's nose.

"I'm afraid so," Kate said ruefully.

"He was such a handsome man, Katie. Such a handsome man. And he loved me. It wasn't a case of the aristocrat seducing the little Irish maid. We loved each other. He would have done anything for me. Anything."

"I know that," Kate said softly. "I've heard how he defied his parents and set us up in a cottage on the estate."

"That he did. And threatened to leave Amberley with us forever if they wouldn't let us stay. If only there hadn't been a war . . ." Mary's voice trailed away, leaving all three of them thinking of how different things might have been had the war not intervened.

Only Erin gave voice to her thoughts. "If there hadn't been a war I might not exist."

"True." Kate gave her daughter a warm smile. "Because had I not gone to Canada I wouldn't have met my darling Jim."

"That's your husband? God rest his soul," Mary said. "So, out of evil comes good." She stared at Kate, her brown eyes searching her face with great intensity. "What I am to say to you now may hurt you, but you mustn't let it. You are my first-born child. I believe that with all my heart. You are the fruit of my love for Giles and his for me. But I can never acknowledge you. I can never say to my children and my grandchildren and my great-grandchildren, this is my daughter."

Kate hung her head and wept. And Erin, watching her mother, wept with her.

Mary stroked Kate's head, the brown age-marked hand smoothing her weeping daughter's hair. "It isn't for want of love of you, Katie. I have always loved you. Even when you died, as I thought, I prayed for your soul's rest every night of my life. But my family here knows nothing of my life in England. Nothing of Giles. Nothing of you."

"I don't see how it could possibly hurt now," Erin said. "Surely they'd understand."

Kate frantically shook her head at Erin.

"No, Mom. I won't be quiet. I don't see why you should have to suffer. None of this was your fault. Why should you find your mother after all these years, only to have her tell you she can't acknowledge you?"

"I can't give you the reason," Mary whispered. "It affects too many lives. On both sides of the Irish Sea."

Kate's hand flew to her mouth. "Oh, God. Then Lucy wasn't imagining it. You were married."

Mary's eyes flashed. "Did Lucy tell you? She swore to me she would never tell."

"Lucy's not as clear-minded as you are," Kate said. "Her mind gets muddled. She let out a hint of something and I put two and two together. Is it true?"

Mary nodded. "God help me, it is."

"I hope someone's going to explain what's going on here," Erin said, "because you've lost me way back."

"*Please,* Erin," Kate said fiercely. "I'll explain later, but we must get this said before someone—"

"My niece, Bridget," Mary said, her voice cracking as she spoke.

"Before Bridget comes in. Is there any proof?" Kate asked Mary.

Mary's eyes met Kate's. "There is. Locked away in a tin in my old hatbox on top of the wardrobe. I've been terrified for years that I might end up in hospital and the family would go through my things and find it. But I could never bring myself to burn it or throw it away."

"Would you give it to me? I'd take good care of it."

Mary gazed at Kate's face. "So you would, child, considering it proves who you are. And *what* you are. But I'll only give it to you if you promise never to use it against him."

"Against Giles? Why should I? He's my father, after all."

"You never know. There could be money involved. A great deal of money, if the estate's as rich as it was when I was there."

Slowly, Kate shook her head. "I'm not interested."

"There's many as good as you would be tempted by a great deal of money or land."

Again Kate shook her head. "I promise that I shall never use what you give me against Giles."

Mary stared at her. Then she nodded. "I believe you. You're my flesh and blood, after all."

"And Giles's."

"Is he well?" Mary asked eagerly. "Have you seen him?"

"Not yet. But Erin has. Tell my . . . tell Mary about Giles," Kate said, giving Erin a warning look as she spoke.

"He was wonderful," Erin said. "We got on very well. He's still very handsome, and high-spirited, too."

"By high-spirited I take it you mean impatient. He always was as impatient as a tetchy horse, was Giles. Now, we mustn't waste any more time talking." Groaning, Mary got to her feet and walked stiffly to the door. "Come and help me," she told Kate. "And you, Erin, will you be keeping watch for my Bridget, please? If she comes you'll have to keep her talking, which is never too hard to do with Bridget. But, mind you, don't be telling her who you are."

"I won't."

Erin was on tenterhooks while her mother and Mary were in the bedroom. All she could hear was the sound of a chair being dragged across the room and much huffing and puffing. Then a shout of triumph, "I have it!"

Aware of the murmured conversation from the bedroom and feeling rather left out, Erin stood in the center of the small front room, gazing at the photographs of members of Mary's family that crammed the mantelshelf and the top of the sideboard.

My family, Erin thought, with a flood of warm feeling. Then she grew cold when she realized that none of them could meet.

By the time Kate and Mary came back Erin had examined every single photograph. "I take it that all these are yours," she said to Mary. "You have a very large family."

Mary smiled. "Larger by two today," she said, looking at them both. Instinctively, all three merged and stood in the center of the room, hugging each other.

The gate opened and shut. Toby started barking outside.

Mary's eyes distended with fright. Kate took charge. "It will be all right," she said. "But first, I want a picture. Erin, stand there with Mary," she commanded, snatching up her camera.

"Mom, there's no time," Erin protested.

"Do as I say."

The camera flashed. The doorbell rang.

"She has a key," Mary said.

"Take our picture, Erin." Kate stuck the camera in Erin's shaking hands and went to stand beside Mary, her arm around her waist.

Again, the camera flashed.

Bridget rapped on the front window, unable to see through the net curtains. "Auntie May, are you in there? I left my key at home."

"I'm just coming, dear."

"I'd like to write to you," Kate said to Mary. "How can I do that?"

"You may send letters to me in care of Father O'Malley. He knows."

Kate's eyes rounded with surprise. "He does?"

"Ah, 'tis easy to see you didn't continue in the Catholic faith, my darling Katie. The confessional, Kate. You have given me your address in Canada. Wait until I write to you with Father O'Malley's address. Then you can write to me there."

"Auntie May!" Bridget yelled. "What are you up to in there? It's started to rain again. I'm getting soaked."

"Sure I'm coming, Bridget. Will you hold your horses? I've visitors in here." Mary held out her arms to Kate. "God bless you, my darling girl," she whispered against her neck.

"Good-bye." Kate was trying not to weep. "I love you."

"And I love you, too."

Then it was Erin's turn. She found herself enfolded in the thin, surprisingly strong arms. "I look forward to hearing of your engagement to my friend's grandson," Mary said.

"I've only known David a couple of weeks," Erin protested, smiling.

"Ah, but the Lord has his ways."

Bridget was still hammering on the door.

"We can't keep her any longer or she'll yell the place down." Mary went to the door and opened it. "Come on in, Bridget," she said. "These ladies were just going."

Bridget stepped inside, a large-boned woman with red, flyaway hair that was dampened by the rain. "I didn't know you had company," she said, staring at Kate and Erin.

Mary held out her hand to Kate. "Good-bye to you, Mrs. Benson," she said, as grand as the lady of a noble house. "God bless you."

"Good-bye, Mrs. Callahan," Kate murmured, her eyes lowered. "Thank you for all your kindness."

"Just you write to Father O'Malley. He'll explain it all to you. Good-bye, Miss Benson." The brown eyes, sharp and bright as a sparrow's, looked directly into Erin's. "I'm glad you brought your mother to me."

Mary watched them as they hurried down the garden path. When they were out of sight she turned to her niece and said, "Now come on in, Bridget, and make me my tea."

"Who were those ladies, Auntie May?"

"Oh, just two women from Canada looking for their ancestors."

Chapter Thirty-five

Kate and Erin walked swiftly up the narrow country lane, neither speaking, both intent on setting a distance between themselves and Mary's house. Then, when they had turned the corner, they stood in a gateway by the side of the road, surrounded by green fields.

Beyond the gate, a lane led to an old ruined farmhouse. It was roofless, open to the elements, a symbol of all the abandoned homes in western Ireland and of the people who'd been forced to leave them to seek their fortune—or just enough to avoid starvation—in faraway lands.

Erin looked at her mother and saw that she was openly weeping, the tears pouring down her face mingling with the soft rain. She put her arms around her. They stood together at the side of the empty road.

"I'm glad she's here in her own country," Kate said after a while, easing away from Erin. "She seems to belong here."

"Yes. I must say I find it hard to imagine her at Amberley. It would be like putting a wild violet in a conservatory." Erin did not add her other thought: that she also found it hard to think of Mary with Giles. If fate hadn't intervened, would their love have lasted? she wondered. "Are you okay, Mom?"

Her mother nodded. "I feel numb at the moment. I expect it will all hit me later on." She turned to look down the road. "I wonder if I shall ever see her again."

"I don't see why not. Next time we plan to come to Ireland we can write to this Father O'Malley and make arrangements to see her on her own."

"But it will still be like this, won't it? All hurried and secret."

Erin hesitated. Then she said, "I'm afraid so. Are you sorry I found her?"

Her mother looked astonished. "Sorry? My darling Erin, how could I possibly be sorry? I'm just sad that it can't be more than this, that's all."

"What was all this talk about marriage and proof—" Erin stopped when she saw the look of alarm in her mother's eyes.

"David's coming down the hill."

They went to join him and walked with him back to the church. "Everything okay?" he asked, once they were in the car.

Erin glanced at her mother, who had chosen to sit in the back seat this time. "We're both feeling a bit shell-shocked, that's all," she said. "But it went very well. Mary was on her own, thank goodness. She was far livelier than I'd expected. Very clear-minded. Don't you agree, Mom?"

"Definitely. I suppose I was expecting an Irish version of Lucy."

"God help us," David said.

Kate smiled. "No, really. She—she seemed perfectly content with her life. I only hope that our visit won't make her feel unsettled or unhappy."

"Do you want to sit here and talk?" David asked, "Or would you prefer to go back to the hotel right away?"

Kate leaned forward. "I'd like to go back, if you don't mind. I'm feeling a little shattered."

David started up the car.

"Just a minute," Erin said. "Before we go anywhere I want one thing explained to me," She twisted around to look at her mother. "Were Mary and Giles married or not?"

David's head whipped around. *"Married?"*

Kate gave Erin one of her scorching looks.

"What?" Erin said, her voice rising. "Does that look mean you don't want to talk about it with David here or you don't want to talk about it, period?"

"This is my business, Erin," Kate said, her mouth pinched, "and I don't choose to discuss it at present."

"I'm sorry, but if what I suspect is true, this affects us all."

Kate's eyes flared at Erin. "You heard my mother. She entrusted the document to me. To me, only."

"Excuse me," David intervened. "But what sort of document is this?"

"It's—"

"Shut up, Erin!"

Erin gripped her bottom lip between her teeth.

"Forgive me, Mrs. Benson," David said, "but if we're talking about Mary and Giles having been married, there would be tremendous repercussions, particularly legal ones."

"Exactly. That's why I wish Erin had kept quiet about it."

"I'm sorry, Mom, but I don't think it should be hushed up."

"You're not thinking this through, Erin. Number one, it's none of David's business. Number two, this document is going to be placed in my safety deposit box in Canada, never to see the light of day again."

"Until, perhaps, you die, Mrs. Benson," said David the lawyer.

"Then I sincerely hope that Erin will carry out my wishes. Which are, Erin," Kate said, leaning forward again to confront her, "that this document be kept secret forever."

"Then why on earth did you take it from Mary, if you wanted to keep it secret?"

"I took it for two reasons. Because it eased my mother's mind to have it taken away, and because it proves that I am the legitimate child of Giles Hogarth and Mary Foley or Mary Hogarth, as she truly was."

The car windows were getting steamed up. David switched on the demister. "So," he said, "this document *is* a marriage certificate."

Kate released a deep sigh. "Now see what you've done?" she told Erin. "Yes. The marriage of Giles and Mary."

"And I take it that this marriage took place long before Giles's other marriage."

"The certificate is dated 1935, the year of my birth."

"Seven years before," David said. "So Giles's marriage to Lady Cynthia might not have been valid."

"But Giles thought Mary was dead."

"I know he did. But I've a feeling he would have needed absolute proof of her death before he remarried for the marriage to be legally binding."

Kate put a hand to her head. "I can't take any more of this. Would you please stop talking about it and drive me back to the hotel."

Erin opened her mouth to protest, but David said, "Your mother is right. Everyone's feeling too emotional at present to be able to discuss this rationally. Better to leave it until later."

The return journey was practically silent, with everyone occupied with their own thoughts.

As they took the Limerick bypass, David said, "I take it that no one's interested in any sightseeing."

"I'd rather not," Kate said. "But you two do whatever you want to do. I don't want to spoil your day for you."

When they got back to the hotel, the three of them stood in the lobby in an awkward silence. No one wanted to be the first to speak.

"I think I'll have a rest," Kate finally said. "I'm feeling really tired. Why don't you both go out and have a look around?"

"Are you sure you'll be okay, Mom?"

"I'm sure."

"I'll just go back to the room for a minute," Erin told David. "Meet you in the lounge, okay?"

"Okay."

When they reached their room, Erin closed the door. "I just want to say—"

Kate took off her jacket and threw it on her bed. "If it's about the certificate, I don't want to discuss it."

"Don't cut me short, Mother, please. I just want to say that I do understand how you feel about it. But please don't come to any hasty decision yet. Why not discuss it with David? After all, he is a lawyer."

"He is also a Hogarth and very much involved with the family. I'm telling you now that I don't want to discuss this with anyone, especially David."

Erin knew when she was up against a brick wall. Her mother could be incredibly stubborn. She also knew that she must be feeling emotionally raw. "Would you like me to stay with you?" she asked, her voice softening.

"No. But thanks for asking, sweetie." Her mother gave her a faint smile. "I feel as if I could sleep for twenty-four hours."

"Then do so. I won't disturb you."

Kate sat down in front of the dressing table and stared at her face. "Trouble is, I'm not sure I can sleep."

"Have you got some sleeping pills with you?"

"Yes. I brought them for the plane, but you know how I hate taking those things."

Erin crossed the room and leaned over her mother. "One's not going to hurt. You've had an incredibly emotional day. I think you could do with a good sleep."

"You're right."

"I'll just clean my teeth. I'm going to change into pants and my Reeboks, in case we decide to go walking."

"You should. Don't miss out on the chance. After all, this is your grandmother's country."

They exchanged strained smiles with each other in the mirror.

When Erin quietly closed the door behind her, her mother was already lying down on the bed.

"She's exhausted," she told David, when he asked her if her mother was okay.

As they sat drinking lager in the lounge, there was a strange uneasiness between them. A combination of the shadow of the marriage certificate and being in unfamiliar surroundings together.

"What would you like to do?" he asked.

"Nothing too strenuous."

"We couldn't have chosen a better hotel for that. Bunratty Castle is less than five minutes away."

"By car?"

"No. By foot. And next to the castle is the folk museum with all the old buildings and also the famous pub, Durty Nelly's."

"Wow!" Erin bounced up. "Let's do it."

"Which?"

"All of it. Just as long as I can walk. I'm feeling incredibly tense."

"I'm not surprised." David stood very close to her, so that she could smell the faint fragrance of his spicy cologne. "Anything I can do to help?"

"Walking will do it."

David grinned. "Okay. I get the message. Tell me," he said, his expression serious. "Have you any regrets about all this? Your quest, I mean?"

"No. None at all. I asked Mom the same question and she said the same thing. My only regret is finding out about the marriage. It makes everything so much more complicated." She gazed up at David. "What are we going to do about it?"

"We're not going to do anything about it for now. For all we know, it might not even be a valid document. The subject is off limits until your mother wants to discuss it."

"But there's too much at stake to—"

David put his fingers across her lips. "No. Pretend you know nothing about it, or you'll never be able to relax."

"Okay. You're right. Let's go, then."

As they strode across the car-park, David took her hand in his.

They could have spent a day, at least, exploring Bunratty Castle and the Folk Park, with its old barns and simple dwelling houses, and the street of old shops that Erin felt sure she'd seen in a couple of films set in Ireland. But it was growing late, so they decided to keep the castle for the next day and just concentrate on the Folk Park.

After an hour, they still hadn't seen half of it, but the rain was getting heavier and beginning to soak through their rain jackets.

"Tea, I think," David said, leading her into a cozy tea shop with red gingham tablecloths and curtains. The ubiquitous aroma of smoldering peat hung in the air. The peat fire glowed red in the hearth, an antidote to the damp chill that seemed to have seeped into Erin's very bones.

Soon, she was warm inside as well, as she devoured floury scones spread with golden butter and homemade strawberry jam washed down by several cups of hot, strong tea.

David released a contented sigh. "Ah, to be sure, that was a treat," he said with a fairly good attempt at an Irish accent. He smiled across the table at her. "Last stop Durty Nelly's?"

"Let's keep that for later." Erin pushed back her chair and yawned. "I'm feeling really sleepy. Must be the effect of the misty day and the fire." She stretched out her hands to the warmth of the peat fire.

"Not to mention three scones and a piece of gingerbread."

"Half a piece. We shared it."

"So we did."

David asked the waitress—who wore an old-fashioned dress with long skirts and a white apron—for the bill. "Will your mother be awake yet?"

Erin looked at her watch. "I doubt it. She was going to take a sleeping pill." Their eyes met. The green in David's seemed more pronounced than usual. Must be the Irish influence, Erin thought, smiling to herself.

"What's funny?"

"Nothing. I'm just feeling very relaxed, that's all."

"Good. That was the general idea." David leaned back in his chair, his posture loose and easy, but his eyes remained watchful.

The waitress brought the bill, acknowledging David's generous tip with a warm smile, and they pulled on their damp jackets to leave the cozy warmth for the chill outside.

As they started off down the path, Erin instinctively moved into the circle of David's arm. The rain was no longer the "soft rain" the Irish liked to call it. By now it was a hard rain, beating down on them. They hurried to the castle and then ran for cover beneath a large tree that grew near the castle entrance.

Although it was only just after six o'clock, the dark clouds and the gray curtain of rain made it seem more like late evening. Everyone else must have taken shelter inside the buildings, for the place was deserted.

David leaned his back against the old stone wall and reached for her, his hands pressed on her back, drawing her close to him. She could feel the entire length of his body against hers. Then, without saying a word, he pushed her away a little, so that he could unzip first his jacket and then hers. Opening both jackets so that less cloth came between them, he pulled her close again, wrapping his jacket around her. Their bodies met, their moist mouths clung, open to each other.

Everything in Erin seemed molten, liquid. As David braced his back against the wall, it was she who now pressed closer to him, in her longing to become one with him. He held her wet face in his hands, lifting it to his searching mouth, their tongues intermingling to add more moisture.

"Please," Erin said, her voice harsh with longing.

"Want to make a run for it?" David asked.

She nodded. Then wished she hadn't when the heat of his body was taken from her.

Hand in hand, they ran down the path and along the sidewalk, back to the hotel.

They burst into the foyer, acknowledging the reception clerk's courteous greeting with a quick, "Hi!" Rushing through the lounge, they broke into a run as soon as they reached the corridor to David's room.

He cursed as he fumbled with the card-key, his hand slippery wet, then he flung the door open. They didn't even bother to turn on the light. The curtains were partly open, but it was so dark no one could have seen in. Besides, they were too far gone now to care.

Laughing, they kicked off their shoes and stripped off their wet clothes, leaving them in a heap on the floor.

"My God, you're beautiful," David breathed.

"You can't even see me," Erin protested.

"I can see you all right." He came closer to her. "I can also touch you." Erin shivered as his hands encircled her breasts.

"Hang on a minute," he said, and bent to fumble with his wallet. Then, after a moment, "Okay."

The time spent beneath the tree had formed the urgency of their desire. There was no need to wait. Their bodies were eager, ready, primed for each other. As they merged in the rhythm of love, they moved as one, two halves of one single body, surging toward infinity. Erin knew a blinding moment of realization: that this was what she'd been waiting for all her life. Then all thought was lost in the mindless mutual soaring, soaring, soaring . . . until it became unbearable to wait any longer and they burst into a million cascading fragments of shuddering ecstasy.

Chapter Thirty-six

The ringing of the telephone woke them. David sat up, cursing to himself as he fumbled around, trying to find the phone. Still half asleep, Erin groaned, missing the warmth of his body against her spine.

"Who was that?" she asked, when David replaced the receiver.

"A private investigator I hired to find Harrington. Sorry the phone woke you, but I told him to call me as soon as he had some news."

Erin sat up, clutching the sheet around her. "And does he?"

"Not only has he found him, but he's actually spoken to him. When he told Harrington who'd hired him, Harrington said he wanted to speak to me urgently."

"Where is Harrington?"

"He's at his niece's place in Eastbourne. I've got the number. At least, I think I have. I had to write it down in the dark."

"Put the light on."

David switched on the light, making Erin blink. They exchanged smiles that held the slight embarrassment of waking up in bed together for the first time. David bent his head to kiss her. A soft, lingering kiss this time.

"Hello, lover," he said.

Erin put her hands on his head to draw him closer, feeling his hair springy beneath her fingers. "Hello, lover. What's the time?"

"You don't want to know."

"That bad, eh?" She peered at the bedside clock. "Quarter past eight? That can't be right."

"Sorry, but it is."

"Yikes! My mother will be wondering where on earth I am."

"She'll know you're with me."

Erin grinned at him. "That's what I'm afraid of." She relaxed against the pillows and gave him a lazy smile. "I'm not quite sure what to say to you."

"I know what you mean. Don't say anything. As far as I'm concerned there are no words to describe it."

"That's how I feel. Only . . . I wasn't sure if it was the same for you, or not."

He leaned over to circle her face with his fingers, stroking each eyebrow, the length of her nose, across her lips. "It was, my darling, it was." He kissed her with exquisite sweetness, his hand caressing the length of her spine. Then he drew away.

"Don't stop."

"I don't want to, but we have to think about your mother."

Erin sighed. "You're right. And you probably want to speak to Harrington as soon as possible."

"I think I should, don't you? The fact that he's eager to speak to me makes me think it could be really important."

"I'm glad he's safe with his niece. I know it's stupid, but I began to have all sorts of nasty thoughts about what might have happened to him. Brrr." A shiver ran across Erin's shoulders.

"Simon tends to have that effect on one, I'm afraid."

"He certainly does. Yet he can also pour on the charm, which makes it hard to decide if you're just imagining things about him, or not."

Erin jumped out of bed. Then she gave a little screech as she realized that she was standing by the window, fully exposed to view. She sprang behind the curtain as David wrapped the bedspread around himself to draw the curtains closed.

"That'll teach us not to be so impatient that we don't bother to close the curtains," he said, laughing. "The local inhabitants will never be the same again."

"Oh, get lost," Erin said, throwing a pillow at him. David's room seemed to have taken on a rosy glow, which she was sure wasn't just a result of the lights being turned on.

David released the bedspread and then drew her to him, wrapping it around them both. "Happy?" he asked, gazing into her eyes.

"Deliriously."

"I know this may sound a little premature, but I think . . . No, I *know* that I'm in love with you, Erin Benson."

Erin felt a rush of sweet relief. "I feel the same way about you. Oh, David." She drew in and then released a long, deep breath., "Is it possible in such a short time, do you think? We've only known each other, what, a couple of weeks."

"I never would have thought it possible. But, then, I've never felt the same way about anyone else as I feel about you."

"I know. It's strange, isn't it? Sort of scary. As if it's not real."

"It's real, all right." His hands curved around her bottom, pulling her against him, so that the bedspread slipped down from them.

"No, David," Erin said, laughing. "We have to stop this. We've got to get dressed, remember?"

"Oh, yeah. Right. Too bad you're such a spoilsport." He gave her a lopsided grimace that made her laugh even more.

"Can I use your shower?" she asked.

"Sure. But you realize you're going to have put on those damp clothes again?"

"Yuck, so I will. Oh, well, that's life. It was worth it." Erin went to the bathroom door. "Why don't you call Harrington while I'm in the bathroom?"

"Okay. Let me in there first, then."

As Erin stood in the shower, steam rising around her, she thought of nothing but David and his love for her. It was like a miracle. She had sensed that this was not a man who casually threw "I love you" around. Several men had said it to her before. Before today, however, only Rob had really meant it. But Rob's concept of love had been very different from hers. It had never encompassed longevity and the prospect of marriage and children. She had the feeling that David felt the same way as she did about love, despite the fact that he'd come from a broken home.

Or maybe because of it.

When she came out of the bathroom, wrapped in one of the thick white toweling robes, David was sitting in his robe on the edge of the bed, writing on the message pad. He looked up at her. "Just a moment, darling. I want to get this down before I forget something."

As he continued to write, Erin pulled on her clothes, shivering as she dragged on the damp jeans, with their mud-stained hems.

"Okay," David said in a brisk, businesslike voice. "It appears we were right. Harrington was bundled out of Amberley by Simon, who didn't even allow him to see Giles before he left. Simon's excuse was that Giles was far too sick to be looked after by an old man. What interests me most is that Harrington told me that Giles had been very worried about your visit."

Erin's heart plummeted. "That's what I was afraid of. I think we know why now, don't we? Giles must have been worried sick when I told him who I was. He knew that he'd been married to Mary. He must have been terrified that the truth would now come out." She sat down beside David on the bed. "I still don't know why he made that announcement to the family. If I'd have been him, in the circumstances, I would have had me thrown out of the house."

"Who knows why he acted as he did? Maybe he had a spasm of guilty conscience."

Erin sighed. "So I suppose he decided not to see me again, or my mother at all."

"But that's what I'm trying to tell you, if you'll only let me get a word in," David said. "Apparently Giles slept very badly Sunday night, but when Harrington came to wake him the next morning, Giles told him that he felt very calm and that he was going to accept what fate had sent him. He said that he was actually looking forward to meeting your mother and was looking forward to hearing from you."

Erin's hand went to her throat. "Oh, my God. So it wasn't Giles's decision not to speak to me, or to you, when we called."

"Apparently not."

"That bloody Simon."

"So it seems. Harrington's convinced he's up to no good with Giles."

Erin shivered. "You don't think—"

"No, no. Simon's too clever to do anything like that. But there are ways of making an old man tractable. Ways that can include cutting him off from the outside world and sedating him just a little more than his doctor ordered." David's expression was grim. "It wouldn't be the first time that happened in a family."

"What on earth can we do?"

"I could try to speak to Alexander again, but he wasn't very willing to listen to me the last time."

"And we suspect that Mrs. Edwards is working with Simon."

"She was certainly engaged by him. She may be quite innocent of any actual wrongdoing, of course, but if Simon's holding the reins, it would be hard for her to say no, unless it was something illegal he asked her to do."

"We need to get to Giles."

"How do we do that, short of breaking in? And that's impossible. Getting into Amberley is like getting into the proverbial Fort Knox. Sophisticated alarm systems, spikes on the walls . . ."

"There's certainly no point in appealing to Simon, is there?"

"Definitely not. If you went to him, all it would do would be alert him to your plans."

"If appealing won't work, how about threatening him?"

"With what?"

Erin grimaced. "Good point. We can't prove a thing, can we?"

" 'Fraid not. Even Harrington's evidence isn't worth a dime."

"Then we're stumped. But we can't let Giles be manipulated by that bastard!" Erin cried. Then she felt waves of alternating heat and cold run over her entire body as she realized what she had said. "Oh, my God."

"What?"

"Bastard."

"So you said, but what about it?"

Erin gazed at him, willing him to think her thoughts, but she saw that she was going to have to explain. "Simon may not literally be a bastard, but his father probably was."

Now she could see that David understood. His eyes darkened. "If you're talking about the marriage certificate, it may not even be valid."

"Of course it's valid."

"Even if it is, I can't verify it until I can see it for myself."

Erin jumped up from the bed, the inaction getting to her. "If only I could get my hands on it, I could make a copy without my mother knowing. Maybe I could get hold of it when she's sleeping."

"That would be sneaky."

"So what? If it helps Giles it's worth being sneaky."

"Why don't we just tell your mother the truth?"

"About Simon, you mean?"

"Yes. Don't you think she'd be concerned if she knew that Simon was keeping her father from seeing her?"

"She might." Erin suddenly felt more positive. "I think she would. But—"

"No buts. Let's just try it and see what happens. I'd better get dressed. Why don't you go and find your mother. Tell her where you've been," David added, with a wicked grin.

"Like hell!"

"She'll probably guess, anyway. You have that after-love glow about you."

"Oh, yeah. How would you know?"

David grinned at her. He got up and stood in front of her. Her eyelids fluttered closed and she lifted her face to his.

"None of that now," he said with mock severity. "If we start again, we'll never stop." He opened the door for her. "Get away from me, you temptress."

"I don't want to go," Erin complained, her hand on the door.

"I know you don't, but you must. I'll meet you both in the bar. Come as soon as you're ready."

When Erin opened the door to her room, her mother

jumped up from the edge of the bed, where she'd been sitting reading a copy of *Ireland of the Welcomes*. She was already dressed for dinner in a smart suit of green raw silk.

"Where have you been? I'm starving."

"Sorry. I was with David. We went to Bunratty Castle and the Folk Park. Why?" Erin looked at her watch. "Oh, I didn't realize it was late. Sorry, Mom. I thought you might still be asleep."

Her mother's brown eyes were examining her very carefully. "I've been awake for two hours. I was starting to worry that something had happened to you."

"There was a lot to see and the shops were open late." Erin turned away, remembering how her mother used to say, "I can always tell when you're lying, Erin Benson," when she was a kid. "I have to change. It was really wet out there."

"So I saw. I walked around the hotel, just in case you were in the gardens."

"I won't be a moment," Erin murmured, her head hidden in the closet, as she looked for something to wear. "David's going to meet us in the bar for a predinner drink."

"I could do with one."

Her mother was in a ratty mood. Probably reaction, Erin thought as she stripped off her damp clothes. That didn't auger well for their hopes that she might help them work on Simon.

But later, in the dining room, when she took her cue from David, Erin discovered that he had no intention of jumping in and discussing the marriage certificate right away, as she certainly would have done. He seemed intent on making the evening as mellow and enjoyable as possible for all three of them. And he succeeded.

By the time they were drinking Irish coffees to round off a superb meal of oysters, oak-smoked salmon, grilled trout, and decadently rich and creamy desserts even Erin had forgotten about Simon, until she heard David say, "I don't want to have to spoil a perfect evening, but we have something very serious to discuss with you, Kate."

She had asked David to call her Kate after they'd shared that plate of oysters at the start of the meal.

The laughter died from Kate's eyes. "What?" she asked, her voice filled with suspicion.

"I haven't been entirely truthful with you about Giles," Erin said.

"He doesn't want to see me, does he?" Kate said flatly. "I can understand why." She patted her bag, which hung from the back of her chair.

"On the contrary," David said, leaning forward. "At first, we thought that might be the case, but tonight I was in contact with someone who was able to convince me that it's not."

"And who was this person?"

"Harrington. That's Giles's—"

"Harrington!" Kate said, greatly surprised. "He's the other witness on the marriage certificate."

Now it was David and Erin's turn to be surprised. "He is?" Erin said incredulously.

"If he's one witness, who is the other?" David asked. "No, don't tell me. I can guess. It was my grandmother, wasn't it? Ah, now I get it. You knew about the marriage *before* you visited your mother today, didn't you? Lucy told you."

Kate's cheeks reddened. "I'm sorry, but I couldn't tell you before. Lucy became so muddled that I wasn't sure what to believe. It was only when I was with my mother that I knew that Lucy hadn't imagined it." Smiling, Kate told them what Lucy had said about the marriage, complete with all the fanciful embellishments about the Queen in red silk.

David roared with laughter. "Perfect. That sounds just like Lucy, bless her heart. No wonder you didn't believe her." His face became serious again. Moving aside his tall glass of Irish coffee, he leaned forward. "What I am going to tell you now is in the strictest confidence. It must never be told to another living soul, you understand? If it were to reach the media, for instance, it could be disastrous for my cousin. I don't want to mention his name. I think you know who I mean."

Kate nodded, her eyes round with interest.

With Erin's assistance, David told Kate of their suspicions and of his talk with Harrington this evening.

"But that's terrible," Kate whispered, in obvious distress, when they had finished. "Do you think he—your cousin—knows about *this*?" She patted her bag again.

"No, I'm quite sure he doesn't," David said. "But what he is afraid of is that, having fallen out with his grandfather over his renunciation of the title, Erin's arrival on the scene might cause Giles to transfer his affections to her and, of course, to you, his daughter."

"By affections do you mean something tangible, like money?" Kate asked.

David nodded. "Possibly. I'm sure that's what my cousin is concerned about. Money, property . . ."

"But . . . isn't the property all tied up with the title?"

This time it was Erin who explained, proud of her new knowledge about the Maybridge title.

For quite a while after Erin had finished, Kate remained silent. Finally she said, "Forgive me for being a bit dense, but just out of interest, if this"—she nodded her head at her bag—"this thing is completely legal, who would then be Giles's heir to the title?"

David looked at Erin and Erin looked at David.

"Unless Erin had a son," he said with a wry grin, "I would still be the heir."

Erin held her breath for a moment and then released it slowly. "You mean that if S. wasn't the heir anymore, my son—if I had one—would be the next in line?"

"That's it," David said.

"But that can never be," Kate said, sitting up very straight in the velvet-backed chair. "I promised my mother that I would never hurt Giles with what she gave me. But even more importantly, even if Giles died, it must still remain a secret. Otherwise, you know what it would mean to my mother's family in Ireland, all those children and their children after them. . . ." Kate's eyes filled with tears. "Forgive me, Erin, but I could never do that to them."

"Hey, no need to apologize to me, Mom," Erin said. She stretched across the table to touch her mother's hand. "I would never ever ask you to break your promise. I'm not interested in a stupid title, for me or my son—if I ever have one."

Erin looked up to catch David looking with great intensity at her. Her face fiery red, she bent to pick up her fallen napkin.

"What we need is ammunition to fight the enemy, so that we can get into Amberley," David told Kate. "You hold that ammunition." He nodded to her bag.

"Oh, no." Kate hastily unwound the strap from her chair and took the bag on her lap, clutching it against her. "He's the last person I'd want to know about this."

"But don't you see, Mom," Erin said eagerly. "He's the last person who would ever want to divulge the secret of . . . what's in there."

"Then what would be the point?" Kate demanded.

"We can use this as a lever to keep him from locking Giles away in Amberley," David said. "That one piece of paper—or just a copy of it—would mean that your father will be restored to his normal vigorous life. But without it, I'm sorry to have to say, you may never even get to meet him."

"You mean you wouldn't use it to actually disinherit . . . this man we're talking about, but just as a threat?"

David nodded.

"That sounds a bit like blackmail to me."

"Blackmail is when something is used against someone for some sort of evil gain," David said. "This is being used for good."

"You couldn't tell Giles that Mary is alive," Kate said. "I swore to her that I'd never tell him."

"There's no need to tell him," Erin said. "You could have been given the certificate years ago. Or a lawyer might have found it and sent it to you."

"Is there absolutely no other way?" Kate asked.

"I've tried," David said. "I've even confronted the man himself, but to no avail. As the next of kin, he has all the angles covered."

"I want to meet my father before it's too late," Kate said, her fingers running over and over the brown leather bag on her lap. "And I don't want him to come to any harm."

Erin glanced at David, and then stirred the cream round and round in her Irish coffee.

"Very well," Kate said at last. "You can have it."

Erin's eyes blazed at David across the table.

"Thank you. I want only to examine the original to ensure that it is authentic," he told Kate. "Then I'll make a copy and return the original document to you."

"So long as you swear to me that you won't use it to hurt Giles or Mary, in any way," Kate told him.

David took Erin's hand in his and held it very tightly. "I promise I won't use it in any way to hurt Giles or Mary," he told Kate in a low voice. "I swear that on my love for your daughter."

Chapter Thirty-seven

Five frustrating days passed before Simon agreed to met with David again. He was unfailingly courteous, even suggesting that they have lunch together at the Atrium in Westminster on Tuesday, but David told him that what he had to discuss was too private for a meeting in such a public place.

"When you hear what it is, I think you'll agree," he added, to make Simon stew a little.

At first Erin had wanted to deal with Simon by herself. "After all," she told David, "this is actually between him and me."

David agreed, but he'd been able to persuade her not to try to see Simon alone. Besides, he doubted that Simon would ever agree to meet her, if she called him herself. When David had accepted the offer of an evening meeting at Simon's house, he deliberately omitted to mention that Erin would be coming with him.

Erin stood before the house in Hampstead, looking up at the elegant facade. "Very nice," she said, lifting her eyebrows at David.

"Oh, everything in impeccable taste for Simon," David said, "including his wife," he added, as Olivia appeared in the doorway, dressed in a deceptively simple black cotton dress, which fitted her slim figure perfectly, and black-and-silver sandals.

"We heard the car," Olivia said, as they mounted the steps. "Oh, good. You were able to find a parking spot nearby. That makes a change." She turned to Erin. "Why, Miss Benson, what a surprise! I don't think you mentioned to Simon that Miss Benson was coming here with you, did you, David?" Her voice was as cold and smooth as glass.

"No, I didn't. Are you going to invite us in, Olivia?"

She looked a little flustered, as if she wasn't sure that she should. "Of course." She stepped back to allow them to go inside and then offered her smooth cheek for David to kiss. "Simon's speaking to Brussels. An unexpected call," she explained. "We'll wait for him in the drawing room."

She led them into a high-ceilinged room furnished and decorated in the Regency style, with graceful furniture and blue-and-ivory-striped curtains at the tall windows.

"What a lovely room." Erin said impulsively, responding to its cool, airy beauty.

"Thank you," Olivia said. She held her face and body in a stiff, unnatural manner as if she were afraid that if she let go, she might fall apart.

"Hello, hello." Simon came into the room, all vigor and smiles. "Sorry about that." He stopped short when he saw Erin, but the smile remained fixed. "Miss Benson, what a surprise!"

"That's exactly what I said." Now Olivia was smiling, too. A carbon copy of her husband.

Erin shook hands with Simon. As she took his hand she thought of it as a salute fencers made before they engaged in a duel. The thought gave her an exhilarating shot of adrenaline.

Once they were all settled into seats selected by Simon—the striped sofa for David and Erin, two Empire chairs on either side of the white marble fireplace for Simon and Olivia—and had received their drinks and been offered a dish of cheese puffs, Simon leaned forward and said solemnly, "Now what can I do for you, David? Obviously this is a serious matter or you wouldn't have been calling me all week, when I'm in the middle of this EEC problem."

"It's about Giles," David said.

"What else? But I thought we had already said all there was to say on the subject the last time you were here." Simon spoke in an eminently reasonable manner.

David smiled. "All *you* had to say, but that didn't mean I dropped my investigation."

"Investigation? Sounds like an American movie. You'll be telling me next that you hired a P.I."

Erin bristled at the hint of a sneer in Simon's voice, but she said nothing. She and David had agreed that he would make the preamble and she would then take over.

"That's exactly what I did." David deliberately exaggerated the hint of American in his voice.

"What on earth for?" Olivia asked.

"To find Harrington."

"Harrington!" Simon leaned back his dark head and laughed, exposing white teeth. "Why go to all the trouble and expense when I told you he was on holiday?"

"He was not on holiday. He has been fired. Thrown out of Amberley with no notice whatsoever."

"Obviously the poor old fellow forgot to mention the very generous severance pay I gave him in lieu of notice."

"I understood that Harrington was in Giles's employ, not yours, Simon."

"My grandfather is very loyal to his old servants. Harrington was a danger to him. He was forgetting to give him his medication. Or he was unable to persuade Giles to take it."

"No one could make Giles do anything against his will," David said. "Unless, of course, he was sedated sufficiently to make him quiescent."

"That's ridiculous!" Olivia said. "How dare you suggest such a thing."

Simon quietened her with one upheld hand. "Are you suggesting that I have given orders for my grandfather to be oversedated?" he asked very quietly. "As a lawyer, you should be aware of the seriousness of such an accusation, particularly as it has been made before a third party, namely Miss Benson."

"Then refute it by allowing me and Erin access to Amberley, so that we may see for ourselves that Giles is well and—"

"But Giles isn't well," Olivia said. "That's the point. That's why Simon got rid of Harrington. He wasn't looking after Giles properly."

"Then why won't he allow us—or me, at least—to visit Giles, to see for myself how he is."

Simon was no longer smiling. "I will not allow it because the very sight of you infuriates my grandfather.

His heart is weak. We cannot allow anything to upset him."

"So you adamantly refuse to permit me to visit him at Amberley?"

Simon gave a little half smile. "Adamantly is exactly the word I would choose."

"That is your last word on the subject?" David asked, glancing at Erin

"Absolutely. Now why don't we stop all this nonsense and have another drink." Simon glanced at his watch. "I'm afraid I have a meeting to attend in three-quarters of an hour."

"At ten o'clock? A little late, isn't it?"

"Ah, us poor politicians are kept working until all hours, you know."

David settled back in his chair. "It will be at least four years before this new Labour government has to call an election, right?"

Simon seemed surprised at this new turn in the conversation. "Quite correct."

Erin, too, was surprised. Surely David wasn't about to embark on a political discussion now.

"So that will give you plenty of time to mend all the rifts and dissensions in the Tory party and pull them together," David continued. "To end all the scandals and media accusations of Tory wrongdoing."

"It's already happening under my leadership."

"What are your chances in the next general election, do you think?"

Simon beamed. "With the way things are going already, I confidently predict that we shall rout the Labor party at the next election."

Erin stirred impatiently, but David ignored her. "What would you say if I were to tell you that Erin has something in her possession that has the potential to bring you down? I mean you personally, Simon."

Simon glanced at Erin and then back at David, his expression suddenly wary. "I would say that there is nothing anywhere in this world that could have that effect."

"Such confidence." David stood up, a move that surprised both Simon and Olivia, who glanced at each other. "As this matter is an extremely delicate one between you and Erin, I suggest that Olivia and I go into another room and leave you two alone to discuss it. Perhaps I could read the girls a story."

"The girls are fast asleep and I'm not going anywhere." Olivia was bursting with indignation.

"I can't stay," David said. "There is a potential source of conflict in this for me, legally. There's also an element of ethical conflict, as well. Erin must discuss it with Simon by herself."

"Simon has no secrets from me," Olivia protested. "Have you?" she asked her husband, her voice rising in a hint of suspicion.

For a moment, Simon looked totally perplexed. Then he smiled to cover his bewilderment. Erin felt a fleeting pang of pity for him. Then, remembering Giles, she hardened against him.

"Take David into my study," Simon told his wife. "Let's put an end to all this nonsense."

If looks could have killed, Erin would now be lying on the ivory carpet, stabbed by Olivia's glacial eyes. She stalked to the door, flung it open, and went ahead of David.

Before he went out, David half turned to give Erin an encouraging look. Then he closed the door behind him, leaving her feeling suddenly very nervous.

Simon had sat down again. He gazed up at her, a faint smile playing around his mouth. "I never realized that David could be quite so melodramatic. So, what is this . . . this thing you have that could bring me down?" The mocking smile widened.

In response, Erin opened her small black bag, took out the photocopy of the marriage certificate, and handed it to Simon. Then she sat down opposite him, in the chair Olivia had vacated, so that she could observe his face.

He scanned it. Then he reread it more slowly. She had to admit he was good. Not a muscle moved in his face. Not one word did he say until he had finished his thorough examination of the paper. Then he set it aside on the delicate oval table beside his chair.

"This is not the original, of course."

"No. David has placed that in a safety deposit box in the bank."

"I doubt the validity of this document."

"David has examined it closely. He will tell you that it is legal."

"He would, of course." For the first time Simon expressed some feeling. "Our David has shown his true colors at last," he said in a voice tainted with bitterness.

"David has nothing to gain from authenticating a valid marriage certificate."

"Doesn't he? You're an intelligent woman. You must realize the repercussions of such a document. If it were valid—which I am quite sure it is not—your mother would be Giles's only legitimate child. Am I correct?"

Erin raised her chin and looked at him directly. "Yes, you are."

"And the marriage between Giles and my grandmother would be invalid, which would make my father illegitimate."

"Exactly." Erin was trying hard to hide her smile of triumph, but she was not entirely successful.

"You and David must be enjoying yourselves enormously with this."

"Not really, no."

"How did you find this . . ." Simon picked up the paper. ". . . this thing?" he said, flinging it contemptuously aside.

"I don't choose to tell you. But I will tell you that both witnesses are willing to swear an affidavit to its validity."

"Lucy and Harrington?" he said with exaggerated incredulity. "What court of law would give credence to *their* testimony, two senile old half-wits?"

Erin's face tightened with anger. "I should imagine that the certificate coupled with their testimony would be enough." She smiled. "Just imagine what a heyday the press would have with it. I can just see the headlines, can't you? *Earl's Love for His Chambermaid. Hogarth's Father a Bastard. Hogarth not Heir to Title He Renounced.*"

"Very clever, Miss Benson. It's easy to see that you

are a member of the media yourself." He made it sound as loathsome as being a member of the Mafia.

"We're sort of cousins, aren't we?" Erin said.

"I'm not admitting to anything."

"For heaven's sake, stop being so damned cagey. We're related by blood, if nothing else. You can't deny that."

"I certainly could. How do I know you are who you say you are?"

"Oh, for Pete's sake, Simon. Give it up." She was tired of all his posturing. "I want to ask you something. What effect would the publication of this certificate have on your political career?" Simon opened his mouth to reply. "I want an honest answer, just between you and me," Erin added quickly before he could speak.

A dark-red flush spread along the edges of his cheekbones. "If it could be proved valid, it would be a total disaster. Although it would ascribe no immorality to me, personally, it would impute my family. Because I pride myself on being able to change the party's sleazy image, the media would descend on me like a pack of hounds on their prey."

"And how would it affect you personally?"

"Not that much, really," he said dryly, "except to give a blow to my pride. After all, I've already renounced the title."

"But if you were to have a son, he would never inherit, would he?"

A spasm twisted his lips for a moment. "That is true," he said softly. "In fact, unless you were to produce a son before Giles dies, David would become Giles's direct heir. Which is why I say he has shown himself in his true colors."

"That is also one of the reasons he didn't want to be in on this conversation."

Simon leaned forward. "I really do have a meeting to go to, Miss Benson. As they say in your part of the world, let's cut to the chase. How much do you want to keep this matter secret? On the understanding, of course, that I still don't accept the validity of the marriage certificate."

"I don't want any money, thank you, Mr. Hogarth."

"No, of course not," he muttered. "How stupid of me. Naturally, you will receive a great deal more by marrying the heir to the entire estate. I would point out you, though, that the estates adhering to the title are pretty well worthless. The only property worth anything is Amberley. And it is worth a great deal. It is packed full with valuable treasures; paintings, tapestries, gold-plate. . . . Of course, it is usually left to the heir, but it can be willed to someone else, if the present title-holder wishes."

"So I understand. I must tell you that I am acting on my own behalf entirely. David and I haven't known each other long enough to be thinking of marriage, let alone talk about it."

"Oh, if you're going to use that certificate against me, Cousin Erin," Simon said in a mocking tone, "you must make the best of it. Grab David before someone else does. Don't you want to be a countess?"

"Not one bit, thanks very much. I'm a Canadian, remember. I'm not into all this title stuff."

Simon gave her a quizzical, half-smiling look. "I almost believe you. It seems we have something in common, after all." He drew in a deep breath and released it. "All right. Let's hear it. What *do* you want from me?"

Careful, Erin, careful, she told herself. Don't make it too easy for him. "For starters, both David and I went immediate access to Giles so that—"

"Of course you do. You want to make sure that he knows you have the evidence against him. Now I understand why he didn't want to see you again."

Erin bit her lip, wondering once again if that were so. Despite what Harrington had told David, it was possible that Giles wanted nothing to do with her and her mother, wasn't it?

"We want to find that out for ourselves, not secondhand, through you," she said. "That's number one. Number two, we want Harrington reinstated, if that is Giles's wish. The rest we'll talk about with you, once we see how things are at Amberley."

"And?"

"That's it. What it amounts to is that we have Giles's best interests at heart."

Simon smiled. "Please spare me these protestations of affection for Giles. Even to protect myself, I'm not going to give my grandfather into the hands of two confidence tricksters."

"Think of the alternative, Simon."

"What alternative? Obviously you're going to use this document for your own advantage." He frowned. "I must admit I'm not quite sure what you're going to do with it. You haven't made that at all plain."

Erin stood up. "That's how it's going to be for now. Once we've been to Amberley and seen Giles we'll have a nice family meeting and discuss the future, okay?"

Simon bent to pick up the photocopy from the floor. "I take it I may keep this."

"No, you may not." Erin held out her hand. "Give it to me, please."

Simon did so, looking more and more puzzled. "What is this? Some sort of nerve warfare? I won't know when you're going to spring its publication on me, is that it?"

"Let's just say it's an insurance policy. I'm asking you not to discuss it with anyone else, including Giles, if you don't mind."

Simon gave a harsh laugh, and then shook his head at her. "I'm not likely to do so, am I?"

"Will you tell Olivia?"

"I suppose I shall have to."

"I suggest that you hold off until we've talked again."

"What's the point?"

"It's just a suggestion."

"What do I tell her? She must suspect that something of a family nature is going on between us."

To have Simon Hogarth asking her what to tell his wife gave Erin a tremendous feeling of power.

"Why not tell her for now that I'm threatening you with the disclosure of your grandfather's love affair with my grandmother?"

"Very well. But you haven't told me what you intend to do."

"Wait and see." Erin folded the paper and put it into her bag. "One thing more. I'd like you to make a telephone call."

"To whom?"

"To Mrs. Edwards at Amberley. Tell her that David and I will be there by nine o'clock tomorrow morning and that we are to be permitted to see Giles."

"I could rescind such an order as soon as you left here."

Erin patted her bag. "Somehow I don't think you would. Please tell Mrs. Edwards we'll be there by nine A.M. sharp, okay?"

Simon remained by his chair, immobile, as if he were frozen. Then he picked up the telephone and made the call. Evidently Mrs. Edwards questioned him, because he barked, "That's what I said," into the phone and then slammed it down. "Mrs. Edwards will be expecting you," was all he said to Erin.

"Thank you." Erin hesitated. Then she said, "I've just had a great idea. Why don't we all spend this weekend together at Amberley? Then you and Olivia could meet my mother, Giles's daughter. I know she'd just love to meet your children." Before he could come up with a reply, she held out her hand. "Good-bye, Simon. I think we're all going to work very well together as a family in the future, don't you?"

As she walked from the room, Erin hugged the memory of Simon's totally dismayed expression to herself.

Chapter Thirty-eight

Giles awoke to the sun streaming in through the crack in the gold-damask curtains. For the past week he seemed to have found it increasingly difficult to wake up in the morning. It was like struggling up from the bottom of a deep pool, forcing himself through layers of weeds, before he surfaced with a great gasp of air.

He pressed the button on his intercom, but no one answered. It appeared he had been deserted by his servants, or whatever they liked to call themselves nowadays, just as he'd been deserted by his family.

So much for his supposed granddaughter's promise of bringing her mother to see him. Had he frightened her off somehow? he wondered. His telephone was dead. Something wrong with the line. They were repairing it, Mrs. Edwards had told him. They were taking a bloody long time to do so, that's all he knew. And when Mrs. Edwards tried to call Erin she said there was no reply at the number she'd left. Nor was David in his office this week.

He felt desperately alone. Cut off from the world. As if Amberley were a tomb and he buried deep inside it.

That was another thing. Why was he feeling so bloody awful? When his estate manager, John Callaway, had met with him yesterday, Giles just told him to do whatever he thought best with the tenants in Pondside Cottage who weren't paying their rent. Normally he would have asked for every little detail and discussed it with Callaway. He was losing his touch. Old age was getting to him at least.

That quack of his said his heart was under too much strain and he must take this medication, but he'd rather be dead than sleep away half the day, as he'd been doing this past week.

His new houseman arrived at last, smiling as always. "Good morning, my lord," he said, sweeping back the curtains. "It's a lovely bright day today."

Giles merely grunted, "It's about time." He missed Harrington, dithery though he was. He and Harrington had practically grown up—and grown old—together. They had shared a great many experiences and they understood each other.

A few days ago, Simon had brought this young chap Colin to him without any warning, announcing that Harrington needed a rest. By then, Giles had been feeling too lethargic to do anything about it. But he knew that something odd was going on. He just couldn't work out what it was. The old brain-box seemed to have closed down.

"You're going to have visitors today," Colin said.

"I am? Who?"

"Mrs. Edwards knows all about it. She said she'd come and see you as soon as you're shaved and dressed. We'd better wear the navy blazer today, hadn't we? Suitable for the lovely day and for visitors."

"Going to be difficult for both of us to get into it, isn't it?" Giles growled. Silly ass. This ridiculous "We" talk—Will we have our egg poached today? Will we be going to the village today?—got on his nerves.

Colin laughed. "I can see we're in a jocular mood today, my lord."

A few days ago, Giles would have kicked him out, but now he felt it wasn't worth the bother.

When he'd finished his breakfast and Colin had removed the tray, Mrs. Edwards came in to see him. She didn't seem to be quite her usual bright self. The ready smile was absent.

"I hear I'm to have visitors today," Giles said. "Who are they?"

"Mr. Simon phoned late last night. I didn't want to wake you. He told me that Miss Benson and Mr. Lennox were coming to see you."

"Miss Benson?" Giles felt a surge of excitement. "So she didn't go back to Canada after all."

"Apparently not."

"You said she had gone back."

"If you remember, my lord, I said she *might* have gone home to Canada, because I couldn't reach her by telephone."

Yes, Mrs. Edwards was definitely put out about something.

"When are they coming?"

"At approximately nine o'clock this morning, my lord." Mrs. Edwards pursed her lips together

"Nine o'clock?" Giles repeated incredulously. "But that's only a few minutes from now. What the devil are they coming so early for?"

"Perhaps Miss Benson has a plane to catch."

Giles's excitement died. Of course. That would be the explanation. She was coming to say good-bye. "I'll see them in the morning room," he told Mrs. Edwards. 'Better make a pot of coffee and some biscuits."

"Not lunch, my lord?"

Giles sighed. "Doubt they'll have time for lunch. Not if she's flying back to Canada today."

They arrived at twenty past nine, so that Giles had begun to worry that they might have been involved in an accident on the M25.

"Miss Benson and Mr. Lennox," Colin announced and showed them into the morning room.

They stood in front of him, hand in hand, both beaming broad smiles at him. Then Erin broke free to fling her arms around his neck, kissing him on both cheeks. Her lips felt soft and she smelled of some lovely lemony perfume that reminded him of Tuscany in August.

"It's wonderful to see you," she said. There were tears in her eyes.

"Well," Giles said, trying to clear his throat. "It's not my fault you haven't seen me. Where the devil have you both been all week?"

Erin straightened up and exchanged glances with David. When she turned back to Giles her eyes seemed even brighter than before, as if he'd said something of great significance that pleased her enormously.

He was right, of course. Erin was convinced now that it hadn't been Giles who had cut himself off from her.

She waited for David to explain, knowing that he would couch his explanation with the necessary diplomacy. While they were driving down to Kent they'd agreed that, although Giles must know that Simon had kept them apart, there was no point in driving a complete wedge between him and his grandson.

"It seems that Simon was concerned about too much excitement for you," David told Giles. "Apparently he gave orders that you were not to receive calls from anyone but himself. Both Erin and I have been trying for days to get you."

Giles's blue eyes sparked fire. "The devil he did! What right had he to do such a thing? But what about all those times I asked Mrs. Edwards to ring you?"

David gave him a rueful smile. "I'm afraid Mrs. Edwards must have been under orders not to make any calls for you. For the same reason: to avoid you undue stress."

"Bloody nonsense! Sounds like a damned conspiracy to me. This time Simon's gone too far."

Knowing that David found it hard not to agree, Erin spoke up. "I think Simon was concerned that meeting with me wouldn't be good for you," she said, choosing her words very carefully.

"So concerned that he gave orders to my staff behind my back and canceled all my telephone calls? To me, that sounds more as if he were being concerned about himself. He didn't want any more relatives in the picture, that's the essence of it."

David and Erin said nothing. What was the point of denying the truth?

Giles fell back in his chair, already weary from the emotional exertion. "I've been feeling bloody tired all the time," he said. "The least little thing seems to wear me out."

"Perhaps your medication needs a little adjustment," Erin suggested. "New medicine often does. Why don't we call Dr. Alexander in and you can talk to him about it? Has he been to see you this week?"

"No, hasn't been near me."

Again Erin glanced at David. So the doctor hadn't

been checking on him. "Would you like David to call him in while we're here?"

"Good idea. I can't abide doctors, but maybe you're right about those pills."

Erin breathed a sigh of relief. Everything was going so much easier than she'd expected.

"You're going to stay for a while, then?" Giles asked.

"If you'd like us to."

He released a long sigh, relaxing his shoulders as if he'd had them hunched up. "I thought you were here at this unearthly hour because you were coming to say good-bye to me. Going back to Canada."

"Oh, no." Erin smiled down at him and took his hand in hers. "We'll stay as long as you like." She hesitated and then said, "As a matter of fact, there's someone else here to see you as well."

"I'll go and make that call to Dr. Alexander," David said and left the room.

"Someone else?" Giles didn't look too pleased. "I'm not sure I feel like seeing a stranger."

"She's not really a stranger." Erin gave him a little smile.

His eyes met hers and then widened in an expression of excitement mixed with anxiety. "She's not really here, is she?" he whispered.

"Yes, she is. She flew in from Winnipeg last week. That's one of the reasons I've been so desperate to speak to you. For a while I was beginning to think you were having regrets about saying you'd like her to come to Amberley."

"Oh, no. The only regrets I have are for the way she was treated by me and my family." His mouth twisted as if he were in pain. "How can I face her, knowing what was done to her?"

"She's come all this way to meet you. You can't turn her away now. She's waiting in the library. I'll go and get her."

When Erin went into the library, her mother was standing in the center of the room, staring up at the painted ceiling. She turned when Erin came in. "It's exactly as I remember it," she said. "Not just the ceiling, but the entire library. I used to love this room. The old globe and the folding steps and all those books. Even the smells I remember vividly: old leather and wood smoke from the fire."

"It was the ceiling that was the biggest clue, though, wasn't it? Not many libraries have ceilings like that."

"Here we are going on about ceilings as if nothing else mattered," her mother said, the tremor in her voice betraying her nervousness. "Is he all right?"

"He's a little frail and rather tired, but he wants to see you. I warn you, though, he's worried about how you're going to feel about him, considering the way you were treated."

"With cause," Kate said caustically. "But what's the point now? Too many years have passed. Was he trying to avoid seeing us?"

"Definitely not. It was all Simon."

"I can't wait to meet this famous Simon Hogarth."

"You won't have to wait long. I suggested he come down for the weekend. You should have seen his face."

"And will he, do you think?"

"That depends on Giles. We must make sure that he feels in control of his own home again. From now on, he will be the one to decide who comes to Amberley. Let's go, Mom. We shouldn't keep him waiting. He's nervous enough, as it is."

"*He's* nervous? How do you think I feel? what on earth shall I call him?" she asked in a panic.

But Erin was already way ahead of her, leading her across the hall. To make matters worse, Erin led her into the morning room and said, "I'm going to leave you two alone together," and did just that.

Kate stood near the door, feeling like a kid in the principal's office.

"Don't hover in the doorway," said a voice from the wing chair by the fireplace, which held a Chinese vase filled with tall flowers from the garden. "Come over here so that I can see you."

Drawing in a deep breath, she walked briskly across the room—trying to give the appearance of being far more confident than she actually felt—to the other chair beside the hearth and sat down.

Now she could see him properly. He looked like an

old general, with his long, lean body and Roman nose and bright blue eyes, which were examining her just as thoroughly as she was examining him.

"You're like your mother," he said.

She opened her mouth to deny it, knowing she didn't have her mother's soft face, but then remembered that she must never divulge that she'd met Mary. "Am I? In what way?"

"The eyes. Those brown eyes, only Mary's were as gentle as a deer's. Yours look more like those of an angry bear at the moment."

"I don't mean to be angry," Kate said. "I'm feeling terribly nervous and I get a little sharp when I'm tense."

He chuckled. "Just like your father, eh?"

So he was going to acknowledge it right away. She liked that. "I shouldn't imagine you'd ever feel nervous."

"Don't you believe it. I've just learned to hide it well over the years." He surveyed her again, so that Kate felt her cheeks redden beneath his scrutiny. "Forgive me for staring. The more I look at you, the more I see of both Mary and myself in you. Poor woman, you've inherited the Hogarth nose, I see."

Kate lifted her chin. "Jim used to call it my aristocratic nose. Little did he realize how right he was," she added, giving him a wry smile.

"Jim was your husband. Your daughter told me that he had recently died. I'm sorry."

Kate blinked rapidly. "Thank you. It hasn't been easy to adjust. I still miss him terribly."

"One never completely recovers from such a loss. When I came back from the front to find Mary and our child dead—as I thought—I felt as if my life had come to an end. But it's like an old wound. Eventually it heals over. However, the scar remains forever to remind you where it was."

To her embarrassment, Kate found herself crying and couldn't stop. "I'm so sorry. This is really stupid. I thought I'd got over this weeping, but it still creeps up on me at the most unexpected moments."

"Don't apologize. Come over here and sit beside me." He patted the chaise longue beside his chair. Kate did as she was told. "There, that's much better, isn't it?" He spoke to her as if she were the small child he remembered. Kate's heart swelled.

"What did I call you?" she asked him. "I've tried so hard to remember, but I can't."

"My mother wouldn't allow you to call me anything but Sir in Amberley, but when we were alone, the three of us, in the cottage, you called me Daddy."

"Did my mother continue to work in the house after—after she became your mistress?"

He seemed to flinch at the word. For a moment she thought he might tell her the truth, but then his mouth snapped shut again. She could understand why. He had the memory of his second wife and their son and all their descendants to think of. Just as Mary was protecting her second family. Kate had made her promise and she would never break it. But she couldn't help wondering how he would react if she were to say outright, *Mary is still alive. I was with her a few days ago.*

Even as she thought it, Giles said, "Mary was my one true love and always will be. Not a day goes by that I don't think about her." He leaned forward and touched her cheek with his long fingers. "And now I see before me the child we created. Something I thought I should never ever see in my lifetime." Tears filled his eyes and stole down his cheeks, but he was smiling and he did not turn his head away to hide his weeping from her. Her heart went out to him.

"I wasn't sure if I was right to come. Erin was very insistent."

"A true Hogarth. She doesn't give up easily."

"Her father was like that, too."

"Then she has a double dose of it. From what she's told me, there's no doubt you would never have found me without her tenacity."

"And David's kindness."

"Hmm!" He didn't seem quite so sure about that. "I gather from the way they were looking at each other that things are becoming more serious between them."

"I sincerely hope so. I like David very much."

"Do you, indeed? He's part Scottish and part American, you know."

"A good combination, I should think," Kate said. Erin had told her about Giles's ambivalent feelings for David.

"You think so? Well, we shall see. He's far too damned independent for my liking."

"I should have thought you'd appreciate such a quality."

Giles chuckled. "Not when he doesn't agree with me. But enough about David. I want to find out all about you." The penetrating blue eyes stared at her until she wanted to look away, but her gaze remained steady.

"Can you ever forgive me for not looking after you and your mother properly?" he finally asked her.

"Once I knew how it had happened, I could."

"Had I realized the extent of my parents' enmity I would have sent you and your mother a thousand miles out of their clutches." He put his hand over his eyes. "I still can't bear to think of what they did to you. Poor child. Turned from your home without your mother and sent to a strange country to live with strangers."

Kate saw his anguish, still raw after more than fifty years, but she knew she must ask him now, while she had the chance. "Didn't you make inquiries? Ask for the list of dead passengers on that boat that was sunk, *The City of Benares*?"

He turned bloodshot eyes to her. "My parents were so sympathetic I believed them implicitly. I didn't come home from Africa until several months after the ship sank. My mother told me they'd made all the arrangements. I was so devastated, I didn't even want to know what those arrangements were." Tears spurted from his eyes. "God, what a bloody fool I was to believe them!"

"You mustn't let it upset you now," she said hurriedly. "The people who adopted me were extremely kind. They loved me very much and gave me a good education. I had a wonderful marriage and a loving daughter. What more could I ask?"

"You could have had what was yours by right. Two parents who loved you. A place at Amberley, where you belonged."

Kate held her breath for a moment, knowing that he was thinking of the marriage with Mary, but again she refused to question him further, knowing where it could lead. "It would never have worked, not while your parents were alive," she reminded him.

And by the time they were dead, she had been adopted by the Bartleys in Winnipeg and her birth mother had married an Irish schoolteacher named Seamus Callahan.

"What about now?" Giles asked her. "Could I persuade you to stay here with me at Amberley?"

She shook her head sadly. "I'm sorry, but I'm a Canadian. If I stayed here I'd be pining for the space and the big prairie sky and my lovely garden—"

"Plenty of lovely gardens at Amberley."

"I know that," she said and was surprised to realize that she did remember the gardens from her childhood. "That's probably why I've always loved flowers and gardens. But my garden is small, manageable. I don't need several gardeners to look after it. I grew up in a small five-room bungalow in a modest part of Winnipeg. I like to do things for myself, not have them done for me. I'd feel alien here in a big stately home."

"Amberley should have been your home," he said emphatically. "You should have been raised here."

"Well, it's yours and that's what matters."

"Are you going back to Canada right away? Could you stay at Amberley for a while? I should like to get to know my daughter," he said wistfully.

"I'd love to stay for a *little* while," Kate said. "We've a great many years to catch up on. Just as long as you realize that I must eventually return to Canada. That's where my home is," she added gently, sensing his disappointment. "I'm just beginning to get my life together again and I want to continue that process."

She looked up as the door opened and Erin put her head around it.

"Now here's someone," Kate said to Giles in an undertone, so that Erin wouldn't hear, "who might be prepared to stay on in England. She could even become a regular visitor at Amberley, if you could just learn to like David."

Epilogue

June 2000

The family were sitting in Lord Maybridge's study watching the general election results coming in on the large-screened television.

"I'm afraid it's going to be a whopping defeat for the Tories," David said. "Far worse than even the Labour Party predicted."

"Poor old Simon," Erin said, shifting baby Carolyn into the crook of her arm.

A grunt came from the couch, where Giles lay stretched out, covered by a warm blanket. "Poor old Simon, my arse! Serve him bloody well right. All that nonsense about giving up the title. Now look where it's got him. Back again as leader of the opposition. In fact, they might not even keep him on as leader after this."

"Daddy, Daddy." Little Jamie hammered on his father's knee with his fist to get his attention. "Gray-Grampa said 'bloody.' "

"So what if I did?" Giles growled. "I hope you're not bringing that child up to be a sanctimonious sissy, Erin."

"Not much chance of that when he spends so much time with you, is there?" David said with a grin, his gaze still on the television.

Giles muttered something beneath his breath. He held out his hand, which now shook constantly, to his great-grandson. "Come and sit up here beside me, Jamie, and I'll teach you some more good words."

"Don't you dare," Erin said, laughter bubbling in her voice.

Giles bent to whisper in three-year-old Jamie's ear.

Jamie looked up at him with large round eyes, and then whispered back in Giles's ear. Giles nodded.

"Shall I say it, then?" Jamie asked.

"Yes, yes. Go on."

"Will Mummy be cross?"

"Terribly."

Jamie looked from Giles to his mother, not quite sure about this.

"For heaven's sake, Giles, stop teasing the poor boy. Go on, say it, Jamie. I won't be cross."

"You're a buscom wench. There, I said it!"

"You mean buxom, Jamie. Thanks a lot," Erin said to Giles. "And, Jamie Lennox, I'm going to give you horrid wet kisses as a big punishment." Erin caught up Jamie with her other hand and kissed his face as he wriggled in her grasp.

"Daddy, Daddy, save me from Mummy." Jamie ran to David and clambered onto his knee. "She's kissing me again."

"Is she? Lucky you. She doesn't give me lovely kisses like that. Here, hold still. I'm trying to watch the television. See, there's Cousin Simon on the screen. He's making a big speech to all his supporters."

Next morning, Giles was looking particularly fragile. "Didn't sleep too well," he explained to Erin when she went to see him after he'd been dressed and shaved. "I phoned him last night. Then I lay awake thinking for most of the night."

"By him, I take it you mean Simon? Was he okay?"

"You know Simon. Didn't let on that he was crushed. Talked about living to fight another battle another day and all that political claptrap."

"David and I were talking about that last night. David said he wouldn't be at all surprised if Simon eventually got to be Prime Minister. He's still a young man, politically speaking. Was it thinking about Simon's defeat that kept you awake all night?"

"In a way. I was thinking what a bloody stupid gesture he'd made, renouncing the title even before I was dead. Then I started to wonder if he'd actually do it, when the time came."

"And?"

"I wouldn't put it past Simon to decide he wanted the title after all when I die."

"'You're not going to die for a long time." Erin plumped up his pillow. "Have some breakfast."

"Stop humoring me as if I'm one of your infants. You're going back to London this afternoon, aren't you?"

"Sorry, we have to. Work calls."

"Not for you, it doesn't. Aren't you on maternity leave from the studio?"

"Yes, for another three months. I'm very tempted to give it up and just be a stay-at-home mum, but I'm afraid I might regret it later on, when I couldn't get back in again."

"Well, if you have to go back to London today there's no time to waste. I want to speak to you and David. Get him, will you?"

"Okay." Erin started to leave the room.

"Wait a bit. One more thing to say." Giles struggled for breath.

"From the sound of it you're saying far too much this early in the morning."

"I had a long talk with your mother on the telephone last night."

"Did you really? She'd have enjoyed that."

"She promised to drag herself away from that confounded flower shop of hers to come and see me."

"That's great news! Now she can see her new granddaughter."

"That's what I told her. I also reminded her that it had been almost a year since I last saw her."

"You're right, it is. She's been so caught up in her work I'm sure she hadn't realized how long it was. Especially as David and I were in Winnipeg last fall. When's she coming?"

"Next week. She said she could get some sort of last-minute flight. Stand-something?"

"Standby. That's wonderful. It'll be great for you to have her here at Amberley again, won't it?"

"That's what I want to speak to you and David about."

"What?"

"Amberley."

Erin went to fetch David. "I'm worried about him. He's in a very strange mood. Apparently he phoned my mother last night and asked her to fly over."

"When?"

"That's the point. Next week. Or as soon as she can get away. She must have realized it was urgent, because she said she'd come on standby."

They exchanged looks. David put his arm around her. "It had to happen sometime, sweetheart. Even his doctor is amazed at how long he's survived. That's all your doing."

"And yours. He's come to rely on you for almost everything. He's very concerned about Simon."

"About his defeat, you mean?"

"That and the consequences of it. He thinks Simon might decide to keep the title, after all."

"So what? We made the decision not to do anything about that when we had Jamie, didn't we?"

She raised her eyes to his. "He wants to talk to us about Amberley."

When they returned to Giles's bedroom, they found that his new houseman, Barry, had helped him get dressed and settled him in his wheelchair.

"Sit down, both of you," Giles said.

They sat opposite him on the green velvet chaise longue.

"There's something I've been wanting to tell you for a long time. Something I *should* have told you many years ago." Giles paused every few words, seeking for breath.

Erin glanced at David, but said nothing.

Giles's mouth quivered. "It's about Mary. Your grandmother, Erin. For more than sixty years I have lived a lie." His face crumpled and he turned it aside to avoid them seeing his tears.

Erin went to him, gently turning him toward her, so that she could look into his eyes. "We know," she said.

"No, you don't know the full extent of my—my treachery."

"Yes, we do. We know that you and Mary were married."

The tired blue eyes seemed to ignite with an inner fire. "How the devil did you find that out?" he barked.

For a moment, Erin was tempted to tell him the truth, but she had not only her own but also her mother's promise to keep. And even though Mary had died last year—how strange that Giles, the elder and more fragile of the two, should outlive her—the promise must be kept for the sake of Mary's large family in Ireland.

"I'm afraid," she said, "that both Lucy and Harrington became less careful in their old age."

"Damn Lucy! Now you may understand why I dreaded her coming here to Amberley," he told David. "I never knew when she would spill the beans on me. Wait till I see her!"

"I don't think she'd know what you were talking about nowadays," David said, with a sad smile. "But I sincerely hope you won't stop her coming here, Giles. She loves staying at Amberley."

"How long have you known?" Giles demanded.

"Since that summer when I first came to Amberley and met you," Erin said, returning to her seat.

"I don't understand why you haven't done something about it, then. After all, it would mean a great deal to you both, now that you have a son. Jamie should be my heir, not Simon." Giles's vehemence brought on a coughing spell.

This time David spoke. "We knew that. When Jamie was born we talked about it for a long time. We decided that we didn't want it for him."

"And what if he wants it for himself, when the time comes?"

"At the moment, it is the decision of the family, particularly Kate, that the children not be told about the marriage between you and Mary Foley." David sighed heavily. "As a lawyer, I had to struggle very hard with this. My duty really should be to divulge it, but the wishes of your daughter and granddaughter were that the marriage certificate be locked away and forgotten about. And that is what we have done."

"Certificate?" Giles asked. "You mean you actually have the marriage certificate? Where did you get it?"

Again, Erin struggled with the truth. But what was the point of raising his hopes only to dash them again? "Lucy had it," she told him.

"Ah, yes, Lucy." He nodded, apparently accepting the explanation. "Mary must have given it to her for safe-keeping after we were married, I suppose." He twisted the fringe on the edge of his rug round and round his pencil-thin fingers. "My poor Mary," he whispered. "God knows what happened to her." Then he rallied. "Don't you think I should make some sort of public acknowledgment about it?"

"No." Erin shook her head vehemently. "Absolutely not."

He released a small sigh. Erin wasn't sure if it was one of relief or sadness.

"That makes my decision even more inevitable then," he said. "I want to get this done right away. I've called Browning and he's coming here this morning."

"Browning?" The last time Erin had met Giles's solicitor was two years ago, after Harrington's funeral, when Giles had changed his will to remove the bequest to his faithful servant.

"I'm going to leave Amberley to you, Erin."

Although Erin wasn't completely surprised, the abruptness of the announcement took her breath away.

"Well, don't I get a thank you, at least?" Giles demanded.

"I'm sorry. I was so utterly flabbergasted that I couldn't speak. Hasn't Amberley always been left with the title?"

"It has, until now. But I think this is the fair way, don't you? Simon gets the title—and I'll leave him sufficient funds to keep him very comfortable, so you needn't feel sorry for him. After all," Giles added, rather sheepishly, "he is still my grandson. And if he does decide to give up politics and keep his title, I don't want the next earl to be a pauper."

"Of course. But he'll be absolutely stunned when he finds out he won't be getting Amberley."

David hadn't said a word, but now he spoke. "I'm not so sure he will be. It will only serve to confirm his darkest suspicions. He once accused us of wheedling our way into your affections."

Giles stretched out a frail hand. "Oh, you've done that, all right. *Both* of you." Then he hurriedly cleared his throat. "I offered Amberley to your mother first, Erin. I thought that she should have first offer. She turned me down flat and said that you and David should get it. Particularly as Jamie loses out on his right to become the Earl of Maybridge."

Now it was David's turn to clear his throat. "Well, actually that isn't so, Giles. Unless Simon has a son, I'll still be his heir. If the title comes to me, it would mean that Jamie would eventually inherit it from me."

Giles's face lit up. "By God, so he could. Now wouldn't that be poetic justice! But there's still the possibility that Simon will have a son."

"Not unless he divorces Olivia," Erin said.

"Not likely to do that, is he?" growled Giles. "She and his children are the world to him. Outside of his damned politics, of course. They'll always come first with Simon. But why haven't he and Olivia tried for another child, that's what I want to know?"

"If you promise not to mention it to either of them, I'll tell you," Erin said.

"Scout's honor," said Giles, giving the appropriate sign.

"Olivia can't have any more children. Doctor's orders. She's had her tubes tied to prevent any chance of a pregnancy. She told me so when I had Jamie." Erin remembered that emotional time, when Olivia had broken down and told her that she couldn't give Simon any more children. It had drawn them closer together at the time, but Olivia soon grew aloof again.

"Ah, so that explains it," Giles said. "Poor old Simon. So you will get to be my heir eventually, David, my boy."

"Not until Simon dies. And as I don't particularly want the title, that suits me just fine."

"Spoken like a true Scottish-American," Erin said, grinning at David.

"Well, title or not, I intend to leave Amberley solely to Erin, my granddaughter, hoping to ensure that it will keep the two of you together."

David looked at Erin, his eyes filled with tenderness. "I can assure you we don't need Amberley to keep us together."

"Glad to hear it. Make sure it stays that way," Giles said with mock severity. "I know how you feel about Amberley, David. This will help to make sure that you keep *all* the things you love."

"Thank you, Giles."

"Yes," Erin said, bending to kiss his cheek. "Thank you. You know how much we both love Amberley." The thought of her children growing up in this lovely place brought tears to her eyes. "We shall look after it properly, I promise you."

"I know you will. It makes me feel much easier knowing that."

That afternoon, when Mr. Browning had left, Erin telephoned her mother.

"Sorry to call so early in the morning, Mom, but I wanted to make sure I caught you before you left for work."

"Hi, darling. Has he spoken to you yet?"

"Yes, that's what I'm calling about. It was quite a surprise."

"Will he last until I come next week?"

Erin thought for a moment. "I think you should just come right away, Mom."

There was a slight pause. "I thought so. All this sudden planning for the future signified something was happening."

"I think Simon's defeat also precipitated things. You know, Giles said it served him bloody well right—"

Her mother laughed. "Sounds like him," she said affectionately.

"But I think that secretly Giles was a bit disappointed. I think he'd have been pretty proud to have had his grandson a Prime Minister."

"I'm sure he would."

"Mom, did he mention anything about the marriage to you?"

"His marriage to Mam? Yes. He told me." Kate drew in a little sob. "I think it was terribly brave of him to tell us. But that also made me realize that he feels he hasn't much time left. What did you tell him?"

"What we'd all agreed. That we don't want the title

for Jamie, at least not by using the marriage certificate. That the certificate is locked away. What I didn't say was that we were hanging on to it to make sure that Simon doesn't cause trouble, now or in the future. We don't want any lawsuits about Amberley, for instance."

"Good point. I'll phone the travel agent right away and get a flight to London as soon as possible. They can manage the shop without me for a while. And Mom's perfectly content in the home. I'll ask Pam to drop in every now and then to check on her."

"Great. Give me a call as soon as you know what flight you'll be on. I can pick you up from Heathrow."

As soon as Kate had put down the phone, she went out to her garden, walking across the damp lawn to gaze at the wide flower bed she'd recently filled with red geraniums and myriad variations of pink, red, and white sweet williams. Behind them grew tall zinnias, with flowers from nature's glowing paintbox: orange, yellow, and scarlet.

She had always loved flowers. The gardens at Amberley had been a part of her early childhood. Perhaps she'd tried in a small way to re-create their beauty in her garden in suburban Winnipeg.

As she gazed at the flowers, Kate's eyes filled with tears. She was about to embark on yet another voyage across the Atlantic, again by air, in contrast to that first terrifying and bewildering one by sea so many years ago. But her tears were not wholly sad ones, for she had found her mother and father and, for a brief couple of years, spent time with them both.

Now she was on her way for what could be her father's final days, but life would continue. Sixty years ago, the child who'd been conceived at Amberley had been sent on a lonely voyage across the sea to Canada. Soon she would return to Amberley, the estate that was hers, by right. And now that estate was to become the rightful home of her child and her child's children.

Aware that her life had come full circle, Kate was filled with warm contentment.